PRAISE FOR KATA

THE READERS OF BROKEN WHEEL RECOMMEND

"A manifesto for booksellers, booklovers, and friendship. We should all celebrate these little bookstores, where our souls find home…one of these books you want to live in for a while."

—Kristin Harmel, *New York Times* bestselling author of *The Book of Lost Names*

"*The Readers of Broken Wheel Recommend* is one of the more surprisingly improbable and delightful books I've read in years. What begins as an unlikely international friendship based on a mutual love of books becomes a sweet and soulful discovery of America. Quirky, unpredictable, funny, and fresh—a wonderful book."

—Nickolas Butler, international bestselling author of *Shotgun Lovesongs* and *Beneath the Bonfire*

"This classic fish-out-of-water story will steal your heart. It's smart, sweet, absorbing, and endearing, just like the town of Broken Wheel. It's a story for everyone who believes in the magic of books to enlighten, heal, and restore. A treat for readers everywhere!"

—Susan Wiggs, *New York Times* bestselling author of *Starlight on Willow Lake*

"A heartwarming tale about literature's power to transform."

—*People*

"Charmingly original…sweet, quirky."

—*Washington Post*

"[A] heartwarming and utterly charming debut by Swedish author Bivald. This gentle, intelligent Midwestern tale will captivate fans of Antoine Laurain's *The Red Notebook*, Nina George's *The Little Paris Bookshop*, and

Gabrielle Zevin's *The Storied Life of A.J. Fikry*. An ideal book group selection, it reminds us why we are booklovers and why it's nice to read a few happy endings."

—*Library Journal*, Starred Review

"Touching and lively, Bivald's genuine homage to the power of books vibrates with fondness for small-town life and fascination with its indelible connections."

—*Booklist*

"Between the book references and the idyllic setting, readers won't want to leave Broken Wheel either."

—*Kirkus Reviews*

"Swedish author Bivald's debut novel is a delight. Bivald fills the pages with book references, chief among them Austen and Bridget Jones, but it is her characters that will win readers over... As in Austen, love conquers but just who and how will come as a pleasant surprise."

—*Publishers Weekly*

WELCOME TO THE PINE AWAY MOTEL AND CABINS

"Katarina Bivald talks about her characters like you talk about your best friends. She gives her story absolutely everything she has. You'll care when you read because she really, really cared when she wrote."

—Fredrik Backman, #1 *New York Times*
bestselling author of *A Man Called Ove*

"Remarkable...unquestionably a page-turner and full of wisdom. A brave, unusual book, which powerfully portrays friendship and love."

—Felicity Hayes-McCoy, author of *The Library at the Edge of the World*

"Hopeful, heartening, and humane, this is the novel I needed to read right now."

—J. Ryan Stradal, author of *The Lager Queen of Minnesota* and *Kitchens of the Great Midwest*

"A novel of irresistible characters that make you believe in the power of hard-won wisdom and second chances, *Welcome to the Pine Away Motel and Cabins* is a delight!"

—Linda Francis Lee, author of *The Glass Kitchen*

"Bivald's charming, heartwarming, and thought-provoking novel will linger long after the last page is turned."

—*Booklist*

"In a story about the lives a single person can touch, the highlight is fittingly Bivald's memorable characterizations, as she makes each person and their needs distinct and complex. This is a winning novel about the lasting impact of love."

—*Publishers Weekly*

"A celebration of life in which friendship, community, and a room for the night are gentle antidotes to prejudice."

—*Kirkus Reviews*

"The novel perfectly captures the joys and trials of small-town living... A story full of both hope and heart."

—*Shelf Awareness*

ALSO BY KATARINA BIVALD

The Readers of Broken Wheel Recommend
Welcome to the Pine Away Motel and Cabins

The
Murders
in Great
Diddling

A NOVEL

Katarina Bivald

Originally published as *Morden i Great Diddling*, © Katarina Bivald,
2022. Translated from Swedish by Alice Menzies.

Published by Poisoned Pen Press, an imprint of Sourcebooks
P.O. Box 4410, Naperville, Illinois 60567-4410
(630) 961-3900
sourcebooks.com

Originally published as *Morden i Great Diddling* in 2022 in Sweden by Bokförlaget Forum.

Cataloging-in-Publication Data is on file with the Library of Congress.

Printed and bound in the United States of America.
VP 10 9 8 7 6 5 4 3 2 1

"*A crow thieves; a fox cheats; a weasel outwits; a man diddles. To diddle is his destiny. 'Man was made to mourn,' says the poet. Not so: he was made to diddle.*"
—Edgar Allan Poe in "Diddling, Considered as One of the Exact Sciences"

"*O my darling books! A day will come when others will buy and possess you. Yet how dear to me are they all!*"
—Antoine-Isaac Silvestre de Sacy (1758–1838)

PROLOGUE

AN EXPLOSIVE TEA PARTY

"WHERE IS BERIT GARDNER?"

Daphne Trent looked out across the neat lawn where the villagers were drinking tea and mingling in the afternoon sun. She knew an event that was about to spiral out of control when she saw one.

It had been an idiotic idea to throw a tea party for the residents of Great Diddling. She had hoped that a few scones and tea cakes would placate the locals and help calm their passions, but so far the opposite had proved true.

The whole event had been thrown together with just a few days' notice, yet almost everyone had turned up. She suspected their curiosity was to blame. Most of them had never seen Tawny Hall up close before, and they had come to have a nose around—at the house, the strange author, possibly even Daphne herself, not that they had any interest in actually talking to her. As though she were responsible for the things her nephew got up to!

Daphne had actually noticed several people turn away from her as they got too close, repelled like magnets of the same pole. One man muttered to himself as he walked by, a long harangue that was deeply offensive not only to Reginald's mother—who had married into the family—but to his grandmothers and great-grandmothers and the women who had come before them. And that, Daphne thought angrily, included her own relatives. The man had the decency not to meet her eye at the very least. He was too busy glaring at Reginald for that. What was his name? Was he one of the Smiths? Had his mother worked at Tawny Hall? She couldn't remember.

Daphne forced her best hostess smile back onto her face. It was something she could usually manage in her sleep, the perfect balance of politeness and charm, bland yet personal. But today it was a real struggle to keep the corners of her mouth turned upward. Her skin felt tight and uncomfortable as she nodded to villagers she wasn't sure she had met before.

A large half-moon had been mown into the south lawn to accommodate the guests, but beyond that, the meadow grass and flowers swayed at knee height. A white gazebo had been erected on the edge of the mown area, and the Hartfield women from Sisters' Café on High Street were serving pastries, shortbread, and muffins, with towering trays of cucumber, salmon, and cheese sandwiches. Freshly baked scones jostled for space alongside still-hot tea cakes laden with butter, cream, and jam, and there were several large thermoses of tea, plus a few smaller silver pots of coffee for those who preferred it.

One of the sisters held out a scone to Daphne, and she forced herself to take it. Her smile grew more strained than ever, but fortunately the woman didn't seem to notice. Mary, that was her name.

Mary continued to make her way among the guests until she reached Daphne's nephew, Reginald. She offered him a cup of tea, and he took it seemingly without even stopping to consider what the owners of the café— two women he had recently threatened to evict—might have put in it.

Daphne watched on expectantly as he drank two deep mouthfuls, but nothing happened. She turned away with a sting of disappointment.

She knew that Reginald had sent word to several shops in the village on Wednesday, serving them notice on their contracts. He had suggested that the properties on High Street would be put up for sale, but he hadn't said anything about the new owners nor why they had no interest in keeping the little supermarket, the hobby shop, and the café as tenants.

A delegation of villagers had come to see Daphne in an attempt to get her to talk some sense into her nephew, but what they failed to understand was that there was nothing she could do. The properties were his, just like Tawny Hall would be once she was dead.

Her books would one day be his too.

Daphne had spent her life at Tawny Hall. It was her home, but it also meant so much more to her than that. The house gave her a sense of history, binding her to the men and women who had come before, as though she was a chapter in a fascinating story that had begun long before she was born. There was magic in the walls here, an intoxicating mix of time and place, memory and opportunity. Sometimes, as she sat in the library, she actually found herself forgetting what century she lived in.

But the spell hadn't proved strong enough to stand up to Reginald. In the face of his hostility, the glittering exterior fell away, leaving nothing but the damp, the dust, the cobwebs, the faded wallpaper, and the books that had been shoved, in panic, into every nook and cranny in an attempt to prevent them from taking over the house completely.

Given half a chance, he would get rid of the lot of it. He would throw out the furniture and her collection—or "the junk" as he called the memories she had gathered over a long and rich life. He would get rid of her.

On the other side of the lawn, Reginald raised his teacup in a mocking toast. Daphne turned away, but she could still feel his eyes on her.

His presence forced her to see herself through his eyes. Old and wrinkly, with thin lips and small eyes, loose skin hanging from her arms—how did he know that when she always wore long sleeves?—and, worst of all, ridiculous, in her old-fashioned dresses and the wig she wore to hide her bald spot.

Daphne still thought of herself as young and beautiful, but it was as though Reginald could see the portrait of Dorian Gray hidden in the attic.

Oh, why had he come here? She had been so happy here before Reginald turned up and ruined everything.

Daphne took a bite of her scone. It seemed to grow in her mouth, and she sipped her champagne in an attempt to wash it down. Even that tasted stale, like old apples and rot and the relentless passage of time, and she searched irritably for somewhere to put her plate.

In the end, her secretary and right-hand woman, Margaret, took it away. She returned a short while later carrying a new bottle of champagne, and she filled Daphne's glass without a word.

"Bit of a tense atmosphere," said Margaret, as prosaic as ever. She was the kind of person who would look out at the Flood, turn to Noah, and say, "Looks like a spot of rain."

"Yes, it is rather," Daphne agreed.

Right then, much too late, she remembered the angry man's name. He was a Samson, not a Smith. The owner of the little supermarket in the village.

"How are we for champagne?" she asked.

"Stock levels are good," Margaret replied.

Then there's nothing more we can do, thought Daphne. Where was Berit Gardner?

She surveyed her guests' glum faces and found herself wondering just how many of them were fantasizing about killing someone. She counted in her head.

At least five of them wanted to kill her nephew.

And at least one wanted to kill her.

1

"STAYIN' ALIVE, STAYIN' ALIVE, BAM-BAM-BAM-BAM, stayin' aliiiiiiive."

Berit Gardner hummed to herself as she ironed a white shirt on the table in her spartan kitchen. She was wearing her best going-out jeans and had a corduroy jacket and two scarves waiting for her on the back of the chair.

She was looking forward to the tea party at Tawny Hall with a mix of anticipation and fear, considerably more of the latter.

What if she didn't find them there?

What if she didn't hear anything at all?

She had never looked forward to a mingle before. There was something about people trying to show off their best sides that virtually guaranteed it would be boring, and she had no reason to think that today would be any different. On the contrary, there was a real risk she would come away having wasted the afternoon chatting about the weather.

No, she told herself. There were stories to be found here, she could feel it. She had known that since the moment she first laid eyes on the little cottage. It felt right. As though she had returned to a long-lost home or finally reached the place she had been heading toward all her life.

In truth, it had started before she even arrived. The minute she saw the ad, she had felt a pang of something she had been longing for, something she had missed.

Even the names had something special about them. She said them aloud to herself now, trying to conjure up some of their magic.

"Great Diddling," she said. "Albert Lane. Wisteria Cottage."

It was that sense of magic and adventure that had convinced her to plow all of her savings, every last penny of the unexpected royalty payment, into a cottage in the middle of nowhere in a tired, rundown village in Cornwall.

And now she was going to attend the tea party. She would smile; she would mingle; she would make small talk about the weather if that was what it took. And she would find them.

Berit swallowed. Strange. She was nervous. Another unfamiliar feeling.

She glanced down at her watch. Half two. Almost time to head over to Tawny Hall.

What the…?

She moved around the kitchen table and leaned over the sink to get a better look out through the little window onto the street.

Sure enough, there was a young woman standing on the gravel path leading to her cottage, and she had a suitcase.

How long had she been there? Now that she thought about it, Berit wondered whether she hadn't heard a knock at the door a while back. Yes, she had heard something, but it had been so quiet that she had barely paid any notice to it.

Right then, she realized her mobile phone was ringing. She found it in the living room, buzzing wildly, the name DON'T PICK UP!!! flashing on the screen.

She picked up anyway. She always did.

"What do you want now?" she asked, making her way back through to the kitchen and peering out through the window. The young woman was still there.

Berit's literary agent, Olivia Marsch, ignored her whining tone. Her own was so professionally cheerful, it wouldn't have sounded out of place coming from a preschool teacher. "How's my favorite author?"

"Ha!" Berit muttered. She knew full well she wasn't Olivia's favorite. Her agent was unfailingly fair in that regard; she loved her authors in strict order of their sales figures. Berit wasn't sure, but she suspected that she was currently Olivia's seventh or eighth favorite and that she was dropping rapidly in the ranks.

"Has your new assistant arrived yet?" asked Olivia.

Berit froze. "My what?"

"Your new assistant. I've sent her to help you. She can stay in your spare room."

"In my spare room?"

Either she had gone crazy or the world had, thought Berit.

"You're always complaining that there are too many people bothering you, so she can help with that."

"I don't need a damn assistant."

There, she had said it. Now all she had to do was stand her ground. Conversations with Olivia were a little like trench warfare: you simply had to pick a position and then hunker down.

"She's already on her way. Left civilization early this morning."

"Hold on a second," said Berit, leaning forward over the sink again until her nose pressed up against the glass. The sun-bleached curtains left behind by the previous owner tickled her forehead. "What does she look like, this assistant of yours?"

"Young woman. Mousy, shoulder-length hair. Terrible posture. Remind her to stand up straight if you have the time—not that it's ever made any difference when I've done it. When I last saw her, she was wearing a thin, beige coat. All very boring."

The young woman outside had shoulder-length brown hair and a boring beige coat.

"Oh Christ," Berit muttered.

"No need to thank me. Only the best is good enough for my authors."

"She looks about fifteen!"

"Turns nineteen this summer. Or is it eighteen? No, nineteen."

"And what the hell am I meant to do with her?"

"Give her plenty of food and water and take her out for a walk three times a day. How do I know? You're the one always complaining about being overworked and isolated in your little house in the sticks. And not even the fashionable sticks! Honestly, I've never heard of anyone moving to inland Cornwall. How are you going to write your warm, cozy novel about a woman in the media who inherits a cottage in Cornwall if it's not even by the sea? Where's the hot fisherman going to come from, I ask you? Not that you've considered any of that, I'm sure. You authors are always so impractical."

"I'm not going to write some Corni—"

"That's why I'm sure you'll find some use for her."

The young woman had taken out her phone and was now standing with it clamped to her ear. Trying to reach Olivia, no doubt.

Berit looked down at her watch again. It was now eight minutes to three, which meant she was officially late.

"I need a follow-up novel, Berit."

"I'm not going to write it."

"August at the latest. The readers are expecting a new book from you next year."

"I'll never be ready by then."

"That's why I'm sending help! Someone who'll be happy and grateful to cater to your every whim. Grateful. She loves your books so much she's actually willing to put up with you. I warned her, but she said, 'Whatever it takes to read another book by Berit E. V. Gardner, I'll do it!' You can always send her back if you're not happy."

"Wait!" said Berit. "I don't even know her na—"

But Olivia had already hung up.

Sally had two options.

One, she could admit defeat and head home.

Two, she could walk the three meters to the door and knock again.

Sally stared at the door in front of her. It was pale blue with a white frame, and the paint had started to flake away. Beside it, there was a wooden sign with the words *Wisteria Cottage* painted in the same shade as the door. The flowers from which the house took its name framed everything, making it look like something out of a Beatrix Potter story. Sally half expected to see a talking rabbit, hedgehog, or duck appear from the bushes at any moment.

Berit Gardner probably hadn't heard her first timid knock, but Sally didn't want to try again in case it seemed like she was pestering her. Then again, she had caught a glimpse of a face in the kitchen window, and logically that face should have seen her too. Yet the door remained stubbornly closed, and she was still standing on the gravel path, going through her options.

Sally couldn't go home. She couldn't go back and say that Berit hadn't even let her inside. It was ridiculous. It was…undignified. She was practically a grown-up now.

OK, she told herself. She would march right up to the door and knock firmly, loud enough that it made a sound this time, and then she would look Berit E. V. Gardner straight in the eye and say, "Hi! I'm Sally Ma—"

No, it was probably best not to mention her surname just yet, which put her in a bit of a tricky position. She could hardly just go up to the author and introduce herself as "Sally," as though she was some chirpy American waitress. OK, forget the name. She would simply say, "Hi, I'm your new assistant."

But that plan wasn't exactly socially acceptable, either. Just turning up and claiming that you had come to work for someone. Sally was pretty sure her new boss should at least know she had been given an assistant.

She swallowed. She was tired and hungry after the journey from London. The closest train station was a twenty-minute drive away, and there hadn't been any taxis when she arrived. The only bus went once a day, fifteen minutes before her train arrived, and so she hadn't had any choice but to grab her suitcase and start walking. She would probably still be lugging it behind her now if it wasn't for the man around her age who had slowed down, stuck his head out of the window, and asked if she'd run away from home.

Sally had been a hot, sweaty mess, and she couldn't think of anything to say. As it happened, that didn't matter because he didn't wait for an answer before he went on.

"Liam Slater. Driver, knight in shining armor—or a grubby Vauxhall, anyway. Available for hire or sale, cash or down payment. Generous terms, low interest rates, no hidden fees."

When she failed to speak, he had leaned over the seat, opened the passenger-side door, and told her to get in.

"You visiting someone?" he asked once she was in the car.

"I'm not sure."

Thinking back to that moment now, Sally shuddered with embarrassment. He must have thought she was a prize idiot.

"Wisteria Cottage, Albert Lane," Liam had repeated to himself. "That's the author's place, isn't it? The Swedish one? Kind of weird?"

"Berit Gardner."

"She a friend of yours, then?"

"Not…exactly. I'm going to be working for her. Maybe."

"What, she hasn't made up her mind yet? Is it like a trial thing? Don't worry, I'm sure you'll do great. She'll love you. But she can't be much of a boss if she just left you at the station like this! Everyone who lives 'round here knows that the bus and the train times don't match up. Why didn't she come to get you?"

"She doesn't even know I exist."

Liam had stared at her then.

"It's, um…a surprise," she continued. "That I'll be her assistant, I mean."

She had expected some sort of criticism or confused remark, but he had just tipped his head back and roared with laughter.

"Amazing. So ballsy. You know, you remind me of Eleanor. Eleanor Hartfield. She runs the café here in the village. That's exactly the kind of thing she would've done when she was younger. She's crazy too."

Sally had felt a little wounded to be called crazy, and she must have shown it because Liam had quickly reassured her that he meant it as a compliment.

"Eleanor says all the best people are crazy," he said just before he dropped her off outside the cottage. "This is it. Wisteria Cottage, as agreed. Don't worry about the payment. I'll invoice you."

She had missed him the minute he drove away, the sudden silence in the absence of his voice making her feel lonelier than ever.

She stared at the door.

There was a third option, she realized now. She could stand here forever, or at least until the neighbors called the police. She had definitely seen a head of gray hair pop up behind the rose bushes next door.

Right then, the door swung open.

She recognized Berit Gardner immediately from her headshots, the steel-gray hair, cut short, the almost childishly blue eyes. The author looked just like she did in pictures. She looked...well, friendly.

But that was simply a first impression. As Berit Gardner studied Sally now, those same blue eyes took on a stern, almost hostile coldness. Sally got the sense that the older woman viewed everything through a clear-eyed, merciless lens and that she wouldn't hesitate to say exactly what she thought about the world, Sally, and anyone else unfortunate enough to get in her way.

"So, you're my new assistant, are you?" said Berit. She didn't sound especially enthusiastic.

"I, uh...guess so," said Sally. "I mean...yes, I am."

"And I'm sure you have a long, well-established track record as an assistant?"

"Y... No."

Great, thought Sally. She couldn't even manage simple sentences anymore. From the corner of her eye, she saw a head of gray hair disappear behind the rose bushes in next door's garden.

"Name?"

"Sally."

Berit raised an eyebrow.

"Sally M-Marsch."

"I suppose there's some sort of relation there?"

"She's my mum."

Sally wasn't sure, but she thought she caught a glimpse of something human in Berit's eyes. Humor, compassion, possibly a combination of the two.

"My condolences," she said after a moment.

Sally looked up at her for a moment. "Thanks. I think." She steeled herself before she next spoke. "Miss Gardner, I—"

"Call me Berit. Not that it matters. I don't need an assistant, and I certainly have no intention of taking one on just because Olivia wants to wash her hands of you."

Her words didn't upset Sally. What Berit had just said was true. *"This will be a wonderful opportunity for you, sweetheart."* That was what her mother had said once she realized there would be a gap of several months between Sally finishing a language course and enrolling at university. Olivia would never have been able to cope with having her around for that long.

Berit cast a demonstrative glance down at her watch.

"I'm late," she said.

Sally felt her shoulders slump even lower. She couldn't force the author to take her in. In that respect, sadly, she was nothing like her mother. If Berit didn't want an assistant, then Sally would just have to... Well, she wasn't quite sure. Head home, she guessed.

She glumly turned to look at the road, so tired that she shivered, despite the warm spring air.

"I s-suppose I can catch a train back to London this evening." Sally was irritated with herself for sounding so pathetic, but there was nothing she could do about it. She was hot, sweaty, hungry, and weary, and she felt about twelve years old. Her shoulders were also aching after dragging her bag for miles. "I'll just tell Mum that...well, I'll come up with something."

Berit folded her arms.

"Do you know if there's anywhere I can get something to eat in the village?" Sally asked. "I don't want to be any trouble, but it'll probably take me a while to walk back to the station and I'm not sure when the next train is and... Well, thanks anyway." She fumbled for the handle on her suitcase and desperately tried to blink back the embarrassing tears.

"Oh, for God's sake," Berit muttered with a sigh. "Come in, then. But hurry up. We're going to a tea party."

Sally braced herself against the sink with both hands as she stared into the little bathroom mirror.

She looked exactly like someone who had spent the day lugging a heavy suitcase from London to Cornwall. Her hair was plastered to her flushed face, her clothes crumpled and sweaty.

She quickly splashed her face with cold water. From the ground floor, she could hear Berit's restless footsteps on the creaky wooden floor.

You can do this, she told herself. *Just stick to the usual strategy: find a wall and pretend you're invisible.*

She reluctantly made her way downstairs. In the living room, Sally's eyes were immediately drawn to the enormous Edwardian desk that dominated the space. It was incredible, all sleek mahogany and polished brass, with an abundance of drawers. The handsome, dark-green leather writing pad practically seemed to invite creativity, and the desk itself had been angled so that anyone sitting at it would have a view out onto the charmingly overgrown garden through the french doors.

Despite all that, the surface of the desk was empty. Not a single pen or sheet of paper in sight. No sign of the stack of books—whether for reference or inspiration—that every author should have. No computer or charging cables, no Post-it Notes, nothing at all to suggest that any writing was ever done there.

In the middle of the room, Berit waited impatiently with a scarf in each hand.

"The party is up at Tawny Hall, and I suspect half the village will be there."

Sally swallowed. "I'm not very good at parties," she confessed, subconsciously taking a step closer to the wall and shrinking back.

Berit ignored her and impatiently waved both scarves. "Which do you like best?" she asked.

The first one, which Sally suspected Berit preferred, was a shade of deep green. The second was a beautiful, shimmering golden yellow.

"The yellow," she blurted out.

Berit arranged the green scarf around her neck and then patted her pockets.

"Notepad. Pen. Hip flask. You never know when it might come in handy."

She then moved toward Sally, getting right up close. Sally blinked in confusion, holding her breath. Berit's eyes looked bluer than ever, and Sally noticed that she made no attempt to hide her fine lines with makeup.

"Stand still," said the author.

She draped the yellow scarf around Sally's neck with an elegant flourish.

"If you ever feel out of place, you should never try to be invisible," she said. "Nothing draws more attention to a person than trying not to be seen. What you need to do is control what they see. Control the story. There. Now you're the girl with the yellow scarf."

Berit patted her pockets again. "Right," she said. "Let's go."

2

SOMETHING AWFUL IS ABOUT TO *happen*, James Elmer thought as he looked around the tea party.

Nothing had gone to plan lately, but that probably shouldn't have come as a surprise. The same had been true all his life. Ever since he failed his first school test at the age of seven, he had known that life was nothing but one long line of disasters that would catch up with him sooner or later.

He didn't mention any of this to Penny, of course. James Elmer was a firm believer that failure was contagious. People shunned losers in favor of winners, and that was why he had long since learned to hide his fears behind a cheery optimism.

"Relax," said Penny, proving that she had never quite grasped just how much of a struggle life was for him. Things that were simple for others always required a huge amount of effort from James Elmer.

Just take the building work at the hotel. He had drawn up a detailed budget, but the project had already cost far more than planned. The construction firm hadn't stuck to their quote. What was the point in even having a budget if you didn't follow it?

Penny gripped his hand, and he realized he had been fidgeting with his tie. It was now rather lopsided, and he felt an itch to straighten it, but Penny was still holding his hand.

Everywhere he looked, people were wandering around in the sun as though nothing was about to happen. James swallowed and fought back a powerful urge to run home and hide.

"Here. Have some champagne," said his wife. "It'll help perk you up. You'll see."

"I need to talk to Reginald Trent."

It had to be a misunderstanding, he told himself. He could still fix this.

Penny snorted. "Reginald Trent is a bastard, simple as that. He'll never be reasonable. You're kidding yourself if you think there's any point trying to talk to him."

James ignored her. If he could just talk to Mr. Trent, businessman to businessman, he was sure they could straighten things out. He felt himself break out in a cold sweat when he thought about what Penny would say if she knew what he had done.

"Is that the author?" Penny asked. "She looks like a bit of an oddball if you ask me."

He followed her eye.

A middle-aged woman had just arrived with what he assumed might be her daughter. Penny was right. The author wasn't much to look at. She was strangely dressed, in a men's jacket and jeans. It was one thing for teenagers to wear jeans all the time, he thought, but this woman was around his age, if not older. At least forty, possibly even in her fifties. Her hair was gray, and she had made zero effort to liven it up with a bit of color.

The young woman by her side looked much more like his imagined idea of an author. She was dressed entirely in gray, with a dramatic yellow scarf adding a hint of interest. Her trousers were neatly pressed.

James nodded approvingly.

Penny knocked back her first glass of champagne and immediately helped herself to another.

"Come on, let's have a bit of fun," she said. "I've never met an author before."

James shook his head. If she wanted to have fun, she had married the wrong man.

The minute Berit saw Tawny Hall, she instinctively reached down to her jacket pocket. She dug out her notepad and pen and began writing.

The clean, straight Georgian lines were softened slightly by the ivy and the climbing roses, by the sun glittering in the dark windows. The tea party was in the garden, but the house seemed to draw the eye in, suggesting that the real adventure lay indoors.

This was a house with a life of its own, Berit thought. A house with a personality.

A soft, almost girlish voice rang out across the lawn. "Berit Gardner!" it shouted with perfect pronunciation.

Berit turned and saw their hostess coming toward them with outstretched arms. She was wearing a long, white dress that billowed out around her as she sailed over the grass. Her face was hidden behind a white hat with a theatrically large brim, its yellow ribbon the only hint of color.

Berit reluctantly put away her pen and paper. Then she froze. She knew what was coming.

Sure enough, Daphne leaned in to kiss her on both cheeks—something that, as a Swede, Berit had always found excruciating. Her strategy was to stand perfectly still and let it happen. Trying to actively take part and work out which cheek to offer up always ended in disaster, as witnessed by the countless occasions on which she had almost kissed a complete stranger on the lips.

A cloud of Chanel No. 5 enveloped her as the brim of Daphne's hat hit her forehead.

"Welcome!" said Daphne. "I simply must get you to sign your books for my collection."

The hostess glanced back over her shoulder to the woman clutching an armful of books just behind her. Daphne took one from the top of the pile and handed it to Berit.

Berit dug her pen back out of her pocket, opened the cover, and scrawled her illegible signature across half of the endpaper. She then closed it and opened the next, repeating the process until she had worked her way through every book. It still felt absurd to see her name in print, not to mention how odd it was for someone to want her signature on something other than a contract or a credit card payment.

Daphne clapped her hands in delight. "Wonderful!" she said. "Now we can enjoy ourselves."

She seemed oblivious to the fact that no one else seemed to be having much fun. In fact, the atmosphere around them was palpably tense, with the villagers shooting hostile glances in their direction as they passed. No one was smiling.

Four glasses of champagne appeared on a tray in front of them, and Berit studied the woman who had supplied Daphne with both books and alcohol.

"This is Margaret Brown, my secretary," Daphne explained.

"Sally Marsch," Berit countered. "My assistant."

"How do you do?" said Daphne, to which Sally mumbled a polite "How do you do?" in reply.

Of the two women, Daphne was clearly the dominant personality, but Berit found herself drawn to Margaret. Once she started looking at her, it was incredibly hard to stop, perhaps because the secretary seemed so determined to remain professional and in the background. In her own way, she was almost as theatrical as her employer.

"I'm so glad you moved to my little village," Daphne cooed. "I've been the only bookworm here all my life. Sometimes it feels as though I'm the only one who even knows how to read." She gave a loud, joyless laugh before she went on. "You may already have noticed, but Great Diddling isn't exactly a stronghold of culture. No theater, no bookshop, no library."

"Maybe not," said Berit. "But there are definitely stories here, I can feel it."

"Tall tales, perhaps. Lies and pure fiction."

"Precisely."

Berit recognized the first two villagers who came over to introduce themselves as the owner of the local hotel and his wife. She had eaten lunch there once, a meal accompanied by the din of the construction site to the rear of the property. It was a mistake she hadn't repeated since.

The man was in his forties, wearing a tweed suit. He was pale, almost anemically so, though he also had that typically English ruddiness that caused his face to flush at the slightest hint of emotion. Right there and then, he seemed nervous to the point of panic, his cheeks scarlet. The woman with a hand on his arm had frazzled, bleached hair and long, neon-pink nails.

Margaret leaned in to Daphne and whispered something in her ear.

"Allow me to introduce James Elmer," said Daphne. "And this is his wife, Penny. This is Berit Gardner, the famous author who recently moved to the village. Extremely talented!"

Berit pulled a face. "Not that talented," she muttered uncomfortably. As a Swede, she was even more uncomfortable with praise than with cheek kissing.

"How do you do," said James. "Nice to have a bit of culture in Great Diddling. That sort of thing is important, so important. I'm afraid I haven't read any of your books myself, but I'm sure they're…um, very rewarding. Interesting, that's the word I was looking for. I'm always telling Penny that I should start reading more, but it's just so hard to find the time when you're as busy as I am."

He began nervously fiddling with his jacket, and his wife reached out and steadied his hand.

"Oh, thank you," he said as he realized what he had been doing.

Margaret waved to the next person waiting to be shown off to Berit, or perhaps it was Berit being shown off to them. At events like this, it was always hard to know who was the circus animal and who the audience, she thought.

Margaret leaned in toward Daphne again to remind her of the woman's name, but Daphne seemed distracted. Her eyes were on a tall, well-dressed man, following his every move.

"Sima Kumar," Margaret eventually spoke up. "Chair of the local council."

Sima was young, much younger than Berit would have expected for someone in such a prominent position. She was smartly dressed, in gray trousers and a pair of sleek pumps that kept sinking down into the lawn, and she looked at Sally and Berit as though she was trying to work out what she could do for them.

Something about her slightly superior smile and the impatient look in her eye told Berit that she was used to being the smartest person in the room—and that she was terrible at hiding it.

Sima also happened to be strikingly beautiful, though she seemed completely unaware of that fact. Her thick, dark hair framed her sharp cheekbones and large, deep-set eyes, and she had dazzlingly white teeth, her smile both charming and confident.

She followed Daphne's eye, and her expression changed when she saw what Daphne was looking at. Sima's professionalism crumbled, and Berit saw several powerful emotions fighting for dominance. Passion, or possibly desperation, plus something dark, restless, and anxious. Her face paled and then she blushed.

"My nephew, Reginald Trent," Daphne said to Berit.

Berit studied the man who seemed to have provoked such a powerful reaction. He was in a gray summer suit and wore his arrogance like an extra accessory.

"He's some sort of banker in the city," Daphne explained.

"He has a lot of interesting ideas for the future of Great Diddling," said the hotel owner, whose forehead was now slick with sweat. "I'm hoping I can have a word with him later."

Reginald Trent walked past an older woman who had been moving between the guests, pouring more tea and trying to foist sandwiches on them.

"You swine!" she hissed, loud enough for everyone to hear.

He wheeled around, but all he saw was a kind, grandmotherly figure with curly white hair and a meek smile.

"Cucumber sandwich?" she asked.

Berit looked around hungrily, keen to take in every last detail of the people around her. There was certainly a lot to process. No one seemed happy. No one was smiling. Several people were openly glaring at them.

There's desperation here, thought Berit. Dark undercurrents that might have unsettled a different person but from which she drew a lighthearted, almost indecent sense of inspiration. Something had begun to bubble inside her as invigorating as the champagne.

She and Sally had moved closer to the tea tent, but while Berit felt invigorated by the conflicts dancing in the air around her, Sally looked more and more tired. She was clutching an empty plate in her hand and seemed about to fall asleep on her feet.

A young man appeared out of nowhere in front of them. "Hey, so I guess you got the job? I told you it would all work out."

Berit stared at him in confusion for a moment, then realized he was talking to Sally.

He held out a hand to Berit. "Liam Slater. I'm a friend of Sally here."

"He gave me a lift," Sally explained. "From the station. There weren't any buses."

"Sally's going to do a great job for you," said Liam. "I could tell the minute I saw her. You won't find a better person for the job."

Liam was hyperactive, constantly moving and talking, like a boxer darting around the ring to avoid a more powerful opponent's blows. Berit studied him. She suspected that those blows had been both literal and figurative at various times of his life.

He gave her a quick, troubled glance, as though he could sense her pity, and started chatting faster than ever.

"Do you like books? I mean, of course you do, both of you. You're a famous author, right, and you're a famous author's assistant, so you have to. Well, you're going to get a kick out of Tawny Hall, let me tell you. Have you been inside yet? I'm sure Daphne won't mind me showing you around." He grinned. "Not that she needs to know. She's busy with the other guests. She won't notice if we just nip inside."

"No, thanks," Sally blurted out. "We—"

Berit cut her off. "We'd love to have a look around."

Liam led them over to the main entrance and opened the tall, heavy doors.

"Cool, huh?" he said, gesturing to the space in front of them. His voice echoed around the grand hall. "I help out with odd jobs here sometimes."

The floor was filthy, dull with years of dirt and dried-on mud, and books had been piled high against the wall opposite, climbing like vines toward the ceiling and threatening to collapse on unsuspecting passersby. The table beneath them was almost completely obscured by novels, so much so that Berit didn't spot its handsome carved legs at first.

A broad staircase led upstairs, splitting in two directions. It had to be at least three meters wide, but most of the steps were cluttered with books. Berit thought it looked like they had started at the edges and slowly eaten their way inward until there was nothing but a narrow passageway in the middle.

Sally moved over to one of the tallest piles and studied the spines.

"Oh, I love this book," she said, pointing at a dog-eared paperback.

From somewhere deeper in the house, Berit heard Reginald Trent's voice. He sounded mocking and dismissive, and she could also hear another voice mumbling in reply. Reginald was talking to someone face-to-face.

She cast a quick look around. Sally was still distracted by the books, and Liam was distracted by Sally, and so Berit decided to leave them to it.

She popped her head into a dark hallway and saw Reginald and James Elmer standing in a doorway. Reginald towered over James, effortlessly tall and threatening.

"But we had an agreement," James said stubbornly.

"You can't prove that."

James stared at him. "But…but this is wrong." It sounded as though he couldn't believe someone would deliberately act dishonorably in business.

Reginald leaned against the wall with a condescending smile, and Berit felt a sudden urge to wipe the grin from his face.

"You can't do this to me," James protested. "It's my hotel."

"You should have thought about that earlier. I seem to recall you being grateful for the money."

"I was desperate. The renovations… You promised…"

Reginald shrugged. "Things change. If you're upset, you can take it up with my lawyer."

"I can't afford a lawyer. This is crazy. I'm in the middle of the renovation work. All my assets are tied up. I—"

It was so painful to hear James's begging, anxious tone that Berit almost felt grateful when a third voice joined the conversation. His wife, Penny, came storming through another door at the end of the corridor, and she marched straight between her husband and Reginald as though she wanted to physically protect James.

"If you've got something to say to James, you'll have to go through me." She turned to her husband. "I've told you, he was a snake when we were kids, and he's a snake now. You definitely don't want to get into business with him."

Reginald grinned. "I think you'll find he already has."

Penny's eyes darted between the two men.

"What do you mean? James, tell him you'd never have anything to do with him. Tell him you'd rather do business with a rattlesnake. Tell him to go to hell."

"I'm sure your dear James can make his own decisions," said Reginald. "He's man enough to look after the business on his own, isn't he? And believe me, there's nothing you can do about it."

Reginald Trent was taller than both the Elmers—significantly taller in the case of Penny—but that didn't stop her from getting right up close and looking him straight in the eye.

"Believe me, there are plenty of things I can do," she said.

He raised an eyebrow, and she leaned in even closer.

"If you don't leave James alone, I'll kill you."

3

THE WORDS ECHOED IN BERIT'S mind as she, Sally, and Liam exited
the house. The sun was still shining, the grass was still strikingly green, tea
was still being served in charming little teacups, and yet everything felt
irrevocably changed.

A death threat did that to a tea party, Berit thought drily.

I'll kill you.

And she had meant it too, Berit thought. It wasn't just a figure of
speech.

Berit was shaken enough to not even reach for her notepad. Beside her,
Sally looked almost dead from fatigue.

"Are we leaving soon?" she asked hopefully.

"Soon," Berit promised, even though she knew they would have to stay
a while longer.

Something is going to happen here, she thought.

The inspiration was still there inside her, but it had gone from bright
and bubbly to dark and restless. Something was seriously wrong in Great
Diddling. All around her, the tensions were growing. One way or another,
they would find an outlet that afternoon; Berit was sure of it.

Reginald Trent had rejoined the tea party, looking for all appearances
completely unaffected by the threat levied against him. Berit wondered if

it was because he was so used to angering people that he hardly noticed it anymore, or if he just didn't think a woman had it in her to kill him. He might be underestimating women at his own peril, Berit thought.

She kept a firm eye on all his movements, so when he left the party again a short time later, Berit followed him.

There seemed to be an invisible boundary for the guests, right where the lawn gave way to a set of wide, shallow steps. The villagers stuck to the neat grass on one side, but Reginald marched up the steps toward the house with quick, determined steps.

Berit gestured to Sally to stay where she was, and then she too crossed that invisible line as she tiptoed after him up toward the house.

Reginald Trent disappeared through a pair of french doors, and Berit hurried closer. She passed several withered orange trees in large stone pots and noticed the weeds that had sprouted between the paving stones. Behind a faux Roman statue, someone had stashed a broken plastic chair.

She walked along the edge of the building toward the doors where Reginald Trent had disappeared, when something seemed to be calling out to her.

Come here, it whispered. She pressed her nose up against a window and saw a series of familiar shapes in the room on the other side. Bookshelves, she thought, torn between the need to find out what Reginald was up to and the beautiful sight in front of her.

The room was enormous, and the bookshelves too. They had to be at least four meters tall, stretching from floor to ceiling. Berit had just reached out as though to touch the books through the closed window when she heard a voice from the adjacent room.

"I'll get the money; you don't need to worry about that, Gerald. Like I told you, it won't be a problem. You can tell Raglan Harris that if he's willing to let me in on the deal, I won't squander that opportunity. You have my word."

Over on the lawn, Daphne used her hand to block out the sun, squinting to see what on earth Berit was up to. Berit ignored her and crept farther along the building. Her years as an author had left her practically immune to any social conventions.

Daphne's nephew was standing between an open window and an old desk that was angled to face the room, a mobile phone to his ear. Berit could make out more bookshelves beyond him, but these were of an entirely different nature. They looked to be full of old leather volumes, the type of books used as decor rather than anything else. Old reference books bought to give the room a certain gravitas, no doubt, and that had been gathering dust ever since.

"My aunt? Hardly. She's the sort of person who doesn't know the price *or* value of anything. Yes, I've spoken to her. I even tried your line about blood being thicker than books, but she just said that wasn't true, that some books are incredibly thick and that blood is rather thin. Yes, I know she's right, but what the hell does that have to do with anything?"

"Don't worry; I'll come up with something. How long do I have? I'll fix it, I swear."

Berit made her way back over to the lawn. Once she was safely among the other guests, she dug out her notepad and jotted down a few key words: *acting, undercurrents, Gerald, Raglan Harris. Desperation.* She underlined the last one several times.

Daphne, Margaret, and Sally joined her, and she reluctantly put the notepad away. Of all the unwritten social norms that plagued Berit's life, the one that forbade people from taking notes at parties was the most annoying. Apparently, it was "impolite."

In general, she didn't let what other people thought influence her behavior. After all, everyone knew that writers were a strange bunch of people. You might as well use it to your advantage.

But there were limits, she supposed, so she pretended to listen to Daphne, Margaret, and Sally chatting politely about something meaningless—the weather, no doubt—while she looked around her in increasing alarm. The feeling that something was very wrong with this tea party grew stronger.

On the far side of the neat lawn, a single elm stood on a slight rise. A flock of starlings lifted off from its branches, and Berit watched them swarm up into the sky.

And then, the ground shook. Irritatingly enough, her immediate reaction was one of confusion. The second was indignation.

Her brain fought to process all the sudden, illogical sounds: the dull blast, the shattering glass, the ringing in her ears. She looked all around to make sure Sally hadn't been hurt, then turned to the scene in front of her.

Berit took in the cloud of dust swirling above the pots, the broken glass on the patio, the shards of wood and scraps of leather.

And then, unbelievably, the torn pages. They floated through the air above the orange trees and the boxwoods like some new species of bird, fluttering in the breeze and getting caught in the branches, landing softly on the paving stones only to swirl away again. The edges were all ripped and warped, the paper charred and shriveled into strange shapes, but they were also free in a way they had never been while glued between heavy leather covers.

Someone started screaming hysterically, piercingly, and the ringing in Berit's ears continued. As did the shrieking.

"My books!"

Margaret had to grab Daphne to stop her from running toward the devastation.

"Oh my goodness, my library! My books! I need to… Let go of me!"

Margaret gave her a slap, and in the sudden silence that followed, she said, "It's not your library. It's the Old Library. Or rather, it was."

Berit had always wondered whether a slap could really calm someone down when they were hysterical, and some twisted part of her brain made a mental note for future books that it could.

Daphne slowly raised a hand to her cheek, swaying slightly as she tried to regain her composure. "Forgive me," she said. "Yes, of course. I don't know what came over me."

"Stay here," said Berit, moving toward the house. She carefully picked her way across the broken glass, grateful she was wearing a pair of sturdy walking boots.

Every window in what Margaret and Daphne had called the Old Library had been blown out, leaving that part of Tawny Hall open like a doll's house. She could see straight through to the hall on the far side, oddly naked now that it was open to the elements. Other than that, the damage was surprisingly concentrated. A Turkish carpet at one end of the room seemed to have come through the blast intact—though it would probably be ruined if it started raining.

Berit forced herself to turn her attention back to the middle of the room.

She closed her eyes.

Looked again.

Swallowed.

"I think…" she began. She had to pause to clear her throat, which irritated her, as though shock were a sign of weakness. When she continued, her voice sounded oddly distant: "It looks like we have a body in the library."

4

DETECTIVE CHIEF INSPECTOR IAN AHMED of the Devon and Cornwall Police saw the crowd of people gathered outside Tawny Hall before he saw the house itself, and it felt like their heads turned in unison as he turned onto the gravel track to drive up to the property.

There had been several 999 calls following the blast, but none had been as calmly informative as Berit Gardner's: "My name is Berit Gardner, and I'd like to report a murder."

He pulled up by the outer cordon that had been set up to keep the press and the public back from the scene. The blue and white tape cut straight across the grounds in a large ring around the house. An officer in uniform had been stationed by the road, and Ian Ahmed held up his ID to be allowed through.

Detective Sergeant Bill Stevens caught up with him on the driveway.

"I see you're back from your vacation," said Stevens.

"Got back two weeks ago," replied DCI Ahmed. *And three days*, he thought. But who was counting?

Stevens was a few years older than him, pushing fifty, but he lacked the drive and ambition to climb the ranks. DCI Ahmed felt both guilty and grateful for that. Stevens was competent, conscientious, and easy to work with, a man who had no trouble following orders.

And much happier than me, Ian Ahmed thought without any real jealousy or resentment.

"Seriously nice house, this. The garden out back is magnificent," said Stevens. "Neglected, but that's not really surprising. You'd need an army of gardeners to stay on top of a place like this. But just imagine what you could do with it."

Stevens had three adult sons that he worshipped, a wife he clearly adored, and a garden that got any time or attention left over.

"Do any of those belong to the victim?" asked DCI Ahmed, nodding to the cars parked in front of the house.

"The Jaguar, I think."

Ian Ahmed nodded. "Run the plates, and get someone to put up an extra cordon around it for the time being. Make sure no one searches it until we've worked out a forensic strategy."

He felt rested and expectant, eager to finally get to immerse himself in a real case. It was his first since he got back from a hiking trip to Mont Blanc, returning first to the bureaucratic, administrative grind.

Returning to his romantic life too. He had been seeing a crown prosecutor from London on and off for a while now, and she had traveled down to Cornwall yesterday for a weekend of rest and relaxation. She had brought a few bottles of expensive wine and a head full of thoughts about a recent case she had closed. Ian Ahmed had listened, asked a few informed questions, and massaged her feet. Ever since he dated his first detective, he had come to realize that working women always seemed to have aching feet.

It had been a mutually satisfying weekend that had come to an abrupt end when his phone started ringing, and Ian Ahmed was acutely aware that he hadn't really minded having to leave to get back to work.

Nor had she. If anything, she had seemed relieved. She had opened her laptop before he even left the house, curled up with it on the sofa wearing nothing but one of his oversized T-shirts. She would head back to London before he got back to the apartment, he thought.

"Who was first on the scene?" he asked.

"A young constable," said Stevens. "Name of Philips, I think."

DCI Ahmed took in the scene as Stevens led him around the back of the property. The lawn had been mown in a half-moon shape, and a large tent had been set up at the far side. It was deserted, and the ground was dotted with napkins, plates, and champagne glasses that had been dropped in the chaos following the explosion. A broken tea cup looked jarringly forlorn in the grass, smashed to pieces in the panic and jostle. He stepped gingerly over it.

Stevens took him up a short set of stone steps, giving DCI Ahmed his first glimpse of the destruction. Shards of glass, scraps of paper, and other nondescript pieces of material were scattered across the paving area.

The grand house towered over their heads, the chaos an insult to its straight, classic lines. He couldn't rid himself of a fanciful notion that the house was displeased about the destruction but not the death.

There was something indifferent about old houses like this, thought Ahmed. As though they had been standing for so long that it didn't matter to them whether someone died within their walls.

Personally, he had the same wild, furious reaction he always did when faced with the fact that someone had taken another person's life. He never got used to the sight of sudden, violent death.

Ian Ahmed allowed himself this moment of private rage before he forced the detective inside of him to take over. Logic, control, clearheaded thinking, that was what was needed to lead a major crime investigation. But he knew from past experience that he would need the anger, too. It would fuel him during the long days to come.

"Ever investigated an explosion, Stevens?"

"Can't say I have, sir."

"Me neither. That's the constable, isn't it?"

A young officer in uniform was hurrying toward them. He had the uncomfortable air of someone competent and conscientious who had suddenly gained far more responsibility than they were used to.

Perhaps he knew—DCI Ahmed certainly did—that their actions today would be picked apart, questioned, and analyzed going forward. Whatever they did or didn't do now could be decisive in securing a conviction when the case came to trial many months and countless hours of work from now.

That was enough to make anyone break out in a sweat.

The constable looked much too young for his uniform, but so did most of the new recruits these days. DCI Ahmed knew he probably hadn't been much older when he first joined the force; it was just that he could no longer remember ever having been that young.

He gave the officer a reassuring smile.

"DCI Ian Ahmed," he said. "And you are?"

"Philips, sir. Peter Philips."

"Relax, constable. Just tell me everything you've done so far in the order that you did it."

"Yes, sir."

The constable spent a few seconds trying to gather his thoughts, then he took a deep breath, as though to steel himself. "The call from control said they'd received several reports of an explosion at Tawny Hall, just outside of Great Diddling, and that there was a suspected fatality."

DCI Ahmed nodded. They had got the first call at 4:32. He had listened to the recording of it so many times now that he knew it by heart: "My name is Berit Gardner, and I'd like to report a murder."

"The woman who made the call identified the victim as Reginald Trent," the constable continued.

DCI Ahmed nodded toward the building. "Is he the owner of the house?"

"He was a guest here, sir. His aunt owns it, Daphne Trent. She also witnessed the explosion."

The three police officers turned instinctively toward the mangled doors.

"There are plenty of witnesses," Stevens muttered. "As I understand it, they were having a tea party at the time."

"Dangerous things, those," DCI Ahmed remarked drily.

"Yes, sir," the young constable replied, slightly taken aback.

"How sure are we of the victim's identity?"

"It was the woman who made the first call who ID'd him, sir. The victim's aunt confirmed it too, but I didn't want to go in until you'd arrived, so I haven't checked for a wallet or any other forms of ID."

"Has anyone else been in the house?" asked DCI Ahmed.

"No, sir. I wasn't sure it was safe."

Ian Ahmed nodded. "You have a point there. Stevens, can you try to get hold of someone who can give us a yes or no? We need to know it's structurally sound before we send forensics in.

DCI Ahmed turned to the young constable again.

"You spoke to the witnesses when you first arrived at the scene?"

"Yes, sir."

"Did they tell you anything other than what they said in the call?"

"I didn't ask. I assumed you would want to talk to them yourself, sir."

"But they hadn't touched anything? No one entered the room?"

"The call handler told them not to, and they said they'd followed those instructions."

DCI Ahmed thought back to the recording. He remembered the operator's voice: "I've dispatched a patrol car, so please wait at a safe distance until they arrive. Don't touch anything, and don't remove anything from the crime scene."

Berit Gardner had replied, "I wasn't exactly planning to go in and start grabbing things."

"How did the woman who called it in seem to you?" asked DCI Ahmed.

"How she seemed, sir?"

"Your impression of her. Was she in shock?"

"Right, sir…I mean…I didn't think…"

"You're doing great, Philips. No real mistakes and plenty of initiative." He patted the young man on the shoulder. "Just give me your subjective impression of her."

The constable seemed to grow several centimeters once the weight of responsibility and possible criticism was lifted from his shoulders.

"No, sir," he said slowly. "I didn't think she seemed shocked. I actually thought she was oddly calm."

Calm and controlled, that was Ahmed's own impression of Berit Gardner. She had answered all of the call handler's questions methodically, in detail, with a hint of sharpness in her voice. As though she was more used to asking the questions than being subjected to them. It was only toward the end of the call that she had revealed anything resembling shock. Or possibly impatience. "For God's sake," she had said, "just send a car out here. A man has been murdered and you're playing twenty questions."

"And…is calmness suspect, sir?" Philips asked.

"Not in and of itself," said Ahmed.

Shock could take many forms, and agitation was no guarantee of innocence. The vast majority of murderers were agitated in one way or another. Most violent crimes were impulsive, driven by intense emotion, which explained the often excessive brutality. Once the dust had settled, perpetrators could be just as shocked by what they had done as anyone else.

Though, on the other hand, it also wasn't uncommon for perpetrators to call the emergency services themselves or to be among the first witnesses.

DCI Ahmed turned to the crowd of onlookers and studied their faces. It looked like half the damn village had turned out to watch the show, and he was starting to feel like a circus animal.

Berit Gardner was somewhere among them.

Stevens followed his eyeline.

"What should we do with them, guv?" he asked.

"They'll get bored soon enough. When forensics gets here, tell them to cover the windows to block out the weather and any prying eyes. Apparently it's going to rain."

Philips and Stevens both looked up at the sky. There wasn't a cloud in sight.

DCI Ahmed glanced over the grass, toward the crowd.

"What did you say her relationship was to the victim?" he asked.

"Whose, sir?" asked Philips.

"Daphne Trent, the owner of the house, where the victim was currently living. You mentioned that earlier, I think?"

"His aunt, sir. On his father's side."

DCI Ahmed nodded. "When you talk to the guests, I'd like you to pay attention to anyone who asks a lot of questions about the investigation or expresses an unnatural interest in our work in any way."

"You think the perp hung around to get a better look at their work?" Stevens asked. "Like a pyromaniac?"

"Or to keep an eye on what we're doing."

Berit thought it seemed as though the police officer in charge was staring right at her, and that made her uneasy. As though he could see straight through her—and from a distance at that.

It was obvious that he was in charge of the investigation. Even those who weren't talking to him seemed acutely aware of his presence. The chaos took on a sense of order with him nearby.

She could still see the destruction in front of her, and it felt just as incomprehensible now as it had earlier. Berit had automatically tried to process the chaotic scene, but that had only made everything even more incoherent, as though her brain was locked in battle with her eyes. Shards of glass. The lamp in the corner, which was more or less intact. Don't look at the body. The Turkish carpet, which would be ruined if it rained. The interior walls, suddenly so vulnerable. She had never realized just how much of an impact the senses had on each other before. Unable to hear anything, the devastation in front of her had been even more disorienting.

It bothered her that she was incapable of describing the experience, as though her shocked state had caused her to fail as an author. At the same time, however, she couldn't escape the feeling that trying to make literature from another person's death would mean she had failed as a human being.

Beside her, Sally was pale and quiet.

"Are you OK?" Berit asked, much more gruffly than she intended.

Her new assistant nodded unconvincingly.

Berit turned back to the house again. People in white overalls had gathered on the driveway, and they were busy setting up a tent in front of the damaged section. The detective chief inspector was standing slightly back from others, talking to someone on the phone.

She watched as he ended his call, turned to the crowd, and started walking straight toward her, ducking beneath the police cordon far more nimbly than she ever could.

He was tall and thin, more wiry than muscular, with the natural self-confidence of someone used to making a lot of important decisions, and quickly—and no doubt having to justify them afterward, she thought.

"Berit Gardner?" he said. "You made the first 999 call."

It sounded more like a statement than a question, so she didn't say a word.

He introduced himself. "I'm Detective Chief Inspector Ian Ahmed, with the Devon and Cornwall Police. I'd like to ask you a few questions if you have a moment?"

She waved a hand impatiently. "A man is dead. Of course I have a moment. I'm not exactly going anywhere, am I?"

"Would you mind taking me through everything that happened? I know it can be frustrating to have to repeat yourself, but I'd like to hear it in your own words, to avoid any misunderstandings."

His voice was warm and kind but with an unmistakable note of strength and determination. A man who inspired confidence and commanded respect. Berit got the sense that he was as good at reassuring shaken witnesses as he was at interrogating suspects, and she realized with a jolt that he still hadn't decided which category she belonged to.

"Start a little before the beginning," he said.

Berit nodded. "As we do in novels." She told him all about the tea party, the explosion that she had gone over to the window and seen… She hesitated there, unsure which words to use. The victim? Mr. Trent? The remains? "The body," she eventually rounded off.

"And you recognized Mr. Trent?"

She nodded.

DCI Ahmed fixed his eyes on her. "We'll have to carry out a formal identification before we can release any names. I hope you understand that, just in case the press gets in touch. Out of respect for Mr. Trent's family."

"I'm not going to talk to the press," she snapped.

"Thank you," he replied. "You told my colleague that the explosion took place sometime between 4:29 and 4:31. How sure are you about that?"

"I checked my watch before I called 999. It can't have been much more than a couple of minutes after the explosion, and I'm guessing it was probably less than that. Perhaps even as little as thirty seconds."

"And you didn't go into the room yourself? Think carefully now."

"It happened less than two hours ago. I'm perfectly capable of remembering what I did. The answer is no. I stopped around half a meter from the win... From where the windows used to be. I remember reaching out to open it, even though I could see it wasn't there anymore. Idiotic."

"Human," he corrected her.

"Yes," said Berit. "But those are so often one and the same, aren't they? In any case, I didn't get any closer before I saw...him."

"And you didn't touch anything? Or move anything?"

"No. I could see right away that there was nothing I or anyone else could do for him."

"So what did you do next?"

"I called 999. And then I followed their instructions, waited for the police to arrive, spoke to a young officer, and waited for you to turn up. And then I waited for you to spare the time to speak to us."

"I apologize for the wait. There are always hundreds of things that need to be done at the start of an investigation."

"Yes," Berit replied, a little embarrassed. "I don't suppose it matters."

"How did you know Mr. Trent?"

"I didn't. I'd never spoken to him."

"How long had he been in Great Diddling?"

"No idea. You'll have to ask Daphne Trent or Margaret Brown. I'm sure they'll know."

"Are you close to them?"

"No, not at all."

"But they invited you to their tea party?"

"Yes."

DCI Ahmed studied her again. When she didn't volunteer any more information, he continued:

"Why is that? Perhaps you're becoming friends?"

"Daphne Trent likes my books. I just moved to the village. I think she invited almost everyone."

"Aha, you're an author! Have I read anything you've written?"

"How on earth could I possibly know that?"

"No, of course. I'll have to look you up later."

Berit doubted he would have much time for reading in the near future.

"You must be Sally Marsch," said the detective.

Sally nodded.

"How old are you, Sally?"

"Nineteen."

His eyes darted between Berit and Sally.

"And she is your—?"

"I'm her assistant," Sally filled in.

Berit felt herself blush, so utterly Swedish that her soul rose up in protest at the idea of DCI Ahmed thinking she considered herself important enough to need an assistant. As though she thought she was anyone special!

"She's my agent's daughter," Berit explained.

"I won't keep you," the detective said to Sally. "Unless you have anything else to add to what Ms. Gardner just told me?"

"Please, call me Berit."

Sally shook her head.

"Then you're both welcome to go home. Try to get some rest, OK?" He smiled at Sally, and she smiled back wanly. "A warm bath often helps. Or a blanket and a nice cup of tea."

Berit thought that both sounded like strange suggestions for a sunny Sunday evening in the middle of May. It had to be at least twenty degrees Celsius in the sun, and her blazer was still draped over her arm. Then she noticed that Sally was wearing her drab beige coat again, shivering despite the sunshine.

"It's the shock," DCI Ahmed said quietly. Berit was irritated she hadn't thought of that herself. "Try to get her to eat. Tea and toast, something like that. A few carbs should do the trick."

A middle-aged man with a friendly face and a smart suit came over to them.

"Detective Sergeant Stevens," said DCI Ahmed, somewhere between a greeting and an introduction.

"Sorry to bother you, guv," said the man, "but Daphne Trent is refusing to answer any questions."

Daphne Trent was standing with her arms folded, glaring at DS Stevens. When she noticed DCI Ahmed, she glared at him too, as though he was guilty just by being there.

"What exactly is she refusing to answer?" Ahmed whispered to Stevens.

"Where she was at the time of the blast? What she thought of the victim?"

"Her age, sir."

"I've never been so insulted in all my life!" said Daphne.

"Christ, Stevens. What did you say to her?"

"That I didn't believe she was forty-seven. My wife is forty-seven."

"I tried to be reasonable," said Daphne. "But forty-seven is my final offer. I'm afraid I can't help you if your bullheaded sergeant can't understand that."

DCI Ahmed was on the verge of smiling when he noticed the expression of the woman standing next to her. She was watching Daphne with a look of concern, and he realized that the theatrical behavior was likely covering up a good deal of shock, possibly exhaustion.

"My colleague never did have an eye for beauty," he said, reaching out to touch the older woman's arm, both to support and encourage her. "That's something I've often noticed over the years. I don't see the problem, Stevens. Ms. Trent here is clearly forty-seven and not a day older. Make a note of that."

"Righto, sir."

"And apologize to the young lady."

"Yes, sir. My apologies, sir."

"Good. That's one misunderstanding straightened out." DCI Ahmed gave Daphne a warm smile. "I'm afraid it may be a while before we can let you back into the house. Is there anything you need? A chair? A glass of water? A nice invigorating cup of tea?"

Daphne reassured him that she was just fine, that Margaret would get her anything she needed, and that if it came to it, champagne was far more invigorating than tea.

"I understand Mr. Trent was your nephew?" DCI Ahmed said.

"Yes, that's right."

"But he didn't live here on a permanent basis?"

"No, he had a flat in London. But he spent his summers at Tawny Hall when he was younger, and he was always welcome back here as a grown man. My home was his home. I often told him that. Come anytime. No need to call ahead."

"How long had he been here this time?"

Daphne turned to the woman beside her. "Margaret Brown, my secretary," she explained.

The secretary, a competent, reassured women with the air of someone who remained coolheaded in a crisis, answered for her: "Since Sunday. He arrived in the morning, just before lunch."

Daphne nodded. "Completely out of the blue. Like I said, he was always welcome."

"The two of you were close?"

"He was the only family I had left." She took out a pretty lace handkerchief and dabbed her dry eyes.

The two aren't necessarily the same, Ian Ahmed thought to himself.

"I gave him the blue room," Daphne said. "The best room in the house."

"I'm sure he was very comfortable there," DCI Ahmed said politely. He looked closely at the two women. "Did you keep any explosives in the house?"

It was Margaret who answered first. "No," she said decisively. "I would never allow something so dangerous to just lay about where anyone could get at it."

"I think having a little dynamite about the place could come in handy," said Daphne. "You never know when you might need to get rid of something."

"Was there anything else you can think of that might have exploded?"

"No," Margaret said firmly.

"Gas?"

"In the kitchen," said Margaret. "But that's at the other end of the house."

DCI Ahmed nodded and thanked the two women, then made his way back beneath the cordon.

He would eat his police ID if Daphne Trent was telling the truth about being close to her nephew. The charade with the handkerchief hadn't fooled him for a second. No, the woman wasn't grieving in the slightest. She wasn't displaying any genuine emotions at all.

His thoughts were interrupted by the police constable who had been first on the scene. He approached the senior detective slowly, unsure of himself, hesitating before he spoke.

"How can I help you, Philips?" the DCI asked.

"I, um, was wondering, sir, if there was any chance that you'll…um, need people to help with the investigation going forward? Whether there was anything I could do?"

DCI Ahmed studied the young man. "My first introduction to a murder inquiry involved standing guard at a crime scene where a woman had been found dead," he said. "I was there all night, with nothing but her ghost for company. I know how you feel. Once you've seen how someone's life has come to a premature end, you want to be involved in getting justice for them."

DCI Ahmed patted him on the shoulder. "We're going to need help interviewing the locals, and you have a friendly face. Who knows, maybe they'll open up to you. Every investigation ultimately comes down to getting the public to trust us. Without that, we'd never be able to do our job."

Once DCI Ahmed had walked away, the young constable turned to DS Stevens.

"Is he always like that?" he asked.

"When I first started, he had me working as the family liaison officer," said Stevens. "He said the family was at the heart of every murder investigation, that we did it for their sake. To give them closure and that sort of thing. He said I would learn a lot by dealing with them."

"And did you?"

"Sure. I learned that it's usually someone in the family who did it."

5

AN ENGINEER FROM THE FIRE brigade inspected Tawny Hall and determined that it was safe to go in.

"A big old house like this can handle far more than that little bang," he said, unperturbed by the aftermath of the blast. "No structural damage. Walls and ceiling, all OK. Feel free to send your guys in."

With that, he walked away, whistling to himself.

While the forensic team got to work on his crime scene, DCI Ahmed asked Daphne Trent's secretary to show him to the victim's room.

"You're welcome to use the kitchen again now," he told her. "And everything else on that side of the house, including your own rooms, of course. But I'm afraid I'll have to cordon off Mr. Trent's bedroom and the hallway outside the room where the explosion took place until we've finished our work here."

Margaret nodded. "The library is on that corridor, and Daphne is going to need some books out of there sooner or later. But I'm sure we can find a way around that."

DCI Ahmed handed her his card. "In case you think of anything else. Or in case you need anything."

Margaret thanked him and calmly went off to continue her tasks, competent, quietly assured, and completely unfazed by the sudden intrusion of a murder in her life. Ian Ahmed had to remind himself again that a lack of shock wasn't in itself suspicious.

The blue room may well have been a fitting name at one point in time, but that was no longer the case. The wallpaper had presumably once been a rich shade of royal blue, but it was now so dusty that it looked almost dark gray. The curtains in the tall windows were so sun bleached that they had turned a shade of dirty white, with only slivers of their former pretty, pale blue visible at the edges that had hung in the shadows.

An enormous cherrywood bed took up much of the room. Neatly made, DCI Ahmed noted—by Mr. Trent or someone else? They would have to look into whether there were any staff other than Margaret Brown and exactly what her duties were.

It would have been easy enough for someone who lived or worked at Tawny Hall to plant the explosives. But what about the guests? Had any of them been inside the house, or had the party stayed outside? He added that to the list of questions they needed to answer.

Other than the bed and the nightstand, the only other piece of furniture in the room was a huge cherrywood wardrobe. Five suitcases of varying sizes had been lined up against the wall, lying flat for easy access, rather than to take up as little space as possible. Not exactly what you'd expect for a nephew on a brief, spontaneous visit to his aunt.

DCI Ahmed opened one of the cases and found several suits inside, still in their dry-cleaning bags. The next contained white T-shirts and underwear, all ironed and folded, plus a number of neatly rolled pairs of socks.

If Reginald Trent had been at Tawny Hall for a full week before he died, why hadn't he unpacked his suitcases?

DCI Ahmed opened the wardrobe and immediately found the answer. The dead man had left his things in his cases because the wardrobe was full to the brim with books.

"Detective Ahmed."

He was making his way back to the rear of the house when that Swedish author called to him from the other side of the cordon. Ian Ahmed waved her over and watched as she ducked beneath the tape and walked toward him with an open notepad in her hands. It was as though they had swapped roles, he thought, and it was her turn to question him.

"I realized I might have been unnecessarily taciturn before," Berit said. "The shock, I assume."

She sounded as brusque as ever, but he decided that was probably just because she'd had to admit her weakness. He was on the verge of reassuring her that it was only human when he remembered that she didn't like showing her human side either. He also remembered the stricken way she had looked at Sally when he pointed out that the young woman was in shock. Maybe there was a soft heart under all that impatient brusqueness, he thought.

"You don't live in Great Diddling, do you?" Berit asked him.

"No, I'm based at the Crownhill Station in Plymouth," he replied. "For my sins."

"I'm not from around here either, but I have been living in the village for the past few weeks and I've noticed a few things. That gives me, if you'll excuse me saying so, a certain advantage over you. I'm also an author. We… observe things."

"I'm sure you're an excellent observer, Ms. Gardner." He wasn't lying. DCI Ahmed had the unnerving sense that she could see straight through him.

Berit tore out a sheet from her notepad and handed it to him. It was a list of names.

Berit Gardner
Sally Marsch
Liam Slater
The Hartfield sisters?
James Elmer
Penny Elmer

"These are the people I know were inside Tawny Hall at some point during the tea party," she explained. "Other than Reginald Trent, Margaret Brown, and Daphne Trent, that is."

"Of course."

He noted that she had included herself and Sally on the list.

"The Hartfield sisters were doing the catering. They must have been in the kitchen at some point, but I didn't actually see them there. Hence the question mark."

She tore out a second sheet, featuring another list, shorter this time.

One of the Hartfield sisters
James Elmer
Penny Elmer
Daphne Trent

"This is a list of people I know disliked Reginald Trent," she said.

"You've included his aunt on this list," he said.

"Oh yes, she couldn't stand the man. She spent most of her time at the tea party glaring at him as though she wanted the ground to open up and send him tumbling down into the fiery pits of hell."

"Or die a violent death in an explosion?" DCI Ahmed suggested.

"Or that."

Berit handed over a third sheet featuring a single name.

Penny Elmer.

"And this list?" he asked.

"People who threatened to kill Reginald Trent. I heard it firsthand, just half an hour before the explosion."

Penny Elmer had her husband's jacket draped over her shoulders. An expression of his urge to protect her, DCI Ahmed thought to himself, though when he saw them standing together it actually seemed more like she wanted to protect him.

She was a half step in front of her husband, standing in an aggressive stance with her chin thrust out and her hands on her hips.

Behind her, James looked uncomfortable.

"I don't understand," he said in a weak, whiny voice. "Surely it was an accident? A gas leak or something?"

"We're investigating every angle," said DCI Ahmed.

"But surely you don't think someone deliberately caused the explosion?"

"We haven't ruled anything out yet."

James seemed torn between his instinct to respect authority and his need to know more. In the end, the latter won out.

"But…why would someone want to kill Reginald Trent?"

DCI Ahmed glanced from James to Penny and back again. "You can't think of any reason?" he asked.

"No, no reason at all," James said quickly. The man was a terrible liar.

Penny disagreed. "The man was a snake. I can think of at least a dozen people who wanted him dead."

She was much harder to read than her husband, and DCI Ahmed got the sense that she was hiding behind her blunt honesty.

"But they wouldn't really," James protested. It sounded as though he was trying to convince himself as much as anything. "I know he rubbed people up the wrong way, but they wouldn't actually kill him. He was a…driven businessman, that's true, and he might have stepped on a few toes during his visit here, but that's no reason to plant a bomb! This is all so bizarre. Bizarre."

"Did you talk to him during the tea party?" DCI Ahmed asked.

"I wouldn't exactly call it a conversation," said Penny. "More an argument."

James glanced at her, his face stricken. DCI Ahmed caught a flash of fear in his eyes when he thought she wasn't looking. But a fear of what?

"I didn't like Mr. Trent," Penny said. "And the same is true of half the village."

"In fact, you threatened to kill him, didn't you?"

"I might have said something along those lines. He put me all out of temper. But I didn't *kill* him. I would never. I mean, you don't, do you? It was just a heat-of-the-moment thing."

"Because you were angry with him. Furious, in fact."

"Of course I was! The man was a snake."

"But not enough to kill him?"

"No! And I sure as hell wouldn't have killed him with a bomb. That's insane. If he had been killed by a knife run violently through his cold, selfish heart or if he'd been beaten repeatedly with a blunt instrument..." She seemed to relish the thought and then remembered who she was talking to. "But not a bomb! I wouldn't even know how to make one."

"That's right," her husband said eagerly. "Penny is hopeless with all these technical things, aren't you, darling?"

"Hopeless," Penny agreed.

"What was the argument about?" DCI Ahmed asked suddenly.

"What argument?"

"With Mr. Trent. You said that you argued?"

"Oh, that. Well, nothing, really. It was just one of those things. Like I said, the man was a snake."

He waited, just in case silence would produce results where questions did not. People were often uncomfortable with silence and rushed to fill it. James fidgeted nervously with his tie, and Penny grabbed his hand. For a moment, it looked like he was about to say something, but Penny gave the hand a warning squeeze.

"Thank you for your time," DCI Ahmed said eventually, handing them both a card. "In case you think of anything else."

"Of course, of course," James said much too quickly. Ahmed was sure he saw relief in his eyes before they hurried away from him.

What could Reginald Trent have done to them that was so threatening? One thing was clear at the very least: far more had gone on between them and Reginald Trent than they were willing to admit to the police.

Or to each other.

Penny had also been right when she said that she wasn't the only person who disliked Reginald Trent.

DCI Ahmed felt the locals' eyes on him, so powerfully that it made the hair on the back of his neck stand on end. When he turned around, he found himself gazing straight at a wall of sullen faces.

Several of them were openly glaring at him, and no one was crying.

So far, he hadn't met a single person who seemed upset by Reginald Trent's death.

6

BERIT SLEPT FITFULLY.

She tossed and turned all night while she dreamt of flying book pages and villagers that were never what they seemed. At dawn, she gave up trying to sleep and went downstairs and made herself a cup of coffee.

She took the coffee into the living room and opened the french doors to let in the smell of cold grass and warm sunshine. A beautiful day was dawning, making her thoughts of bombs and murder seem like the overheated fantasies of a restless mind.

Her body ached. She sat down in front of her beautiful desk and wearily leaned her elbows on the luxurious, green leather. She took a sip of coffee and closed her eyes.

Her body might be tired, but her head felt clearer than it had in months, and her entire mind hummed with an energy that she recognized so well. She felt like crying, so intense was the relief.

She might love the desk in front of her, but the truth was that it had been a very long time since she had last written on it.

Six months, to be precise.

Berit could still remember the afternoon in mid-November when she realized that her head had suddenly gone quiet. The voices had vanished. It was like waking up blind one morning. A missing sense, a moment of panic.

She had continued to sit down at her desk every single day, as though the voices and inspiration would come back to her so long as she was waiting in the right place, and she had kept that up until the very sight of the damn thing made her want to scream.

The solution to her problems was right here in Great Diddling; she knew that. She hadn't felt so inspired by a place since she first moved to London at the age of twenty. Berit had made the move for the literature and the stories, for the history and the books and, like Helene Hanff, she had found the exact version of London she was looking for.

Her first home there had been a charming bohemian flat in Bloomsbury. She had shared it with four other young women, and since then she'd never been short of ideas. That flat was full of characters. The owner's father had been an actor with the Royal Shakespeare Company, and he always spoke a little too loudly during his visits in a rich, powerful, extremely well-articulated voice. It meant that a simple line like "Yes, I think I'll have a splash of milk" sounded like a soliloquy.

She had drawn on him in a short story she had written about a lonely, retired actor who still projected everything he said though there was no longer anyone there to hear him. Sooner or later all of her flatmates had ended up in her work in one way or another—all but one of them, who also happened to be the one person who fascinated Berit most. That particular flatmate had been so carelessly self-absorbed, so completely selfish, in a way Berit had never experienced before or since. If there was only one biscuit left, she would eat it, and if there was hardly any milk left in the carton, she would take what she needed for her tea and then pour the rest down the sink. If any of them ever met a handsome man, she stole him too. The girls quickly learned not to take anyone home with them and to always keep a spare pack of biscuits hidden in their rooms. She had eventually met a man who owned a hotel in Tenerife, and she had moved there to run the hotel with him. Berit couldn't imagine her in a customer relations job. It was just too unrealistic to use in a novel.

Berit had lived constantly with her nose in a notepad, frantically scribbling down everything she saw and heard. She would sit at her tiny desk by the damp, dirty wall for hours after the others went to bed, eagerly trying to jot it all down before she forgot it. Berit could still remember the scent of the paper and ink—hunched so close to her notepad that the words became a blur—the scratching sound of her pen.

She had managed to write ten books in the end. Most had been positively reviewed, and on the whole, they had brought her enough pleasure that she never thought about doing something else. She didn't earn much money from her writing, of course, but she hadn't minded having to live cheaply to be able to do what she loved. Berit had been free, she realized now, quietly satisfied with the life she had chosen.

And that was how she had assumed it would continue, until a gang of unruly pensioners on a trip to Brighton had taken over her thoughts and upended her carefully constructed life. Berit had been picking up the pieces after the end of a relationship, and in her fragile state, life had felt unusually gray and dull. Perhaps that was why she'd felt the need to create something so crazy and absurdly funny.

The book was an immediate hit, and Berit soon discovered—much too late—that success was far harder to bear than failure had ever been. At first, she had agreed to everything. She had gone to every book festival, answered every question, visited every bookshop and book group that invited her, until she woke up one day and realized that her mind had gone blank. Her head was eerily quiet. The voices, the vague outlines of potential stories, the fully-fledged imaginary friends that had always chatted to her, the alternative universes where she had lived half of the time—all gone. And in their place there was nothing but a stubborn, constant, unbending reality.

Never again, she had promised herself.

Since that quiet, frightening day in November, she had begun to pick and choose which emails she responded to, turning down requests and ignoring her agent's phone calls. Five months later, when that failed to make any difference, she had left her beloved London.

Left? No, it had been more of a panicked escape.

She had bought the cottage in Great Diddling without even seeing it in person and left London for Cornwall as soon as she'd gotten the keys to it. It had been the right decision—she had been sure of that the minute she set foot in the cottage. The minute she saw Tawny Hall. The minute she stood among the villagers and eavesdropped on their conversations.

And then the earth shook and everything shattered.

She took a deep, shaky breath. The gentle summer wind brought with it the sweet scent of her neighbors' roses, even more intoxicating than usual in the crisp, early morning. Had she found her stories only to lose them right away?

No. Her entire being rose up in protest.

The blast had crystallized certain things in the villagers that she had previously only caught glimpses of. It hadn't just broken the windows; it had torn the masks from several of the villagers' faces, and in their shock afterward, Berit had seen their true, unguarded feelings.

Hatred, uncertainty, fear, love, a desire to protect—everything that makes people interesting and that we do our utmost to hide. Yesterday it had all been suddenly, violently revealed.

She had to admit that the murder itself fascinated her. Curiosity had always been one of her biggest driving forces, and faced with a real-life, genuine mystery she felt a powerful longing to work out exactly what had happened.

But could she do it?

She knew more about the people in Great Diddling than the police, that much was clear, and she could find out even more. She could go where the police couldn't and listen in on conversations that would turn silent the moment the police showed up. Watch and observe everything around her, the way she always did. Spend time among the people of Great Diddling and see what she could find out.

Berit ran her hands over the smooth desk. Then she reached for her notepad.

It all began with a single question, she thought, and she wrote it down on the blank page in front of her.

What does it take to kill a person?

She jotted down her first thoughts. A few related questions sprang from that first, big one. Little by little, the pages of her notepad began to fill up. Words, boxes, circled text, and arrows danced before her eyes. The garden was so quiet that she could hear the scratching of her pen on the paper.

Something was ringing.

Sally's brain felt like cotton wool, and she had an awful taste in her mouth.

There was something hard digging into her cheek, and she reached beneath her head on the pillow. Ah. Her phone.

The ringing continued, and she reluctantly squinted toward the screen and answered the phone call.

"Were you there?"

Sally flinched at her mother's loud, sharp voice. Her own sounded rough when she replied:

"Huh, where?"

"At the tea party of course! All the papers are talking about it today. It's all over the news—bombs, murder, and Cornwall."

"Yes," Sally croaked, closing her eyes.

Her mother seemed to be holding her breath. "With Berit?"

"Mmm."

Olivia exhaled. "Oh, this is perfect. We can use this. Author caught up in real-life murder…helping the police with their inquiries…an explosive mix of reality and fiction."

Sally rolled over onto her back and stared up at the ceiling.

"Where are you staying?" Olivia asked suddenly.

"At Berit's."

"So you managed to get in at the very least." Her mother sounded reluctantly impressed. "And she let you join her at the tea party? Good work. Is she writing?"

There wasn't a simple answer to that question. Berit had taken her notepad to the tea party, and Sally had seen her scribbling in it several times, but her desk was also so neat and tidy that she doubted much work was ever done at it.

"I've seen her with a notepad," she replied.

"Good. Excellent. OK, here's what I need you to do: make sure she keeps writing. Are you taking notes?"

Sally reached out and found her bag on the floor and dug out an old notepad and a pen. She jotted down what her mother had said: get Berit Gardner to keep writing.

"I need her to write me a follow-up. These are tough times in the publishing industry; you know that as well as I do."

Sally knew. She had heard it all before.

"She seems a bit…uh, scary," she said.

"Pfft, she's a softie deep down. A dreamer who thinks she's a cynic. The woman can't help but take care of every loser, lost soul, and wreck of a person she meets. She's got an absurd aversion to all forms of status and a complete lack of insight into the way the world really works." Her mother seemed to be searching for a concrete example, eventually blurting out something she thought spoke volumes about the kind of person Berit Gardner was: "She's the kind of person who'd stop to talk to the receptionist while the head of the publishing house is waiting for her." The impatience in her mother's voice was clear. Then she added: "I'm trusting you with this, Sally."

Sally blinked in confusion, subconsciously straightening up on her bed. Her mother never trusted anyone with anything, especially not her chronic disappointment of a daughter.

"Make sure she includes some quirky minor characters. The readers loved those in her last book for some reason."

Sally made another note: Quirky minor characters.

"And for God's sake, make sure there's a plot this time. Remind her that people actually like that sort of thing. A happy ending too, if you can."

Sally kept writing: Plot and Happy ending.

"Oh, and tell her to add a cat. Or a lost dog."

More scribbling: Cat. Or dog.

Her mother hung up on her, but Sally stayed sitting on her bed long after the call had ended, going through various scenarios in which she tried to tell Berit that she needed to add a cat to her next novel.

None of them ended in anything other than utter disaster.

Sally quickly pulled on a pair of jeans and a gray sweater and tiptoed down the stairs. Berit sat by her desk, so still that Sally initially thought she must be sleeping. Then she asked suddenly without turning:

"Could you have blown up the library?"

Sally froze. "Me?" she asked. Her voice sounded guilty in her own ears, as if she somehow had something to do with the explosion.

"I'm wondering if it's a generational thing," said Berit.

"Planting a bomb?"

"Or a city versus country sort of thing."

Sally stared at her in confusion as Berit continued:

"I grew up in a suburb of Stockholm, but I spent every summer on an island in the archipelago. I remember watching my dad use dynamite to get rid of a tree stump one day. It might sound crazy, but I'm not sure I'd ever seen him as happy as he looked right then. Mum was worried, of course—and annoyed. But the point is that I saw it happen. I think I could probably manage to blow something up without any real trouble. Assuming I had the explosives, of course. Maybe you could manage it too, but not without having to search for step-by-step instructions first, like dynamite + blow up + murder. The police would be onto you in the blink of an eye. I'm fairly sure they can see what people have been Googling these days."

"I wouldn't *want* to blow up a library," Sally protested.

"Or maybe you'd watch some of those how-to videos on YouTube to learn how to set up a simple timer."

"Those videos are really helpful," Sally agreed.

"And get caught right away. But I should think that plenty of forty- or fifty-year-olds would know what to do without having to resort to Google or YouTube. Especially if they've done military service, which almost all men of my generation did—at least in Sweden. And anyone who grew up in the countryside and blew up things like tree stumps, like my dad. But you? No, I really don't think so."

"I can do other things! Anyway, there's nothing good about being able to blow people to pieces."

"Hmm," Berit murmured, unconvinced. "Which takes us to the question of who had the opportunity to plant the bomb. Half the village was at the tea party. It can't have been especially difficult to sneak in and plant the device, not for someone who knew what they were doing…"

"What about the motive?" asked Sally.

Berit ignored her. "Would you be able to kill someone?" she asked instead.

"Are you talking about millennials again? Because I'm pretty sure we're as good at killing as any other generation."

"No, I meant you personally. And not theoretically but mentally."

"I...don't know." Sally considered the question for a moment. "No." She sounded disappointed, as though this was proof of yet another character flaw.

"Not on purpose, in any case," Berit agreed. "No one can do much about accidents. But I'm wondering how many people are really capable of killing someone in cold blood. Soldiers have to be trained to do it instinctively and yet... I think plenty of us would actually be capable of it—if we were really pushed."

"I suppose so," Sally said hesitantly. "Though we don't. Kill people, I mean. Most of us will never kill anyone."

"No. When you think about it, it's a surprise it doesn't happen more often."

"That's not what I meant."

"Look at it this way: plenty of people hate their neighbors, their exes, parents, bosses, and colleagues. We've all got people who drive us to distraction. But very few of us ever actually do anything about it. Is that because we're fundamentally conservative in nature? Because we don't like trying new things? We reluctantly move to the other side of town, rarely change jobs—even if we can't stand our boss—and approach new people slowly and cautiously. Maybe it just never occurs to us to kill anyone."

"So you're saying we don't kill people for the same reason we don't move to a new country? That's insane. People don't commit murder because it's...well, wrong," Sally argued.

"Possibly," Berit mused. "An internal resistance? Yes, probably. But I wonder whether we ever really know what another person is capable of."

She seemed lost in thought, and for several minutes she sat quietly in her chair, staring at the overgrown rhododendron bushes in front of her.

"People and circumstances," she eventually said. "That's where we need to start. Someone was pushed so far that they did something completely out of character." She grimaced. "Or at least I hope it was out of character."

Sally was confused. "What do you mean 'start'? Start what? I thought you were here to write."

Berit got to her feet. "I think the best thing I can do right now is pay a visit to Tawny Hall to see how Daphne is doing," she said.

"Are you sure? Can we really just turn up like that, without warning? We barely even know her, and her nephew just died. Visitors are probably the last thing that poor woman wants."

"Daphne isn't grieving her nephew any more than you or I," Berit said dismissively, turning to Sally. "Possibly even less. Besides, no one expects an author to be polite or considerate."

She was right about that anyway, Sally thought grumpily.

The walk to Tawny Hall took half an hour, and it seemed to invigorate Berit. By the time she arrived, she was full of energy and determination. The young constable seemed reluctant to let them pass the police cordon. Before Berit could suggest that they give DCI Ahmed a call and ask him, Margaret Brown appeared.

She flinched slightly when she spotted Berit, but when she spoke, it was to the constable.

"Daphne asked me to check whether you needed any more tea."

"No, thank you."

"Or sandwiches?"

The young man quickly shook his head.

Margaret looked questioningly at Berit and Sally.

"We just want to make sure Daphne has everything she needs," Berit said.

Margaret seemed confused. "Of course she has," she replied. "I make sure of that."

Berit waited until Margaret grimaced and impatiently muttered, "Oh, come on, then." To the constable, she said, "I'm sure it's fine. And if not, you can always blame me."

He lifted the cordon, and Berit and Sally ducked underneath it.

"She's up in the attic," Margaret explained over her shoulder as she led them up to the house. Her face was completely expressionless. "She's convinced she's going to find something that proves vital to the investigation. She is determined to do anything she can to help the police get justice for her nephew."

The words sounded ridiculous and melodramatic in Margaret's mouth.

The attic was probably bigger than Berit's entire cottage. The ceiling had to be almost three meters high in the middle, sloping downward on both sides, and the only light came from a large single window at the gable end. It was the middle of the day, and the air was hot and stuffy.

Despite its size, the attic was packed to the rafters with junk. Berit spotted an old sailor's chest overflowing with costumes, including a cape, several wigs, and a Victorian ball gown.

They found Daphne in the middle of the room, wearing a black Chanel dress and slippers. She was surrounded by a number of large boxes and chests, which she had somehow managed to drag into the light from the window. The lids of several were open, and one had tipped over. All seemed to be stuffed to the brim with old letters, photographs, invitations, and yellowed paper. Some were so well preserved that they looked like they could have been sent yesterday, others faded and delicate, and everything seemed to have been tossed inside without any real order or system. In the box closest to Berit, for example, she could see both a thick, creamy envelope with old-fashioned cursive on the front and a gaudy, modern postcard from the Costa del Sol.

"It's all here," said Daphne. "The whole family's correspondence. I'm sure I'll find something that can shed some light on everything!"

She didn't elaborate on what "everything" was, but Berit assumed she must be talking about the murder.

"What are you hoping to find?" she asked.

"Something about the village, of course. I just know it was someone local who murdered my nephew and destroyed my library."

She sounded far more resentful about the latter.

"Office," Margaret corrected her. "You've always said that room wasn't a real library."

"That's irrelevant," Daphne snapped. "They couldn't have known that my library would survive! Such unforgivable negligence!"

"Who do you think could have done it?" asked Berit. She took a seat in an old armchair, then coughed as a cloud of dust enveloped her.

"How am I supposed to know? That's the detective's job. But I will say that I noticed that Samson chap from the shop glaring at both me and Reginald during the tea party. Awful man. I know my father had problems with one of the Samsons too. His father, perhaps? Something to do with the cricket field, I believe."

"There's a cricket field?" Berit asked in surprise. She had never noticed anything of the sort on any of her many walks around the village.

"Not anymore," said Daphne. "My father sold the land to a developer."

"Samson owns the supermarket," Margaret interjected. "Which is one of the properties Mr. Trent had threatened."

"Threatened?"

"He wanted to evict the whole village!" said Daphne.

"Not quite," said Margaret. "Only four properties."

"And they all blamed me, of course! As though I had anything to do with his business. My father always said that the only thing the men around here were good for was drinking and fighting. I open up my garden to them for the first time in decades—out of sheer hospitality and goodwill—and one of them immediately blows my nephew to smithereens!"

"I wonder whether the police will be looking into his dealings in London," said Margaret.

Dealings in London, thought Berit. She took out her notepad and flicked back to the pages she had used during the tea party, and there it was: Gerald. Raglan Harris.

"He had all sorts of dealings here in the village too," said Daphne. "Margaret, tell her about the tourist board."

Margaret's face grew serious. "They had some sort of meeting on Wednesday," she said. "A lot of people were upset, I've heard. Reginald was there, and he didn't do much to calm things down. The very next day, the village sent a…delegation up here. I think they were hoping Daphne might be able to do something to make him change his mind, but the properties are all Reginald's. We tried to explain it to them, but…"

Margaret's version was much too prosaic for Daphne, who threw her hands up in the air and took over: "But they wouldn't listen! They hated Reginald, and now they hate me!"

Berit wondered how much of Daphne's performance was based on real feelings. She couldn't help but feel that it was all just an act.

It wasn't just that Daphne seemed determined to be playing a part in a melodrama; it was that she was so focused on being the lead role. However upset she might seem, Berit could feel her private satisfaction at finally being surrounded by people who gave her their undivided attention. She had always assumed that a woman of Daphne's class and background would hate having the police snoop around, but if anything, she was enjoying it.

Berit wondered how Daphne really felt about living here, isolated up at Tawny Hall with nothing but her books for company.

"I threw the tea party in an attempt to calm things down," she continued. "To pour oil on troubled waters, so to speak. Odd turn of phrase, that. Who wants oil on water? Like one of those ships that are always running aground and leaking everywhere. All those poor birds you see on TV."

Margaret cleared her throat, and Daphne remembered what she had been talking about.

"I just wanted to do something nice for the village," she insisted. "People were upset—you saw that for yourself yesterday."

Berit nodded. "Yes, I noticed," she said. "Which businesses had Reginald threatened with eviction?"

"The supermarket, the hobby shop, and the café." Margaret sounded so matter-of-fact, as though she was reeling off a list. It was clear that none of the businesses meant anything to her.

Berit jotted down the names in her notepad.

The sun was shining in through the window at the end of the building, making it look as though the dust that had been stirred up was dancing in the air. The attic had grown even hotter during the short time they had been up there, and Daphne was sweating in her black dress. She seemed to have decided that enough was enough.

"Take these boxes downstairs so that DCI Ahmed can go through them," she said. "Now that I think about it, it is his job."

She turned and disappeared down the steep wooden stairs, leaving

Margaret, Sally, and Berit to struggle with the boxes. They took one each, following her down another narrow staircase and out through the back door. DCI Ahmed was over by the white tent that had been erected outside the old library.

He watched their strange procession with mild bemusement, his eyes lingering briefly on Berit before he gave Daphne a smile.

"What can I do for you, Ms. Trent?" he asked.

"It's more what I can do for you," she said, pointing to the boxes. "This is all the correspondence between Reginald and myself, among other things. Between the village and Tawny Hall too. Dating back years. I'm sure you'll find the motive in these boxes. There are more up in the attic."

"Sorry?" said DCI Ahmed. "Find what?"

"Threatening letters. Old family secrets. Grudges that have been nurtured for generations. Isn't that how this sort of thing usually works?"

"Right," said the detective. He sounded weary, but he quickly composed himself. "I'm very grateful, of course. Ms. Gardner, if I could have a word?"

Daphne looked pleased to have done her civic duty and suggested that they retire to the parlor for a drink. Sally followed them in, while Berit remained standing where she was.

She was half expecting to be given a dressing down for coming back to Tawny Hall, but he simply smiled and said, "I just have a quick question. How did you know it was a murder?"

"How did I know it was a murder?"

"That's what you said in your 999 call yesterday. Your exact words were: I'd like to report a murder."

So he had listened to it. Berit hoped she hadn't sounded too incoherent. But there had been so many questions, and her ears had still been ringing from the blast.

"The man was blown to pieces practically in front of me," she replied. "So it was fairly obvious to me that he didn't die of natural causes."

"You never considered that it might have been an accident? A gas leak, for example?"

"Ah, that's what you're getting at. No, I didn't. We don't use much gas in Sweden, so that didn't even occur to me, despite the fact that I've been in England for a long time." She thought for a moment. "Surely it's also the wrong end of the house?"

He nodded and handed her his card. "In case you think of anything else, Ms. Gardner."

"Please, call me Berit."

"So you're from Sweden?"

"My mother was Swedish, and I grew up there. But my father was English."

"Did your parents also find love across the borders?" DCI Ahmed asked, pointing to himself. "Ian Ahmed. My mother is from England, my father from Iran."

"I hope your parents were happier together than mine," said Berit.

He shrugged. "As happy as people ever are."

Neither he nor Berit made any attempt to finish the conversation.

"What do the E and the V stand for?" he asked. "I understand you use the name Berit E. V. Gardner on your books?"

She wondered whether he had Googled her.

"That was my agent's idea," Berit replied, a little defensively. "She thought it sounded more literary. Pretentious nonsense, if you ask me. Elizabeth Victoria. My mother chose my rather ordinary first name, my father my grander middle names. That should have been the first sign that it would never work out between them. Dad was a dreamer, but Mum was as practical as an alarm clock."

DCI Ahmed hesitated. "I've been thinking about something you said, about having a head start on me. You were right. The minute an investigation gets underway, we're already behind." He nodded to the card he had given her. "If you see or hear anything, or if you remember anything else, please just give me a ring."

He had turned to leave when Berit spoke up.

"There was one more thing."

"Oh?"

"Daphne might want to blame the villagers, but Margaret mentioned Reginald Trent's dealings in London. And I overheard something yesterday."

DCI Ahmed looked amused. "You overheard something?" he asked.

"Well, I happened to be hunched outside an open window. Belonging to the office that Daphnes calls the 'old library'. It was around half an hour before it all blew up. Reginald Trent was talking to someone called Gerald about a deal he desperately wanted to pull off. It sounded like he needed to find money and couldn't go to Daphne for it. He mentioned someone else too—Raglan Harris. As I understood it, this Raglan Harris chap was behind the whole thing."

"London. Gerald. Raglan Harris. Deal," the DCI repeated. "Thank you. I'll remember that." He looked seriously at her. "If that phone call had been half an hour later, if you'd still been standing by that window! You could have been hurt, seriously hurt."

Berit shrugged. "You never learn anything if you don't eavesdrop occasionally."

Impulsively, he reached out and touched her arm. "It's not a game, Ms....Berit," he said. "Don't do anything stupid. *No more eavesdropping under open windows*, do you hear?"

"Of course not," she lied.

DS Stevens came up to DCI Ahmed as Berit was walking away from him. He took off his jacket, his shirt already drenched with sweat beneath his arms. It was oppressively hot.

"It's going to rain," said DCI Ahmed.

There wasn't a cloud in the sky, but he said it so confidently that it felt like only a matter of time until the heavens opened. The air was still, as though nature itself were holding its breath in anticipation of catharsis.

"The bomb expert has arrived, sir," Stevens said.

DCI Ahmed nodded and followed him to the back of the house. A number of step plates had been laid out on the ground, forming a walkway from the driveway to the site of the explosion.

He took a couple of deep breaths. He had only managed to get a few hours' sleep last night, but he could feel the energy flooding through his veins. It was the same feeling he usually got during a long hike. There was a certain freedom that came from being so utterly focused on a single thing. His private life, the crown prosecutor in London, the office politics and endless meetings—right now, none of it mattered.

The bomb technician in charge was probably around ten years older than him, and at least sixty pounds heavier. His hairline had long since crept backward, and what little hair he had left was cropped short.

"Nice day for a little bang, huh?" he said with an inappropriate cheeriness that irritated Stevens right away.

Ian Ahmed recognized the type. It was the sort of behavior common among older police officers, soldiers, doctors, and other healthcare professionals: people who had seen too much death and suffering and developed a kind of childish gallows humor in order to cope. *Sometimes you simply had to laugh in order to avoid losing your mind*, he thought. *And sometimes you laughed because you already had.*

The technician seemed perfectly at home in the aftermath of the explosion. He moved across the wreckage as though he was in his own living room, and DCI Ahmed followed him, albeit more slowly and cautiously.

The room was larger than he had expected, and it felt even more spacious now that it had no windows. Standing in the middle of it, Ian Ahmed realized there was a certain order to the chaos, a direction and movement to the destruction that he hadn't noticed before. Some areas of the room were completely unrecognizable, whereas others seemed oddly intact. He wondered what patterns the bomb technician could see, things that hadn't yet revealed themselves to him. As he asked the question, the man's face grew serious for the first time.

"You develop an eye for it over the years," he explained. "Bombs are selectively destructive. More comes out unscathed than you might think. And definitely more than whoever planted it expects."

"A bit like a fire," said DCI Ahmed, earning himself a nod from the expert.

"We'll have to wait on the test results, obviously, but I'm pretty sure it was some sort of putty explosive. Not a huge amount of it, either."

"A kilo?"

"Less than that. The blast was pretty small."

DCI Ahmed looked around and raised an eyebrow.

The bomb expert grinned. "Relatively speaking," he said. "But that's the interesting thing here. Most newbies get overexcited, you see. They don't know what they're doing, so they use way too much explosive and blow up way more than planned—including themselves half of the time. But that's not what we've got here. This damage is really localized. No more than a few meters' radius."

"Enough to kill a person, though."

"Doesn't take much," the bomb expert agreed.

"So what would it take to achieve this? Pretend you're explaining to an idiot."

The man's amused face told DCI Ahmed that he already was.

"Well, you need the explosives, obviously. In this case, like I said, probably a putty explosive. They got that name because they're pretty moldable, an explosive mixed with mineral oil to produce...well, a putty. My guess is that they used hexogen, but we'll know more once the results come back. The soft consistency means you can cut it up into smaller pieces and mold it around whatever you're trying to blow up. Really easy and relatively safe. Nowhere near as unstable as dynamite. Anyway, the explosive is what goes boom, but you also need a primer, which is what makes the explosive go boom. Like a percussion cap, you know?"

DCI Ahmed nodded.

"And then you need some sort of timer or detonation mechanism, often hooked up to an energy source like a battery."

"Will you be able to tell what set it off here?"

"Sure. There are always traces." The bomb expert made his way over to a collapsible table outside. Various warped, unrecognizable objects had been laid out in a row, all carefully labeled. "Look at this," he said.

"What exactly am I looking at?" DCI Ahmed asked.

The bomb expert gave Ahmed a condescending glance.

"I'm fairly sure," he said, "that this is all that's left of a mobile phone. The bomb was probably detonated remotely. All you need for that is a reliable phone with some juice in the battery. I've heard that old Nokias are the terrorists' phone of choice. It wouldn't surprise me if that's what we've got here."

He nodded down at the table again.

"Ask the woman who lives here whether there was an old grandfather clock in the room. If there was, I think that's where the bomb was placed. And check this out."

He pointed at an object that looked like the twisted remains of a laptop.

DCI Ahmed whistled. "What I wouldn't give to be able to access that." He studied it dejectedly. "No chance of that, I guess."

"Don't be so sure. The hard drive could have survived. Let your tech guys have a look. Some of those guys are goddamn magicians."

What he had said was true, but DCI Ahmed doubted they would be able to do much with this particular laptop. Still, it was interesting that they had found it here rather than in the victim's bedroom. He wondered how many people had known that Reginald Trent liked to work in the old library.

"Where might a person get hold of explosives these days?" he asked the bomb expert.

"If you've got the right permits, you can just buy it."

"I think we can probably assume that whoever planted the bomb didn't."

"Well, in the past, my standard answer was always the military, but there's less of the stuff in circulation now, and they've really tightened the checks. My best bet would be to look into whether any construction firms have reported any missing explosives. They lose this stuff all the time, though of course it's not certain they report it."

The bomb expert shook his head. "It's enough to drive you crazy. But at least we'll be able to find out where the explosives were made. Every batch has its own unique composition, and it's all registered these days. We'll be able to trace the putty back to the factory where it was produced, I guarantee that."

DCI Ahmed nodded, impressed. His eye was drawn to a small object on the table. Using the sleeve of his sweater, he rubbed at it and realized it was brass.

"That's a cuff link," said the bomb expert.

DCI Ahmed took a closer look and realized it was in the shape of a small anchor.

"Looks like your victim liked boats," the bomb expert said.

7

DIDDLE / ˈdɪdəł / :
verb
to cheat or swindle (someone) so as to deprive
them of something.
to pass time aimlessly or unproductively.
(...)

GREAT / ˈgɹeɪt / :
adjective
of an extent, amount, or intensity considerably
above average.

Great Diddling was nothing like the charming seaside villages that came to mind when you thought of Cornwall. There were no picture-postcard houses or huts selling ice cream or Cornish pasties, no boat trips from the harbor, children playing, or bright bunting between pastel-colored houses. The village had neither a bakery, a bookshop, nor a beachside café.

Berit studied the little supermarket on the other side of the road. Its windows were grubby and full of sun-bleached posters for the National Lottery. *Yesssss! Woo-hoo! Yippeeee! Hooray!* she read, in colors that had long since faded. The text beneath claimed there were four winners every second, but Berit had a sneaking suspicion that the villagers of Great Diddling weren't among them.

She closed her eyes and focused on her other senses.

"What are we doing?" asked Sally.

"Taking in the atmosphere."

The screeching of a car's tires and a child screaming somewhere nearby. The clinking of china, probably from the café or the antiques shop. The air smelled like cigarette smoke, rubbish, and old frying oil.

"Um, why?"

"Research."

A car horn sounded, making Berit flinch, but she kept her eyes shut. It was uncomfortably hot in the sun, and she realized she should have chosen the shady side of the street.

"Into what?"

Berit's eyes snapped open. "The village, of course."

She strode across the road, held the door for a weary mother with an overtired child, and stepped into the shop, where a middle-aged man was standing behind the counter. Mr. Samson, she presumed. He was the kind of person who lacked any apparent redeeming features. He was scruffy, rude, and impatient, and Berit had to struggle to keep an open mind when she talked to him.

"I don't know why you're bothering me," he snapped once Berit had introduced herself and told him what she was doing. "Reginald Trent was a bloody snob from London, and his aunt's a crazy upper-class hag, but I don't have time to go 'round blowing them up."

"I understand your father was no fan of the Trent family either?" she said.

"My dad? What is this? Do you think this is some sort of detective show, and we're a bunch of inbred idiots who've kept up a feud for generations?"

Berit studied him calmly. Her silence seemed to get on his nerves, because he continued almost immediately.

"Fine. My old man used to work up at the house, I remember that, but I couldn't tell you what happened. He got the boot, I assume. Happened often enough. Probably turned up drunk or something."

"Is that something he did often?"

Samson laughed. "More often than he did sober. I hope you don't think I've got some kind of personal vendetta against anyone who ever fired my dad, because if I did, I would never have time to do anything else."

"Was he bitter? At how he was treated by Reginald Trent's father?"

"Not my old man, no." Samson shook his head. "He got sacked from every job he ever had, but he didn't go around whining about it. The man was a happy drunk. So long as there was someone to buy him a pint, he didn't grumble. Working was for other people. And you can say what you want about Great Diddling, but there's always someone willing to buy a pint for a poor sod that's down on his luck. Anyway, dad's been dead and buried for years."

"I heard that Reginald Trent was threatening to evict you?"

"Reginald Trent talked a load of crap," said Samson. "Yeah, he threatened us, but it was just talk. He was like an empty barrel: makes a lot of noise but completely hollow inside. My lease isn't up until 2040. I'll be dead before anyone can kick me out."

"There are ways of getting around a rental contract," said Berit. "Drastically raising the rent, for example, or making you close for renovations."

"True," he conceded. "I'm barely breaking even as it is. If the rent went up, that would be the final straw—for the other shops too, I bet. But look around you. This place is more effort than it's worth. If Reginald Trent had tried anything, I would've thrown the damn keys in his face and moved on. Dad's dead; mum is just sitting around in a home. There's nothing keeping me here but this bloody shop."

He gave a joyless laugh.

"Believe me, if I was going to blow anyone to pieces, it'd be myself."

The owner of the hobby shop barely seemed to have noticed Reginald Trent's threats against his business. The man didn't even seem to know what decade it was. He was tall and thin, wearing a suit designed for a much shorter man. It looked as though he had simply started growing one day and failed to notice that he never stopped.

He didn't know who Reginald Trent was and hadn't been at the tea party. He generally showed up at the tourist board's meetings—one had to do one's bit, he said—but hadn't been at last week's, as he was laid up in bed with a cold. He blew his nose in an old handkerchief, tried to convince Berit to buy the model plane in the shop window, and quickly lost all interest in their conversation.

As she and Sally left the shop, they almost ran straight into a reporter from Channel 4, broadcasting live from outside the shop. A white van with the company logo on the side was parked directly over the road.

Outside the café, she noticed one of the sisters who had been responsible for the catering at the tea party. The same woman who had called Reginald Trent a swine before immediately reverting to the grandmotherly figure Berit saw now. Her white hair was pinned up in an elaborate, old-fashioned style, and she was hunched over a chalkboard writing the day's specials.

Tea and cake: £7 (10% discount for emergency services)

And beneath that, in small letters, *Special price for locals.*

When the Hartfield woman noticed the reporter from Channel 4, she quickly bent back down and rubbed out the old text, writing:

Tea and cake: £10 (10% discount for emergency services and journalists)

"How much for locals?" Berit asked her.

"Five pounds."

Berit gave her an amused shake of the head and made her way into the café.

A woman in her seventies was sitting just inside the door. She was thin and wiry, as though the years had concentrated her somehow, and her sharp, blue gaze fell first on Berit, assessing her in a glance, and then moved on to Sally.

On the table in front of the woman, there were three playing cards, and she turned one of them over. The queen of hearts.

She looked Sally straight in the eye. "Follow the queen," she said.

Her voice was low and dark, and Sally watched as though hypnotized as the card switched places before her eyes. The woman turned a card over, the queen of hearts again, now on the left. She then continued to move the three cards, getting quicker and quicker. Sally's card seemed to be on the right, then in the middle, then to the left. When the woman eventually stopped, Sally was confident. She reached out and pressed a finger to the card on the right. The woman smiled approvingly and turned over the card Sally had picked out.

"The queen of hearts," she said. "You're a natural. What do you say, shall we make this a bit more interesting?"

Sally looked intrigued, but Berit ushered Sally deeper into the café, to where the grandmotherly woman from outside stood behind the counter.

Sally ordered an egg and bacon sandwich, a scone with jam and cream, a large pot of tea, and two biscuits. No, three. Four. A lot of food, in other words, but the sum total still seemed rather high in Berit's view. Sally paid by card and then studied the receipt in confusion. The woman behind the till had entered the wrong total, she realized, but when she pointed it out the older woman simply squinted down at the barely legible receipt and started mumbling to herself. "Whoopsie daisy," she said and "Oh, goodness me" and "Do you think I could accidentally have put the sandwich through twice?"

Sally gazed longingly at her tray.

"Good grief, if only I knew how to fix this...?"

"Don't worry," said Sally. "It's fine."

The woman beamed at her. Berit paid cash for her coffee, then carried it over to the table where Sally was sitting, choosing the seat closest to the woman by the door and angling herself so that she could study her properly.

This must be the second of the Hartfield sisters, Berit thought.

If she were a character in one of her novels, Berit never would have put her in a setting like this. The woman belonged somewhere far more exciting. In a big city somewhere. Abroad. For some reason, she pictured North Africa. Marrakesh, possibly Cairo. She could imagine loud conversations in foreign languages, car horns blaring, the smell of strong coffee in the air...

The woman held out a hand. "Eleanor. Eleanor Hartfield," she said. "You're the author, aren't you?" She had a strong, firm handshake, and she nodded to the woman behind the counter. "That's Mary."

"Berit Gardner," said Berit. "And this is my assistant, Sally Marsch."

"Yesterday must have given you plenty to write about, hmm?" said Eleanor.

"A thing or two," Berit replied.

There were loud footsteps from the floor above, and Liam appeared from a door behind the counter a moment or two later. His face was deathly pale, with dark circles beneath his eyes, and his hair looked dirty. Mary handed him a wrapped egg and bacon sandwich as he staggered past. The grease had already soaked through the paper.

"Hi, Sally!" he said in passing, managing a bleak smile before he stumbled outside.

Sally watched him walk away through the window before turning her attention to her sandwich, which she wolfed down as though she had never seen food before.

Berit took a sip of her coffee.

"I heard last week's tourist board meeting got a little lively," she said. "Were the two of you there?"

"Of course," Mary replied from behind the till. "We were supposed to be deciding on next year's campaign, but we never actually got 'round to that."

Berit thought she noticed Eleanor give her sister a warning glance, but it was so quick, she couldn't be sure she hadn't just imagined it.

"The tourist board is just an informal group of people who care about the village," Eleanor explained. "We usually just meet over a pint at the pub, that's the sort of meeting it is. But there he was, dressed like some hotshot from London. Expensive suit, even more expensive shoes. So shiny you could practically see your reflection in them."

"Heaven knows that man liked his own reflection," said Mary.

"He thought he was so much better than everyone else, and he wanted us all to know it."

"I understand he threatened to evict several tenants?" said Berit.

"He said he'd evict everyone," said Mary. She sounded as though she was still upset about it. Eleanor gave her another warning glance, more obvious this time, but her sister ignored it. "Us, Samson, even poor old Lewis from the hobby shop. Reginald said he was the future and we were the past. He looked me straight in the eye as he said that. Me!"

"When it comes to old Lewis, he's not exactly wrong," said Eleanor. "The world has definitely run away from him. He'll never sell that model plane."

Mary opened her mouth to speak, but Eleanor continued before she had a chance.

"Samson didn't like what he had to say one bit," she said.

"No, he called Reginald a bad name," said Mary, smiling at the memory.

"Several, in fact. And Reginald wasn't happy about that. He said a few choice words himself. Something along the lines of Samson and the rest of Great Diddling being inbred idiots with an unhealthy fondness for our own sheep." She chuckled. "Yes, he really got going on the subject of villagers and sheep." Eleanor sounded reluctantly impressed.

"So what happened?"

"Samson and at least five of the other regulars at the pub decided to go a few rounds with him."

"They must have been pretty drunk if he managed to take them all on," said Berit. "He didn't have any visible injuries at the tea party, not even a black eye. And he wasn't moving like someone who had just been in a fight with five men."

"Sima broke it up," said Eleanor. "Taking charge like always. If it wasn't for her, nothing would get done around here."

Interesting, thought Berit.

She remembered Sima from the tea party. Definitely a woman used to taking charge of things, she thought. And full of passion when it came to Reginald, too.

"As he was leaving, he said, 'See you soon' in a real unpleasant way. Menacing."

"What, to the regulars? As a threat?"

"I don't know," said Eleanor. "I almost got the impression he meant it for Sima."

"Did he threaten the café too at the meeting? You're one of the tenants he wanted to evict, aren't you?"

Eleanor shrugged. "It was all just talk," she said dismissively. "If he had really wanted to get rid of us, he would have sent his lawyers rather than giving a speech at the pub."

"So you weren't worried?"

"Not us," said Eleanor. "We're not even from here. Over the years we've run bars, restaurants, a casino, a security firm, an art gallery, and plenty of other things all over the world. I've lost count of how many times we've started over somewhere new. If he had managed to evict us—and I'm not saying he would have, because we had a solid contract—we could just have gone elsewhere. To a new village, even a new country."

Mary folded her arms and thrust out her chin, and Berit found herself wondering whether she was as prepared to up sticks as her sister.

"So Reginald just left the meeting? No one followed him to, I don't know, finish the argument outside?"

"Oh, I did," Mary said.

Berit looked surprised at her.

"Not to fight, of course. Just to see where he was going."

"Didn't he go back to Tawny Hall?"

"That's the thing. He didn't go in the right direction for that. So I followed him. He went to the hotel, but he didn't go inside. He went around the back. I followed him, of course."

"Why is that?"

"Because it was suspicious! There's nothing back there but a building site. Hardly the right place for shoes as shiny as his."

"Could he have been meeting someone? The hotel owner, perhaps? James something?"

Mary nodded eagerly. "James Elmer. He wasn't at the meeting, you see—he never comes. He doesn't like it when people bend the truth."

"And that's all the tourist board really does," Eleanor filled in.

"Did you hear what they were talking about?" asked Berit.

"I wasn't eavesdropping," said Mary. "I was too far away. I couldn't get any closer either. Not at my age, not in the dark, with all the junk they've got lying about. I could have tripped and broken my leg. But it wasn't a friendly chat, I could see that much. James was trying to convince Reginald to do something. Or not do something. I'm not too sure. 'You promised.' I distinctly heard him say that."

"How did Reginald reply?"

"He laughed."

Another customer came in, and Mary turned her attention to him.

"Have you ever lived in Marrakesh?" Berit asked Eleanor on a whim.

"No, but I did live in Tangiers for a few years, so I've been there. Explored the labyrinthine medina." A dreamy, absent look took over her face. "I used to take the train from Tangiers to Casablanca and then inland, to Fez and Marrakesh. I liked sitting at Café de France, drinking spiced coffee and listening to the men doing deals at the tables around me. Sometimes I did deals of my own too."

"Sand. Sand, everywhere," Mary called over from the till as the man paid. "That's all I remember from Tangiers. Nothing I tried to grow ever survived. The desert wind buried everything in sand."

Eleanor started shuffling the cards in front of her again, and Berit took the opportunity to really study her. The older woman had a restless energy that was starting to make Berit uncomfortable, but she couldn't quite pinpoint why. The word *indifferent* popped into her head for some reason. Indifferent, and potentially destructive.

If Eleanor was a character in one of her books, she would have made her bold and rash, possibly even foolhardy. The sort of person who would throw herself off a cliff in an attempt to find out what it was like to fly.

Mary served the new customer his tea and scone, then came back over to their table and set down a flyer in front of Berit.

"If you're really interested in the tourist board, you should come to our next meeting. There's a new one on Wednesday, given the latest… developments."

The flyer announced that the meeting would be held at the local pub, the Queen's Head, Arms, and Legs on Wednesday, 15 May at 7:00 p.m. *Come along to the Great Diddling Tourist Board meeting to hear all about a fantastic new idea that could change the village forever!*

This time, it was impossible to miss the warning glance Eleanor gave her sister.

Sally looked around the hotel reception and thought, for the fifth time, that nothing was happening there. In the armchair beside her, Berit was sitting with her eyes closed.

"What are we doing?" Sally asked.

"Listening."

"Can I ask you something?"

Berit's eyes remained closed. "Why not?" she answered.

"Why have you spent a whole day talking to these people?" she asked. "I know what happened to Mr. Trent was awful, but surely it's the police's job to get to the bottom of that?"

"True, but we can help," said Berit, her eyes still closed. "People are… willing to share certain things with an author. We might be utterly selfish and self-obsessed a lot of the time, but we're also very good listeners."

"Because deep down you still care?"

"Because we know that everything can be used in a book at some point."

"That tourist board must be really good at what they do," Sally said suddenly. She was thinking about the banner she had seen on the high street. "Given they've managed to get the village voted best in England, I mean."

"Nominated," Berit corrected her. "The small print is key."

"OK, but I'm sure it could have won. So much important has happened here!"

There seemed to be little pieces of history everywhere she turned, with brass plaques providing information about everything from the episodes of the TV show *Poldark* (both versions!) that were filmed in the village to the fact that Winston Churchill had paid a visit during the evacuation of Dunkirk. The brown booby, a rare seabird, had been spotted locally in 2016, and the building next to the hotel had once been home to Queen's

Roger Taylor. Queen had actually played their first ever show in Great Diddling, right in the middle of the high street.

"I can't believe that Winston Churchill actually came here during Dunkirk," said Sally.

Berit opened her eyes and looked at her. "Of course he didn't. He would never have left his booze and cigars at such a crucial point of the war."

"But I read it on one of the brass signs…" Sally protested, realizing, far too late, that she should have been more skeptical. "Oh," she said.

"Precisely," said Berit. "Fascinating place. Utterly fascinating."

Sally slumped back in her armchair. It was so big, it felt like it was about to swallow her whole. "Can I ask you something else?"

"I'm sure you will."

"How long has my mum been your agent?" she asked.

"Ten years."

"Do you like her?"

"She's extremely good at her job."

Sally knew that all too well. Her mother was a difficult act to follow.

"How are you supposed to know if you could be good at something?"

"You can't," Berit replied. "All you can know is whether you find something fun or rewarding enough to put in the time it takes to do the job."

"Have you ever been bad at something?"

Berit looked surprised. "Of course I have. More often than I have ever been good."

"But…isn't it awful, trying your best at something and then just failing?"

"How else are you supposed to learn?"

"So what do you do when you fail?"

"Either you keep trying or you quit. In my experience, success is usually more about desire than talent. Incredibly talented people give up all the time, and many mediocre people become successful simply because they're prepared to fight for what they want."

Desire. Sally wasn't sure she had much of that either. Not the way her mother did, anyway. Olivia was steely and unbending, while Sally constantly doubted herself and everything around her.

"Do you want to be an author?" asked Berit.

"God, no!"

"Smart. Well, whatever you decide to do, the only sure way to become good at something is to make mistakes. Lots and lots of mistakes."

Sally shuddered at the very thought, but Berit seemed almost longing. "There's nothing better than being a beginner at something," she said. Sally gave her a skeptical look. "You'd rather be starting out as a writer than be established and successful?"

"Other than the money, absolutely. In the beginning, every mistake you make is interesting. Every time you do something wrong, you learn something new. The most depressing thing about getting older is that you start repeating the same mistakes you've already made. It's incredibly annoying. No, believe me, new mistakes are the most fun."

Berit leaned forward in her armchair and peered through to reception. "Here's a piece of advice you can have for free," she continued. "Whatever you do in life, don't bother comparing yourself to others. Just find something you enjoy doing, work hard, and continue to make new mistakes, and I guarantee your life will never be boring."

Sally nodded. In the warm, safe environment of the hotel lobby, she could at least be honest with herself about her goals. She wanted to be a literary agent. No, more than that. She wanted to be a great literary agent, and she wanted to do it her own way.

Right there and then, in Great Diddling, hundreds of miles away from her mother, she felt for the first time like she might actually have a shot at it. Sally didn't know how, or not exactly, but she knew where to start. She would learn everything she could about Berit E. V. Gardner, and she would make herself indispensable.

She settled back into the chair and closed her eyes.

"So what are we listening for?" Sally asked eagerly. "It's so quiet here. I don't hear anything."

"*Exactly*," Berit said.

8

DCI AHMED WAS BACK AT his desk at Crownhill Station in Plymouth. He had just given his superiors an update on the case and was now trying to think through the next steps.

It was already 7:00 p.m., but on the other side of the glass wall, the major incident room was a hive of activity. The first full day of a murder investigation was always hectic. There were over twenty specialist officers from CID involved in the case, but that number would most likely double before it was all over—and that didn't even include all the forensic technicians, staff at the lab, or the pathology team.

To Ahmed, it was an inspiring sight and one of the main reasons he had never seriously considered changing jobs. He often doubted himself during the course of an investigation, and God knows he often doubted the structure and administration of the police force as a whole—the almost manic use of acronyms, the hierarchies, and the endless management and budget meetings—but he never doubted his team. They were systematic and organized, collectively relentless in their pursuit to identify and arrest the perpetrator, laying the foundation for a successful prosecution to get them off the streets.

He was busy going through the report detailing Reginald Trent's belongings when there was a knock on his door. The pathologist opened it herself and held up a brown folder as though it was some sort of entry ticket.

"My report," she said.

The pathologist was a highly competent British Indian woman. She and DCI Ahmed had worked together several times in the past, but they had never really clicked. He sometimes wondered if it was because they were so often lumped together as "different" on account of their backgrounds and if they on some illogical, deeply subconscious level blamed each other for it.

It was unusual for her to have brought him the report in person, and there was a note of surprise in his voice as he thanked her.

"I was passing by anyway," she explained. "And since you detectives usually want the postmortem results yesterday, preferably before the murder even takes place, I thought I'd bring them over."

Ahmed started scanning through the documents inside. After a moment, he looked up. "Any surprises I should know about?"

She took that as an invitation to sit down opposite him. He cursed himself for not offering her a seat earlier, overcompensating for his mistake by asking whether she would like any tea or coffee. The pathologist declined and crossed her legs.

"Not exactly," she said in reply to his earlier question. "The immediate cause of death was severe head trauma, but he also sustained extensive damage to his internal organs, spine, and limbs. No significant amount of alcohol in his blood, and no trace of any other drugs. No sign that he was dead or injured before the explosion, either. He was sitting behind his desk when he died."

Ahmed looked down at his own.

"His desk was probably much sturdier than yours," she said.

"Solid oak."

"Sounds plausible. It protected the lower half of his body, anyway. Almost all his injuries were from the waist up, and he was facing the bomb when it went off. I'll be able to give you a more precise answer once I know what type of explosive was used, but I think he was probably at least a couple of meters from the bomb. Maybe three. It would have been much harder for us to identify him otherwise."

So, the bomb technician's theory about the grandfather clock might be correct, thought Ahmed. Reginald Trent could have been looking straight at it when it suddenly disintegrated before his eyes.

"So what exactly was it that killed him?" he asked. "Was he hit by something or…?"

"The shock wave."

"He was killed by…air?"

She looked impatient, as though he was acting dumber than he really was.

"Pretend I'm an idiot," he said. If there was one thing Ian Ahmed had learned over the years, it was that most experts were patient around people who didn't know as much as them, providing you openly acknowledged both your own limitations and their superior knowledge.

"OK, think of it a little like this," said the pathologist. "If you dive into a pool from a few meters, you'll cut through the water without a problem. But if you try the same thing from a higher altitude, it'll be like hitting concrete. It's the same principle with a shockwave. Normal pressure air, no problem at all. Sudden high-pressure shock wave, big problems. Putty explosives have a detonation speed of over seven thousand meters a second. Close up, the shock wave that produces is powerful enough to rip the skin from your face. Slightly farther back, it destroys internal organs. Even at a relatively large distance, it can hit you like a rugby tackle. In Reginald Trent's case, the immediate cause of death was a brain injury caused by the shock wave, but he would have died anyway from the combination of damage to his lungs, blood vessels, and spine."

DCI Ahmed nodded in thanks, wondering aloud whether Trent would have had time to be surprised.

"Probably not," the pathologist replied. "Death would have been instantaneous."

"Dangerous business, spending too much time at your desk," he said in an awkward attempt to lighten the mood. His was a cheap model from Ikea and wouldn't provide any protection whatsoever; he was sure of that.

"Not exactly," said the pathologist. "It's dangerous spending time around explosives. Reginald Trent would have died even if his desk weren't there. Though if you mean sitting down too much, you're right. That's incredibly bad for you. Personally, I use a standing desk."

She cast one last critical glance at the chaos on his desk before getting to her feet, gave him a slight nod, and left the room.

Ian Ahmed spun around in his chair to look out through the small window. The dark rain clouds made the buildings on the other side look even more neglected than ever, but he felt an odd urge to get out into the bad weather, to be anywhere at all but his office, sitting behind his potentially lethal desk.

He shook his head, turned back to his computer, and, putting the pathologist's report aside for the moment, brought up the list of possessions again. Everything Reginald Trent had had with him at Tawny Hall had been cataloged and documented and was currently being held until his next of kin were given permission to come and collect it. There was no mention of a cuff link shaped like an anchor.

He double-checked the list of objects that had been found at the crime scene, all carefully photographed and documented, and saved the image of the sooty cuff link to his phone.

Stevens came into the office with Detective Inspector Linda Rogers, who had recently joined the team. She had previously been with first the firearm squad and then financial crimes, and she would be helping them to get to the bottom of Reginald Trent's business dealings. She was in her early thirties, short and muscular, with a face that was completely expressionless when relaxed.

DCI Ahmed thought there was something extremely intimidating about a woman who could both understand numbers and fire a gun.

He quickly got up and cleared a stack of papers from a chair, then gestured for them both to sit down. "OK," he said. "What do we know? Let's take it from the beginning."

Stevens launched into a recap. "The victim is one Reginald Fergus Giles Trent, a forty-seven-year-old male. Registered as living in a flat in Mayfair, London. Next of kin is an ex-wife. Two kids, poor little sods. He was visiting his aunt at the family estate of Tawny Hall, Cornwall, at the time of death."

"Has someone notified the wife?"

"Ex-wife," Stevens reminded him, but Ahmed didn't think it made much difference now. Death would rob her of a man she had once loved more completely than a divorce ever could.

"The Met Police informed her yesterday. We've been in touch with her to request a meeting, and she's agreed to meet you tomorrow."

DCI Ahmed nodded. Rogers remained expressionless.

Stevens continued. "Reginald Trent arrived at Tawny Hall at 3:00 p.m. on Sunday, May 5. Several people saw him arrive. Namely, Ms. Margaret Brown, resident of Tawny Hall; Ms. Daphne Trent, owner of Tawny Hall; and Mrs. Rose, cook, cleaner, and general housekeeper. Thirty minutes later, one Liam Slater arrived to help Mr. Trent with his suitcases. He thought it was beneath him to carry them himself, apparently."

"There are two sorts of people in this world," Rogers muttered. "The ones who carry their own bags and the ones who don't."

She clearly belonged to the first group, DCI Ahmed thought to himself. Her contempt for Trent was obvious.

"He hadn't given them advance warning that he was coming—other than a phone call when he left London, that is. He drove to Tawny Hall in his own car, alone. It's still parked outside the house. Leased, not owned.

"Reginald Trent came and went during the day, but he ate most of his meals at Tawny Hall, an arrangement that no one seemed especially happy with. Mrs. Rose works four days a week, and when she isn't there, Margaret Brown is in charge of the cooking. The two women split the food shopping between them."

"Any other staff?" asked DCI Ahmed.

"Just one. Liam Slater, who helped with the bags."

DCI Ahmed looked at the list Berit had given him. "Then he had plenty of opportunity to visit Tawny Hall before the tea party, too," he said.

"He'd been there several times in the days leading up to Sunday," Stevens agreed. "Helps out with various jobs around the house, apparently. Mrs. Rose mentioned that they used to have a gardener who worked there a few days a week during spring and summer too, but he retired a couple of years ago and hasn't been replaced yet."

"Never will be, either," said Rogers. "The time when places like Tawny Hall could afford a gardener is long gone."

Stevens nodded. "Shame, with that garden. In any case, Liam does all that stuff now. Cuts the lawn and weeds the flower beds and that sort of thing. Margaret Brown says he does as he's told."

"Who stands to inherit Trent's estate?"

This time, it was Rogers who answered. "His kids. They're five and seven, so everything will be held in trust until they're twenty-one, and child maintenance will be paid to his ex-wife while they're still in school. Nothing strange about that, though there is one interesting point: Reginald Trent would have inherited Tawny Hall when his aunt died. It's an entail trust, which means she had no choice in the matter. She's just the tenant-in-possession."

"Hmm," said DCI Ahmed. "So who inherits it now?"

"His children. Or rather, the eldest son."

"Daphne Trent said he had property in the village?"

Rogers nodded. "He owns—sorry, owned—four properties in Great Diddling."

"And the tenants include a man called Samson, who runs the supermarket," DCI Ahmed added. "Daphne Trent suggested he might have a long-standing grudge against the family."

"I'll look into it," said Stevens.

DCI Ahmed nodded. "Are those four properties what brought him to Great Diddling?"

No one answered. It was a rhetorical question. One of the many things they simply didn't know.

"What did he do for a living?" he asked.

"He had a business," said Rogers. "Proper Consulting Limited. Turnover of just under a hundred thousand last year."

"Is that a lot?"

"In his circles? Absolutely not."

"A former colleague reached out on the tip line," said Rogers. They had held their first press conference earlier that day, providing a number the public could call if they had any relevant information. "Apparently he spoke to Reginald on the phone the Friday before he left for Cornwall."

"What did they talk about?"

"He didn't give any details, but he said that something felt 'off' during their chat."

"Off?"

"As though Reginald had gotten himself mixed up in something he'd regret. That was what he said."

"Interesting. Reach out to him and see if he has time to meet us tomorrow, while we're in London."

"We, sir?" asked Rogers.

"You're coming with me. Stevens can stay here and continue the work in Great Diddling. Look into this Samson bloke."

Stevens nodded.

"And see if you can find any dog owners."

The instruction didn't seem to come as a surprise to Stevens. Everyone knew that dog owners were the best witnesses, always out and about at odd times of day. In crime dramas on TV, they were always the ones who found the body, and the same was broadly true in real life.

Which was exactly the reason Stevens had never given in to his sons when they nagged him for a dog. Stevens had said on multiple occasions that there was no damn way he was going to let the missus or the boys stumble over a body in the woods. It was bad enough that he had to see that sort of thing at work.

"Reginald Trent arrived at Tawny Hall on Sunday afternoon," DCI Ahmed said. "A week later, he was dead. We need to find out what the hell is going on here."

Stevens nodded. Rogers looked even more expressionless.

DCI Ahmed ended the meeting just as the heavens finally opened outside.

James Elmer refused to talk to Penny as he did his crossword in bed.

She was standing listlessly by the window, watching the raindrops hitting the glass.

He hadn't said a word to her all evening, and when Penny had tried to get him to tell her what he and the project manager from the building company had been talking about earlier, he had just snapped and said it was "business," as though the hotel had nothing to do with her.

It was only her home, for God's sake.

Penny pulled on a worn pink dressing gown. It was an old hotel bathrobe she had attempted to liven up with a bit of dye, but her little craft project hadn't exactly been a success. She then left the room to make them both a cup of tea, maybe even a bite to eat.

Her route to the kitchen took her past reception, and Alice, the girl behind the desk, said when asked that she didn't mind either a cup of tea or a smoke. The two women left the reception unmanned and went out for a smoke beneath the overhanging roof in the backyard.

Alice was chatting away about the date she'd been on recently, but Penny hardly heard a word. She could see Alice's lips moving, exaggeratedly, as though in slow motion, occasionally pausing to take a deep drag on her cigarette and to blow a nonchalant smoke ring, but the words just seemed to float straight past her. Cheap gin. Great kisser. Old Ford. It was his fucking mum's.

The only thing she could hear, over and over again, was her own voice: *I'll kill you.* She could still see the look of surprise on Reginald's face, but it was no longer quite as satisfying as it had been at the time. Because it was always followed by the next image: shards of glass flying through the air. She felt a series of shivers pass down her spine, a little like remembering something stupid you'd done when drunk.

Only this was worse. Much worse.

Beyond the overhanging roof, the rain was drumming down on the ground. The building site would be a mud bath tomorrow, she thought, and she pulled her bathrobe tighter around her.

Penny stubbed out her cigarette and debated lighting another, left Alice still smoking outside, and headed through to the kitchen to find something to eat.

She opened the fridge and spent a moment or two studying the contents. The sight of all the food usually cheered her up, but today, she just looked blankly at the sliced cheese, ham, eggs, butter, and milk. Penny's mother had been a single parent, making do with one meal a day to ensure that Penny ate a decent breakfast, lunch, and dinner. There hadn't been any late-night snacks while she was growing up, that's for sure.

She buttered a couple of slices of white bread, so fresh that the knife left marks on the pale crumb.

She had spent her entire life working hard so that she would never have to go hungry again, and then she had met James and discovered that she no longer had to work quite so damn hard all the time. Penny refused to give that up. Never ever.

She wasn't going to give up James. The little sod could forget about sneaking out behind her back for meetings with the building company at all hours of the day. Or worse—with Reginald fucking Trent.

Penny slapped the two slices of bread together and angrily took a bite from one corner. She took another, then a third, realizing to her surprise that she was crying.

She could still fix this, she thought, angrily blinking away the tears. She just had to find a way to save James and the hotel.

It was gone eleven when Daphne knocked on Margaret's door. They had been living together at Tawny Hall for several years now, but this was the first time Daphne had ever come to her room like this. Margaret had always taken that as evidence of an inherited respect for the private life of her staff, but perhaps the murder had changed that.

Margaret's room might look spartan, but she was secretly very pleased with it. She had everything she needed: a bed, a small armchair in one corner, and a narrow desk where she kept her kettle, tea bags, and biscuits. She bought those when she went down to the village to do the weekly shop.

But there was only one place to sit.

Daphne looked around the room. "You take the bed," she said. "And I'll take the armchair."

Margaret stiffly did as she was told. She felt like a young girl being put to bed, and that irritated her far more than any of yesterday's chaos.

Daphne helped herself to a biscuit.

"I've been thinking," she said. A crumb dropped to her lap, and she picked it up between her index finger and thumb and flicked it away across the carpet. "You and I had the most contact with Reginald in the days leading up to his death. And neither of us exactly liked him. I think it is safe to assume that the police aren't done with us yet. We should think carefully about how we proceed."

You and I. Us. We.

Oh, she was good, thought Margaret.

Daphne nibbled her biscuit and didn't quite meet Margaret's eye. "So perhaps we should agree on what we're going to tell them," she said.

"Not the truth, in other words?" Margaret asked, purely to see what Daphne would say.

Daphne had a much stronger motive than she did, which also meant she had far more reason to worry about the police. Reginald was her nephew, and in the police's eyes, surely members of family were often prime suspects?

"Don't be so childish, Margaret," Daphne said impatiently. "I'm not suggesting we lie to the police, mind you. Just that we could, perhaps, be a little...selective about what we say. After all, we hardly need to unburden ourselves to them. They're hardly interested in our boring, quiet lives. Besides, the whole truth has never pleased anyone. Half the truth, yes. Parts of the truth, of course. Enough truth that it isn't, strictly speaking, a lie? Certainly. But that's more than enough."

"Right," Margaret said after a brief pause. She thought her voice sounded strange, but Daphne didn't seem to notice.

"At the end of the day," Daphne continued, "neither of us killed him, did we?"

Margaret could still see the shards of glass flying through the air whenever she closed her eyes. The grotesque torn pages everywhere. She didn't want to think about what that kind of force could do to a fragile human body.

She shook her head. "No," she agreed.

Daphne crossed her legs and brushed a few invisible crumbs from her lap. "We'll have to keep an eye on them," she said. "The police, I mean. On what they find out and who they talk to. And then we'll simply have to improvise."

Margaret nodded.

The rain was pattering against the small window. A cozy sound, she thought, at odds with such an unpleasant topic of conversation. She debated asking Daphne whether she had murdered her nephew, but she decided against it.

All she wanted was for things to go back to normal. Daphne needed her. Margaret would take charge, and everything would be fine.

In the dark café, Eleanor stood listening to the rain on the windowpanes. Outside, High Street was virtually deserted, empty but for a lone dog walker who turned up his collar against the foul weather and hurried away.

Mary had been baking all evening, and the sickly scent of fresh biscuits hung heavy in the air. There were trays of biscuits on every available surface, and Mary had now turned her attention to bread.

With flour up to her elbows, Mary furiously kneaded her dough. It went thud, thud, thud as she brought it down on the work surface, flattening it out with her palms. A lock of hair had come loose and was now clinging to her sweaty forehead. She used her forearm to push it back, leaving a streak of flour across her soft skin.

"You shouldn't have tried the *too old to understand the card machine* trick with that girl," said Eleanor.

"What are you talking about? She happily paid *forty-two* pounds!"

"It's not her I'm worried about; it's the author. That woman sees everything."

"Then she'll have seen it was an honest mistake. I offered to correct it." Mary grinned. "The confused-granny act works brilliantly with the police when they come in too. No one likes to cause a fuss. But I don't do it too often, so you don't need to look so worried. A few times a day, that's all.

Now with the journalists, that's different… They're so busy on their phones that they don't even know how much they've just paid."

Mary's cheeks were flushed, her face full of life, and her eyes glittering more than they had in a long time.

Eleanor gave her a pleading look. "Come on, let's clear out of here before it's too late. It was a mistake to use our real names here. Who knows what they'll find if they start digging."

Mary folded her arms. "I'm not moving again, Eleanor. It took us years before we got around to hanging the curtains here."

There was something touchingly fragile about her, beneath all the stubbornness. *She's getting old*, thought Eleanor tiredly. *And I am too.*

Mary would turn seventy-five this winter. It was just in Eleanor's eyes that the two of them never aged.

"I'm too old to live out of a backpack again," Mary continued in a whiny tone she wouldn't have used even ten years ago. "My joints hurt when it's cold, and I don't like having cold feet either, and we never stayed anywhere long enough to buy rugs or—"

"Morocco was warm."

"And sweaty, Eleanor! There were no seasons. It never rained!"

Both gazed out at the downpour outside. Eleanor hadn't realized it was possible to miss such miserable weather, but apparently Mary could.

"I just don't know whether we can stay," she said in desperation.

Mary beamed at her, convinced she had won the argument. "You'll come up with something," she said. "You always do."

9

BERIT TURNED ON THE COLD tap first, then the hot, tentatively checking the temperature. The water rarely got above lukewarm in the cottage, but you could never completely relax. The shower had a bad habit of suddenly scalding unsuspecting users.

Once she was finished in the bathroom, Berit pulled on her dressing gown and went downstairs to make coffee. The rain had grown heavier, streaming down the windowpanes and turning the garden into an otherworldly landscape of puddles.

Cradling her mug in her hands, Berit opened the french doors and took a deep breath. The scent of rain, earth, and damp grass mixed with the aroma of hot coffee, and she closed her eyes. Several raindrops hit her face, but she didn't care. The inspiration was like adrenaline flowing through her veins.

She hummed to herself.

The rain always got her mind whirring. There was nothing more perfect for a voyage of imagination than a rainy day. She wrapped herself in a warm blanket and pushed the chair as far back against the wall of the cottage as she could.

So far, the people of Great Diddling had evaded her attempts to wrap her head around them.

Everyone was playing a part, she thought. There was something theatrical about the entire village. She laughed suddenly. Winston Churchill, indeed!

Fat raindrops landed on her wool blanket, shimmering on the surface, but they hadn't yet managed to soak through.

Her thoughts kept returning to the theater, so she delved deeper into the theater metaphor. Playing a role suggested there was both a stage and an audience and, just as importantly, a backstage area and a dressing room where that role ended and a person's real, authentic self took over. What happened to a person when they played a particular part for a long period of time? Could anyone really keep up that sort of performance for years on end?

It was different if they were two, she thought. A shared endeavor. Maybe you could play the part all your life then and still remember who you really were.

After all, there was a great deal of freedom in being able to control how other people saw you in writing your own story.

Two *or more*, Berit thought suddenly. Maybe everyone in Great Diddling was in on the same play, and the outsiders were the ones being fooled by it?

And then, of course, there was the silence. As the rain continued to pour down in front of her, Berit thought long and hard about *that*.

Detective Inspector Rogers drove the way she did everything else, thought DCI Ahmed. Confidently, competently, and assertively—verging on aggressively.

It was raining, and the windscreen wipers had been working nonstop all the way from Cornwall when they stopped off at a petrol station just outside of Reading to grab a quick bite to eat. The sandwiches were dry and tasteless, but the tea was hot and strong, and the meal deal came with a bag of crisps. DCI Ahmed tipped his out onto the table and tried to use them to build a house of cards.

"I'm guessing you'll be leading the interview with Trent's ex-wife?" said Rogers.

"Unless you have any better ideas?"

Rogers quickly shook her head. "People aren't my strong suit. There's always too much emotion. I prefer real things, like numbers. In interviews, I tend to assume that everyone is lying to me."

"Not the worst strategy," said DCI Ahmed. "A lot of people do."

"Yeah," Rogers replied. "And about the stupidest of things. At least with numbers, they only lie about important things. And they're never crazy or completely arbitrary or psychotic or drugged up. That's why I prefer good old-fashioned motives like money and greed."

DCI Ahmed's potato-based house of cards came crashing down, and he swept the crisps into his hand, got up, and dumped them in the bin. Rogers followed him out to the car.

They arrived at the former Mrs. Trent's house just before eleven.

DCI Ahmed was more inclined than Rogers to look for an emotional motive behind the murder, and in his experience, there was nothing more deadly than jealousy—though upon meeting Reginald Trent's ex-wife, he was immediately forced to concede that she didn't seem particularly jealous.

She took in his crumpled shirt and wet coat with an amused look on her face. Her own clothes were deceptively simple, in the way that only expensive, high-quality clothing can be.

"Detective Chief Inspector Ahmed, I presume?"

"Mrs. Trent. I'm sorry for your loss."

"We're all adults here, Mr. Ahmed. There's no need to pretend."

He introduced DI Rogers and noted with interest that Mrs. Trent seemed to feel an instinctive sense of antipathy toward his colleague. Rogers, in turn, endured her patronizing scrutiny far less stoically than DCI Ahmed had. The two women were like amusing mirror images of each other, he thought. Hands on hips, eyebrows raised in skepticism, mouths curled into disdainful smirks.

In the end, it was Rogers who regained control of herself first. She took half a step back, giving way to DCI Ahmed, letting her hands hang by her sides with palms turned outward in a subtle, nonthreatening gesture. Mrs. Trent relaxed, subconsciously turning her attention back to DCI Ahmed.

He shot DI Rogers an approving look.

Mrs. Trent led the way through to a large, open-plan living room full of concrete and glass, minimally decorated with bare surfaces and cool lighting. She was an attractive woman, with high cheekbones, smooth skin, and thick, glossy hair that even Ian Ahmed could see was the work of an expensive salon somewhere. On the whole, Mrs. Trent gave off an exclusive, if slightly strained, air. Money couldn't entirely mask the passage of time, and he wondered what she looked like when she laughed—and whether she ever really did.

Despite her words earlier, he couldn't help but search for signs of sadness in her. There really didn't seem to be any, and that unsettled him, not that he was the right person to judge. Ian Ahmed conducted all his relationships so that no one would be upset when they ended. That wasn't so much a choice as a necessity; he was just too dedicated to his job to be a good partner to anyone. There had been plenty of women who said they understood that he had to prioritize his work, but they all seemed surprised and hurt when it transpired that that also applied to them. Emotions were never logical, he thought.

"Do you know whether your ex-husband had any enemies?" he asked.

"God, this is just like being in a bad film," she said.

"I know it must sound a little melodramatic, but the fact remains that someone killed him."

Mrs. Trent got up and walked over to the drinks cabinet—three concrete shelves with hidden spotlights illuminating the bottles—and poured herself a large whisky with a splash of soda. She then held up the glass and raised a shapely eyebrow, but DCI Ahmed shook his head.

"Reginald was fine," she said without warning. "Not that I realized that when I was younger, of course. We have such strange ideas before we turn forty."

DCI Ahmed wondered briefly whether the crown prosecutor would grieve him if he died, though he quickly decided she wouldn't. He hoped she would, at least, remember him with more fondness than Mrs. Trent was currently showing toward her ex-husband.

"But he was never satisfied," she continued. "Nothing was ever enough. There was always someone who earned more than him, never enough praise at work. And there was always another woman who was younger and prettier than me."

"Did he hurt you?"

It was the first time Rogers had spoken, and Mrs. Trent froze. She gave the detective a suspicious glance, as though she was searching for mockery or pity in her words, but Rogers's face remained blank.

"He hurt my pride," Mrs. Trent said after a moment. "If it happened again now, I wouldn't care. I'd just get even. There are plenty of younger men out there, too. Are you sure you don't want a drink?" she asked DCI Ahmed.

He shook his head, and she turned to Rogers instead.

"What about you?"

"No, thank you."

"Just have a damn drink. I don't like drinking alone."

Rogers accepted a glass of good whiskey ruined with soda water and took a small sip to placate her, though she put it down as soon as Mrs. Trent turned her attention back to DCI Ahmed.

"Did your ex-husband ever mention anyone by the name of Gerald?" he asked. "Or a man named Raglan Harris?"

She shook her head. "Not to me, no. But they're probably business associates. He didn't have any real friends. Money and success were all he cared about."

Mrs. Trent absentmindedly swirled her glass, making the ice clink. DCI Ahmed found himself wondering whether she found the sound calming.

"Reginald was chronically dissatisfied," she went on. "And greedy. My best guess is that he screwed someone over once too often. Anything to make a quick profit. He wasn't the most honest man, and he definitely wasn't smart enough for all the things he was trying to do."

DCI Ahmed nodded, and Mrs. Trent continued.

"Do you know the worst part? I really did love him at one point in time. He didn't have any patience for weakness, but neither did I. And at least he wanted something out of life. I'd met so many men before him who were blasé about everything, but Reggie had ideas. He used to say that the only way to succeed was to grab the bull by its horn. He was like that. Hungry. Always on the hunt for the next opportunity. Yes, he was a bloody idiot, but he was my idiot."

There it was at last, a real emotion. DCI Ahmed felt oddly grateful for that. And it would definitely make it easier for them to build a picture of who Reginald Trent had been. The main purpose of this trip to London was to find out more about Reginald's business dealings, but it was just as important to him that they were also starting to get a sense of Reginald in his natural environment, as it were. He stood out too much in Great Diddling, and other people's opinions of him constantly kept getting in the way. For the first time, he'd got a glimpse of the real Reginald. He hoped he would learn even more from his apartment. You could learn a lot about a person from where they lived.

He took out his phone and brought up the image of the cuff link.

"Do you know whether this belonged to Reginald?" he asked.

Mrs. Trent leaned forward and gave the image a quick, uninterested glance.

"I doubt it," she said. "The whole sailing thing really wasn't Reggie's style. The man could get seasick on a pond. Is it gold?"

"Brass."

She laughed. "Then it's definitely not his."

DCI Ahmed nodded and returned his phone to his pocket.

Mrs. Trent waved her hand dismissively, as though to say they could go now, and he did as she wanted. He and DI Rogers put on their damp jackets and showed themselves out.

On the street outside, their unmarked Ford Fiesta stuck out like a sore thumb among the gleaming, black, chauffeur-driven cars. Though strictly speaking, DCI Ahmed thought as he got back into the passenger seat, he had a driver too. He always preferred not to drive, if possible. Being a passenger gave him more time to stare out through the window. He did his best thinking that way.

"Not exactly the stereotypical grieving widow," Rogers said as she started the engine.

DCI Ahmed knew that grief could take many forms, but all he said was: "No sign of their kids there, either."

It seemed unnatural to him to have such a clean, stylish home if you also had two children under ten. Mrs. Trent had sole custody of the two children, though her ex-husband had had visitation rights. Neither of them had reported any issues with that arrangement, and DCI Ahmed wondered now whether it was because they simply didn't care enough to fight about it.

Rogers shrugged. "These people are rich. They've probably shipped them off to boarding school."

At first glance, Reginald Trent's flat revealed next to nothing about him. Subdued shades of gray and white dominated, with thick carpets on the floors. The furniture was expensive and blandly modern, the only personal touch a magnificent landscape by Turner.

DCI Ahmed spent several minutes studying the beautiful painting. He wondered whether Reginald Trent had ever done the same, though considering what they knew about him so far, he suspected he had mostly been interested in its value.

He thought back to Trent's bedroom at Tawny Hall, to the meticulously organized suitcases, wondering aloud how the personality behind this room could have coped with the chaos and mess at Tawny Hall.

"What personality?" Rogers asked. "This place is like a personality vacuum."

DCI Ahmed went through to the kitchen and opened the fridge, driven by an inherent sense of curiosity. He was a firm believer that looking through a person's fridge could give a raw, honest picture of a person's life.

But the only thing he learned was that Mr. Trent had had a taste for expensive mineral water and takeaway sushi when he was at home. The small containers of soy sauce that came with the sushi were all lined up on the top row of the shelf, and there were a lot of them. Other than that, the fridge was clean and empty.

DCI Ahmed opened a few drawers at random and found precisely what he had expected: individually wrapped chopsticks. He always saved the extra ones too.

In the bedroom, they found more gray and white decor, the wardrobes full of yet more suits and shirts. Two shelves had been given over to expensive, tasteful silk ties, and there was a box of cuff links. Every pair was gold, and none were shaped like anchors.

He looked around the room. There were no books, no records, and only the one photograph. Two children, looking depressingly neat and tidy. In DCI Ahmed's view, kids were supposed to be anything but.

Rogers picked up the framed photo and held it up to DCI Ahmed.

"See?" she said. "Private school uniforms."

Rogers wandered off to check the other rooms. A few minutes later, she shouted from another room, "Sir! Over here!"

He followed her voice through to what seemed to be a home office and found Rogers standing in front of two filing cabinets with a brown folder in her hand. For the first time since they arrived in London, she had an eager look on her face.

"Jackpot," she said. "We have to take everything with us and really go through it, but check this out." She handed him the folder marked *James Elmer*. It contained several annual reports from the hotel in Great Diddling.

And a loan agreement.

DCI Ahmed let out a low whistle. "So James Elmer owed money to Reginald Trent," he said. "Good work."

That alone justified the long drive to London.

"Extremely good terms too," DI Rogers said. "Both the interest rate and the repayment sums are incredibly generous. If James Elmer needed money, I can see why this must have seemed irresistible."

"But…?"

"There's a clause here that says Reginald Trent could demand the entire sum back at any time, with the hotel as security if James couldn't repay him. And if Reginald had demanded the loan back, there's no way James Elmer would have been able to do it," she said. "The hotel is already mortgaged to the roof. That's probably why James Elmer went looking for private options in the first place. It's a crazy contract. No sane person would agree to it."

"But someone desperate might," DCI Ahmed suggested.

DI Rogers looked doubtful. "They had to be incredibly stupid. Or naïve. Or both." Her tone of voice clearly stated that someone like that had no business signing anything.

"Is there anything else in there?" asked DCI Ahmed, trying a long shot: "Anything about a man by the name of Gerald? Or Raglan Harris?"

"Let's have a look."

She returned James Elmer's folder to the drawer and started rifling through the others.

"There's one for someone called Gerald Corduroy-Smith," she said. "But it's pretty much empty. Just some initial correspondence, including a very formal letter from Mr. Corduroy-Smith talking in vague terms about some business opportunity he'd like to discuss. If Mr. Trent could spare a few moments of his precious time, at a time that works for his busy schedule, at his earliest convenience, etc., etc."

"Didn't this former colleague we're about to meet mention something about Trent being up to something fishy?"

"What? You think it could be this brilliant opportunity Mr. Corduroy-Smith is talking about?" Rogers checked the date on the letter. "It was sent on April 23, so it could fit."

"OK, let's load everything into the car," said DCI Ahmed. "And then we can head over to see what his colleague has to say."

Mr. Cantwell, Reginald Trent's former colleague, reminded DCI Ahmed that the class system in the UK was alive and kicking. His teeth were completely white and straight, his hair well cut, his skin clear and irritatingly smooth. At first glance, his dark suit looked like any other, but there was something subtly different about it, distinguishing it from the kind of off-the-rack suit worn by mere mortals.

He made them wait for several minutes as he continued talking on the phone.

"Terrible business, this," he said when he eventually ended the call and shook his head. And that seemed to be the amount of grief he could spare for his former colleague.

He got up and gave them both a firm handshake, pointed to an armchair for DCI Ahmed and made a real show of pulling out another seat for Rogers.

"Thank you," she said politely but indifferently over her shoulder, as though she were talking to a waiter.

Cantwell seemed irritated by her tone as he made his way back around the desk to sit down.

DCI Ahmed smiled. "I understand you spoke to Mr. Trent shortly before his death?" he said.

"Yes, he phoned me. Strange call. Incredibly strange…"

He paused for effect, trying to pique their interest. Mr. Cantwell didn't seem the least bit nervous to be talking to the police, but DCI Ahmed was willing to bet his meager savings that that wasn't because he didn't have anything to hide. No, it was because he considered himself untouchable, the detectives insignificant.

"What was so strange about it?" DCI Ahmed asked.

"He was…agitated," said Mr. Cantwell. "He had some business opportunity in the pipeline, though Reginald always did. I'm the same. That's just how we are. There's always a next best thing, eh?"

His self-awareness was surprising, as was the slight hint of self-deprecation that shone through.

"Was it a property deal?" Rogers asked.

"Yes…" Cantwell hesitated. "At least, he *was* finally on the verge of selling those worthless properties in Cornwall, but that wasn't what had gotten him all worked up, that's for certain."

"Do you know who the buyer was?" Rogers asked.

Cantwell directed all his replies to DCI Ahmed. "That's the thing. I didn't quite grasp all the details, but he'd found himself a buyer. Represented by a man Reggie called Gerald Corduroy-Smith. The name was clearly fake."

Rogers leaned forward in her chair.

"Oh?" DCI Ahmed said calmly.

"You have no idea how many Something-Smiths I've met over the years, but if you scrape the surface, they're always from a long line of plain old Smiths."

"But you think Mr. Trent was preoccupied by something other than the sale of those properties?" said DCI Ahmed.

"This Gerald chap had an investment opportunity for him, and it was that opportunity Reggie wanted to talk about. But something about it seemed off."

"In what sense?" asked Rogers.

"I'm not sure." Cantwell sounded irritated. "I can't put my finger on it. But something wasn't right."

"Did you suspect it could be fraud?" Rogers pressed him.

"That was my first thought, but how would that work? Why pretend to be interested in buying a handful of properties in a backwater like that? What would anyone stand to gain?"

"Did you share your thoughts with Mr. Trent?" asked DCI Ahmed.

Mr. Cantwell shrugged. "It was his money, not my place to say anything. I doubt it would have gone down well. Besides…"

"Yes?"

Mr. Cantwell seemed to have changed his mind. "Oh, nothing," he said. "But I'll tell you one thing. There was someone else involved. Reggie sounded like a loved-up schoolgirl when he talked about him."

"A man by the name of Raglan Harris?" asked Rogers.

Cantwell seemed annoyed that they already knew the name. "Yes, that was it. I Googled the man right away, of course, but I couldn't find him. Now, I know that's not suspicious in and of itself—plenty of the big fish prefer to fly under the radar, so to speak—but I'd never heard of him, and that is rather odd. I was so curious that I did a little asking around, but no one I spoke to had heard of him either."

He looked at DCI Ahmed and said, slightly awkwardly, "I'm sorry I can't tell you more about Reggie's business dealings, but the truth is, we hardly kept in touch after he left the company. It was his choice as much as anyone's. No one likes to be reminded of what they've lost. Oh, he wasn't fired," he added quickly when he saw Rogers surprised look. "He, shall we say, left to pursue other opportunities."

Mr. Cantwell paused to make sure they understood what he meant. They did.

"Brexit was a real readjustment for all of us," he continued. "And I'm afraid Reggie didn't quite keep up with the times. That's how it's always been: some stars rise, but others fall."

He smiled confidently, safe in the knowledge that he would always be among life's winners. DCI Ahmed found himself hoping that Mr. Cantwell got a taste of failure someday.

"But I do know that he was renting a desk in a serviced office." Cantwell shook his head. "Tragic, really," he added in a stage whisper. "Outside of the City."

DCI Ahmed raised an eyebrow at Rogers, who nodded. She had found the address in his papers.

"I actually think he was fishing to see whether I might be interested. When he called, I mean." Cantwell went on. "In this unique investment opportunity of his. I deflected the topic rather quickly, so he never came out and asked, but that was the impression I got. He was just a bit *too* enthusiastic, you know. But now I'm afraid I really do need to get back to work, so unless there's anything else I can do for you…?"

He got up and held out a well-groomed hand. DCI Ahmed glanced at Rogers to check whether she had any further questions, but she shook her head, so he rose and took Mr. Cantwell's hand.

"Thank you for taking the time to talk to us."

Cantwell was back on the phone before they had even closed the glass door behind them.

In the lift on the way down, Rogers turned to DCI Ahmed.

"I know what he was going to say when he seemed to lose his train of thought. The reason he didn't warn Reginald Trent that it might have been a scam."

"Oh?"

"It's because he wasn't sure whether Trent was the victim or the scammer."

"A unique business opportunity, eh?"

"Exactly."

The words "serviced office" made DCI Ahmed think of depressing office spaces on the outskirts of big cities, but Reginald Trent had rented an office in one of the shiny, new tower blocks in Canary Wharf. To the west, the skyscrapers of the City of London—the business district at the heart of Europe's financial markets—glittered in the distance.

"The banks all have important-sounding addresses in the City," Rogers explained, "but their main offices, where people actually work, are out here."

DCI Ahmed looked around and shuddered. The area was completely soulless.

Rogers explained that Reginald Trent's building had probably been built as the headquarters of some major corporation, and when the owners failed to rent it out at the extortionate rates they were hoping for, they had compromised by opening it up to those needing office space on a more ad hoc basis.

"Or even just a virtual office. You can probably get a PO box here without ever setting foot in the building. Or the country," she added.

Sarah Clarke, the manager of the serviced offices, was between twenty-five and thirty. She hadn't yet grown dissatisfied with her job, but she was no longer quite so proud of it either. Her desk was positioned so that she was facing away from the magnificent views, as if she was so used to them that she no longer needed to see them.

But DCI Ahmed couldn't help but look. Every building in the area was made from glass, so modern that it was hard to remember that the sluggish river down below had seen riches come and go in the area for centuries.

The rain was still stubbornly coming down, and London was blanketed in a damp, impenetrable grayness. If the sun suddenly stopped shining, he thought, this would be the last place where people noticed. The rest of the world would panic, but the inhabitants of London would keep calm and carry on.

"It was Reginald Trent who rented the space," said Ms. Clarke. "He signed all the paperwork and checked Mr. Gerald Corduroy-Smith in as a temporary guest during his last week."

"Is that allowed?"

She shrugged. "For a fee, we're happy to provide an extra desk or workstation."

"So how does it work, on a practical level?" he asked. "With these offices in general, I mean."

The manager took them through everything quickly and professionally. "Our tenants sign a contract for the period and number of rooms they're interested in, and that gives them access twenty-four seven. Reception is manned around the clock, and any visitors have to be signed in, for security reasons—not that we ask for ID or anything. It's a balancing act. Having visitors needs to be a painless process for our tenants here. For an additional fee, we can provide access to a secretary or to our exclusive Italian espresso machines. Our concierge helps the tenants with whatever they need: catering, dinner reservations—anything, really."

"Would we be able to see Mr. Trent's office? Is it still empty?"

"Of course. He paid until the end of the month."

Her tone of voice suggested that life and death were of less importance than a fully paid contract. She got up from her desk and showed them to the room Reginald Trent had rented. It was considerably less impressive than her own office, little more than a glass box surrounded by other glass boxes, probably around five by five meters. A thick gray carpet dampened all sounds, and the only hint of color came from a green monstera plant in one of the corners.

DCI Ahmed stood still for a moment, trying to get a feel for the space. All he could think was that he would never want to work somewhere like that. The room was cramped with two desks in it, and the glass walls amplified the feeling of being locked in a cage.

"Did Mr. Trent pay extra for a secretary or the coffee machine?" he asked.

"The coffee machine but not the secretary."

"Did you ever meet him or Mr. Corduroy-Smith?" Ahmed asked.

"Of course. We strive to provide a personal service here. I spoke to Mr. Trent several times. He never did manage to wrap his head around how the espresso machine worked."

DCI Ahmed smiled. Ms. Clarke didn't.

"Could you describe Mr. Corduroy-Smith?"

"Of course," Ms. Clarke said, and after the briefest of pauses to collect her thoughts, she did so competently and effectively: "Around sixty. Five foot nine. Medium build. Tanned, with short, gray hair. Well dressed, in a gray suit. Everything about him seemed just right."

"Just right?"

"You can always tell when something is a little off." She took in the detective's creased white shirt and dark windbreaker. "By a person's clothes, I mean. And Mr. Corduroy-Smith was just as he ought." Her tone of voice hinted that she saw all sorts here.

"What was the dynamic between him and Mr. Trent? What I mean is, who was in charge?"

"Mr. Corduroy-Smith was," she replied without hesitation.

"How could you tell?" Rogers asked.

"It was always Mr. Trent who called about the espresso machine."

As the kettle boiled, Sally studied the list on her notepad. Sally had spent the rainy day writing down everything she had learned about her new boss so far. The heading of the list was Things Berit E. V. Gardner Does, and the first point: "Swears, often, in two different languages."

Berit was always muttering things Sally didn't understand, but which she assumed must be Swedish. She had heard her say "*jävlar!*" and "*helvete!*" when the shower was the wrong temperature, for example, and the author also seemed fond of saying "bollocks to that" when she didn't feel like doing something, like the washing up.

She spoke perfect English, with just a slight Swedish accent that gave her speech a lilting, melodic rhythm.

She also read copiously. She always seemed to be reading when Sally came down in the mornings, and she was still reading when she went to bed—often with multiple books on the go. Sally had counted at least ten lying about the house, still open at the page where she had left them. Right now, for example, Berit seemed to be midway through books by Diana Athill, Bernardine Evaristo, Laurie R. King, Jules Verne, Siegfried Sassoon,

Edith Wharton, Zadie Smith, Jan Morris, and Julian Barnes—and those were only the titles on the living room table.

She sang when she thought no one was listening. She liked old Irish songs and strange Swedish tunes. Sally had asked her what the Swedish songs were about, but Berit's answer had left her none the wiser. One was about picking cherries in a garden, for example, which had given Sally a mental image of Sweden as a dreamlike Japanese landscape full of delicate pink cherry blossoms—at least until Berit announced that there were more apple trees than anything. She hadn't explained what "diggi-lo, diggi-ley" meant, which led Sally to believe it must be something rude.

And she had extremely strange eating habits. When Sally checked the pantry this morning, there had been nothing in but two rows of Heinz tomato soup, two more of Heinz mushroom soup, some cardamom rusks, and a few bags of coffee. In the fridge, there was nothing but cheese, butter, milk, champagne, and gin.

On Sally's initiative, they now also had tea, marmalade, eggs, bacon, onions, carrots, ground beef, pasta, sliced bread, and chopped tomatoes. She had been hoping that a slightly better diet might stimulate Berit to write more, but so far it hadn't had any effect.

She looked down at her list again. The last point was staring her straight in the face.

Berit Gardner still wasn't writing.

She was cutting a pitiful figure outside in the rain, her face cold and wet. Sally could see water dripping from her nose and hair, but Berit herself didn't seem to have noticed. Both her notepad and her hands were safe and dry beneath her blanket.

Sally decided to see this as an opportunity. Perhaps she had finally found something she could do for Berit. She would try to work out a way to help her move past her writer's block, thereby proving to both Berit and her mother that she had what it took to be an agent.

She filled a mug with hot water and left the tea bag to steep for a moment or two before taking it out to the veranda and handing it to Berit.

"You're stuck," she said.

Berit wrapped both hands around the mug and leaned over it, letting the steam rise onto her face. "Is it that obvious?" she asked.

"You've stopped doing research," Sally pointed out. "Are you going to that tourist board meeting tomorrow?"

"Maybe," Berit said.

Sally took that as a yes. Every one of the villagers they'd met so far would make an excellent quirky secondary character, just like her mother wanted. Now all Sally needed to do was find a way to plant the idea of a cat.

"If you've run out of ideas, it might help to talk about it…?" she said.

"You might be right," Berit said. "Maybe I should give DCI Ahmed a call. I need to tell him about what we overheard at the hotel."

"But we didn't hear anything! And what do you mean *DCI Ahmed*? I thought you were writing a book!"

"Writing a book? I'm solving a murder."

Sally closed her eyes. Her mother would kill her.

"Have you noticed that we've been working on this case for two days now," said DI Rogers, "and no one has shouted at us yet?"

DCI Ahmed glanced over to her, but her face was as hard to read as ever.

"You want people to shout at us?" he asked. He rubbed his face. It had been a long day.

"I just think that someone should care enough about him to want to do it," she said. "We haven't met a single person who seems to miss him at all. Not even here in London, where he lived and worked."

"*If there is any person in the town, who feels emotion caused by this man's death, show that person to me,*" DCI Ahmed said to himself.

"What was that, sir?"

"Charles Dickens, *A Christmas Carol*. You're right, Rogers. People seem oddly unmoved by his death."

"So why are we doing all this?" Rogers pressed him. "Why spend all this time and money when no one even cares?"

She seemed to sense just how unkind her words sounded, because she added defensively: "I know we have to investigate every murder, regardless of who the victim is—even when it's just a criminal who dies." DCI Ahmed pulled a face at the *just a criminal* comment, but Rogers didn't notice. "Even when everyone else hated the victim, there's usually a mother or girlfriend or someone who can't stop crying and who yells at us to bloody do our job and catch the person who did it. I'm just saying that someone should care when a person dies."

Ian Ahmed nodded, tipping his head to the cold window, closing his eyes. He agreed. Someone should care.

"Get some shut-eye, sir," Rogers told him, but instead he took out his phone and called DS Stevens.

Ms. Clarke had given them the check-in lists, and the plan now was to comb the CCTV in the area for footage from the times when they knew Gerald Corduroy-Smith had been at the office. Once they had a better idea of what he looked like, they would release his name and picture to the public. DCI Ahmed asked Stevens to pass on his instructions to the rest of the team.

Stevens's own day in Great Diddling had been far less productive.

"Samson, who owns the supermarket, is a dead end," he said. "And Daphne Trent now claims that Reginald was trying to kill *her* and blew himself up in the process. Says she was the real target."

Ahmed told Rogers about Daphne's theory. She shook her head. "No trace of explosives in Reginald Trent's room or car."

He nodded. "Any news from the village?"

"No one is saying anything. You know how it is. These small villages are more difficult to get to talk than the bloody organized gangs. Everyone is protecting someone. And no one is talking to the police. In villages like these, everyone has something to hide. It's going to be a bloody nightmare to get them to open up."

"Go home for the day," Ahmed told Stevens. "We'll find a way to get them to talk to us tomorrow."

He hung up and checked his voicemail. *Speak of the devil,* he thought. Berit Gardner had left a message asking him to stop off at her cottage whenever he had time, to go through the cast of characters. Maybe she could help give him a clearer picture of the village. At least the trip to London had given him a far better idea of who Reginald Trent was, he thought.

May as well get it over and done with, he thought, asking DI Rogers to drop him off in Great Diddling rather than Plymouth.

It was after eight by the time they pulled up in front of the cottage. DCI Ahmed got out of the car, but he didn't immediately close the door. Instead, he leaned back in to talk to Rogers.

"It's not true that no one cares about Reginald Trent's death," he said.

"No?"

"*I* care."

Then he frowned. *The cast of characters?*

10

BERIT GARDNER OPENED THE DOOR before DCI Ahmed even had time to knock.

She studied him, really studied him, in a way that left him unsure of what he might be giving away, and then said, "Come in. You look like you could do with a drink."

A mercifully short time later, Ian Ahmed was sitting in the most comfortable armchair with a generous gin and tonic in one hand. His body was aching from spending so much time in the car, his head weary from the hustle and bustle of the city.

It had finally stopped raining, and the air flooding in through the open french doors smelled fragrant and fresh. Berit was pacing back and forth across the floor in front of him. She seemed to be on the verge of saying something several times, but she simply shook her head in irritation at the last minute.

DCI Ahmed pressed the cold glass to his forehead.

"In your message you said you wanted to talk to me about something," he reminded her.

Berit nodded. "There are several ways to describe the writing process. Some compare it to the way an artist might work, talking about sketches, the first layer of paint, the way depth and shadows gradually emerge. Others talk about getting to know characters the way you would real people, from the immediately obvious things like age, gender, their profession and class to the deeply personal level of hopes, dreams, disappointments, fears."

"Forgive me, Berit, but did you ask me here just to talk about your next book?" Ahmed asked in confusion.

She waved her hand dismissively and slumped down on the sofa. "Of course not," she said. "What I'm trying to say is that many people seem like caricatures of themselves—or simplistic sketches—until you get to know them better. I can't see any of them clearly yet."

Displeasure made Ahmed sit up in the armchair. "Are you writing a book about Reginald Trent's murder? Because if you are, Ms. Gardner, I have to warn you that—"

"Call me Berit. And no. I'm not a true crime writer. What I'm interested in is human psychology. Like I said, I've observe things. I just haven't managed to make sense of what I've observed. It struck me that you also have a need to understand the people around here, and I thought we might be able to work together."

"And how do you imagine that might work?" he replied, unconvinced.

"We share our thoughts. Bounce ideas. That sort of thing. I'm not asking for access to any confidential material or anything like that. I just want to compare my view of the people in Great Diddling with yours."

"Why don't you start by telling me some of your thoughts?" Ahmed suggested. "Who haven't you managed to get a clear picture of yet?"

"Mary and Eleanor Hartfield," she replied right away. "They run the café on the high street."

"The Hartfield Sisters?" He smiled. It was like something from *Arsenic and Old Lace*. "They must be at least seventy."

"A person doesn't have to be young to set off a bomb."

"No, I guess, but..." He trailed off. "What do you find so suspicious about them?"

"They're too perfect. Mary's whole friendly, confused-grandmother thing is an act; I guarantee it. And as for Eleanor...she's not who she claims to be either."

That still didn't exactly move them to the top of his list of suspects, DCI Ahmed thought.

"Anyone else?" he asked.

"Daphne Trent is hiding something," said Berit. "I'm sure of that. She seems desperate to cast suspicion on the other villagers."

"When Stevens spoke to her," Ahmed said, "she suggested that she was the real target. That Reginald Trent had accidentally blown himself up while planning her death."

"Could he have?"

"Explosives are dangerous. Accidents do happen. It's possible. What do you think? You met the man."

Berit thought for a moment, with a focus that seemed oddly absent, as though she was turning something over in her mind.

"No," she eventually said, "I can't imagine that Reginald Trent was competent or crazy enough to have built a bomb."

"You're assuming that the killer must be one or the other?"

"Well, it's not exactly the most common choice of murder weapon."

DCI Ahmed turned toward the window. With the lights on, it was nothing but a dark mirror of the room inside. They looked relaxed. Drinks in hand. Impossible to tell from looking at them that their thoughts ran to murder. Berit adjusted her position on the sofa, her perfume mixing with the scents of the garden outside.

DCI Ahmed leaned forward. Perfume had always fascinated him. It was both an expression of someone's personality and a suit of armor. No fragrance smelled the same on any two people, which meant there were practically an infinite number of scent combinations out there.

DCI Ahmed often remembered a person's smell just as clearly as he did their face, and he would definitely remember Berit's. He would have guessed that she was a practical soap and water kind of woman, but he could make out notes of pomegranate and persimmon, lotus and mahogany, plus something else he couldn't identify.

"The trouble is that there are just too many possible explanations right now," said Berit. "Far too many people hated Reginald Trent and had reason to want to kill him. The man seemed to positively enjoy provoking people.

An extremely pathetic form of attention seeking but hardly unusual nowadays. Everyone has to 'say it as it is' and be 'controversial' and 'provocative,' as though the only thing that matters is annoying others."

Ahmed took a sip of his G&T and studied Berit openly. He made no attempt to hide what he was doing. After all, she was doing the same to him.

Her stern, determined face told him she had no time for idiots. That was why her quick smile came as such a surprise. The amused glimmer in her eye, the almost sarcastic twitch of her mouth, told him that while she normally didn't suffer fools gladly, she might be willing to make an exception for him.

Remarkably, she didn't seem the least bit uncomfortable in his company. Most people found it slightly unsettling to spend time with an on-duty police officer. DCI Ahmed assumed that was because most people had committed at least a few minor crimes—and one or two sins. Some dealt with that nervousness by becoming quiet or bullish, others by oversharing or being embarrassingly helpful, and then there were those who seemed to be struck by an irresistible urge to tell terrible jokes.

Berit did none of these. She was leaning back on the sofa with her head against the wall, and she met his eye with an amused look on her face.

Was that because she hadn't committed any sins or because she had made peace with them? For reasons DCI Ahmed couldn't quite explain, he heard himself asking her that very question.

Berit laughed. A surprisingly deep, hearty laugh.

"I'm a writer," she said. "I've already used all my faults, shortcomings, crimes, and sins in my books."

"Do you only write about your own?"

"No, not at all. Other people's faults and shortcomings are incredibly useful. And much more interesting. At this point in my life, all my own sins bore me."

"No criminal past you'd rather hide?" Ian Ahmed asked.

"Hide! If I had a criminal past to draw on, I would have written far more bestsellers than I have. My agent would be over the moon if you could find one."

"I'll do my best."

Berit hesitated again. "There's one more thing," she said.

Ahmed smiled. "Go ahead, Columbo," he said. His headache had finally begun to ease. The gin and tonic she had mixed him really was exceptionally good.

"I think I might have missed something. Or rather, misunderstood it. That damn tea party." She shook her head, frustrated. "There were just so many strong feelings! They all sort of just blur together. After all, so many of our strongest emotions are so easily mistaken for one another—hatred, fear, desperation. Love. And Reginald Trent was so obviously obnoxious that I saw only the hatred. An unforgivable mistake."

"Not quite unforgivable?" Ahmed suggested, but she waved her hand dismissively at him.

"I should have looked more closely. After all, love is usually the deadliest feeling of them all… Although men are usually the perpetrators rather than the victims, of course."

Ahmed disagreed. He'd seen many men kill their wives, girlfriends, even daughters, and in his eyes, love seldom had anything to do with it. Control, jealousy, anger, a twisted sense of honor, perhaps—but not love.

"Are you saying someone at that tea party *was in love* with Reginald Trent?"

That would be news indeed, Ahmed thought. Not even the ex-wife had seemed to, even though she had claimed to in the beginning.

"In one case…yes, perhaps, I almost think it *was* love. But it's all so muddled together I can't be *sure*. You know James Elmer?"

Ahmed nodded. "The hotel owner. You told me he had a fight with Reginald Trent at the tea party." He now had a pretty good idea what the fight was about.

"That argument distracted me too," said Berit. She sounded annoyed with herself again. "It was so dramatic that when I thought back to that moment afterward, it was all I remembered. But the fact is that James was nervous even before their argument. I noticed that during the tea party."

"He may well have had reason to be nervous," Ahmed said. "I can't get into the specifics, but he had a…business relationship with Mr. Trent."

Berit nodded. "I know. They argued about it on the evening of the tourist board meeting. Reginald Trent had threatened James in some way. Mary from the café saw them, but she couldn't hear everything they said. My point is that I'm not sure it *was* nerves. I'm wondering whether what James Elmer felt at the tea party was *guilt*."

"Guilt?"

"Did you know that they're currently doing a lot of work at the hotel?"

"Renovations?"

"No, an extension. Small cottages, behind the hotel. For summer guests from London. They've been blasting for two weeks, but as far as I can work out, it all went completely silent on Friday. No explosions since. And on Sunday, James was nervous or guilty about something *before* the blast that killed Reginald Trent. I'm not saying that they're necessarily connected, but, well, you see?"

He did.

11

THE OFFICE AT THE HOTEL was far too small for three people. DCI Ahmed and DS Stevens were sitting on one side of the desk, James Elmer on the other, squashed up against the wall. Stevens thought Elmer looked nervous before they even began.

"Have you had breakfast?" James Elmer asked, glancing down at his watch. It was a few minutes after ten. "We can whip something up for you, if you're hungry. Scrambled eggs? Bacon? Toast? Tea?" He craned his neck and shouted through the door: "Penny! Can you get the kitchen to send some tea?"

"Not for me, thanks," said DCI Ahmed. Stevens also shook his head.

"No? No tea, Penny! So, gentlemen, what can I do for you? Anything to help the police, eh? Not that I think I can help you all that much. I barely knew Mr. Trent."

"I understand you're in the process of renovating the hotel?" DCI Ahmed asked evenly.

James shuffled a few papers at random, very nearly knocking over an old cup of tea. "Yes, or rather we're expanding. Summer cottages. The comforts of a hotel, combined with the freedom and privacy of having your own space. All without needing to fly or leave the country. It's so much nicer to holiday where people speak English, don't you think?"

"I'm sure," DCI Ahmed said drily.

James Elmer looked panic-stricken. "Or other languages! They're nice too."

"You've been carrying out blasting work to prepare for the foundations, is that correct?"

The hotel owner's face paled. "Yes," he whispered.

"And I'm assuming you have all the necessary permits for that?"

"Yes. Or I'm sure the building company we're using does. I try to stay out of their way."

"Explosives are controlled substances, which means they have to be used and stored properly, subject to all sorts of rules and regulations," the detective continued, much more sternly this time.

Stevens could see the DCI's words register in James's eyes: controlled substances, rules, regulations.

"And there are substantial penalties for any departure from established practice—including for those who fail to report any irregularities."

Penalties. Irregularities. Sweat was starting to break out on James brow. He looked like a rabbit caught in headlights.

"The theft of explosives is incredibly serious and should be reported to the relevant authorities right away, as any responsible citizen surely knows."

"Yes, I… We assumed it was probably just kids," James blurted out.

Bingo, thought Stevens.

James Elmer got up, as though he thought he would feel better if he kept moving. Sadly, the office was much too cramped for that, and he only managed to take half a step before knocking a box over. He bent down to pick up everything that had spilled across the floor, changed his mind, and then slumped back down onto his chair.

"I never thought something like…this would happen. And anyway, what choice did I have? It was just one thing after another with this building project."

James lowered his head to his hands as though all was lost. DCI Ahmed looked like he had all the time in the world.

"Why don't you start from the beginning, Mr. Elmer?" he suggested. "You'll feel much better once you've gotten it all off your chest."

"Things had only just got underway," James said. "We had just started blasting to prepare for the foundations."

There was a childish eagerness to his voice as he talked about the explosives. Stevens recognized that enthusiasm for things that went boom from his sons. They had been wild when they were younger, he thought with nostalgia, remembering the various chemistry projects the boys had thrown themselves into with real zeal. The bathroom had never been the same since.

"But we ran into trouble with that too," James continued. "Stanislav came to me on Friday morning and said there'd been a break-in. All that was stolen was a bit of explosives. A tiny bit, hardly any at all. And possibly a detonator or two. I was afraid a police investigation would ruin everything. Who knows what they might find once they started digging, you know?"

"That you'd taken a few shortcuts, perhaps?" Stevens suggested.

"No! No, nothing like that. Everything was by the book. But Stanislav was…well, his quote was by far the cheapest, so…"

"So you couldn't be sure he hadn't missed something?" said DCI Ahmed.

"I was worried," James conceded. "And then he asked what I wanted him to do, as though we had any choice! He didn't even mention that we had to notify the police. He just stood there, waiting for me to make a decision."

"And your decision was to do nothing?"

"Yes." James's voice was barely audible. "We thought it was just kids," he repeated.

Stevens stared at him in disbelief. "Let me get this straight—you thought one of the local troublemakers had gotten ahold of some explosives, but you didn't think to warn us about it? Jesus Christ Almighty."

"I didn't think anything like this would happen!"

"Do you want to consult a lawyer?" Ahmed asked. "We can continue at the station."

James shook his head.

"When did Reginald Trent loan you the money?"

James stared down at the phone. "Loan?" he repeated, his voice reaching a falsetto. *The man's guilty*, Stevens thought.

"As I understand it, Reginald Trent had lent a considerable sum of money to the hotel?"

"Yes."

"And he then asked you to repay the full amount?"

"It wasn't fair!" James spat out the words. "He promised I'd be able to pay it back at my own pace. The contract was just a formality, he said. He promised!"

"With the hotel as security?"

James nodded. "Thirty percent of it."

"That bomb solved things nicely for you," Stevens commented matter-of-factly.

"It didn't solve anything," James snapped. "You're here, aren't you? This is going to be a huge headache for the hotel. And we're already behind schedule." He must have seen something in their faces because he leaned forward over the desk. "You think I killed him! You think I stole my own explosives!"

"Break-ins can be faked," said Stevens.

James looked around as though he didn't know where to start. "Do you really think I'd have gotten myself in this mess if I could have avoided it? That I'd use explosives that were sure to be traced back to me and the hotel? I've been living in hell since I saw that blast on Sunday. I tried to convince myself that it wasn't necessarily our explosives, but deep down I knew you'd turn up sooner or later. I just never thought…I didn't think you'd suspect me of *murder!*"

Stevens glanced over to DCI Ahmed but couldn't tell whether he believed him or not. His boss's face was as calm and attentive as ever.

"I love this hotel," James continued. "I bought it myself. My dad had nothing to do with it. In fact, he told me it would never work out. I was going to prove him wrong. Eventually."

"Reginald Trent threatened that," said DCI Ahmed.

"Yes, and I tried to talk to him. I begged him to change his mind, but I didn't murder him. If you think the break-in was faked, why don't you talk to the construction crew? They're the ones that reported it to me, and let me tell you, some of them certainly seem dodgy."

"We will," said DCI Ahmed. "Do you own a pair of cuff links shaped like anchors?"

James looked up at him in confusion. "Anchors? No, I don't. I've never liked boats. My dad used to go fishing."

DCI Ahmed got to his feet. The room felt even more crowded with him standing.

"We'll be in touch," he said. He managed to make it sound like part promise, part threat.

"Do you think he was telling the truth, sir?" Stevens asked as they made their way out to the car. He had just been in touch with the department and asked them to start going through the employees at both the hotel and the construction firm.

"He was convincing; I'll give him that."

"But the man's an idiot."

DCI Ahmed couldn't argue with that assessment. "We still can't tie James to the crime scene," he said instead.

"He was at the tea party. Half the village saw him there."

"I know, but where did he keep the explosives and the mobile phone and everything else he would have needed? He didn't have a bag with him, and we can't prove that he was up at the house on any other occasion."

"That doesn't mean he wasn't."

DCI Ahmed nodded. "Issue a new appeal to the public. Tell them we're interested in anyone they might have seen in the vicinity of or on their way to Tawny Hall between Thursday and the tea party on Sunday."

"Yes, guv."

Stevens's phone started ringing, and he moved off to one side to take the call.

Once he hung up, he turned back to DCI Ahmed.

"They've only just made a start on the staff lists, but they've already uncovered one interesting name."

"Anyone we know?"

"Liam Slater. Seems like he works for the construction crew too. And he's not unknown to us, sir."

"Got a record, does he? What for?"

"Theft."

At five to twelve that morning, Liam Slater was brought in for questioning. At ten past, Berit and Sally found out.

They were sitting in the garden when a head of gray hair suddenly appeared over the box hedge. It belonged to their neighbor Ms. Green, who didn't waste any time telling them what she knew.

"I happened to be on High Street as they were loading him into the police car," she said. Her cheeks were flushed with excitement, her eyes bright. "That Detective Ahmed said, 'If we could trouble you with a few questions, Mr. Slater,' which is a damn sight more polite than anyone usually is with that lad. His colleague didn't look all too pleased, let me tell you. Probably thought it was a waste of politeness."

A head of white hair popped up above the rose bushes in the garden on the other side.

"Politeness is never wasted," said its owner, Mrs. Smith. "It says more about the person showing it than the one receiving." She nodded approvingly, as though DCI Ahmed had just earned a gold star in her eyes.

"Either way, they took him off to the station. I know that's where they went because I heard them mention it. So they could 'talk more privately' is what the detective said."

"Well, I was just on my way back from visiting a friend on Mills Lane," said Mrs. Smith.

Berit couldn't help but notice that her neighbor's hair, usually so perfectly coiffed, was now standing on end and that there were twigs clinging to the collar of her cardigan. Perhaps, thought Berit, from the rose bushes outside the cottages at the lower end of Mills Lane.

"And I saw several police officers searching the building where he lives as I was heading home. He lives there with his mother, you know, in one of the flats at the top end of Mills Lane."

Mrs. Smith crinkled her nose as she said "top end." Berit knew the locals drew an invisible line roughly halfway down the street. The blocks of flats at the start of Mills Lane were all tired and shabby, but the cottages at the bottom end were charming.

"Awful woman," said Ms. Green.

Mrs. Smith nodded eagerly. "I've always said that Liam Slater might not be God's best child, but what can you expect with a mother like that?"

"As I said," Mrs. Smith continued, "the police were conducting a thorough search of the place, but I don't know whether they found anything. Other than furniture that reeks of cigarettes."

"That woman smokes like a chimney," Ms. Green agreed.

"And drinks like a fish."

"Well, I think Liam seems nice," Sally spoke up. "And I don't care what his mum is like."

"You would if you'd met her," said Ms. Green.

"Did the police take anything from the search?" asked Berit.

The two old women turned their attention from Sally to Berit.

"Just some clothes," said Mrs. Smith. "A pair of black jeans and a dark sweater, I think. They had them in those clear plastic bags."

"Evidence bags," Ms. Green nodded solemnly. "I've seen it on TV."

Sally and Berit got up and went inside, and as soon as they'd closed the door behind them, Sally blurted out, "Liam would never hurt anyone; I'm sure of it."

She was still so young that she hadn't yet been forced to learn that people could be perfectly nice and pleasant toward some while also hurting others, thought Berit. It was a realization many adults struggled with too: the fact that someone who treated you well might not necessarily do the same for everyone else.

"There are loads of people who could have broken in to the building site," said Sally.

"Some," Berit agreed. "But far from everyone. Whoever took the explosives needed to know where they were kept and whether there was a lock or an alarm. And they also had to come up with the idea in the first place."

"Liam didn't kill Reginald Trent; I just know it," Sally insisted.

Berit nodded and went out into the hallway.

"Wait here," she called back over her shoulder. "I'll be back well before the tourist board meeting."

Something in Sally's face made her stop in the doorway. "Well?" she said impatiently. "What is it?"

"They're all going to be gossiping about him, aren't they? At the meeting, I mean."

"Of course they are, and we're going to listen to what they have to say. You're coming too. I might need your eyes and ears."

Berit paused on the street outside the Queen's Head, Arms, and Legs and looked around. She shook her head. The pub was only a short walk from the hotel, and she was fairly sure that James and Penny Elmer must visit from time to time. She couldn't imagine that the construction workers would want to drink in the same bar as their employers—not if they could help it, anyway.

The other pub in the village felt much more promising. Unlike its competitor, it hadn't won any awards, and it was considerably more run-down. The walls were a shade of dirty yellow, the glare of the ceiling lights harsh, and Berit could see a group of idle young men hanging around the pool table to the rear of the room. Everyone stopped talking as she came in.

Over by the bar, she noticed a man who looked slightly older than the others. He radiated a sort of calm authority, an impression that was only reinforced by the fact that he was sitting alone.

Berit marched straight over to him. "You work for the construction firm, don't you?"

He gave her an amused glance. "Who's asking?"

Berit decided to take that as a yes, and she hopped up onto a barstool, ordered two pints of beers, and turned to face him.

"I'm not with the police," she assured him.

The man laughed. "Lady, no one thinks you are."

Berit sipped her beer. "I suppose you've heard that they've taken Liam Slater in for questioning?" she asked.

"Why else do you think I'm here in the middle of the day? They're turning the site office upside down as we speak." The man swigged his beer.

"Have you spoken to the police?"

"Sure. I've got nothing to hide. I went straight to Mr. Elmer when I realized someone had broken into the office. His hotel, his responsibility, y'know? Just keep working, he told me, so that's what we did. And that's what I told the cops."

"When did you discover the break-in?"

"Now you do sound like a cop," he said. "But since you're buying…" He looked pointedly at his already half-empty pint. She ordered another one for him, and he smiled approvingly. "On Friday morning, and I went straight to Elmer about it, just like I told the actual cops. So if you're not a cop, what are you?"

"An author."

He paused, his glass halfway to his mouth. "What, you're writing about me?"

"How did you know someone had broken into the office? What I mean is…had they forced entry? Or did you only realize once you noticed something was missing?"

"The doors to the cupboard where we keep the explosives had been pried open. Are you going to mention how dark and handsome I am?" He tapped on her notebook. "Stanislav Kowalczyk, that's me. Write it down."

He spelled it out for her, and Berit jotted it down, adding *dark and handsome* beside his name. Stanislav read it over her shoulder and nodded happily.

"As long as we're talking," he said. "I might have something for you. Or rather, Tomasz might. He's young, dark, and handsome for real, but there's no need to mention him in your book." He beckoned to a bored-looking man in his twenties. "Hey, Tomasz, tell this lady what you told me just now."

The young man turned to Berit with a blank expression. "I was on my way out on Thursday, came over here for a few beers around ten. There was nothing weird in the office when I left, but when I got back at eleven, the door was open."

"And you didn't wake Mr. Kowalczyk?"

Tomasz's eyes glittered. "I wasn't exactly sober," he said. "And the door hadn't been broken or anything. I could see that straightaway. I just thought one of the guys had been in to get something and left it open. The door locks automatically if you push it shut properly, but it gets stuck if you don't. So I closed the door, went home, and hit the sack."

"And then I realized someone had stolen the explosives the next morning," Stanislav continued. "I told Elmer right away, before I knew what Tomasz here had seen. We kept the whole thing kind of hush-hush. About the explosives going missing, I mean. That's how Mr. Elmer wanted it. But it meant Tomasz only remembered the open door and told me about it once the cops started snooping about and took Liam down to the station."

"So the explosives were probably stolen sometime between 10:00 and 11:00 p.m. on Thursday," Berit said to herself. She ordered a beer for Tomasz, another for Stanislav, and a round for the other construction workers playing pool. If she kept spending money at this pace, she thought, she really would have to write a bestseller soon.

Berit took a sip from her still almost-full beer. "I don't suppose you knew Mr. Trent personally, did you?" she asked nonchalantly. "You hadn't met him earlier?"

"Of course we hadn't. Where d'you think we would've done that?"

"On another building project, perhaps? Have you ever worked in London?"

"We've worked all over the place, but not for him. And even if we had met him before, we wouldn't have killed him."

"Why not? Apparently the man was an idiot."

The man laughed. "Come on, lady. You can't go round killing rich idiots when you work in this trade." He clinked his glass against hers in an ironic toast. "We'd have no clients left if we did."

As soon as she left the pub, Berit took out her phone and called DCI Ahmed. "The explosives were stolen from the construction firm who have been doing work at the hotel," she said.

"I know. At some point during Thursday night."

"Between 10:00 and 11:00 p.m.," Berit corrected him.

The detective's silence told her that this was news to him.

"Have you looked into the Hartfield sisters, like I told you to?" Berit asked.

"I've been busy," DCI Ahmed replied a touch irritably. "And they aren't exactly top of my list of suspects."

"Do it anyway. They're hiding something; I'm sure of it. There's another tourist board meeting tonight," she said. "If I hear anything, I'll pass it on."

DCI Ahmed was quiet.

"Are you still there?" Berit asked impatiently.

"I can't stop you from going to that meeting," Ahmed replied. "I'm not even going to try to talk you out of going, but…Berit, I know how people can react to unsolved crimes. I've seen the way suspicion, accusations, and mistrust can spread like wildfire when people are afraid. Just be careful, OK? These people aren't characters in one of your books. Any one of them could very well be involved in an extremely real murder."

"I saw Reginald Trent die in front of my eyes," said Berit. "Believe me, I know what's real here."

12

DIDDLE / ˈdɪdəɬ / :
verb
to have sex with (someone)

The pub was crowded when Berit and Sally got there.

The tourist board meeting had just started, but the atmosphere was already tense.

The chair of the local council, Sima Kumar, was leading the meeting. She was standing on the bench that ran along one wall, using it like an improvised stage, trying to drown out the dissatisfied mumbles of the crowd.

"Far fewer of the road signs with the village name were stolen last year than the previous year. We've always maintained that it's good publicity for Great Diddling. It's certainly a name people remember if they see it somewhere," she said, leaving a hopeful pause for laughter.

No one laughed. Several people stared at Berit and Sally. Berit sat down on a seat by a table at the edge of the room and pulled Sally down on the chair beside her.

"In any case," Sima continued, "I'd like to propose ordering some more. With a bit of luck the recent attention on the village will lead to more visitors and more signs being stolen."

"There won't be any more visitors!" someone shouted out. "Not now that we're known as the village that blows people up."

"How are we supposed to prepare for the summer season when there are police officers on every street corner?" someone else said.

"Yeah, and whose fault is all that?" Samson from the supermarket snapped. He had a full pint in front of him, and several empty glasses suggested it wasn't his first. He glared over to the table where Daphne and Margaret were sitting.

Come on, Berit wanted to tell Sima. The room could erupt at any moment, and it wouldn't be like the recent rainstorms, helping to clear the air. No, the villagers knew each other far too well, and that meant the lack of trust was even worse, more personal.

"And what about the journalists? All they're interested in is the murder. It doesn't matter what we do, they're only going to write about Reginald fucking Trent."

"He was a pain in the arse while he was alive, and he's still a damn nuisance now he's dead," said a middle-aged man. The woman beside him gave him a firm jab in the ribs. "No offense, Ms. Trent," he muttered, glaring at his wife.

"The hotel never should have been granted planning permission if you ask me," another man snarled.

"No one asked you!" Penny shouted from the bar.

"I don't understand why we're even bothering with this meeting," someone else said, and several people muttered in assent. "It won't matter what theme we pick. No one will talk about anything else than the murder."

Sima nodded eagerly. "Exactly," she said. "Don't you see? This could be the solution to all our problems!"

"What could?"

"Murder!" said Sima.

Her words were met by utter silence. It hung in the air for a moment or two, with several people exchanging unsure glances with their tablemates. In the end, someone asked what everyone was no doubt thinking:

"Another one?"

"Who did you have in mind?" another person asked, sounding nervous.

"Not a real murder," said Sima. "Fictional murders. If we can't make people forget about the murder—and that's clearly not going to happen in the space of a few weeks—then we should make the most of it. All the papers are writing about us; there's a huge amount of interest from the press."

The faces in front of her were skeptical, the body language defensive.

"Just think about it. What do people love? Murder. And what else do they love? True crime. And what else?"

"Books," Daphne said seriously, at the same time that someone suggested serial killers.

"Books about murder," Daphne insisted.

"Yes!" said Sima. "Books, murder, and charming villages. And what better than a combination of the three? There are so many opportunities! Maybe Agatha Christie spent some time here or DCI Barnaby? We have an opportunity to come up with a campaign that could really spread the name of Great Diddling far and wide once and for all. We've got journalists who are listening and writing about us. We could become a real-life Midsomer."

Before anyone could say anything else, she quickly continued: "I'd like to suggest that this year's theme is books and murder. And I think we should do more than put up a few brass plaques. We could organize guided tours, themed evenings. A book festival, even. Get some crime writers here."

"Oh, great," a man close to Berit muttered, "more writers."

Daphne's eyes locked onto Sima, ignoring the hostile glances the others were still giving her. Daphne seemed to be the only person Sima had convinced. Most people in the pub were still shaking their heads, and Berit suspected none of them believed that books could be enough to lure tourists to the village.

Right then, the door to the pub opened and Liam came in.

"Sorry I'm late," he said. "I hear there's a plan for more murders in the village?" he added with a nod to Sima.

Berit assumed the council leader must have already told him about her plans, and she found herself wondering whether he worked for her, too.

One of the regulars held up his hand and said, "Please don't blow me up! I've got a wife and kids!"

With that, the mood eased a little. There were no doubt certain things an Englishman couldn't joke about at the pub, but being suspected of murder clearly wasn't one of them.

"Susan would thank me," Liam replied. He managed to force a smile onto his face, but he wasn't quite as nonchalant as he wanted to come. He looked pale and tired under all that bravado.

"Harry!" Samson shouted to the man behind the bar. "Get the Oklahoma City bomber here a pint. Put it on my tab."

Harry poured him an ale, and the villagers slowly started chatting among themselves.

"Books, hmm?" said someone.

"And murder," Sima reminded them.

They're hardly going to forget, thought Berit.

"I move that we organize a murder and book festival in early June. Anyone against? Good, then it's settled. I declare this meeting ended."

Sima hopped down from the bench.

"We can have a quiz night here," said the man behind the bar. "Questions about untraceable poison from the Amazon rainforest and other classic methods from history."

"Or a Clue evening?" Samson suggested sarcastically, slurring his words slightly. "Colonel Mustard with the bomb in the library."

No one laughed.

Mary immediately began coming up with ideas for what they could do at the café.

"Could we sell tea and an Agatha Christie cake for fifteen pounds?" she asked Eleanor. "Or give a discount to anyone who brings in one of her books?"

Eleanor leaned toward her. "What are you doing?" she hissed.

"What do you mean? I'm *helping*. We need to get more customers. We need money."

Eleanor looked around and lowered her voice further. "They took Liam in for questioning!"

"And let him go again."

Eleanor put a hand on Mary's arm. "Let's go home," she said. "We did what you wanted. We came to the damn meeting, but now we can go home."

"But we've barely even gotten started yet. We need to form a working group and decide when the next meeting is going to be…"

Eleanor pulled a face at the words *working group* and *next meeting*.

"Get yourself a beer while I help out," said Mary.

Nothing good ever came from helping out, thought Eleanor, fixing her sights on the bar.

As soon as the meeting was over, Sally got up and made her way over to Liam.

He was standing by the bar, surrounded by a loud group of men who seemed to have known him forever.

The people here were different from the people in London, she thought. They seemed both harder and more delicate somehow. They didn't have the same cheerful, indestructible shell as the people in the city, the carefully crafted façade that acted like a suit of armor. No, the villagers were visibly rough around the edges.

One of them was wearing a blue T-shirt advertising Foster's beer with the words *Thank God it's Foster's* written across the back. He boxed Liam on the shoulder, making Liam grimace when he thought no one was looking.

Sally was about to turn around and return to Berit when Liam noticed her. He peeled away from the others and led her over to a quieter part of the bar.

She instinctively reached out and touched his arm.

"Are you OK? It must have been awful. At the station, I mean. Did they believe you when you said you were innocent?"

Liam looked incredibly uncomfortable, despite the fact that he had been laughing along with the men's jokes earlier, as though he found kindness and consideration harder to deal with than sarcasm, Sally thought.

"They didn't exactly take my word for it, no," he said. "I think maybe they had heard it all before."

Sally couldn't even imagine what it must be like to be suspected of a crime and to then be unable to convince the police that you were innocent! "Wasn't there anything you could say to make them realize that you'd never do something like that?" she asked.

"I guess I thought I should just keep my mouth shut and try not to make it any worse," he said.

Sally wasn't sure how it could have gotten much worse. She didn't understand how Liam could be so stoical about the whole thing. Personally, she liked to write to the papers or email her local MP, protest against the injustice and talk to the press, *do* something, but Liam said firmly that none of it would help and that her MP probably had more important things to worry about.

"Leave it; it's fine," he said. "Though if you really want to help there is one thing you could do…"

"Anything."

"I promised Sima I'd help her with some research for this book campaign. She asked me to find a few dead authors who could have lived in the village or visited the pub or something. Not really, of course. Just a bit of fun. For a laugh," he added, in case she hadn't already worked out that the village took a lot of creative liberties when it came to their little brass signs.

"I'll help you," she promised, and when he smiled, it was like he turned back into the Liam she knew from before all of this, her…her friend, the man who'd given her a lift just when she needed it and assured her she would get the job. God, was it only a few days ago? Apparently a few days with Berit Gardner felt like a lifetime.

"OK," she said determinedly. "We can start with Chaucer. Most things do…"

"Can he have visited the pub? Or stayed at the hotel?" Liam suggested.

"Let's keep working on it," she said.

Berit made her way over to the bar and ordered a beer. As she sipped, she took out her notepad and looked around.

A banner hanging from the ceiling announced that the Queen's Head, Arms, and Legs had won Pub of the Year in 2008, 2010, 2012, 2017, and 2019. The lower half of the walls were clad in dark wooden panels, the top half in a homey patterned wallpaper in red, green, and gold. Above the turquoise door to the toilets, there was a sign reading *Gone Fishing*, and the beam above the bar—from which countless glasses were hanging—was shaped like a stylized rowing boat. The dark, exposed beams on the ceiling gave the place a cozy feel.

The man behind the bar was around forty, but he seemed younger. He had a few gray hairs in his dark curls, but they didn't do much to make him look his age. Berit's immediate thought was that he looked like a puppy. All eager cuteness.

And at the moment, he was looking admiringly at something just behind her shoulder.

Berit turned around and discovered Sima, flashing her best professional smile at her and looking frighteningly effective. "Ms. Gardner," she began eagerly.

"Call me Berit."

"I really hope you'll be able to help us, Berit," Sima said. Her tone was polite, but she sounded so confident that Berit would do what she wanted that it felt more like an order than a request.

Sima Kumar is much too used to getting her own way, Berit thought.

"I'm afraid I don't write crime novels," she said.

"But you're an author! There must be so much you could teach us about book festivals and how they work."

"No." With people like Sima, being clear and firm from the very outset was key.

Sima's smile faltered. "I beg your pardon?"

"No," Berit repeated.

"Are you sure? We could organize an event with you here at the pub. With a proper stage, of course. You wouldn't have to stand on a bench all evening. And you could sell copies of your books afterward too, of course. Just think of the publicity! Your name on every press release. We might be able to get you on the radio, maybe even TV!"

Berit shuddered. "No thanks."

"What about a book club at the café? Or just joining our working group? Maybe you know other writers who might be interested?"

"Not if you're planning to hold the festival in just a few weeks' time, they won't," Berit said.

"You were the reason I suggested a book festival," said Sima. "Your writing and Daphne's tea party were the inspiration for the whole idea."

"I thought you said it was Reginald Trent's murder."

Sima's smile faded yet again. "And books," she reminded her.

"Well, you'll have to manage without me," said Berit, turning away. "I'm afraid I'm busy."

Eleanor was sitting at the bar with a pint of ale in front of her, glumly watching as Mary chatted with the little group that had gathered at one of the tables. It looked like their discussion would go on forever.

The author, Berit Gardner, was sitting alone at another table. She kept glancing over to the working group, and Eleanor debated going over to join her.

Eleanor had spent her entire life learning what people wanted and needed, and she recognized hunger when she saw it. This was something she could use. She remembered the interest Berit had shown in her and smiled to herself. The woman had practically done half the job herself.

Now that she thought about it, Berit was almost like a colleague of sorts, and everyone knew that colleagues were the easiest to snare.

Eleanor's gaze drifted over to Mary again. Her face was as eager and engaged as it usually was when they worked together. Eleanor felt a pang of jealousy. Mary had managed to find something that brought her as much satisfaction as their old career had.

Eleanor sighed. Barely a day went by that she didn't miss their old lives. But they were over now, and she would just have to accept that.

She dug a pack of cards from her pocket and leaned forward over the bar.

"Fancy a bet? You give me a beer for free or I pay double," she said to Harry. "Highest card wins."

He drew a card, the eight of diamonds—though she had known that before he even turned it over.

Eleanor drew a king.

"Best of three?" he said, taking another. A queen this time.

She made sure to pull a lower card. No point ruining the tension, after all. His queen easily trumped her six, and the next card he drew was the jack of spades. Not bad at all.

The odds were on his side, she thought as she drew the ace of spades.

But then again, Eleanor had never put much faith in odds.

Harry shook his head and poured her another beer.

On the next stool over, Penny was knocking back vodka shots as though there were no tomorrow.

"Yoo-hoo, handsome!" she shouted, nodding down to her empty glass. "Another, please."

"What exactly are you looking for in all that booze?" Eleanor asked.

"Inspiration," Penny muttered. "Is being a knight in shining armor really that hard?"

"Why, do you need one?"

"No, I need to become one." She leaned in close to Eleanor. "And I need to get my hands on some money pretty fucking sharpish, I'll tell you that much." She seemed to be struggling to focus on Eleanor's face. "D'you know what James's problem is?"

"The police?" Eleanor suggested.

"Nope. It's that he cares what people think about him. He doesn't realize how much power that gives them."

Eleanor studied her with surprise. Surprise and interest.

"The important thing is not to care," she said.

"*Exactly*," said Penny, knocking back her shot.

Eleanor beckoned to Harry. "Two more," she said. "In some ways, Mary is even worse. She might not care what people think of her, but she believes in things. She's got hope."

"Risky," Penny agreed, although with the slurring, it came out more like *rischky*.

"She's hoping the café will suddenly start making money, that everything will work out, and that we'll feel like we finally belong somewhere. You know, rose gardens and rainbows and fluffy white clouds everywhere."

"James hopes too little. He's always convinced things are going to end in disaster and that he might as well give up now, before it all goes wrong. And I mean, yeah, things will probably go to shit. But the point is not to let them see you defeated."

"Never let them know they got to you," Eleanor said.

"D'you know what he said to me after the cops came to the hotel?"

Eleanor shook her head.

"That there's no justice in this world. That's what he said. No. Justice."

"Of course there isn't. What did he expect?"

"That's exactly what I said. But that doesn't mean you can just give up, does it? You have to fight even harder for what you want. And if, by some miracle, you end up getting it, they're going to try to take it from you. And then you have to defend it."

Or leave, Eleanor thought.

Penny nodded to herself. "That's all you can do. Just keep going, and fight back."

"Hear, hear," said Eleanor a bit uneasily. But retreating was a form of defense, wasn't it? "And don't join any working groups."

Penny sighed. "I need to find a way to get my hands on some money for the hotel. We desperately need it." She glanced over to Eleanor. "We're in a bit of a financial…cock-up."

"Who isn't?" Eleanor replied with a shrug. "But this book festival isn't going to help; I can guarantee that. You and I will have to come up with something else."

"Good luck with that," said Penny. "I hope you're a better knight than me."

Daphne shouted for Berit to join her and Margaret at their table.

"Sima is quite right," she said enthusiastically once Margaret had gone off to buy another round. The secretary returned not long later with a beer for Berit, two small glasses of cider, and a bag of salt and vinegar crisps.

"There's nothing better than books and murder," Daphne said, taking a sip of her cider. "You'll have to come and see my book collection one day. I've got first editions of all the Agatha Christie books, of course—speaking of murder. And all the other queens of crime from the golden era too: Dorothy L. Sayers, Ngaio Marsh, Margery Allingham."

"Let Berit discover them for herself," said Margaret. She kept glancing over to Berit with an insistent look on her face, as though she wanted to tell her something.

Berit didn't share Daphne's enthusiasm for the festival. On the contrary. She was convinced the so-called book and murder festival would be nothing but trouble. The more they all acted like Reginald Trent's death was just part of a tourism drive, the more acutely aware she became that someone—possibly even someone in that very room—was a killer.

If she was really honest with herself, and Berit always was, she could probably understand Daphne's enthusiasm. She felt it herself: that longing to throw herself into a project and become part of a new community. Berit had spent a large chunk of her life living on the sidelines, but she had never stopped dreaming about really belonging somewhere. And a book festival! She loved book festivals. What could be better than a group of people who shared an interest in reading?

It was that very longing that made her push back. She knew just how easily she could get caught up in the project, using it as an excuse not to think about anything else. About her writing, or lack thereof. About Reginald Trent and his tragic fate.

About who killed him.

"My family have been collecting books for generations, you understand," said Daphne. "It was my grandfather who started the tradition, and it'll end with me. I'm the last member of the family who cares."

Berit wasn't really listening. From the corner of her eye, she had seen Eleanor make her way over to the table where the working group was sitting. She whispered something in Mary's ear, then slipped a folded scrap of paper into Liam's jacket pocket. Berit wouldn't have noticed if she hadn't been sitting on the sidelines, ready to observe rather than take part.

She needed to keep her distance in order to maintain a clear head.

Berit felt uneasy as she walked home to her cottage. The village was quiet, the streets deserted. Berit had always enjoyed solitude and darkness. Ordinarily, she drew a great deal of creative power from shadows, from a world where nothing was definite, fixed, or real. But today, it simply fueled her fears. She swallowed, painfully aware that her heart was beating much faster than usual.

She was so focused on her imagination and her ability to picture things that her first thought was that the footsteps must be all in her mind.

Berit listened carefully. *No, they were definitely real.*

She sped up, and the footsteps behind her continued at the same pace: calm but determined, with no real urgency. Moving at a speed that would allow whoever it was to keep up with Berit rather than catching her.

It was DCI Ahmed's fault that she was so nervous, she thought, but she refused to be afraid. Berit slowed down, and the footsteps did the same. She thought back to that evening. Who could have reason to follow her home from the pub?

When she reached the door to her cottage, she paused and turned around.

"Hello, Margaret," she said.

Margaret stepped forward out of the shadows. She was wearing a sensible, navy-blue jacket to keep out the evening chill, and the dark color made her blend in with the darkness around them.

"I see Daphne was right when she said you could be a great detective," Margaret said with a smile.

"She said that?"

"She said that you really see people. That you're clearheaded and perceptive. But I don't think she meant it as a compliment."

Berit showed Margaret around to the rear of the cottage, and they sat down in the garden chairs. In the soft glow of the light on the back wall, Margaret's face looked serious and introspective, and Berit realized she must be thinking of something other than the overgrown apple tree and the dark rhododendrons.

"My cottage looks a bit like this," the secretary said without warning. "Though mine is by the water."

"Where is it?" asked Berit.

"Oh, I haven't actually found it yet."

And yet she had spoken about it with such confidence that she made it sound like it definitely existed somewhere. Berit was used to that sort of conviction. Many of her characters felt more real than the people around her. Once something had existed for so long in your head, it became hard to tell whether it was real or not.

"Are there roses?" she asked.

Margaret smiled to herself. "No, it's too close to the sea for that. Salty winds and bare rocks. Up north somewhere."

Berit nodded. She understood the appeal of the gray and the barren, the rugged and the timeless. Personally, she had always loved the Stockholm archipelago in autumn.

"I…" Margaret began. "You and I don't know each other. Not really, I mean. But we're in this mess together, so to speak, and maybe it's because you aren't from around here…"

"An outsider's perspective."

"Yes, something like that. The thing is…this interest the police have in Liam, it's madness. He would never kill anyone. He's been helping out at Tawny Hall for years now. I know he never takes anything seriously, that he's as irresponsible as anyone else at that age, but the idea that he'd kill someone in cold blood…and like that? No, never."

Berit breathed in the scents of the early summer evening, thinking about darkness and shadows and the fact that things are rarely as simple as they seem.

"He's a little wild," Margaret continued. "The kind of person who always gets the blame for everything."

"Sometimes justly so and sometimes unfairly?" said Berit.

Margaret glanced at her. "Do you know what he told the police?" she asked.

"Nothing, most likely. I should think he probably just smirked at them."

"You see? Anyone would realize that this wasn't the right time to mess with the police. But there's no way he can have killed Reginald, which means that either someone else stole the explosives, or he stole it for the killer and is now covering for them. That's the way I see it. Which could mean he knows who did it."

Berit didn't speak. In her experience, silence was often the most effective way to get someone to keep talking.

"He sees it as a joke," said Margaret. "The whole village does. That was what I wanted to talk to you about. Everyone seems to think that if they just laugh the whole thing off, it'll be like it never happened. But someone in this village is capable of committing murder, and I'm afraid that's going to change this place forever."

"Have you always lived here then?"

Margaret seemed taken aback by her question.

"Me? No, not at all. I came here a few years ago. Seven, to be precise." She paused for a long moment before adding, "I came to Great Diddling to get away."

"You didn't come here to work for Daphne?"

"No, she found me later. She has an uncanny ability to find lost souls in need of sanctuary. It creates a real sense of loyalty."

"What did you need sanctuary from?"

Margaret looked straight at her. "I killed someone," she said.

13

THERE HAD BEEN A TIME when Sima was obsessed with the thought of a team.

When she grew up, she was used to being smarter than everyone else, brilliant but also alone. It wasn't until she arrived at university in Oxford that she realized the world was full of gifted young people. And it wasn't until she discovered politics that she'd realized the power that could be harvested if you worked together for something you believed in.

When she imagined the future during her time at Oxford, she had pictured herself leading a team of brilliant people—people who had gone to private schools like Eton, Harrow, Cheltenham; men and women who spoke Latin, French, Arabic, and Cantonese; who had been born with a silver spoon in their mouth and never lacked expensive cutlery since. And her.

She could have accomplished great things; she was still convinced of that. Because she had something the others lacked: an insight into the way the real world worked and what ordinary people thought and felt, plus the ability to get through to them. With her experience and their privilege, they could have changed the world. For real.

But the future hadn't quite worked out that way. Shit happened, and you had to work with what you got.

Her current team, for example, consisted of an unreliable petty criminal with too much wax in his hair, a depressingly beige young woman who seemed desperate to be liked, and an older woman who seemed determined to force tea and sandwiches on everyone.

They were sitting around a small table in the corner of the café. Everyone had pulled their chairs as far in as they could, which meant their elbows were constantly bumping. There was barely room for their teacups on the table, and Mary kept getting up to fetch more biscuits or refill the teapot.

"As I was saying," Sima said once Mary came back, "some of you might have opinions on the fact that we're...bending the truth in some cases."

"Not at all!" Mary chirped. "We can't allow ourselves to be hamstrung by the truth."

"OK, but still. We live in a world where the rich are called entrepreneurs and the poor liars. Where some people are allowed to reinvent themselves whenever they like, and the rest of us are bound by 'the truth,' whatever that is. Everyone knows the game is rigged. What we're doing here is more like...self-defense. We're not liars. We're dreamers. We see the world as it could be, not as it is, and that, my friends, is a higher form of truth."

She paused for effect, looking expectantly around the group. At Liam, who was sitting with his knees as far apart as the cramped space would allow. And at Sally, who was listening politely. And at Mary, who excused herself and got up to brew another pot of tea.

"They say that if you put a frog into a pan of boiling water, it'll jump straight out," Sima continued, her face eager, serious. "But if you put it into a pan of lukewarm water and heat it slowly, it'll stay there and slowly cook to death."

"Sounds like a dumb frog to me," said Liam.

"I've always found frogs so sweet," said Mary. "More tea?"

Sima gritted her teeth. "The village is the frog," she said impatiently. "*We* are. We've sat quietly and watched as shop after shop is forced to close, as the tourist season gets shorter and shorter and more and more people move away. We've given up. The water is getting really bloody hot, but we're just sitting in our little pot, slowly being boiled alive. We need to do something before it's too late. And I promise you, there's nothing I'm not prepared to do for this village."

She looked each of them in the eye, one by one, trying to make them feel the urgency and importance of what they were doing. No one said anything.

"Right," she said. "We'll meet here again tonight, 7:00 p.m. We need to get to work ASAP. Liam, you're in charge of the web page."

"I don't even know what a book festival website should look like."

"I do," said Sally.

"Right. Sally, you're in charge of design. And content. And Mary, you're in charge of..."

"Tea?" Mary said hopefully.

DCI Ahmed glumly studied the woman who was making him a cup of tea.

He and DS Stevens were squashed up together on the small sofa in her living room, and from where he was sitting he could see Mrs. Ainsley searching the kitchen cupboards for mugs, tea, and sugar. She seemed like a friendly, pleasant—if confused!—woman in her seventies, but she was also the main reason their once promising lead had turned to nothing.

The forensic report had confirmed that the substance used in the blast that killed Reginald Trent came from the construction firm at the hotel. The lab had traced the explosives back to the factory where it had been produced and had obtained documentation for the entire distribution chain. Liam Slater's clothing had also tested positive for traces of the same substance. It was a breakthrough, and DCI Ahmed had been feeling good about the case for the first time since he had been called out to Tawny Hall.

And then Mrs. Ainsley had barged into their investigation, confused but unapologetic.

The air in the living room was hot and stuffy. Mrs. Ainsley had insisted on making them tea, though she couldn't seem to remember where she kept her cups. She had to open the lids of several jars before eventually finding the one containing tea.

Stevens glanced over to DCI Ahmed. Both men were thinking the same thing: Just how reliable could this woman really be as a witness?

DCI Ahmed had brought Liam Slater in for questioning again, and this time the young man had sung like a canary—to quote DS Stevens. Suddenly, the man remembered he had an alibi for Thursday night and was only too happy to share it. He'd been helping Mrs. Ainsley fix her computer. And sure, his clothes had tested positive for explosives, but as he'd been working with the blasting all day on Thursday, it wasn't that surprising, was it? DCI Ahmed had watched his case crumble around him.

Unless, of course, Liam had been lying about the alibi.

Ian Ahmed looked around the room. 17 Church Lane was dark and depressingly empty. A protective cover had been draped over an armchair, and there were no coats or shoes in the hallway. Every single curtain was drawn, as though Mrs. Ainsley was trying to block out the beautiful day outside.

One of the windows began thudding in the morning breeze, and DS Stevens got up to close it. He quickly realized that the latch was broken, however, and tried to provisionally fix it for her.

Mrs. Ainsley came back through to the living room carrying a tray. The cups and saucers rattled as she slowly made her way toward them, and Stevens gave up on the window to help her. He sat the tray down on the living room table.

"Liam was here last Thursday," Mrs. Ainsley assured them. "He was helping me with my computer. Nasty little buggers, aren't they? Computers, that is. Always something wrong with them."

"Eh, quite," said DCI Ahmed. "And is Liam Slater a close friend of yours, Mrs. Ainsley?"

"Not especially," she replied. "That lad has always been a little trouble-maker. The little sod used to steal my apples when he was younger. But he does know his way around a computer."

DCI Ahmed phrased his words carefully before he next spoke. "And you are quite sure it was Thursday evening that he came over?"

"Yes," she replied, squinting up at them through the pair of enormous glasses that dominated her face, the lenses as thick as milk bottles.

"It couldn't have been, say, Wednesday evening?" Ahmed asked hopefully.

"No, I have my sewing circle then."

"Or even Friday?"

"That's the all-you-can-eat buffet at the Indian restaurant."

"Between 9:00 and 11:00 p.m.?" DCI Ahmed asked, surprised.

"No. Pensioners' discount between four and six, and heartburn the rest of the evening. I didn't have heartburn while he was here, which means it can't have been Friday."

There was an undeniable logic to what she had said; he had to admit that. DCI Ahmed sighed, thanked Mrs. Ainsley, and got up from the sofa.

Once outside, Ahmed paused outside the cottage and looked around at the sunny, idyllic street. It looked so charming that it was hard to believe someone in the village could have planned the destruction at the tea party.

"Did she seem trustworthy to you?" he asked his sergeant.

"She seemed pretty sure about the days," Stevens said reluctantly.

Ahmed sighed again. "Yes, that's what I thought too."

"But she's definitely a bit barmy," Stevens said. "She doesn't even *have* an apple tree. That's a plum tree over there."

Oh God oh God oh God oh God.

Berit E. V. Gardner was dead on the living room floor.

Sally's brain had short-circuited. All she could think was *oh God* over and over again, frozen to the spot in the hallway. She had just gotten home from the working group meeting and found Berit just lying there on the floor.

Her mother would never forgive her if she let Berit die before she had finished her next novel. If she died afterward, it might actually be good for sales, but not before…

What was she thinking? She couldn't let Berit die at all.

She should ring someone. Her hands fumbled for her phone, as though her fingers had gone numb. Sally took a few unsteady steps into the living room and realized that her feet didn't seem to be working either.

She should call her mum. She had to...shouldn't she call the police first? Or an ambulance?

Her first step should probably be to check that Berit really was dead. She shakingly walked the short distance over to her, dropped to her knees, and noticed—thank God, thank God—that Berit's chest was still rising and falling.

Berit's eyes snapped open, and Sally fell back with an undignified shriek.

"What on earth are you doing?" Berit asked.

"What am *I* doing?" Sally asked, her heart still beating uncomfortably hard in her chest. Her mouth tasted of panic and fear. "What are *you* doing?"

"What does it look like?"

"Lying on the living room floor?"

"There you go."

Sally closed her eyes. "But why?"

"I thought things might look different from down here."

Sally fought the inappropriate urge to laugh uncontrollably. "And...do they?" she asked once she had herself under control again.

"Absolutely. Someone used to smoke in here. The ceiling is stained yellow from the nicotine. There's a dust bunny behind the armchair. And the floor is surprisingly uncomfortable to lie on for an extended period of time."

Sally rubbed her face. It was all well and good for Berit to be lying on the floor, but her heart was still pounding from shock, and she couldn't get her stupid hands to stop shaking.

"It's often possible to gain new perspectives just by changing position," said Berit. "It gives the brain a little shake up, which is good for getting the old juices flowing."

Sally got up on unsteady legs. Tea, she thought. She needed tea.

Her eyes were drawn to the open notepad on the desk. Its pages were full of notes, with some words circled and underlined, arrows linking different thoughts. Berit had been working before she decided she needed a new perspective, Sally realized.

Berit's handwriting was small and neat, a fluid cursive. Sally could only make out around half of the words, written in perfectly straight lines on the creamy, unlined pages. She seemed to have written in full sentences in places, drawn improvised mind maps featuring a handful of words and multiple arrows in others, angrily circled certain things, and added question marks and boxes.

Her eyes were immediately drawn to Liam's name. It was surrounded by thick, dark lines. In another box, she saw the word *relationships*, and there were arrows linking his name to Eleanor, Tawny Hall, and the hotel.

Sally's own name was nowhere to be seen.

She kept reading.

"What do you mean by ineffective defense mechanisms?" she asked.

Berit answered from the floor.

"Everything we use to negotiate the fact that life will inevitably involve suffering. Once upon a time in our lives, we developed different defense mechanisms to protect ourselves from suffering. They might have worked once, but sooner or later, they mostly lead us to repeat the same mistakes over and over again. It's one big muddle of protection, security, self-deception, projection, and denial."

Beside Liam's name, Berit had written: Laughing in the face of adversity? Lowered expectations—defense or self-fulfilling prophecy? Loyalty— constructive or destructive?

"So what are your defense mechanisms?"

Sally didn't really expect Berit to answer, but the author did so without missing a beat.

"Longing to live life to the fullest and be a part of something, but channeling that by watching and observing from the sidelines and by writing about it, which minimizes the risks of getting hurt but also guarantees that I'll never get what I really want."

"And mine?"

Yet again, Berit replied immediately: "A belief that the walls will protect you when in fact they're trapping you."

Sally instinctively took a step away from the wall and looked down at her gray clothing. The things she wore were practically camouflage in many office environments, and she wondered whether she subconsciously chose them in an attempt to blend in with the walls.

"I'm not in love with him," she said.

"I know."

"We're just friends."

"No just about it."

Sally went into the kitchen and filled the kettle. Once it boiled, she took the two cups back through to the living room, setting hers down on the desk and Berit's on the floor by her head.

"Things aren't what they seem," said Berit, still staring up at the ceiling. "The people in Great Diddling have an impressively long tradition of lying."

"Sima says it's all about re-creating yourself. People do it all the time, apparently. We're just open about it here."

"So, you're planning to be part of the working group, are you?" Berit sounded resigned. Resigned but skeptical.

"There's another meeting this evening," said Sally. "We're going to make a home page for the festival."

"Where?"

"At Mary and Eleanor's. They live in the flat above the café."

"Just make sure you're never alone with anyone from the group. And I know I asked you to be my eyes and ears at the tourist board meeting, but I want you to forget all about that. Hear and see nothing."

Sally felt hurt. She knew she might not have done a great job so far, but surely she couldn't have been that bad?

"I don't want you to accidentally see or hear anything that could put you in danger," Berit explained. She seemed to hesitate for a moment, then muttered, "Just be careful, OK?"

She was worried! Berit was worried about her! Sally was so happy at this unexpected show of concern from her boss that she actually promised not to be alone with anyone from the village.

Other than Liam, she thought. But Berit couldn't have meant him.

She took a little dancing step out toward the kitchen.

"Wait!" she heard Berit shout from the living room.

Sally turned around.

"Give me a hand here. I can't get up on my own."

In DCI Ahmed's own private opinion, people didn't change. And they definitely didn't change into four different people in the space of a twenty-minute commute.

The analyst was proud of herself, and rightly so. She had been tasked with going through the CCTV footage in an attempt to find the mysterious Mr. Gerald Corduroy-Smith, a charge that had proved much harder than DCI Ahmed expected given just how many surveillance cameras there were in London.

"That's the problem," she explained. "There are almost seven hundred thousand of them."

"You'd expect at least a few to have caught him."

"They did, absolutely. It's just that we don't know which, and they produce a huge amount of data."

Ian Ahmed nodded. In modern police investigations, having too much information was almost always a bigger problem than too little.

"But I did find him outside of the office building at the time you suggested. And nearby cameras spotted him here and here." She pointed to various locations on the map on DCI Ahmed's computer screen. "Then we got some unexpected help from an owner of a hotel in Earl's Court who saw the picture we released and called the tip line. It's the kind of hotel where it's not unusual for people to stay long term, or to keep coming back. Businessmen, commuters, divorced men."

"No divorced women?"

She shook her head. "They tend to get the house and the kids."

"Interesting that the owner called us," said DCI Ahmed. "I would have thought that a hotel like that wouldn't care who their guests were so long as they pay on time and don't cause any trouble. Not exactly the type to call the police."

"I think the owner likes him, sir. She seemed worried that something might have happened to him. An accident or something."

"So we know where he was staying?"

The analyst passed him a sheet of paper with the name and address of the hotel.

"Good job," Ahmed said, but she wasn't done.

"Since I had a good idea of where he was heading, I decided to request the CCTV footage from the cameras on the right Underground lines at roughly the right time, plus from the street where the hotel is. Even though we already know where he lived, I thought it might be of interest."

DCI Ahmed gave her an impressed look. "And was it?"

"See for yourself."

She highlighted a few files on her computer and opened them in order.

DCI Ahmed leaned over her shoulder and whistled.

"Great work," he said and meant it.

In the first of the clips, Gerald Corduroy-Smith could be seen coming out of the office building. They had used a still from that same footage when they released his image to the public and asked for information. His face was slightly downturned, and he was wearing a hat, but he was still recognizable. A smart man in his sixties, with a fleshy nose, a pronounced chin, and hair that was probably cut short. He had good posture and his suit was, as Ms. Clarke had said, perfect for the area. He moved with confidence and gravitas, and looked every inch the successful business man.

The Gerald Corduroy-Smith visible in the footage from the Tube was entirely different. His hat was gone, his hair suddenly blond and curly, but the biggest difference was his posture. He was now slumped in his seat, looking tired and bored. The cut of his suit looked much less impressive now that he wasn't standing tall, blending in seamlessly with the other weary commuters.

"I asked a colleague who works with the facial recognition software to double-check for me," she said. "As a personal favor. It's definitely the same person."

DCI Ahmed nodded. "Good initiative," he said.

In the next clip, Gerald Corduroy-Smith was standing on the bustling Earl's Court Road. He had taken off his coat and seemed to have stuffed it into his bag. There was a camera hanging around his neck, and he was holding up a map. His movements seemed jerky, unsteady, and he kept stopping. He looked like just another lost tourist, getting in the way on a street corner. DCI Ahmed found himself thinking that he could have walked straight past him without even noticing.

In the fourth clip, captured right outside the budget hotel, Gerald Corduroy-Smith's appearance had transformed yet again. He suddenly seemed much older and slower, softer somehow, a contrast to the shabby street around him. He looked like an elderly gentleman who had fallen on hard times, alone and out of place in the cold, indifferent city around him.

DCI Ahmed thanked the analyst and reached for the phone.

The cynic in him had expected it to be run by a woman of a certain age, single and with a weakness for charming older men, but he was wrong. The hotel was owned by a young Somali couple. It was the woman who had phoned the tip line, but she called out to her husband and put DCI Ahmed on speakerphone. Yes, they knew Mr. Gerald, they replied in unison. A sweet, old gentleman. His children didn't take care of him the way they should, and he was all alone in London. Their own families were still in Somalia, and they sent money home to them every week. They just couldn't understand why the English didn't take better care of their elders. They had been happy to help dear Mr. Gerald.

"When did he check in with you?" asked DCI Ahmed.

"Two weeks ago."

"And how did he pay when he checked out?"

"Pay? He hasn't checked out yet."

Ian Ahmed froze. "Are you telling me he's still there?"

"Yes," they said. "Well, not right now. He had to go and see one of his children. His grandchild was ill, and they needed his help. Then they called him, you know?"

"He didn't happen to mention where his child and grandchild live, did he?"

"Sure. In Dorchester."

"And did he say how long he would be gone?"

"No, he didn't know," they said. "The child was ill."

"Of course. Did he leave anything in his room?"

"A bag. But he took most of his things with him, probably because he didn't know how long he would be there."

"Could you do me a favor? Could you go up to his room and see what's in the bag? I'll wait on the line."

The man went away, but he was soon back.

"It's empty," he said, confused. "But his toothbrush is still here," he added, as though that was some sort of guarantee that Mr. Corduroy-Smith would be back.

"And he didn't pay before he left?"

"We have his card details in the system, so there was no need."

DCI Ahmed nodded to himself. He gave the couple his number and asked them to give him a call right away if Mr. Gerald did reappear, then ended the call. He could picture them so clearly, as though he were right there with them in reception. They seemed like decent, hardworking, likable people. The kind who toiled away without expecting much in return, making sure they gave back more than they took.

He was fairly confident they would never see their dear Mr. Gerald again. Their elusive guest was gone for good, and his credit card would turn out to be fake or stolen.

It was yet another reminder that scammers were never content just to fleece the rich, he thought tiredly.

His mobile phone buzzed. Then again. And again. He picked it up and saw a series of text messages from Berit.

The village is planning a book and murder festival, read the first one. He closed his eyes for several seconds, then read on.

What's Sima's background? Is she from the village? Has she ever reinvented herself?

How's it going with the background checks on Mary and Eleanor? Fluid identities! Re-creating themselves! Everyone sees what they want to see!

He rubbed his face. "Stevens!" he called through the open door, face still in his hands. "Do a background check on our people of interest. All of them. Where they're from, where they've lived, financial statements, the works. Daphne Trent, Margaret Brown, Penny and James Elmer, Liam Slater, and Mary and Eleanor Hartfield."

Stevens put his head through the door. "Mary and Eleanor Hartfield, sir?" he asked, his face unreadable.

"They're not what they seem, Stevens."

"No, sir."

DCI Ahmed's phone buzzed again. His eyebrows shot up. "Oh, and find out who Margaret Brown killed."

14

MARY AND ELEANOR LIVED IN a small flat above the café. When Sima and Sally got there, they found Liam hunched in front of an ancient computer, his fingers already tapping away on the keyboard.

Sima grabbed a chair from the kitchen and sat down behind him.

"I want it to feel luxurious," she instructed, ignoring that she had delegated the design of it to Sally. "And sort of old-timey. Think 1920s, Agatha Christie, dramatic deaths in a charming setting. Holidays and murder— Poirot or Miss Marple solving crimes and drinking cocktails with women in pretty dresses. This could be you! That's what I want it to say."

Liam made the background completely black, so that the swooping, gold lettering really popped.

Great Diddling Book and Murder Festival, they said.

That was it. No details. No pictures. No descriptions.

He sat quietly for a moment, then added a few champagne glasses, some gold glitter and the shimmering silhouette of a flapper against the dark background. She was holding a cigarette in a long holder, the smoke curing up toward the heading.

Liam then added a knife. It was a murder festival, after all.

The most important part of the website was the program itself, and this was where they ran into problems. Mainly because they didn't have one.

But they had to write something. People needed some idea of what they were paying for.

"We have to make them want to come here," Sima said. "Once they're hooked, we can change it."

Mary came in with tea and a plate of biscuits. There was no room on the desk for Liam's cup, so Sally held it for him.

"What do people expect at a book festival?"

"Well, authors, of course," Sally said. "Panel discussions about their life and writing. Interviews. Book signings, perhaps. Some famous names to draw them in. Maybe even an international guest."

"OK," said Sima. "So, let's go with a panel discussion on the Thursday. Give me some crime writers. I'm guessing we can't tell people Agatha Christie will be there."

"What do you mean, some crime writers?"

"Just name any."

"Ian Rankin?" Sally suggested, trying to think of authors who she herself enjoyed. "Elly Griffiths."

Liam jotted both down.

Under the program heading, the text now read:

> Thursday: PANEL DISCUSSION. Hear IAN
> RANKIN and ELLY GRIFFITHS discuss life and
> writing in a cozy pub setting.

"But!" Sally said anxiously. "You'll never be able to get them here. Not at such short notice."

Sima waved dismissively. "Later," she said. "We can worry about that later. Right now, the key thing is to mention names that will convince people to stump up for a ticket. Once they've made up their mind to come, we can always make changes to the program. Sudden cancellations due to illnesses, but fear not, we've found a replacement. That sort of thing."

Sally shook her head. It was crazy. It was…bordering on dishonest. She had never done anything like it in her life.

"Come on, we need more. What are you reading now?"

"Margaret Atwood's *Alias Grace*."

"Is she alive?"

"Yes, but…"

Sima snapped her fingers at Liam, and the text on the computer changed in front of their eyes:

> Thursday: INTERNATIONAL PANEL
> DISCUSSION. Hear IAN RANKIN, ELLY
> GRIFFITHS, and MARGARET ATWOOD discuss
> life and writing in a cozy pub setting.

"All right," Sima said. "Let's move on to Friday. Let's say…'book-related activity' in the schedule. I'll think of something later. We have plenty of time to come up with a book-related activity."

"You have two weeks!"

"Write that there'll be a surprise too," Sima said. "A big surprise. In bold. Maybe add a few exclamation marks too?"

"No problem," said Liam, tapping away again.

The remainder of the program read as follow:

> Friday: BOOK-RELATED ACTIVITY
>
> Saturday: THE BIG SURPRISE!!!

Sally closed her eyes. Nothing would surprise her more than if they actually managed to book any authors, she thought glumly.

The café was closed by the time Berit arrived. She pressed her nose to the glass and saw that the chairs had been stacked on top of the tables. A small Closed sign had been hung on the door, but she tried the handle anyway. Locked.

Was that to prevent confused customers from marching straight in, or did it stem from a general need for security? She chose to believe it was the former and made her way around to the rear of the property. As expected, she found a back door onto the alleyway, and she tried the handle. Unlocked. She opened the door and slipped inside.

To the right, a dark staircase led up to the flat above, and the door at the top opened without a problem. Berit could hear the working group chatting away in a small room at the end of the narrow hallway, but she was more interested in the soft voice coming from the kitchen.

Mary was alone by the sink, humming to herself as she scrubbed the dirty dishes. She had her long hair pinned up, but several of the grips were on the verge of falling out. Her face was even more beautiful when lost in thoughts, thought Berit. The high cheekbones and clear, bright skin in combination with her snow-white hair made her look young and somehow delicate. But she scrubbed the pan in the sink with real zeal, and Berit noticed that her arms were strong and muscular.

The walls of the kitchen were covered in pictures of flowers and plants. Some were cut from ordinary seed catalogs, others hand-embroidered; some were framed, others simply tacked to the wallpaper. A beautiful watercolor of roses hung alongside an amateurish oil painting of wisteria hanging over a window, and one picture seemed to have been torn out of a book on English flora.

The scent of roses in the air was overpowering, and Berit's first, illogical thought was that it came from the pictures on the wall. Then she noticed the large bouquet of roses beside Mary at the sink.

"She's always wanted an English country garden," Eleanor said into Berit's ear, keeping her voice so low that Mary wouldn't hear her. "But this is the best I've managed. So far, anyway."

The two women stepped back into the dark hallway and continued to watch Mary work.

"How long have the two of you been together?" Berit asked, her voice just as low.

"Most people don't notice," said Eleanor. "It's funny, really, how invisible older women become."

"It was something in the way you looked at her."

"Love at first sight, as far as I was concerned," said Eleanor. "Mary needed a little longer, but we left England together just two weeks after we first met."

She and Berit were standing side by side, so close that their shoulders were touching, but Berit still couldn't quite read the look in Eleanor's eye as she watched Mary.

Mary continued to hum to herself. Her voice was light and bright, which produced an oddly ghostly effect in the half-light. The only bulb in the kitchen illuminated the empty dining table, making it feel like none of them were really there.

"Forty years and two marriages," Eleanor said to herself. "Mine, not hers," she added to Berit. "I've always been more pragmatically minded than Mary. She's the romantic. Personally, I can see the advantage of having a man around from time to time. From a purely social point of view."

"Why don't you tell people that you're a couple?" asked Berit. "Surely times have changed?"

"The times might have, but we haven't. We're too old for any of that."

In a way, Berit understood. She had never felt the need to stand before the world and proclaim her love for any of the men in her life. Or the women. Something was lost in a relationship when you subjected it to other people's expectations and opinions.

But more was lost when you had to hide it. She said as much out loud.

"We're not hiding," Eleanor said defensively. She put a firm hand on Berit's arm and led her down the staircase to the alleyway behind the house. She leaned back against the wall as she lit a cigarette, the smoke mixing with the aroma of frying oil from the fish-and-chips shop next door.

"Look," she said. "Everyone sees what they want to see, and we just… let them. There's a lot of freedom in living under the radar. And two unmarried old sisters—we're completely invisible. In a good way! We could probably get away with anything. With murder, even. After all, who would suspect us?"

Berit looked at her sharply. Was she joking—in extremely bad taste, Berit thought—or openly challenging her? *Or both.*

"I would," Berit said. "In a heartbeat. Those innocent and confused faces of yours didn't fool me for a second. You played your parts too well. Too perfectly."

"I told Mary not to overdo it in front of you. You're not quite as stupid as the rest of them."

"Thank you. I think."

Eleanor shrugged. "We've lived our own lives. We've lived all over the world. It's been a good life, all in all. No complaints."

Berit thought she heard longing in her voice. "Why did the two of you move back to England?" she asked.

"Mary decided she missed the seasons here. She missed the rain, if you can believe that." Eleanor shook her head. "You never think that the place where you live now will be the last. No matter how old you get, you always think there's a new adventure waiting out there for you."

As so often before, Berit reflected on the fact that people always used the general "you" when what they really meant was "I."

15

THERE WAS NO POLICE CONSTABLE waiting for Berit when she arrived at Tawny Hall the next day. The police cordon was gone, as were all their vehicles on the driveway. Berit knocked several times on the grand double doors.

Margaret seemed surprised when she opened the door. Surprised and slightly anxious. Perhaps she regretted confiding in Berit the last time they spoke.

"Daphne offered to show me her library," said Berit.

Margaret held the door open—reluctantly, it seemed to Berit—and showed her through to a small room on the ground floor, where Daphne was sitting in an armchair.

"She wants to see the library," said Margaret.

Daphne leapt up, eagerly leading the way down a long, narrow hallway. "Can we get you a drink?" she asked over her shoulder.

"Maybe later," said Berit. It was eleven o'clock in the morning.

It was the same hallway where she had heard Reginald Trent argue with James and Penny Elmer during the tea party. There were books everywhere. Several times, she came close to stumbling on them, while Daphne and Margaret, on the other hand, deftly avoided every pile. Berit quickly mirrored their movements—taking a half step in one direction to avoid a sideboard, swinging back the other way in order to pass the chair she could see peeping out from beneath another heap—and eventually they reached a pair of tall double doors.

Daphne came to a halt in front of them, pausing briefly to build anticipation before flinging them open.

The first thing Berit saw was the wall of pretty, softly curving windows out onto the terrace along one side of the room. The high, custom-built bookshelves rose up on either side of them like a beautiful old vine. Thousands, if not tens of thousands, of books were crammed onto the shelves in seemingly no order at all.

The floor was checkered, but the dust and dirt were so ingrained into the tiles that it took her a while to notice the pattern.

"It's an old ballroom," Daphne explained, her voice dripping with delight, as though the room hadn't lost any of its enchantment despite all the time she must have spent there.

It really is magic, Berit thought. The very air around her seemed to shimmer with stories and adventures. She coughed. And dust.

Several deep chesterfield arm chairs seemed to be made for curling up with a good book, and all over the room, a number of glass cases displayed select books from the collection.

Berit made her way over to one of them and studied the titles inside. *When Hitler Stole Pink Rabbit* by Judith Kerr, *The Tale of Peter Rabbit* by Beatrix Potter, and E. Nesbit's *Five Children and It* and *The Railway Children*.

The next case contained the full Chronicles of Narnia. One of them was open, revealing a greeting from C. S. Lewis himself: "No book is really worth reading at the age of ten which is not equally—and often far more—worth reading at the age of fifty and beyond." His handwriting was neat and delicate, the rows perfectly straight. Berit reached out with her hand as if trying to reach across time, but her fingertips only came up against dusty glass.

On another case, the glass was so grimy that it was impossible to see through. She pulled her sleeve down over her hand and buffed a small circle.

On a yellowed sheet of paper, the words *The Detection Club* were written in jet-black ink. The case contained books by some of its most famous members: Agatha Christie, Dorothy L. Sayers, G. K. Chesterton, Baroness Orczy, Freeman Wills Crofts, and Anthony Berkeley.

"They signed them for one another," Daphne explained. Margaret removed the glass for Berit to see better.

Berit gently opened the various books. Agatha Christie's *Murder at the Vicarage* featured a message for Dorothy L. Sayers, whose *Murder Must Advertise* had a greeting for Ronald Knox, and the copy of *The Floating Admiral* was signed by each of the authors that had contributed to it. Their signatures were all crammed together on the title page. Margaret lowered the glass back into place.

In another of the cases, there was a more eclectic mix of newer titles: William Boyd's *Any Human Heart*, several books by Neil Gaiman and Zadie Smith, plus Sarah Waters's *Fingersmith*.

It was an incredible room, thought Berit, and yet for some reason, it filled her with a sense of melancholy. There was something sad about the way the sunlight filtered through the old glass, while the dust danced in the air. In the soft light, the book spines looked faded and worn with age, giving the books an almost abandoned feeling, as if they had all been placed there many, many years ago, never again to be taken down.

Berit thought about her own novels and whether they would end up in here, forgotten and unread beneath a growing blanket of dust.

Books aren't made to be collected, she thought. *They're made to be* read.

Despite the dust, the room still held some of its enchanting power. Berit could feel it pulling her in. She moved slowly along the shelves, trailing her fingers along the spines, reading a title here, a name of an author there. Some she recognized; many she hadn't even heard about.

"My grandparents started the collection," Daphne explained. "And my parents and I built upon it, adding to their legacy."

"Would Reginald have inherited these books?" asked Berit.

"The books and everything else here," Daphne said angrily.

"Did he share your interest in reading?"

"Ha!" said Daphne. "Hardly. He tried to get me to sell the

collection—before I was even dead. He would have been free to do any-thing he liked with them once I was gone, but that wasn't enough for him. No, he wanted them now, and he just kept nagging and nagging."

"He couldn't do anything," said Margaret. "Legally speaking, every-thing belongs to Daphne until she dies. She has full possession of Tawny Hall, the books, everything."

"It's not easy getting old, Berit," Daphne complained. "I'd known Reginald since he was in nappies, but he acted like I was the weak, helpless one. And in the end, I suppose I was. God help me, but I'm glad he's dead."

"I'm sure God will forgive you. It's not like you had anything to do with it," said Margaret. Her tone was firm.

Berit walked over to one of the french doors and opened it, stepping out onto the terrace. The police had done their best to tidy up after them-selves, but Tawny Hall still bore traces of their work. The step plates had left square depressions in the grass, and the plastic sheet that had been taped over the windows in the old library was fluttering softly in the breeze. A solitary strip of blue and white tape had caught in the dead orange tree, and Berit bent down and pulled it free.

"So what will happen to the books now? Once you die, I mean," she asked over her shoulder.

"Reginald's children will inherit them, like everything else," said Daphne. "They might not preserve the collection, but they also won't bother me the way their father did. And at least now my books won't be going to *him*. You can't imagine what a relief that is."

DCI Ahmed found a space for his latest cup of tea on his cluttered desk and rubbed his weary eyes. He had just come out of a three-hour meeting about the case with the strategic leadership team. It never failed to amaze him just how much of modern police work consisted of documentation, budget meetings, and communication strategies. He promised himself never to climb any higher up the ranks. If he did, it would only mean more meetings and even less time out on the field.

"Do you have a minute, sir?"

A head popped around his door. Their evidence manager was in his thirties, with unruly reddish hair that made him look even younger. His desk was the only one that could compete with Ian Ahmed's in terms of chaos, always piled high with various objects in plastic evidence bags waiting to be logged into the system.

DCI Ahmed gestured for him to come in, relieved to have an opportunity to put the budget report to one side.

"It's about the laptop," said the younger man.

DCI Ahmed straightened up. "Reginald Trent's?"

"Forensics managed to recover quite a bit of data from the hard drive in the end." He pointed to DCI Ahmed's computer. "May I?"

Without waiting for a reply, he grabbed the mouse and opened a folder marked *Reginald Trent—laptop* followed by a series of digits. Document after document soon appeared on the screen.

DCI Ahmed slapped his shoulder, got to his feet, opened the door, and shouted for Stevens and Rogers to join them. He told them both about the folder and divvied up the documents between them, then they all headed back to their respective desks and got to work.

Rogers was the first to find something.

"Have a look at this, sir," she called over from her computer.

DCI Ahmed went over to her and read from the screen.

It was a draft email to Reginald Trent's lawyer, investigating the possibility of appointing a legal guardian for Tawny Hall. His argument was based on the idea that Daphne Trent was no longer mentally capable of running or maintaining the manor. At the end of the document, Reginald had added his own personal take in a "P.S. The old woman's crazy. She's got books everywhere. The roof is leaking in several places, but all she cares about is her collection. Unless something is done soon, I'll be inheriting a damp pile of rubble."

Rogers showed him several other letters and emails. Reginald Trent's plans to challenge the will and Daphne Trent's control of Tawny Hall seemed to have been in motion for several years, but they had gained new intensity in the week before his final visit to Great Diddling.

During that week, an appraiser had also gone out to the manor to take a look around Daphne's collection. "I pretended to be a collector myself," he wrote to Reginald, "and had no trouble gaining access to her collection." He estimated the books to be worth around fifty thousand pounds but wrote that Daphne had also hinted that the most valuable titles were kept elsewhere. If she really did have the books she had mentioned, then the collection could be worth far more, up to six times that sum. He recommended carrying out a complete inventory of everything at Tawny Hall.

DCI Ahmed looked up and met Rogers's eyes.

"Fifty thousand pounds for some books?" he said.

"At least that. Maybe six times as much."

Stevens shared with them his opinion that people had too much bloody money. Some people, that is. He personally had never had that problem, but if he did, he sure as hell wouldn't spend it on books.

"What would you spend it on, Stevens?" DCI Ahmed asked, fascinated.

"My garden, sir. Like any civilized man. When I think of the state of the gardens up at Tawny Hall…! Makes me almost agree with the man. Maybe the old bird really is crazy."

"Well, you'll get another chance to see the gardens soon," Ahmed said. "I think it's high time we paid the, erm, old bird another visit."

Sitting in an armchair in the middle of the enormous library, Daphne Trent looked vanishingly small. But not alone.

All around her, the bookshelves towered up toward the ceiling in mute support. She was gazing out through the window at land her ancestors had controlled for generations, and she seemed to be drawing strength from both the land and the books. Behind her, Margaret Brown was hovering like a protective shadow.

DCI Ahmed looked around, spotted a low stool, and went over to grab it. He set it down in front of her armchair and took a seat. It was much lower than her chair, which meant he had no choice but to look up at her as they spoke.

Daphne smiled. She looked comfortable. Comfortable and trusting.

Ian Ahmed felt a familiar impulse to defend her. People weren't made for conflict, blunt facts, or harsh truths, he thought. They were made for white lies, forgiveness, bending the truth a little, and fooling themselves. But it was his job to tear through the half-truths and white lies like a bulldozer. He still hadn't completely kicked the habit of wanting to spare people's feelings, though with age he had become better at ignoring the urge.

"Why did Reginald want to appoint an administrator to take over Tawny Hall?" he asked.

Daphne's smile faltered. She glanced back over her shoulder to Margaret.

"I don't know," she said after a moment.

"But he did threaten it? Did his lawyer ever get in touch with you?"

"Lots of people get in touch with me," she said. "It would be impossible to keep track of them all."

"What were the conditions laid out in your father's will?"

She smiled proudly. "That I have full rights of occupancy here until I die." She stopped smiling. "And then Reginald inherits everything."

"Did you know that they once found a computer hard drive on a sunken ship," DCI Ahmed said suddenly. "It had been on the bottom of the sea for six months, but they still managed to recover the data from it."

He couldn't detect any anxiety in Daphne's eyes. Just stubbornness.

"It seems the hard drive from Reginald's computer managed to survive the blast. We've managed to recover over seventy percent of the files on it."

"I'm sure it's all very boring," Daphne said.

"Including several emails with his lawyer about Tawny Hall. They wanted to argue for the house to be handed over to an administrator because you had been—and I can't emphasize enough that these are their words, not mine—acting 'unpredictably and irresponsibly.' They planned to claim that you'd neglected the necessary maintenance for several years, failing to repair the leaking roof in order to invest in…" He looked around the room. "A large number of books."

"Only a philistine would choose a new roof over literature," Daphne snapped.

"The roof was repaired," said Margaret. "One small detail that Reginald and his lawyer might have forgotten to mention in their emails. Besides, nothing ever came of those emails. That was several years ago."

"But he demanded an inventory recently, didn't he?"

"Reginald was completely obsessed with the idea that there might be a few valuable titles in my collection."

"And are there?"

"All the books in my collection are priceless."

What was priceless to Daphne was surely a gulf away from what Reginald Trent considered valuable, thought DCI Ahmed.

"First he kept calling me irresponsible for buying too many books, and then he decided the books were extremely valuable—and his."

Margaret butted in again: "Books aren't like artworks," she explained. "Just so we're on the right page, so to speak. There hasn't been the same level of price inflation in the book world that there has been with art. Certain books might be worth thousands of pounds, but we're not talking millions. Entire collections sell for less than a small Renoir."

DCI Ahmed looked around the room. "There must be a lot of memories in a house like this."

"I should think there are plenty of memories in all houses," said Margaret.

"Have you always lived here, Ms. Trent?"

"Yes."

"What would you have done if Reginald had tried to follow through on his threats?" he asked.

Margaret answered on Daphne's behalf:

"Consulted a lawyer, of course," she said. "The will was crystal clear. Reginald Trent had no legal basis for his claims."

"Basis or no basis, he could still have made life difficult for you," said DCI Ahmed.

"Impractical, perhaps," Margaret admitted. "But it would have been just as much work for him. Legal disputes cost money. They also take time. Two things that Mr. Trent did not have. He was in a hurry. He kept talking about some great business opportunity. He needed money and fast. You should be looking into his dodgy dealings, if you ask me."

"We will."

"We agreed to the inventory, of course," Daphne spoke up. "Why wouldn't we? I would have liked to get a better sense of all the titles in the collection."

Margaret looked annoyed at the interjection, then hid it passably well beneath her mask of general indifference. "Yes, well, nothing will come of it now," she said.

"Where were you on the Thursday evening before the tea party?" DCI Ahmed asked. "Between 10:00 and 11:00 p.m., to be precise. Just so I can rule you out of our inquiries."

"We were right here," Daphne replied without hesitation. "Just like always. I was reading."

"And I was trying to get a bit of work done," said Margaret. "I was at my desk over there."

She nodded to a table at the far end of the library. It was slightly less cluttered with books than the rest of the room, as though she had claimed for herself a small free zone.

"And you were together all evening?"

"I went to the kitchen to prepare a snack at some point," said Margaret. "Just tea and some sandwiches. I wasn't gone for more than twenty minutes. I would never have made it to the village and back in that time."

It did seem impossible, DCI Ahmed thought.

"And I wouldn't have even managed to get up from this chair," said Daphne cheerily. "Not with my dodgy knees."

DCI Ahmed got up and thanked them for their time. He was just about to leave when his eye was drawn to a pile of books that seemed slightly newer and glossier than the others. He moved over to it, picking up the top book. Berit Gardner's name was splashed across the cover in large letters. He opened it and discovered her signature—distinctive, bold, and completely illegible. A thick *B* and *G* were all he could make out.

"Have you read any of her books?" Daphne asked.

DCI Ahmed shook his head.

"Borrow one, if you like. She has a real eye for the loneliness of human existence."

Eleanor found Penny smoking by the bins at the rear of the hotel. She looked desperate. Desperate and alone.

Good, thought Eleanor. Desperate people made rash decisions, and lonely people had no one to stop them from going through with them.

She nodded to the pack of cigarettes by the ashtray, and when Penny shrugged, she helped herself. "I've been thinking about what you said in the pub yesterday," she said. "About needing money."

Now that Penny was sober, she seemed much less keen to talk about the economic situation of the hotel. She said in a fair attempt at nonchalance, "Who doesn't?"

"I may have a proposition for you."

Penny shot Eleanor a quick glance, giving herself away. *She's interested,* Eleanor thought.

"How much are we talking?" Penny asked.

"Ten thousand. Maybe more."

Penny whistled. "I'm listening," she said.

Eleanor pushed the cigarette between her lips and patted her pockets, digging out a business card. She set it down on the lid of the bin beside the ashtray.

Fergus O'Malley. Journalist. The *Sun.*

"All you need to do is call him and confess to murder."

Penny tensed middrag. Then she slowly exhaled the smoke. "Nothing more, huh?"

"It's an idiot-proof plan," Eleanor insisted. "Well, practically anyway."

"For God's sake, Eleanor. Don't you think that annoying little detective might start asking questions if I suddenly confess to a bloody murder? I'm too young to go to prison. The uniforms wouldn't suit me."

"It's that exact risk that means you can demand so much money. The papers will easily pay £100,000 for an exclusive confession. Maybe even £200,000 if you can give them a few credible details they can verify. Simple things, that's all. Things everyone 'round here already knows, but the police haven't released yet. You could tell them you stole the explosives from the construction firm, for example."

"I don't care if they're willing to pay a million quid," said Penny. "What good's that going to do me if I'm stuck in prison? And why do I have to be the one to confess? What's your part in all this?"

"I'm going to confess too. I'm planning to sell my story for just as much money to the *Daily Mirror.*"

That shut Penny up for a moment.

"I suppose DCI Ahmed can't arrest both of us for the same murder," she conceded.

"Exactly. Mary's in on it too. So that's a third confession. Safety in numbers and all that." It was that principle that had made Eleanor reach out to Penny. Two wasn't enough. They needed a third for the idea to work.

"We'll never pull it off," Penny protested. "The papers, they'll never pay up when they realize someone else has confessed too. Not exactly exclusive then, is it?"

"They'll be annoyed, but we'll have kept our side of the bargain. None of us is going to talk to more than one paper, so the confession we make to them is still technically an exclusive. It's not our fault if someone else confesses too, is it? What can they do? It's not like they can sue us."

"What can they do? They could not pay us £100,000 for what suddenly feels like a joke. And we can forget about £200,000."

Eleanor waved a hand dismissively. "We were never after the full amount."

"We weren't?"

"No point in being greedy. We just want a small advance. Five percent, maybe ten. Cash. Before the interview."

"Ten grand," Penny repeated. "That would buy James some time… We could pay off some of the interest. The bank would give him a reprieve." Her hand was shaking as she lit another cigarette. "It could work."

"Of course it'll work," said Eleanor, nodding down to the business card. "I've done a bit of groundwork already. He's expecting to hear from you, so all you need to do is make the call."

James was on his way up to bed when he heard Penny's voice from one of the hotel rooms. He froze. The words "I killed him and I'm proud of it!" had caught his attention.

The door was slightly ajar, and he could see Penny inside but not who she was talking to. Room 13. Like virtually every other room, it was currently unoccupied.

"I couldn't stand him, so I blew him to pieces. The little rat got what was coming to him."

The sliver of Penny's face he could see looked perfectly normal. She was actually smiling politely, and that made her violent words even more frightening.

Who was she talking to? James thought, panicking. *And for God's sake, if she had to blow the man to pieces, why is she blabbing about it now?*

Sweat broke out on his back. This was a disaster. He had to *do* something, but what could he possibly do? Everything was spinning out of control. He moved blindly down the corridor, slamming the door behind him and slumping down onto the bed.

When Penny eventually came through, he was still fully dressed on top of the covers. He watched as she got ready in the bathroom and then came back out into the bedroom. He saw her lips moving, but he didn't hear a single word she said.

After a moment or two, Penny switched off the lamp, leaving James staring up at the ceiling in the darkness.

Think, James.

16

"UHH, CAN I HAVE A word, guv?"

It was just after nine o'clock on Saturday morning when Detective Sergeant Stevens popped his head into DCI Ahmed's office.

Ahmed had come into the station to go through his notes on an old case that was due in court soon. He had a meeting with the Crown Prosecution Service next week and needed to refresh his memory. But Stevens was supposed to be at home with his family.

He was wearing jeans and a cotton shirt, the casual clothes strangely at odds with the stressed look on his face, as he hovered in the doorway with his hands behind his back.

Ahmed waved for him to come in, and he reluctantly did.

"What can I do for you, Stevens?"

"I, uh…I thought you might want to see this. Or not want to, exactly. But you probably should. Sorry, sir."

Stevens brought his hands out from behind his back. He was holding the morning edition of three different tabloids, and he placed them gingerly over DCI Ahmed's case files. All the papers had virtually the same front page.

The *Daily Mirror* had gone with I CONFESS in huge letters, followed by "EXCLUSIVE interview with the Great Diddling Bomber."

The words I'M GUILTY were plastered across the front of the *Daily*

Mail. "Exclusive! *Daily Mail* solves horror bomb death, but where are the police?"

The *Sun* had gone with a slightly longer quote: "'THE LITTLE RAT GOT WHAT WAS COMING TO HIM!'—NEW BREAKTHROUGH IN GREAT DIDDLING MURDER. SUN EXCLUSIVE."

DCI Ahmed looked up at Stevens.

"Looks like someone has been busy," he said drily. "Who confessed?"

"Three of them did, sir"

"I beg your pardon?"

"Penny Elmer and both of the Hartfield sisters."

"Are you saying they did it together?"

DS Stevens looked uncomfortable. "Afraid not, guv. It's three separate confessions. They're all claiming they worked alone."

DCI Ahmed looked down at the headlines again and felt his face twist into a grimace. He pushed the papers away—the very sight of them felt like a physical affront—but found his eye being immediately drawn back to them.

"Call Rogers in, then start reaching out to the journalists at each of the papers," he said. "I know they're not usually interested in working with us, but they might this time. Every one of them uses the word 'exclusive.' I'd imagine there are three pissed off journalists and three even angrier editors today."

"Couldn't happen to a nicer bunch," said Stevens.

"Try to find out whether any of the suspects told them anything that didn't end up in print. Finely comb every single article to check whether any of the women have accidentally given anything away. And send someone over there to pick them up too."

"All three?"

"They've confessed to murder. The least we can do is take them in for questioning."

The drive to Plymouth took just over an hour, but once it was over, James

Elmer couldn't remember a single minute of it. He was running on autopilot as he took the A30 toward Bodmin and then turned off onto the A38 toward Plymouth. In Plymouth, he had to drive around the area several times to find the police station, and when he finally did, the sight of the row of parked police cars triggered a niggling feeling of doubt about the whole endeavor.

He didn't even know how he was supposed to do this. Should he just march up to the first police officer he saw or inquire within as to the proper procedure?

James got out of the car and hesitated in front of the ticket machine. Parking was only free for thirty minutes, but surely it would take longer than that? In a rare show of initiative, he paid handsomely for a full day.

He followed the signs to reception, looked around, and then went over to one of the information desks, where a bored-looking officer in his fifties had just finished helping an older woman.

"Excuse me," James began.

"Take a number," said the officer.

"No, I'd like to—"

"You'll need a number. Over there." With that, the man pressed a button to call up the next person in line.

James tried to insist, but a woman with two children angrily elbowed her way past him.

"Some people think they're too good to queue," she muttered, just loud enough for him to hear.

He became acutely aware that he—unintentionally! Involuntarily! He hadn't been thinking!—had managed to cut in line.

"I'm sorry," he blurted out. "I didn't mean to… I… Forgive me."

Blushing, he stepped to one side. The woman's face softened slightly when she saw just how embarrassed he was.

"Never mind," she said. "The system can be very confusing, I know." She gave him a motherly smile and nodded to the machine. "You get your number over there."

"Thank you. Thank you very much. I really am very sorry."

"I'm sure you are, love. Over there, now."

James pressed the button on the ticket machine without really knowing what he was doing, then slumped down onto an uncomfortable plastic chair by the wall. His clammy fingers gripped the little slip of paper.

The numbers on the screen slowly ticked upward. 157 came and went, and 158 kept one of the officers busy for at least fifteen minutes. James found himself wondering what that person's problem could be. The officer didn't seem particularly interested, no doubt because he was being paid the same amount no matter how many people he dealt with. 159, 160. James's hands grew sweaty again. The slip with his number on was already crumpled.

161 came around so suddenly that he was afraid he would miss his turn. He leapt up, making the chair rock behind him.

"Sorry for the misunderstanding before," he told the same officer he had tried to speak with earlier, after repeatedly showing him his number.

The policeman smiled. "No problem, sir," he said. "You weren't to know."

"Well, yes, look, see I, uh, I'd like to confess to murder."

The officer's smile faltered. He stared at James with a look of sorrowful reproach, as though he had expected better.

James could understand that. He expected better of himself. And yet… shouldn't something be happening? Anything at all, really?

"A murder," he repeated, articulating every syllable.

"Sure, sure. The explosion in Great Diddling, I assume?"

"How did you know that?"

"Good one. But now you've had your fun, maybe you wouldn't mind buggering off? Stop wasting everyone's time."

"But I want to confess! I did it!"

The policeman held up three newspapers. "Get in line," he said.

"I have been! Look." James waved the little number again. "I've been waiting almost an hour." He pointed toward the chair where he had been sitting patiently, as though it could back him up. "I'll admit, there was a bit of a misunderstanding earlier, but it is my turn now, I assure you."

The police officer sighed. "Fine, if you insist, sir." He reached for his phone. "DCI Ahmed, I've got a murderer here in reception. No, sir. No, it's not one of the other three. It's another one. No, I don't think he's talked to the press first. Have you?"

James shook his head.

"No, sir. It appears he went straight to us, sir. Very gratifying, yes. All right." He ended the call and looked tiredly at James. "DS Stevens will be down to get you shortly. Take a seat."

"How much longer is this going to take?" James asked.

"With all due respect, sir…if you're here to confess to a murder, you may as well get used to waiting."

"Yes, of course. Sorry. I forgot."

"Right you are, sir. I guess it slipped your mind for a moment there."

They took James Elmer to interview room 1.

DCI Ahmed and his boss, the chief superintendent, was watching him from a small room at the end of the corridor. There were no two-way mirrors like there were on TV, just a series of old monitors that showed them what went on in the four interview rooms. Three of the screens were black. The fourth showed James Elmer, sitting forlornly by the worn table.

DCI Ahmed's boss was watching him with evident displeasure. The chief superintendent was in his fifties, and everything about him seemed to command respect. He was tall and muscular, with thick, silver hair and bushy eyebrows that gave his face a stern, focused look. In his less-generous moments, DCI Ahmed found himself thinking that his boss had those eyebrows and hair to thank for much of his career success. Even today, when he was dressed for golf on his day off, those eyebrows gave him an aura of authority.

At the moment, they were frowning angrily as he leaned in and squinted toward the monitor.

"Let me just make sure I understand," he said. "Four people have now confessed to the same murder, three of them direct to the tabloids?"

"Yes, sir."

"But this man at least showed us the courtesy of coming in personally?"

"Yes, sir."

"Made the confession completely voluntarily, you say?"

"That's right, sir," said DCI Ahmed.

"Lunatic?"

"I think not, sir."

James was sitting perfectly still in the interview room, his hands in his lap. He rubbed them on his thighs from time to time, possibly to dry his palms, but other than that, he was completely motionless. His face was blank, his posture shrunken and apologetic.

DCI Ahmed's boss straightened up. "No need to tell you, Ahmed, that we risk looking damn silly over this whole business."

"No, sir."

"You're planning to bring in the other three?"

"Yes, sir."

"Good! Let's put some fear of God into them. Threaten them with something. Interfering with a police investigation, wasting police resources, being a damn nuisance. That sort of thing."

"Sir?"

"And keep me updated. I want to know everything that happens."

"Yes, sir."

They brought the three women into the station and placed them in separate interview rooms.

Mary Hartfield was taken to interview room 2, Eleanor Hartfield to room 3, and Penny Elmer to room 4. In the small control room, the screens alongside James Elmer's flickered to life.

Mary Hartfield was the very picture of an innocent grandmother, sitting perfectly still and smiling absently to herself. DCI Ahmed wondered where her daydreams had taken her.

Her sister, on the other hand, seemed acutely aware of everything that was going on around her. She reminded the detective of a hunting dog just before it was let off on the hunt: senses primed, almost quivering with anticipation, only managing to stay still through a feat of enforced self-control. She listened attentively to any sound, shoulders leaned back, feet planted on the floor, probably ready to sprint out of the room given half a chance.

Of the three, Penny Elmer was the worst at hiding her feelings. She was frightened, nervous, and anxious, and she clearly hated sitting still. Her hands kept reaching down to her pockets, presumably for the pack of cigarettes they had confiscated. She picked up the little plastic cup from the drinks machine at regular intervals, only to discover that she had already finished it.

"OK, give me something I can use," Ahmed said while staring at the screens.

"Well," Stevens began. "Penny and James Elmer were both born and raised in Great Diddling, though they didn't know each other as children. Penny is a year older. She…"

"Something I can *use*," Ahmed reminded him.

"She knew our victim. In the biblical sense of the word."

Ahmed looked sharply at him. "They had a relationship?"

"When they were younger, yeah. He used to spend his summers up at Tawny Hall and amused himself in the village. Broke one heart after another, apparently."

Ahmed wasn't exactly surprised. Reginald Trent seemed to have been precisely the sort of rich arsehole who would do that sort of thing.

"Penny was pretty wild when she was younger. James isn't her first husband. She's been married twice before. No kids, but seemingly that's not by choice. Otherwise she would have been, and I quote, 'pregnant before she was fifteen.'"

"So the local gossips have started opening up, have they?" DCI Ahmed said drily.

"That's not really gossip, sir. They were just quoting what she herself has said."

"What about James?"

"He didn't associate with Reginald when he was younger. Or Penny, for that matter. They didn't move in the same circles. He actually doesn't seem to have belonged to any circle at all. Strict father, mostly kept himself to himself. Penny is his first wife, and they got together relatively late in life."

"If they grew up in the village, there must be plenty of people who can give us some idea of whether they think they're capable of committing murder," said DCI Ahmed. "Give me a wide range of people—childhood friends, old teachers, new friends, colleagues."

"On it, guv."

"And focus on Penny. She's got both the brains and brawn in their marriage, if I'm not much mistaken."

There was a timid knock on the door, and then it slowly opened. A head peeped in. "Excuse me, sir," said a young constable. "You wanted to see me, sir? I'm the one responsible for the background check on Mary and Eleanor Hartfield."

"Yes, excellent, squeeze in. The more the merrier." He looked at Mary and Eleanor on the screens next to each other. "Right," he said. "Our potentially murderous sisters. What can you tell me about them?"

"That's just it, sir. They're not."

"Murderers? It was just an expression. Even though you shouldn't rule anything out just because they're a bit older than the average suspect."

"Sisters, sir." The voice that interrupted him was still quiet, but this time it was said more firmly. "They're not sisters."

DCI Ahmed stilled. "*They're not what they seem,*" he muttered under his breath.

"Sorry, sir?"

"Damn it, the woman was right."

"Sir?"

"Go on. Are the names real?"

"Oh yes. Mary and Eleanor Hartfield. They got married when same-sex marriage was legalized in 2014, and Mary took Eleanor's surname. She was born Mary Diane Hewitt in Surrey in 1947—the same year and county as Eleanor, in other words. They left England as young women and seem to have spent much of their lives abroad."

"Have you been in touch with Interpol?"

"Yes, and with some success. Their names have cropped up in

connection with various fraud cases in the Netherlands, Spain, Monaco, and France."

"Ever been charged with anything? Or arrested?"

"No, sir. On a few occasions they were asked politely to leave whatever country they were in—unofficially, of course—but they've never actually been convicted of anything. They've never even been charged."

"That's not unusual in fraud cases," said Rogers. "The victims are often reluctant to file a report. No one likes to admit that they're stupid enough to have fallen for a fraudster, and if they do, then they don't exactly want the whole world to know."

"The only people who have made an official complaint were a couple on the Costa del Sol in Spain. One Mr. and Mrs. Hutchley accused Mary Hartfield and her cousin—the famous painter Eleanor Hartfield—of selling them worthless art they claimed had once belonged to Eleanor's artist friends. It seems they invented a whole group of Spanish impressionists and forged some of their paintings. But the couple withdrew their report pretty quickly. The prosecutor in charge thought it was for 'insurance purposes.'"

"Yeah, probably because they didn't want the insurance company to find out that their heavily insured art was worthless," said Rogers.

"Any connection to Reginald Trent?" asked DCI Ahmed.

The young constable shook her head. "Not that I could find, sir."

"Reginald Trent preferred England," said Rogers. "His business was all here. The man barely even went abroad on holiday."

"And Mary and Eleanor have never been suspected of any crimes in England," said the young woman. "Their records are clean. Not even any speeding tickets."

"Do we know anything else about them? Stevens? Any local gossip?"

"Sorry, guv. Everyone goes to their café, but no one seems to actually know them. It's not just that everyone thinks they're sisters—no one knows anything about their lives before they came to Great Diddling, either."

DCI Ahmed thought about Mary and Eleanor hiding in plain sight, practically invisible because of their age and gender, and about Penny and James, one of them almost certainly confessing for money and the other for—what? Love? Maybe Berit was right. Maybe love really was the deadliest emotion.

Despite the warm sunshine outside, Mary was wearing a pink knitted sweater. Her long hair looked like it had been pinned up in a hurry, and one of the hairpins was on the verge of coming loose. Her eyes were the palest of turquoises, as though someone had added a drop of paint to a glass of water.

She looked completely out of place in the depressing room. The only furniture was a shabby table and four plastic chairs, all bolted to the floor, and the video camera that recorded everything they said.

Out of place but not unhappy. She was lost in her own thoughts, and she obviously found pleasure in them. She was gazing at DCI Ahmed with a faraway look in her eyes, smiling serenely to herself.

"The time is 11:21 on Saturday, May 19, commencing interview with Mary Hartfield. My name is Detective Chief Inspector Ian Ahmed, and Detective Sergeant Bill Stevens is also present."

Then he sat back and watched her. He smiled.

"Where are your daydreams taking you?" he asked softly.

She answered without hesitation: "My rose garden."

He nodded. "How long have you and Eleanor been married?"

"Forever. She's the love of my life, you know."

"That's nice."

She heard the condescension in his voice and shot him an amused look. "Nice," she repeated to herself. "Yes, I guess you could call it that."

"You seem to have lived a very…colorful life, Mrs. Hartfield?"

"It's life with Eleanor," Mary said. "It's always an adventure."

"I understand you spent some years living abroad?"

"Too many. It was time to go home. It was great fun, of course. Life with Eleanor always is. But after a while you need your own home. We should have come back ages ago."

"And you decided to settle in Great Diddling."

"Of course," Mary said eagerly. "We belong there."

"Oh? You had some sort of connection with the village? Friends, family, perhaps?"

"Oh, no. It was the name, you see. It meant Eleanor could treat it as a joke, at first. The old café had just gone bankrupt, so we took over the lease and bought their stock. After that, it was just a case of making it cozy."

"Why did you establish yourself as sisters?"

"Eleanor always says that it's never a good idea to be *too* honest with people. It makes them think you're hiding something."

"Did Daphne hire you to do the catering for the tea party?"

"Yes. Well, technically it was Margaret who asked me. She didn't give me much warning, either. Just showed up at the café on Friday telling me she needed tea and cakes for a hundred people this Sunday. We only had two days to prepare. Eleanor complained the entire time, but we got it done in the end, didn't we?"

"I'm sure you did a great job."

"I enjoyed it. I like old houses." She added naïvely, "They're so often full of beautiful things."

Eleanor Hartfield was wearing jeans and a black T-shirt, and she seemed to be quivering with energy. She was thin, slight, and intense. More like a bird than a hunting dog, he thought. Always on her guard, ready to react to the slightest of movements. Her natural impulse seemed to be flight rather than fight.

DCI Ahmed thought back to the time he had cupped a bird in his hands in order to release it. He had been amazed by just how delicate and fragile it felt.

"I'm sorry you've had to wait so long," he said. "I've been chatting with your wife."

Eleanor pulled a face. "So you know, do you? I wish she'd stop blabbing about it to everyone."

"Most people would probably want their wife to be open about who she's married to."

"I'm not most people."

DCI Ahmed smiled. "That's very true. The two of you seem to have lived a unique life together. With a...colorful career."

"Are you planning to charge us with something?"

He wasn't sure whether she meant something from their past or because of their false confessions.

"I'm not interested in your old misdeeds," he said. "I'm fairly sure the statute of limitations will have passed for most of them. Either that or they took place outside of our jurisdiction."

"They did. We've always been good, law-abiding citizens in England."

"Very patriotic."

Eleanor shrugged. "Mary wanted to be able to move back here."

"It must have been quite the change to start running a café?"

"Not really. We've done it before. Plus a bar, an art gallery, a jewelry shop…"

"And you do everything aboveboard now? You didn't move to Great Diddling as part of some new…scheme?"

"We're retired. We're just two old ladies with a café."

"Where were you on the Thursday evening before Reginald Trent's death?" he asked. "Between, say, 9:00 and 11:00 p.m.?"

"Let me see…Thursday. Ah yes, we were making baklava." She sounded triumphant, as if making baklava was the perfect alibi.

"And can anyone corroborate that?"

"Absolutely. Our neighbor, Lillian Hayes, always comes over when we're making baklava. The woman has never been farther than Exeter, so she thinks baklava and Turkish coffee are incredibly exotic."

"What time did she come over?"

"Just before nine."

"And she stayed until…?"

"Twelve at least. Probably just before one. Mary got started on the sherry, you see. Come on, Detective. We both know that neither of us killed Reginald Trent."

"You confessed."

"Only to the papers. And only for the money."

"Whose idea was it to confess to them?"

"Mine."

He believed her. She sounded proud.

"How much did they pay?"

"Ten grand apiece. We need the money. Living honestly is expensive. The only thing we've done is mess with a few tabloids, and they can afford it, believe you me. I hope you're not going to shed any crocodile tears for their sake."

"You also obstructed a police investigation."

"You seem like an intelligent man, Chief Inspector. I'm sure you'll manage to work it out in the end."

DCI Ahmed leaned back in his chair. Something about Eleanor had just sparked a memory to life, but he couldn't work out what it was. A memory, but something confusing and out of place and not really related to her at all…

But what? *Something about her scent*, he thought.

It was interesting in and of itself. Old cigarettes and Turkish coffee, musk and top notes of iris and violet, which he recognized from Mary.

"Do you know what Reginald was looking for in Great Diddling?" he asked, taking a shot in the dark.

"No idea," said Eleanor. "How would I know?"

"Given that you were responsible for the catering, you must have been given relatively free rein inside Tawny Hall, both before and during the tea party?"

Eleanor tensed briefly, then quickly relaxed again. "Yes," she said, "but we were run off our feet. We spent most of our time in the kitchen."

"So Mary never went anywhere else in the house? To the old library, for example?"

Eleanor was far too smart to get caught up on a minor detail the police would be able to disprove. She shrugged nonchalantly.

"She probably had a bit of a nosy around at some point. She loves old houses."

"Yes, of course," said DCI Ahmed. "Because of all the beautiful objects."

"Was it Mary who wanted you to accept the catering job? I understand it was very last minute?"

"No, it was me," Eleanor replied without batting an eyelid.

She was an unsettlingly good liar, thought the detective.

James Elmer looked defeated before the interview even began.

He straightened his shirtsleeves and blazer for at least the thirtieth time, possibly in a desperate attempt to give himself some dignity. DCI Ahmed had seen all manner of reactions in the interview room over the years. When faced with the institutional indifference and suspicion of the police force, many people seemed to struggle to remember who they were outside of these four walls.

Ahmed felt the usual mixture of pity and annoyance that he always felt when confronted with human stupidity. *If love isn't the deadliest feeling, it sure is one of the most stupid*, he thought.

"Why did you confess?" he asked.

"What do you mean? Because I did it. I killed Reginald Trent."

"What I meant was: Why right now? When we interviewed you at the hotel, you seemed determined to—how can I put it?—deny any responsibility. Yet today you came to see us voluntarily."

"I suppose I felt, um…guilty. Yes, that's right. Guilty."

"It must have come on suddenly."

"Yes…" James said guardedly.

"How long has Penny known Reginald?"

James flinched. "What? What does that have to do with anything?"

"They were romantically involved at one point, weren't they?"

James managed to knock his plastic cup over, and he stared down at the table with a panicked look on his face until he realized it had been empty. "It was a long time ago," he said hastily. "It didn't mean anything."

"For her or for him?"

"For either of them."

"Did you know her then?"

"No."

"Do you know her now?"

James gave him a troubled look, but he didn't speak.

"Why did you break into your own construction site to steal explosives?"

"I...had to make it look like a break-in, so I forced the door. With a screwdriver." He looked pleased with himself for coming up with that last detail.

"And where was Penny while all this was happening? Or did the two of you work together?"

"No! Of course we didn't. She wasn't there. She...she was with Alice, in the dining room."

"What were they doing there?"

James Elmer's eyes wandered desperately. "They...they were playing board games."

DCI Ahmed raised an eyebrow. "Board games?"

"Yes! Board games."

Ahmed made a mark on the list of questions in front of him. James looked more stressed than ever.

"When did you plant the explosives in Reginald's office?"

"During the tea party, of course. When no one was looking," he added.

Another scribble.

"And where did you keep them prior to that?"

"What do you mean?"

"You didn't have a bag with you, so where did you keep the explosives until you planted them?"

"I had a bag, I did. I just...hid it in a bush."

"Which bush?"

"How am I meant to know? A random bush."

DCI Ahmed smiled softly. "I would have thought you'd have good reason to try to remember the specific bush. Imagine if you'd forgotten which one it was when you went to retrieve the explosives."

"Well, yes, but I knew at the time. Clearly. It's just that it's been a while."

"One week. Did Penny know that you'd borrowed money from Reginald?"

"No. No, she had no idea. She never trusted him."

"Was it the interview in the *Sun* that made you suspect your wife?"

"No!"

"You suspected her before that, then?"

"What? No. What I mean is that I don't suspect her of anything. Penny didn't kill Reginald; I'm sure of it."

"How can you be so sure?"

"I…I just am."

Ahmed raised an eyebrow, and after a moment or two, the penny finally seemed to drop.

"Because I did it!" James blurted out.

"I can understand the impulse to protect the people you love," said DCI Ahmed. "It's understandable. Admirable, even. But it isn't always helpful."

"Penny didn't kill Reginald Trent," James mumbled, so quietly that his voice was barely audible. "It was me. I did it. Just me. All on my own."

DCI Ahmed nodded. "We're going to need to double-check your version of events." He got to his feet, but before he stopped the tape, he asked, "Where did you plant the explosives?"

"In the old library. I knew Reginald used it as his office. I'd seen him there when I went to try to convince him not to ask for all the money he lent me back."

"What I meant was where in the old library."

"Oh. Right. In the…bookshelves. That's it. I hid it behind a couple of books."

DCI Ahmed glanced at his watch. "Interview terminated at 11:55," he said, stopping the tape.

"Interview with Penny Elmer. My name is Detective Chief Inspector Ian Ahmed, and my colleague Detective Sergeant Bill Stevens is also present. The time is 12:10."

DCI Ahmed gave Penny an expectant look. She met his eye with a stubborn defiance.

She was wearing a low-cut neon-pink top. A tiny daisy was painted on each of her long false nails, and her fingers were impatiently drumming on the table.

DCI Ahmed flicked absentmindedly through the thick file in front of him and then closed it. The name *James Elmer* was written on the cover.

"When did you last play a board game, Mrs. Elmer?"

Penny's eye had been drawn down to the folder on the table, but she looked up at him in surprise. "A board game?"

"You know. Monopoly, Ludo, that sort of thing."

"Ludo? I don't know, when I was thirteen maybe? I discovered boys when I was fourteen, so it definitely wasn't after that. Why are you asking me about board games? What's in that folder?"

"I've just spoken to your husband."

"James? *Here?*" She seemed to be on the verge of getting up and marching out of the room to look for him.

"Why did you lie, Mrs. Elmer?"

Her gaze began to wander. "Lie is a strong word," she muttered.

"You knew Reginald Trent, didn't you?"

"Define 'knew.'"

"You were in a relationship with him when you were younger."

Penny seemed relieved. "Ah, that. Fine, yes, I slept with him a few times about twenty years ago. So what?"

"Is your husband aware of that?"

"James? Probably, I don't know. It was before we met. A long time before."

"Is he jealous?"

"James? No, never." Penny met the detective's eye. "My second husband was incredibly jealous. Thanks to him, I'll never mistake controlling behavior for love again."

"Did you see him when he was in Great Diddling?"

"Who? My second husband?"

"Reginald Trent."

"He was at the tea party. Everyone saw him."

"And you didn't see him other than at the tea party?"

"No." She swallowed nervously.

DCI Ahmed gave her a disdainful look. "I hope the money was worth it," he said.

"The money?"

"I'm assuming the three of you didn't do it for free," he said, emphasizing "three," which made her flinch.

"Why can't you just tell me what James is doing here?" she asked.

"Your husband has just confessed to the murder of Reginald Trent. Officially, that is. To us rather than the press."

"What? Why the hell would he do that?"

"For your sake, I believe. I suppose it's quite noble in a way. Sacrificing himself to protect you."

"That *idiot*," Penny said.

Ahmed nodded. "Agreed."

Penny swallowed. "So what happens now?" she asked.

Ahmed shrugged. "He'll have to stay here for the time being. You're free to go."

She didn't move. It was as though all the energy had drained away from her.

DCI Ahmed got up instead. "It's quite sad, really."

"What is?"

"Your husband's confession. It seems quite romantic at first glance, but when you think about it, it means he must believe you really did kill Mr. Trent. Your husband thinks you're a murderer, Mrs. Elmer. That should give you plenty to think about."

The detective superintendent lowered his chin to his interlinked fingers and studied DCI Ahmed from beneath his bushy brows. It was a gesture that seemed both determined and thoughtful, and DCI Ahmed found himself wondering whether he practiced it in the mirror.

"Do you think he's guilty?" he asked.

DCI Ahmed hesitated. "He had means, motive, and opportunity, sir."

"Keep him overnight. Let's make an example out of him."

"But why kill Reginald Trent in a way that would lead us straight back to him and threaten the business he was trying to protect? It doesn't make sense. I think he's trying to cover for his wife."

"Maybe her husband being arrested for her crime will make her do something stupid then," the superintendent said hopefully. "And in any case, we can't allow four people to confess and not have anything to show for it!"

"No, sir."

"The press is already much too excited about this case. At the press conference yesterday, someone asked whether we shouldn't bring in Poirot. So keep Mr. Elmer in custody overnight, and put out a press release announcing that we have a suspect in custody. That should shake things up."

"Yes, sir."

"And Ahmed?"

"Sir?"

"Make sure you solve this."

Penny, Mary, and Eleanor met outside the station and squeezed into the back seat of a cab. Their driver was chatty, and Penny answered all his questions distractedly. Yes, the weather was nice. No, they hadn't been on a girls' shopping trip. Yes, Great Diddling was the same village where that bomb went off. Here, she looked quickly at Mary and Eleanor. Yes, it really was a memorable name for a village.

The minute they got out of the cab outside the hotel, she let it all out.

"You said the plan was idiotproof!"

"That's just a turn of phrase," Eleanor replied. "No plan is safe from a real idiot."

"They've arrested James!"

"How was I supposed to know that he'd be stupid enough to confess? And to the *police*. He didn't even get paid for it."

"You have to do something!"

"Me?" said Eleanor, ignoring the reproachful look Mary gave her. "It's hardly my problem."

"But—" Penny protested.

"You got your money like I promised you, didn't you?"

"Yes, but who cares about the money when James is locked up!"

"They can't keep him in custody forever. They don't have any proof. They'll probably let him go with a warning in a day or two."

"So you're a legal expert now, are you? What happens if they do find something?"

Eleanor paused. "Why? Do you think he did it?"

"What? No, of course I don't think he did it!"

"Well, then you've got nothing to worry about."

Penny swore under her breath, made her way into the hotel, and marched straight over to the little bar in the lounge and poured herself a large whisky. She then shouted a thanks to Alice behind the reception desk for holding the fort while she was gone. Alice got such a fright that she almost spilled her tea, but Penny didn't notice.

"I can take over now," she said, knocking back her whisky and immediately refilling her glass. "You get going."

Alice grabbed her handbag and practically ran out of the door, almost as though she…

Penny closed her eyes.

Almost as though she had just come face-to-face with a murderer.

The stupid girl must have read the damn interview in the paper. *I should never have talked to that reporter*, Penny thought.

"I only did it for the money!" she shouted after her, but that just seemed to make Alice run faster.

"What did DCI Ahmed talk to you about?" Eleanor asked, deliberately trying to seem calm as she lifted the chairs onto the tables. The café had been closed all day, and neither of them thought it was worth opening for the last hour on a Saturday. Mary grabbed the mop to clean the floor instead.

"My rose garden," she said.

Eleanor was taken aback by her answer. "You told him about that?" Mary smiled. "DCI Ahmed understands the power of dreams."

"You shouldn't have told him anything at all."

"You used to understand dreams too, Eleanor Hartfield."

Eleanor turned away. "I've got far too much to worry about to have time for dreaming," she replied.

17

SALLY WAS IN THE MIDDLE of making a hearty, cooked Sunday breakfast when the phone rang. There were pots and pans everywhere, the sausages already sizzling on the stove.

At the kitchen table, Berit had spread out all the papers Sally had managed to find on that morning's trip to the supermarket. Each one mentioned the withdrawn confessions and the fact that the police now had a suspect in custody.

Sally had texted Liam as soon as she heard the news, but he still hadn't replied. She hoped it would be him calling her now, but instead she saw *Mum* flashing on the screen.

Sally took her phone out to the garden, making sure to close the door behind her.

"Hello?" she whispered.

"What's this I'm reading about people confessing to the murder left, right, and center?" asked her mother.

It sounded as though she thought Berit should have prevented them. Or possibly joined them for the free PR.

"What is Berit doing?" she asked.

"She's at the kitchen table...working."

Sally moved over to the patch of sunshine on the lawn and raised her face to the sky. It was only nine in the morning, but it was already getting warm, the fresh scent of grass heavy in the air. She closed her eyes. *Please, please, please don't let it be Liam they've arrested.*

"Is she working on a new project? If it's a crime novel, she needs to stay on top of this. We can't have a load of other crazies running around talking to the press. That's our job."

"I don't think she's writing that sort of book," Sally said hesitantly.

"I got an extremely odd email from someone called Sima Kumar, claiming there's going to be a book festival in Great Diddling the weekend after the next?"

"That's right. Sima says that everyone loves murder and books. And charming villages. It's the perfect combination."

She wondered how that would be affected by the fact that multiple people in the village had now apparently confessed to murder.

"And Berit is taking part?" her mother asked, a clear note of hope in her voice.

"I…don't think so, no. No, she's not."

"But the festival is right on her doorstep! This is going to get lots of attention; I can just feel it. Sima is right. It's an irresistible combination, and that means Berit needs to be right there in the foreground, explaining precisely why the English are so obsessed with murdering their neighbors in their sleepy little villages. Or something like that."

Sally wondered what her mother would say if she found out that Berit was determined to solve the murder. She'd probably be thrilled, Sally realized. She might even send out a press release about it. Best not to say anything at the moment, she decided.

"She's busy," Sally said instead.

Olivia's voice was dripping with sarcasm when she replied. "Busy writing, I assume?"

"Not…exactly."

"She's tricked you into doing some research for her, hasn't she? Telling you she needs more 'background information' before she can get to work."

"She might have said something like that…but she is working. She's doing research."

"My God, you're like an innocent little lamb, wandering around without a clue. Research! You have no idea how many authors I've lost to 'research.' They can sacrifice years to it. Honestly, you give them one history book and they start thinking they're the next Hilary Mantel. Give them a murder and they probably turn into Truman Capote."

"Yes, Mum."

"What's the program like, then? Hold on, let me have a look at the website." Sally heard the sound of her mother's long nails tapping the keys. "Ian Rankin? I could have sworn he was planning to be in Edinburgh for the whole of the next month."

"The program is… It's still only preliminary."

"Hang on, this Sima woman seems to have emailed me again. She's asking whether any of my authors might be interested in taking part in her unique book festival…blah, blah…wonderful opportunity…more bullshit…a real murder. Well, there is that. No one can take that away from her, I suppose. And a real-life detective chief inspector, she writes. I wonder if he's going to give a talk? Well, she's ballsy, this Sima Kumar; I'll give her that."

"I'm thinking about helping out," Sally said. "With the festival, I mean."

Her mum sighed. "Sometimes I marvel that you're my own daughter," she said, adding disbelievingly. "*Helping out.* You're just one of life's little suckers, aren't you?"

"Yes, Mum."

"She'll never get any writers to come. Or people. Not with two weeks' notice. Oh well, I suppose there's always next year."

"Yes, Mum."

"Get Berit to start writing. No more of this research nonsense."

"No, Mum."

"Good. I'm glad you're there."

Sally froze.

"It would be such a faff if I had to travel to the middle of nowhere in Cornwall to sort this out."

The minute Sally opened the door to the cottage, she sniffed the air.

Then she ran through to the kitchen. Over in the sink, the frying pan of charred sausages was still smoking. The kitchen window was now wide open, but Berit was sitting calmly at the kitchen table reading the papers as though nothing had happened.

Sally opened a new pack of sausages.

"Mrs. Smith popped in," said Berit. "It's not Liam that's helping the police with their inquiries. It's James Elmer."

"*James Elmer?*" Sally asked as she dropped two slices of bread into the toaster and poured more coffee into Berit's cup. "Is he guilty?"

"Who knows," said Berit. She seemed lost in thought.

"Do you think this will affect the festival? I mean, who wants to visit a village with four possible murder suspects."

Berit sipped her coffee. "Oh, there are far more than that."

On the table beside the papers, Berit's notepad was lying open. In the middle of the page, she had written Sima's name and circled it several times, but other than that, the sheet was blank.

"It wouldn't surprise me if this turned out to be good for the festival. At least they're getting some free publicity out of it." Berit shook her head. "I wonder what Eleanor was up to with those confessions."

"You think it was her idea?"

"Out of those three? No doubt about it." Berit smiled. "Mary and Eleanor, they belong in a novel. Most of us eventually give in to life, but not these madwomen. They should have admitted defeat long ago, but they don't seem to have realized. Far too many people grow boring with age, but in Great Diddling the opposite seems true."

"I don't think people get more boring with age," Sally said. "Although possibly a bit more…strange?"

"You might be right," Berit said. "Maybe middle age is the most boring?" She shook her head. "Imagine being in your seventies and still running about confessing to murders!"

Sally paused with the frying pan in her hand. "You like them!" she said.

"Yes," Berit admitted. "That's the problem."

She nodded to the stove. "You're about to burn those sausages again."

Sima pushed her cup and plate away to make more room for her laptop. She had the websites for all the major newspapers, radio stations, and TV channels open in various tabs. Almost all were reporting the news that three people had confessed to the recent murder in Great Diddling and that a fourth person—who had also confessed—was currently "helping the police with their inquiries."

This is fantastic, she thought.

She reached for her phone and tried Ian Rankin's agent again. No answer. She left yet another message about the attention the village had already received, encouraging Mr. Rankin to seize this incredible opportunity to combine business with pleasure at a book festival in the wake of a real murder.

She took a sip of tea, not caring that it had gone cold, and opened her emails, clicking the Compose button. In the recipient field, she added every news channel she could think of, then moved on to the subject box.

PRESS STATEMENT RE: DEADLY BOMBING IN GREAT DIDDLING.

Having thus caught their attention, she got straight to the most important thing:

> Books and murder in scandal-gripped village!
> An explosive mix of fiction and reality!
> The police have drawn a blank. Is it time to call
> in Miss Marple?
> Find all this and more in Great Diddling—
> Cornwall's hidden gem.
> The idyllic village of Great Diddling, Cornwall,
> (known for its many award-winning sights
> and pubs) was recently the setting of a brutal
> murder.
> In the wake of this exciting real-life crime, we
> invite you to explore Great Diddling's rich

literary heritage. Discover the village where
both Agatha Christie and Dorothy L. Sayers
once lived, and where Cornwall's own Daphne
du Maurier met a woman called Rebecca...
All this and MORE at the Great Diddling Books
and Murder Festival. Sign up NOW! Price incl.
board: £350.

She glanced down at her phone. No missed calls and no new messages.

Detective Sergeant Stevens had found his dog owner in the end, thought
DCI Ahmed.

The man's dairy farm was located some twenty minutes outside of
Great Diddling, and Ahmed found the place without a problem.

He turned onto the driveway just after four o'clock on Sunday afternoon. The farm was a handsome stone house with an orangery running
along one side, but all the actual farming activity seemed to be concentrated
around the large, modern agricultural buildings. In a meadow nearby, a
herd of cows was grazing.

DCI Ahmed got out of the car and came extremely close to stepping
straight into a large, muddy puddle.

He was immediately greeted by their primary witness: a lively cocker
spaniel who started jumping up in search of treats, leaving muddy paw
prints on his trouser legs. DCI Ahmed firmly but gently gripped the dog's
paws and lowered them to the ground. He scratched the dog's belly instead,
to her obvious delight.

"Ignore her," said a surly voice from the open barn, where a tractor was
parked. "I take it you're the detective who called?"

DCI Ahmed confirmed that he was. "I'm investigating the murder of
Reginald Trent," he said. "I understand you might have seen something?"

Something to do with Penny Wilson, as he had called her when he eventually got in touch with the police, much too late. DCI Ahmed didn't voice his criticisms, but his thoughts must have been plain to see because the man looked slightly sheepish when he said:

"I s'pose I should've called you sooner, but I didn't think it was important. I'd forgotten all about it by the time the murder took place. But then I read her confession in the paper, right there in black-and-white. And now you've arrested James, haven't you? Well, that got me thinking. Made me remember a thing or two."

"You saw something? At the tea party?"

"What? No. I never went. I don't bother with that sort of thing. Got enough on my plate without socializing. The wife went. I was here with my cows. At least they don't expect me to wear uncomfortable clothes and converse and what have you. No, this was on Friday."

"The Friday before the tea party?"

"Yes, that's what I was saying. I was having a pint down in the village. Had the bitch with me, so I walked home."

DCI Ahmed was fairly sure he was talking about the dog.

"And that's when you saw Reginald Trent?" he asked.

"No, I never saw him." The man seemed to hesitate again.

DCI Ahmed bent down to stroke the dog, who was rolling around by his feet, beside herself at finally being given some attention. After fussing over her for a minute or two, he asked, "But you saw someone?"

"Like I told your sergeant, I'm not one for gossip."

"This is a murder investigation, sir." DCI Ahmed tried to keep his voice neutral, without any hint of threat or authority. Nothing that could rub the man the wrong way.

"I'm sure she had her reasons, but it was Penny. Penny Wilson. She's called Elmer now, I s'pose. I also do a bit of work as a car mechanic, and I've fixed that old banger she insists on driving around in often enough to recognize it anywhere. She was driving up to the big house."

"Do you remember roughly what time it was when you saw her?"

"It was gone eleven, at least. Maybe even close to twelve. I didn't check the time. I might not even have remembered it if I hadn't remembered their past. I thought, *Aha, so is that what Penny's up to these days?* I thought…well,

James Elmer wouldn't be too happy if he knew. And then, well, someone did actually kill the bloke, so there must've been a reason for it…if you see what I mean?"

DCI Ahmed nodded.

He did.

"So you reckon she did it, guv?" Stevens asked when they met up outside of the hotel the same evening.

Detective Inspector Rogers were already there. She was directing two uniformed police officer as they transferred all of the hotel's financial documents into boxes, to take down to the station.

"I don't know," Ahmed said. He studied Penny through the open doors. She was standing behind the reception desk, staring at the chaos in the office and at the officers walking past with box upon box of folders and documents. She had dark bags beneath both eyes and a lifeless expression on her face. The thick layer of makeup she wore only reinforced the weariness below it.

Ahmed thought about the nature of love. Of all human emotions, it was the most unpredictable. He said as much to Stevens, who nodded seriously.

"You're probably right, guv."

Rogers rolled her eyes. "If it's all the same to you, sir, I prefer to follow the money."

A bit further down the street, Sima Kumar was giving an interview over the phone. She was pacing the pavement with her phone pressed to her ear. Her singsong voice sounded cheerily professional as she answered the questions with confidence and wit.

"I didn't know him personally, no," she said, presumably about their victim. "But I do know that he was a respected and admired businessman in the village. Yes, we do very much see ourselves as a real-life Midsomer village." She laughed at something the interviewer said and nodded eagerly even though they couldn't see it over the phone. "It sounds deadly? Yes, I think you're right. One wonders if the Midsomer region has any villagers left at this point. I think part of our fascination with it is the thrill of the contrast between the charming façade and the darkness and danger that lurks beneath it. Another murder? Well, I can't promise anything, but I guess there's always a chance, eh?"

18

LIAM CAME BARRELING INTO WISTERIA Cottage early the next morning.

"Quick! Put the TV on! Sima's on *Good Morning Britain!*"

Berit looked up from her book and her coffee, Sally from her book and her tea. There was no TV in the cottage.

"Fuck's sake," Liam muttered, bringing up the stream on his phone instead.

Berit leaned in close, squinting in order to see the tiny Sima on the screen.

It was patently obvious that she had only been invited on the show to fill a gap and possibly also to give the audience a good laugh at the countryside's expense. The host seemed uninterested and nonchalant, introducing Sima with his eyes locked onto his cue card and barely bothering to look up at her afterward.

"The *Daily Mail* accused Great Diddling of exploiting a human tragedy yesterday," he began. "What do you make of that?"

Sima gazed calmly back at him. "I think maybe the *Daily Mail* is just annoyed that they don't have an exclusive right to exploitation," she replied.

At that, the host looked up from his card as though he was seeing her for the first time.

"Three locals have confessed to the murder, and a fourth is currently in custody," he said after a moment. "You have to ask yourself: Is this village really somewhere a tourist would want to go? Where a tourist *should* go?"

"Obviously I can't comment on an ongoing investigation," said Sima. "But as for your question, I can give you a categorical yes. The people of this country have always loved murder as entertainment. Thomas de Quincey wrote about this very thing in 1827 in 'On Murder Considered as One of the Fine Arts.' He lived in a small, picturesque village when he witnessed the public's reaction to murder. So who knows what people will write about Great Diddling in the future?"

"But you're hosting a 'book and murder festival' next weekend! That's in bad taste, isn't it? What do you say to the victim's family?"

"The victim's family fully supports the festival," Sima replied. She looked the host straight in the eyes and added, "It's what the victim himself would have wanted."

"She's a much better liar than I thought," Liam said, impressed.

Over the course of the next week, Sima was everywhere. She took part in another radio program and appeared on morning TV, talking about the role of the village in the perfect murder mystery. Her media strategy was topped off by the ultimate success: a late dropout and the fact that two of the other guests (a writer-director and an actor) had recently been involved in various murder mystery productions led to an invitation to appear on the *Graham Norton Show*. The shoot was on the Thursday, so by the time it was broadcast on Friday evening, Sima was back in Great Diddling.

Harry, the pub owner, had managed to get hold of a projector, and he hung a large sheet to show the program in the Queen's Head, Arms, and Legs. He was handing out huge buckets full of popcorn when Berit and Sally arrived.

The pub was packed. Half the village seemed to have turned out, thought Berit. She and Sally found two seats at a table by the edge of the room, and Berit went to get herself a beer and some popcorn for Sally.

Everyone cheered when Sima eventually turned up on the sofa beside the actor and the director. She was clearly the least famous of the three, and she went to great lengths to praise and admire them both, offering a touching yet fake naivety without letting herself be outshone in the slightest.

A slight nostalgia settled over the TV studio as she started talking about the love the English had for murder mysteries and the books, television shows, and settings that celebrated them. The actor told an anecdote about working with David Suchet ("Hercule Poirot!" Sima blurted out), and Graham Norton spoke about his latest interview with Kenneth Branagh ("Hercule Poirot!" Sima repeated, making the audience laugh). They all seemed to be in agreement that murder was entertaining.

"But wouldn't you say it's a guilty pleasure?" asked Graham Norton. "And in your case, it's based on a very real—and recent—case. Doesn't that make feel you bad?"

Sima looked him straight in the eye, her face bright and open.

"It's not the murder itself that's entertaining," she explained. "What appeals to us in these stories is *justice*. The solving of the mystery and the punishment dealt out to the killer—that's what keeps us glued to our seats. I also believe that's why the golden age of mystery novels came between the two World Wars. When things are uncertain and dangerous, we need the comfort of stories more than ever. And now we are hoping to bring some comfort, and some stories, to our picturesque little village in the heart of beautiful Cornwall."

On the projection screen, Graham Norton's face grew serious again. "The fact remains that a man died," he continued. "Is it really right to use that as the basis for a festival?"

Sima nodded, her face just as solemn as the host's. She then began talking—at length and with what seemed like genuine honesty—about what a great man Reginald Trent was and how beloved he had been in the village. The festival was dedicated to him, she explained, and a memorial plaque would be put up.

At the mentioning of the plaque, several members of the pub audience booed.

Sima held up her hands. "I had to say that," she said.

Someone suggested the toilets as a suitable location for her plaque, and good humor was restored again.

It was after ten o'clock on Friday evening when DCI Ahmed finally got back to his flat. The sound of voices and laughter from the pubs he passed had followed him home. It was a warm, dry evening in May, and everyone but him seemed to be out having fun.

He pushed the door shut behind him, tossed his keys into the old brass bowl on top of the chest of drawers, and took off his jacket. He had barely needed it on the walk home. *Summer is coming*, he thought with a pang of longing.

Ian Ahmed kicked off his shoes, unbuttoned his shirt, and draped it over the back of a chair in the kitchen. He felt his shoulders relax, freed at last from their buttoned-up uniform.

There were several dirty cups on the worktop in the kitchen, but he ignored them and opened the fridge. The leftovers from yesterday's palak paneer were inside, along with a couple of beers and a bottle of champagne he had bought ahead of his failed weekend with the crown prosecutor, Jalissa. He tossed the curry into the bin and took one of the beers through to the living room.

When he first got the job in Plymouth six years ago, he had spent a good deal of time, money, and energy on getting the flat just how he wanted it. The decor was functional yet personal, designed to suit his needs and tastes, but as he looked around the space now, he realized it hadn't been a resounding success. Yes, this was where he slept—it was his castle, his refuge—but it had never felt like home.

His neighbors were having a party, the music pulsing through the walls, but he didn't mind. If he had to live in the city, then he liked these small reminders that he was surrounded by other people, the fact that their lives were going on around his.

DCI Ahmed didn't have a TV, but he did have a comfortable armchair and a side table where he put his computer whenever he wanted to watch something. He brought up the iPlayer and hit the "Watch live" button on BBC One.

Sima Kumar's face filled the screen. He had met her in person, of course, but he was struck by just how well suited she seemed for TV. She had the sort of interesting beauty that was only enhanced by being on-screen.

"We're holding the book festival in Reginald Trent's honor," she said in a deep, solemn voice. It was hypnotic. "He would have appreciated everything we're doing; I'm sure of that."

DCI Ahmed took a swig of his cold beer as Sima went on, talking about a memorial and just how beloved Reginald Trent had been.

She smiled sadly.

"It's like Reginald always used to say, 'You've got to grab the bull by the horns. That's what separates those of us who are successful from the rest of people.' I suppose you could say that's what we're doing here. We're grabbing the bull by the horns and trying to turn this terrible, awful tragedy into something positive."

Bullshit, he thought. But then he froze. He leaned forward, rewound the live feed and focused on Sima's face.

Lies, lies, lies, he thought. *Memory.*

19

DCI AHMED WATCHED THE CLIP several times as he shaved the next morning. With each viewing, he became increasingly sure of his hunch: Sima Kumar knew Reginald Trent from before, and she had just given herself away.

Back in his student days, his psychology professor had once explained that inventing and remembering things used different parts of the brain. If you paid close attention to a person's face, their subconscious eye movements would reveal whether or not they were telling the truth. Looking down meant they were remembering something, but if they looked up, they were using their imagination.

He went over everything he had seen and heard as he made his way to the station, stopping off at a bakery to buy coffee and croissants—it was Saturday, after all, and his team had been working two consecutive weekends.

The city around him hadn't woken yet. People were no doubt sleeping off their heavy Friday nights, he thought, discarded takeaway cartons bearing witness to countless drunken walks home.

Sima had openly lowered her gaze and glanced to the left while she was talking about Reginald, but DCI Ahmed's hunch wasn't based on that. Twenty years on the force had taught him that his professor was wrong.

In actual fact, it was almost impossible to tell whether or not a person was lying. Innocent people's eyes darted around nonstop, and they also frequently broke out in a sweat, began to stutter, and contradicted themselves. The guilty, on the other hand, could look you straight in the eye and lie as though it was the easiest thing on earth.

By the time DCI Ahmed got to the station, Stevens and Rogers were already there. He pushed the office door open using his elbow, hesitated at the sight of his cluttered desk, and then handed the three paper cups to Stevens, the bag of croissants to Rogers.

"Sima Kumar knew Reginald Trent," he said. "And she lied about it."

Rogers was staring at his chin, and he reached up and felt the small scraps of paper clinging to his skin. He probably should have paid a little more attention to shaving and less to the interview with Sima, he realized.

DCI Ahmed checked HOLMES for the notes from the first interviews on scene at the tea party. "Look," he said. "Sima Kumar clearly stated that she didn't know the victim. She said it again in an interview yesterday. But listen to this."

He brought up the clip on his phone and played it for them. Of his two colleagues, only Rogers grasped the importance of what Sima had said.

"You've got to grab the bull by the horns," she repeated.

"Exactly," he said. Stevens hadn't been in London with them, so DCI Ahmed explained: "Reginald Trent's ex-wife used that exact phrase when she was talking about him. As though it was something he used to say all the time, so often that it automatically came to mind when she was telling us about him. Sima Kumar used the same phrase—"

"Because she knew him well enough to have heard him say it all the time too," Rogers filled in.

Stevens looked doubtful. "A bit weak, isn't it? It's just a turn of phrase. Anyone can use it. Doesn't mean she knew him."

DCI Ahmed ignored him. "I want a full background check on her. Finances, education, friends, social media, call data—everything."

"She's not from the village," Stevens said. "Moved there in her mid-twenties from London." When he saw DCI Ahmed's surprised face, he added modestly, "People talk, guv. She's only lived in the village for ten years.

Not one of them yet, so they felt no compunction about gossiping about her. She's still an outsider. A bit too smart for some in the village, perhaps."

"Where's she from originally?"

"Bristol, guv. Parents still live there. Visits them sometimes but not so often as she should, say some of the old birds in the village."

"Not childhood sweethearts then," Ahmed said. "But they did meet somewhere; I'm sure of it." He looked at Rogers. "Keep digging," he said. "Stevens, you're with me."

Berit hadn't said anything about it, but the truth was that Sally's cooking had improved her days considerably. She had formed the habit of just drifting into the kitchen around 1:00 p.m. to see what was for lunch, and she wasn't the only one. Liam was already sitting at the table when she got there.

"Do you know that we've got *one hundred and ninety-two* people signing up for the Books and Murder Festival?" he said cheerily. "But where she's going to put them all, I have no idea. It's not like the hotel has got a hundred and ninety-two rooms. Shouldn't think they have more than sixty, at most."

Berit sniffed the air and looked at the pot on the stove. Today was London particular soup, and it looked delicious, with split peas, bacon, carrots, and celery, and so thick it really did resemble the London smog. The kitchen smelled of warm soup and newly baked bread.

Her phone buzzed insistently. Olivia had tried to call her ever since she'd seen Sima on the *Graham Norton Show*. She had also texted her repeatedly.

It should've been you on that TV sofa, said one of them.

You're dead to me now, said another.

Olivia was only joking. Or so she hoped.

Berit carried her phone into the living room and put it in one of the drawers of her Edwardian desk. It didn't help. The buzzing continued. If anything it had been amplified by the drawer. It sounded as though some sort of Edwardian ghost was trapped inside the desk.

An extremely angry Edwardian ghost.

She opened the desk and answered the call, without bothering to pick up the phone. "*What?*" she said irritably down into the drawer.

"You hired me to do one job, and that's to make sure your books sell!" Olivia said. "But I can't do my job if you constantly refuse to do yours!"

"I *am* writing," Berit said defensively. "Practically writing. Almost writing. Very nearly writing."

Berit instinctively closed the drawer. She took several deep breaths. It was a beautiful day outside. The sun was shining, and bees and butterflies were buzzing around the overgrown garden. The scent of roses and wildflowers drifted in through the open french doors and mixed with the heavenly smell from the kitchen.

In the desk drawer, her agent was still shrieking. "It should have been you on that sofa!"

Berit opened the drawer. "My job is to write!" she said.

The drawer was worryingly quiet for a few seconds before Olivia replied, her voice now alarmingly light and breezy. "So that's what you're doing right now, is it? Writing? What chapter are you on? You're at your computer, I assume?"

"Not right this second, no. But practically. Soon. Almost. I just need to do a tiny bit more research…"

"No, Berit. No!" Olivia barked. "I forbid it. Listen to me—"

Berit ended the call and slammed the drawer shut. She snatched up her pen and notepad from the desk, grabbed a light jacket, and headed out, only remembering at the last moment to dig her phone out of the drawer.

"Where are you going?" Sally asked from the kitchen, soup ladle in hand.

"To the village."

"Well, what are you going to do?"

"The same thing I always do. I'm going to follow the story to the end."

At the hotel, Penny was looking even more worn than ever. They had released James last week, but that didn't seem to have made her any happier. She was vacuuming while James stood behind the reception desk, neither of them talking and both of them trying very hard not to meet the other one's eyes.

But when DCI Ahmed asked if she had a minute, she shot her husband an anxious glance.

"Perhaps we can talk somewhere more private?" Ahmed suggested, and Penny showed him into the empty dining room. He sat down in front of her and felt DS Stevens's disapproving presence next to him.

"You lied to us, Mrs. Elmer," DCI Ahmed said.

"I didn't lie."

"Withheld from us then."

She stared mutely at him and crossed her arms in front of her chest.

"Why didn't you tell us that you went out to Tawny Hall on the Friday before the tea party? You spoke to Mr. Trent, didn't you? A little detail you forgot to mention to us."

"It wasn't relevant—"

"Wasn't relevant?!" DCI Ahmed didn't raise his voice, but he managed to sound so disbelieving that Penny flinched.

"I didn't talk to him, OK?" she said without meeting his eyes.

"But you did go over there?"

"Yes, and I was planning to speak to him. I'll admit that. But I hadn't exactly thought the whole thing through, OK? When I actually got there, I realized I couldn't very well just knock on the front door and wake Daphne up, could I? So I parked far enough back from the house that I didn't think they'd notice me, and then I just sat there for a bit and…thought."

"About what?"

"If you have to know, about how bloody funny Reginald would have found it if I did turn up to talk to him. Let me tell you, he'd have loved that." She leaned forward, looked to both sides, and lowered her voice: "Do you promise not to repeat any of this to James?"

"So you were in love with him then?" Stevens asked. He sounded disappointed and disapproving.

Penny straightened up, insulted. "What? No! Of course I wasn't! That's a damn lie! Slander and defamation! If you say anything like that again, I'll…I'll *sue*!"

Stevens stared at her in confusion. "Then what don't you want Mr. Elmer to find out? And why did you go over there?"

"Look, Reginald came to the hotel on Thursday evening. He threatened James, and they got into an argument. Well, Reginald argued. James practically begged. I know that gives James a motive, but he would never hurt anyone. Not even a fly. Or spiders. Literally. It's always me who has to deal with them." She shuddered. "Anyway, I knew that Reginald had been trying to talk him into some sort of deal, and I knew it had something to do with the hotel. James was worried. And I thought he probably had reason to be. Reginald could be a real bastard. Not someone you want to get into business with."

"You got into bed with him, though, didn't you?" DS Stevens asked.

Penny waved her hand dismissively. "That was ages ago. He might have been a bastard, but he was handsome. That was more than enough for me those days. Can't blame a girl for wanting a bit of fun, eh?"

Stevens looked like he very much could blame her.

"So what did you do? After you overheard the argument?"

"Well, nothing. At first. But then I started thinking. James loves this hotel, so I drove over to Tawny Hall to ask Reginald to leave us alone. To beg him to leave James alone."

She looked more embarrassed by that confession than she ever had when she confessed to a murder.

"But in the end, you didn't do anything?" DCI Ahmed asked. "You didn't go inside?"

"Didn't even step out of the car. No point, really. Reginald would have loved to watch me beg, but it wouldn't have changed his mind. If anything, it might have egged him on. And then on Sunday, when I heard James pleading with him again, I couldn't hold back. I had to butt in and start shouting and cause a scene—everything James hates."

She looked down at the table. "Such a nice fucking knight in shining armor I turned out to be, huh?" she said bitterly.

Afterward, DCI Ahmed stood for a long time out in the sunshine, trying to wash away some of the tragic misery that always hung around cases like this.

"I talked to her friends, you know," Stevens said. He sounded reluctant.

"Even one of her former schoolteachers. They all said she had a fiery temper, but she's completely useless when it comes to anything technical. Her chemistry teacher said he forbade her from taking part in any experiments in class. She was downright dangerous. As he put it, 'Penny Elmer could probably kill Reginald in the heat of the moment, but the only person she'd be capable of blowing up was herself.'"

DCI Ahmed nodded. "It doesn't feel right. If we'd found him with twelve knife wounds in the chest, that would be another matter entirely. Let's not write it off just yet, but it feels like a dead end to me."

"So what do we do now?"

"We keep working the way we always do. Calmly and systematically. Sooner or later, something will turn up. Stick to Sima Kumar for the moment. See if you can get your old gossips to tell you more."

"What are you going to do, guv?"

"Me? I'm going to do the only reasonable thing you can do when you're stuck. I'm going to have a cup of tea."

The queue snaked all the way down the high street, past the pub, past Great Diddling Antiques and Souvenirs ("Affordable Prices—Always!") and the supermarket, all the way to Ladies' Fashions ("Tradition, Quality, Elegance").

It started close to the café, where Sima and Liam were sitting behind a huge sign reading **GREAT DIDDLING BED & BREAKFAST ASSOCIATION.**

Berit sipped her coffee and studied the scene in front of her.

She barely had time to take out her notepad before something blocked out the sun, and when she looked up, she saw a tall figure standing in front of her.

"Mind if I join you?" asked DCI Ahmed. He was holding a cup of tea and looking at the empty chair next to her.

"Be my guest. They've been at it since ten apparently. And more and more people keep joining the line."

Berit gazed over at the timid-looking woman at the front of the queue. She was so unsure of herself that she seemed much younger than she was, and Sima gave her a reassuring, almost motherly smile, despite the fact that the woman was far older.

"Yes, the thing is…" the woman began. "I have a room, but I don't know whether it's any good. It's a bit…well, old-fashioned. It was my mother's, you see, and I haven't been able to bring myself to change anything since… since she passed away. The house was hers, but I took care of her there at the end, and now…" She leaned in close. "I could really do with the money."

"So what you're saying is that you have a single room with old-school charm?" said Sima. Liam noted everything down on his computer. "Somewhere that evokes memories of the olden days, of an England where family was at the heart of everyday life. I think I've got the perfect guest for you. Next!"

The woman hesitated, and Sima glanced up again.

"I was just wondering…" the woman began, leaning in again. "When will we be paid? Breakfast is supposed to be included, isn't it? And as I said, things are…they're a bit tight at the moment, and…"

"You raise a good point," said Sima, turning to Liam. "We'll have to do a big shop. I'll make a list and you can drive over to Truro to pick everything up for me." She turned back to the woman. "You'll have everything you need by Friday."

The woman seemed relieved.

Berit scribbled down a few key words in her notepad. She could feel DCI Ahmed's disapproving gaze on her, but she ignored him. This material was just too good.

"I came to ask you a few questions about the tea party," he said.

Berit relaxed her shoulders and closed her eyes. Ahmed looked at her in surprise.

"Sunshine. The smell of freshly cut grass. Tea and scones. Tension so thick you could cut it with a knife. I'm there. Go on."

"Oh. Well, I'm particularly interested in whether you noticed anything to do with Sima Kumar. How was she behaving? Did she talk to Reginald Trent? Did they seem to know each other?"

"Sima. Smartly dressed." She smiled. "Although the heels were probably a bit impractical on a lawn. She felt something for him, I can tell you that. Strong feelings. When she looked at him, the first word that came to my mind was *passion*. I remember that clearly."

Ahmed leaned forward eagerly. "She loved him?"

Berit opened her eyes. "Not necessarily," she said. "Might have been hate too."

"But you're certain she knew him?"

"Oh, yes. She knew him all right. What I'd really like to know," Berit mused to herself, "is how a woman like Sima ended up in a village like Great Diddling. A bit overqualified, wouldn't you say? I imagine she used to have bigger ambitions for herself."

"She seems happy enough with her role here," DCI Ahmed said.

"Yes, that's what fascinates me. Did you manage to unearth anything about Margaret's past?"

DCI Ahmed hesitated. "You told me you had no intention of using the murder in your next book," he reminded her. "Is that still the case?"

"Nothing about the murder, no. Or anything related to the investigation. You have my word."

"Well, as far as Margaret is concerned, there's no real secret. It has nothing to do with the current investigation, either. The whole thing was a dead end. She was the administrator at a health center, which meant she was responsible for making budgetary savings—more and more cuts every year. You know how it is, everything has to be streamlined and made more efficient. In the end, things probably got a bit too streamlined. An over-worked doctor who had just joined the team missed an obvious diagnosis. I'm sure it happens all the time, but in this instance the young woman ended up dying. Twenty-three years of age, a new mother. In the eyes of the press and the public, it was because of the cutbacks."

"So what did Margaret do?"

"She took the blame and quit."

"And moved to Great Diddling? Did you get any sense of what she was like as a person before all this happened? She's one of several people who have been avoiding me."

"We spoke to a few former colleagues and friends. They all described her as competent, friendly, helpful, charming. Someone who laughed a lot. Intelligent and reflective. The fact of the matter is that she doesn't have a motive to kill Reginald Trent, and she and Daphne have given each other an alibi for the Thursday evening when the explosives were stolen."

"What were they doing?"

"Reading, at home. In the same room for most of that time."

"What were they reading?"

"I didn't exactly ask for recommendations," Ahmed said exasperatedly. "I remember you saying that whoever killed Reginald must be crazy or competent. What's your impression of Daphne?"

"Oh, she's definitely crazy enough, but she's not the kind of person who would do the legwork herself."

"But could she have got someone else to do it for her?" he asked. "Or encouraged it?"

"'Will no one rid me of this meddlesome priest?'" Berit quoted.

DCI Ahmed nodded. "I've read that Henry II regretted it afterward, but I doubt Daphne would have."

The next woman in line at Sima and Liam's stand was middle-aged, chic, and good-looking. Her hair was neatly styled, and her navy nails matched her skirt. Even her mascara was blue.

"No men," she said. "Twenty years I spent tidying up after my husband, and when he left, I made a promise to myself never to do it again."

"Shouldn't be a problem," said Sima. "So far, only seven men have signed up."

Berit turned back to DCI Ahmed.

"Have you ever been to a book festival? I've been to several, you see, but only ever as an author. I'm trying to understand what people get out of it."

"No, but I did travel around Ireland once, a long time ago, reading Khaled Hosseini's books in the evening. I still can't think about his incredible descriptions of Afghanistan and its history and landscape without also seeing the west coast of Ireland. So in that sense, I do understand the impulse to travel with books."

Berit nodded. "I discovered Georgette Heyer while I was staying at a small guesthouse in Dublin. This was toward the end of a long, fruitless trip trying to gather inspiration for a novel that never happened. I was tired and weary and suddenly felt a long way from home, even though I was just on the other side of the Irish Sea. But then I walked past a used bookshop, and I thought, why not? I found an old edition of *The Grand Sophy* there, with a woman in a yellow dress and a monkey on her shoulder on the cover. Irresistible!"

"Of course," DCI Ahmed replied with a smile.

"It's a brilliant book too, of course. I bought crisps and Coca-Cola and didn't leave the guesthouse for the next three days—other than to visit other shops in search of more books by Georgette Heyer. And to eat lunch and grab a pint at a pub, taking the book with me. I was so caught up in the story that I left without paying. I didn't realize until later, while I was reading in a café, and I was so horrified that I jumped up and hurried back over there…"

The detective's smile grew bigger. "And forgot to pay at the café?"

"Exactly."

He shook his head and turned his attention back to the queue. "I might find it easier to respect what they're doing if it was more about a love of books and less about sensationalizing and exploiting a murder. A man has died, but look at her. She's enjoying this. She's having the time of her life organizing all of this and all thanks to a man's death."

Berit watched Sima closely and frowned. She wasn't sure she *was* enjoying herself. Oh, she was determined to keep up the façade, and she laughed and smiled at all the right moments, but when she thought no one was looking, the smile faltered. She kept glancing down at her phone and didn't seem the least bit reassured by whatever she saw.

Sima isn't enjoying any of this, Berit thought. *She's worried about something.*

Mary reached for another of her teapots, carefully rinsed it beneath the hot tap, and then lovingly dried it off, all without looking at Eleanor.

Her precious collection of unique, unusual teapots had taken over the café. They were everywhere: cluttering the kitchen worktop, the display counter by the till, even the table closest to it. Mary had decided to wash every last one of them so that they would be ready for use during the festival, and she was doing it without a single word to her wife.

On the other side of the window, people were standing in some sort of line. It stretched as far as the eye could see.

Mary picked up another of her teapots. It was small and squat, in the shape of a strawberry, with the lid made to look like leaves. It was also incredibly ugly, but Mary loved it all the same. She remained tight-lipped as she gave it a thorough wipe down, paying no attention whatsoever to Eleanor.

Eleanor held up her hands. "Come on, what is it?" she said. "Why don't you just tell me what you think I should do?"

"OK," said Mary. "I think you should help out with the festival. Once upon a time, it would have been you who came up with the brilliant idea of a book festival. It's just your style. Don't you remember all the art soirees you organized in Malaga?"

"That was different," Eleanor muttered. "My ideas brought in money."

"Oh really, Eleanor," said Mary, shaking her head and laughing. "You know full well they usually didn't earn us anything. You did plenty of things purely because you thought it was fun—and because you never could resist a challenge."

Eleanor gave her a wry smile. "Well, we earned money from some of them in any case."

Mary threw down the tea towel. "How are we supposed to live here if you won't make an effort? You could stand to learn a thing or two about community, Eleanor Hartfield."

Eleanor stared at her. "Community?" she repeated. "Has the world gone mad?"

"Don't you see? The people here, they're just like us. We belong here. Among friends. Neighbors. All we need to do is help organize one little book festival. It's the perfect opportunity for you. You were practically made for this. I know Sima is a politician, but you've forgotten more about cons than Sima has ever known."

"We wouldn't have to be involved in anything if we could just move somewhere else," Eleanor argued. "You and me against the world again, Mary. The way it's always been."

"Oh, come on. We've scraped by all our lives. Isn't it time we aimed a little higher? Don't you want to be a part of something?"

"I'm not sure I know how."

"This village needs help, and Sima can't do it on her own."

James Elmer was standing by the window in room thirteen, watching as the construction firm packed up their tools.

"Are they leaving?" asked Penny.

He nodded.

"Will we get any of the money back?"

"No."

"Sima's book festival seems to be going well at least. Almost two hundred people have signed up so far! We'll be fully booked for several days. But will that be enough?"

James didn't answer.

"We still have the money from the tabloid."

More silence. Always this damn silence.

"Oh, come on!" she said. "Say something. Be angry. Do something. Shout at me."

James turned to her with an exhausted look on his face. "What good would that do?"

For the first time, Penny felt genuinely afraid. "I did it for the hotel, James. For us."

"Don't say anything. I don't want to hear it. We'll just have to keep going like normal. It'll all work out in the end. Somehow. It has to. But just…be quiet, would you?"

Penny swallowed and nodded. She clenched her fists so tight that her false nails dug into her palms, but she didn't speak. And on the other side of the window, the construction workers continued to dismantle their huts.

20

DCI AHMED SPENT HIS SUNDAY in the meeting room with Stevens and Rogers. They had spread the case files across the long table in the middle of the room. Call lists, the postmortem report, lab results, transcripts of interviews, the hotel's accounts, reports from their door-to-door investigation in the village—everything they had managed to compile so far.

On the whiteboard at one end of the room, DCI Ahmed pinned photographs of their suspects. Stevens protested when he saw what his boss was doing.

"It's like we're in a bloody TV series," he said, launching into a long tirade about how unrealistic those police stations were with pictures of suspects stuck to a wall where anyone—including the suspects themselves—might see them. DCI Ahmed knew that Stevens was no longer allowed to watch all those crime dramas with his wife on account of him repeatedly pointing out all the inaccuracies to her.

"No one is going to see the pictures here," DCI Ahmed assured him patiently. "I want to be able to see the links between them."

He grabbed a whiteboard marker and drew lines between the people who were connected to each other.

Eleanor led to Mary, of course, but she also had a connection to Penny, and Penny led straight to James.

Daphne was linked to Margaret.

Liam's name produced multiple lines: to Sima, James, Penny, Daphne, and Margaret.

"Liam is connected to more people than anyone else, and he's also the only person who links several different areas," said Rogers. "The hotel and Tawny Hall; the council, via Sima; the café. He seems to work for everyone."

DCI Ahmed nodded, deep in thought.

"But he has an alibi," Stevens muttered. "Given that he apparently also helps old ladies with their computers. Regular little boy scout, isn't he?"

On the other whiteboard, DCI Ahmed began listing aspects of the case that still bothered him.

Where is Gerald Corduroy-Smith?

Who does the cuff link belong to?

What was Sima Kumar's relationship to Reginald Trent?

"What have you found out about Sima?" Ahmed asked.

"Not much from her childhood in Bristol," Stevens admitted. "But we have managed to track down a few of her fellow students and teachers at Oxford."

"She was part of their gifted students program," Rogers explained. "Brilliant student, sharp mind, politically engaged. Her time at Oxford overlapped with Reginald Trent, so they might have met there."

"But she was three years younger than him, guv. By the time she enrolled, he was about to graduate. The university has over twenty thousand students. We still haven't managed to establish a connection between them there."

"Well, it's a start. Was Reginald engaged in politics?"

Rogers shrugged. "Shouldn't think so. Not really the type, was he?"

"Then Oxford is still our best bet. Keep looking. See if you can find any links between them: teachers they had in common, mutual acquaintances, extracurricular activities…"

"Maybe they were both on the rowing team, guv," Stevens suggested sarcastically.

"I guess I could talk to his wife again," Rogers said. "Maybe she remembers some of his friends from his student days. People keep in touch. Especially in that social class."

"Great. Do it."

DCI Ahmed checked the time. Almost lunch already. He asked Stevens to order in sandwiches and then turned to Rogers:

"How did it go with the hotel's finances?"

"They were struggling even before the building work started. And the construction firm filed for bankruptcy this morning."

"Probably trying to avoid having to pay the fines," Stevens muttered.

Rogers agreed. "I'm sure they'll turn up under a new name elsewhere."

"Will the hotel survive?"

"Who knows?" She shrugged. "The building project was only in the first phase. They've already spent a good amount of money on it, but that's nothing compared to what it would cost to complete the plans. Ironically, having to shelve the whole thing could be what saves them—assuming they can work through the debt, that is." Rogers sounded fundamentally indifferent to the fate of the hotel. It was all just numbers to her, Ahmed guessed.

"Have you found anything we can use?" he asked.

"Doubt it. They've taken a few shortcuts, just as I suspected, but nothing exactly illegal. Let's say they've managed to stay inside the gray area so far. I might find out something more if I keep digging though."

DCI Ahmed thought for a moment. "Let's hold off on it for now," he said. "Focus on former Mrs. Trent and those Oxford friends."

Yet another dead end, he thought. One of many in this case. The air was already stuffy, and the meeting room was starting to feel claustrophobic.

A young constable knocked on the door.

"Sorry to bother you, sir," he said, "but we've got someone asking for you in reception. Even though it's Sunday."

DCI Ahmed closed his eyes. "They don't want to confess, do they?"

It had been a long week.

"No, sir. Claims he's an actor, sir." The young man's face looked excessively neutral. "Calls himself Alec Rushford."

"Well, so long as he doesn't confess to this murder, he can call himself whatever he wants. Come with me, Stevens. Rogers, keep looking for mutual acquaintances of Reginald Trent and Sima Kumar."

Alec Rushford turned out to be a thin, gangly man in his forties. Unfortunately for someone in his chosen profession, thought DCI Ahmed, he had the sort of face that was immediately forgettable. His skin was pale and smooth, as though he had never faced any hardship in life, but a slight hint of discontent hung about him.

A discontent on the verge of becoming chronic too, DCI Ahmed thought. He looked down at the business card in his hand: *Alec Rushford, actor. No part too big or too small.*

"I was in *Midsomer Murders* once," the actor said suddenly. He looked at Ahmed with hungry eyes, as though he was memorizing every detail for some future role.

"What was the part?" Stevens asked. It was clear that he would rather be spending the rest of his Sunday afternoon with his wife than stuck in a cramped room with a pretentious actor.

Mr. Rushford pursed his thin lips. "Cyclist number three," he replied after a brief pause.

"What can we do for you, Mr. Rushford?" asked DCI Ahmed.

"It's more a question of what *I* can do for you! Gerald Corduroy-Smith contacted me about playing the part of financial genius Raglan Harris."

The two detectives stared at him in disbelief.

Mr. Rushford nodded, clearly pleased with himself.

"Yes, I thought that might interest you," he said smugly. "I had to develop his background and motivation myself, but that's no problem for a character actor like me." He seemed more excited by his own performance than the fact that he suddenly found himself caught up in a murder inquiry.

"And did Mr. Corduroy-Smith give you any indication of why he wanted you to take on this commission?"

"I'm sorry, but I have to know: Do you always ask the questions in such a courteous manner? I'd probably add a bit more oomph to the interrogation technique, if you see what I mean. More eye contact too. Really fix my eyes on the suspect. Nerves of steel and an icy intellect, but with an inner darkness that occasionally spills out in a fit of anger. Tell me, have you ever thrown a chair during an interview?"

"They're bolted to the floor," said Stevens. "Otherwise he'd let loose on every suspect like a wild animal."

DCI Ahmed gave his colleague a warning glance.

"Hmm." Alec Rushford gazed around the room with a critical look on his face.

"Well?" DCI Ahmed asked calmly. "Did Mr. Corduroy-Smith give you a reason?"

"He said he wanted to play a prank on a friend." The actor shrugged. "Just a bit of fun between old friends. Quite harmless, I assure you."

"How did Mr. Corduroy-Smith make contact with you?"

"Through an agency I use. I'm just waiting for my big break. It only takes one good part, you know." He sighed. "Sadly, no one seems to be able to recognize talent these days."

"How did he pay you?"

"Cash. Up front, of course."

The man had enough sense for that at least, Ahmed thought amusedly.

"OK, so what exactly did the part involve?" he asked.

Alec Rushford seemed to be on the verge of another lengthy explanation about his character's inner conflict, darkness, and motivations, but DCI Ahmed interrupted him.

"What I mean is: What, exactly, did he ask you to do?"

"Ah, I see. Eat dinner at Alain Ducasse at the Dorchester." He anticipated Stevens's criticism before the detective even had time to speak. "It was work. I was playing a part. I wasn't there to enjoy myself! Besides, the money from Mr. Corduroy-Smith only stretched to a starter."

"I'm sure you did a brilliant job," said DCI Ahmed. "Was Reginald Trent there?"

"No. Or yes. What I'm trying to say is that we didn't eat together. The idea was that I would drop my wallet in such a way that Reginald

Trent found it and then make it look like I'd just come out from the Table Lumière. That's the best table at Alain Ducasse," he said turning to Stevens.

"And it…what? Glows, does it?" Stevens asked.

"It's behind a shimmering curtain."

Stevens shook his head. "The things these people come up with."

"Everything went to plan in any case. I dropped my wallet. Reginald Trent found it. I offered a reward; he declined. Very proper. He was a real gentleman. I'd been given several key lines to use, but otherwise Mr. Corduroy-Smith was willing to trust my improv skills. And that was it. I would have loved to develop the role further, of course, possibly add a little more darkness beneath the surface, maybe a childhood trauma…but sadly it was a one-off appearance."

"And you never suspected there might be something untoward about a job involving you dropping a fake wallet?" asked Stevens.

"No, why would I? It wasn't like I was asked to steal his wallet or anything. On the contrary. I was supposed to treat him to dinner. The advance paid for his meal." He looked affronted again. "Just. I had hoped there would be enough left to cover other expenses, but Mr. Trent certainly wasn't the kind of man who picked the cheaper items on the menu—or who limited himself to a starter!"

DCI Ahmed nodded. "What were the lines you were supposed to work into your performance?"

Mr. Rushford pushed a scrap of paper across the table. "I jotted them down while I was waiting."

In neat handwriting, he had scribbled down the following:

Offer finder's fee

Name mutual acquaintances: Oliver Talbot, Charles Lewis, and Guy Huxley (cousin; his, not yours)

Mention Harrow, not Eton

Mention Oxford, not Cambridge

Look appreciative, flatter him, but don't forget your high status.

"In improvisation classes, we often work with high and low status," Mr. Rushford explained.

"A sort of master and servant dynamic?" DCI Ahmed suggested.

"In very basic terms, yes."

"This Mr. Corduroy-Smith, did he give you his contact details?"

"A telephone number, though I later learned it wasn't his. I tried ring-ing it before I came in to see you, you see."

"Where was it for?"

Alec Rushford looked insulted. The affront made his face more inter-esting but also more childlike. His smooth skin and pale-blue eyes made him look very much like a sulking child.

"A helpline for out-of-work actors!"

Stevens spluttered.

"But I'm not out of work," said Mr. Rushford. "I'm just picky about the parts I take."

"Sure you are, cyclist number three," said Stevens.

21

BERIT HAD BEEN ASLEEP FOR some time when the phone woke her. The sudden sound cut ominously through the silence. Confused, she looked down at her phone, which continued to pump out its deviously cheery tune.

It was half past midnight; it couldn't be good news. Her thoughts automatically turned to DCI Ahmed, which left her even more confused when she heard another man's voice on the end of the line.

"Berit? Come quick. We need your help."

"Who is this?" she asked, sitting up on the edge of her bed.

"It's Harry, from the pub. Can you come?" he asked. "Please, Berit. Hurry."

Three minutes. That was how long it took Berit to throw on a jacket over her pajamas, push her feet into a pair of rubber boots, and run out into the night.

She didn't waste any valuable time looking in the mirror, but as she charged into the pub and caught sight of her reflection in the mirror above the bar, Berit realized that she probably should have.

She was wearing a pair of tartan pajama bottoms, and a loose white T-shirt that said *I ♥ Mr. Darcy*. She pulled her jacket closer and looked around the pub as though she expected to see a dead body somewhere.

The chairs had been stacked on the tables, and half the floor seemed to have been cleaned, the mop leaning against one wall as though it had been dropped in a hurry. The air smelled like soap and stale beer. Sima was sitting at one end of the bar, and for some reason Penny and Eleanor were there too.

"What's going on?" asked Berit.

"Four days from now, 192 people will arrive in Great Diddling expecting a literature festival," said Sima. "But we don't have a single author booked. No publishers will answer my calls, and the agents I've managed to get hold of practically burst out laughing when I suggested that their authors might like to take a break in Cornwall this weekend. I've sent friend requests on Facebook and messages on Instagram, put callouts on Twitter, and left comments on blog posts, but no one ever responds. The festival is less than a week away, and I've got nothing."

"You've got us," said Harry. "And unlimited amounts of alcohol."

Sima shot him a look of gratitude, and despite the crisis, Harry looked overjoyed.

He poured a beer for Berit and another one for Eleanor. Penny was staring down into her still-full glass.

"You'd think an author would *want* to get away for a while," said Sima. "But no one famous will even reply to my emails."

"Writers often aren't the most flexible," said Berit.

Sima looked around. "I've asked you all to come because it is an emergency. Penny and Eleanor, you've already shown some real initiative with the confessions. I might need your creative thinking."

"Fat lot of good that did me," Penny muttered.

"And Berit, I know you said you didn't want to help with the festival, but this is an emergency."

Berit sipped her beer and wondered if she should ask for coffee instead. Even if she had wanted to help, she had no idea what she could do. Yes, she had colleagues she respected and liked, but none that would be willing to drop everything and travel to a small village in the middle of nowhere just because she had asked them to. Not in just one week's time.

They weren't *that* close.

That just left her, but she was neither famous nor interesting enough to be the main draw of an entire festival. She didn't even write crime novels, for God's sake.

Eleanor took a sip of her beer. "What does an author look like?" she asked.

"Like anyone else, I suppose," Berit replied with a shrug. "Possibly a bit more eccentric. After all, we spend most of our time alone, playing with our imaginary friends. Tends to make us a bit…odd."

"Can I ask you something? If Elly Griffiths were sitting right here in this pub, would you have known her? Would any of us?"

Berit considered Eleanor's question for a moment. She had actually met Griffiths once, in a bookshop a few years ago, but she doubted she would recognize her in another context. If their paths crossed on the street, they would probably walk straight past each other.

"I'm not sure I would," she admitted. "It's like Fran Lebowitz once said, 'The best fame is a writer's fame. It's enough to get a table at a good restaurant, but not enough to get you interrupted when you eat.' Most people don't recognize any of us."

"Exactly," said Eleanor.

"Where are you going with this?" Berit asked.

"I've got an idea."

Penny snorted into her beer glass. "I hope it's a damn sight better than your last one," she said. Even this late at night, she was dressed and made up like usual. But she looked tired, Berit thought.

"I could coach a few volunteers from the village enough to get through the panel discussion on Thursday evening," said Eleanor.

Berit paused with her beer halfway to her mouth. Sima stared at Eleanor.

"No problem at all," Eleanor assured them. "All it takes to be someone else is a small dose of imagination and a big dose of balls. And as luck would have it, I've got plenty of both. No one will notice because no one really knows what the authors look like. I will play Margaret Atwood myself, so we will have someone good in the panel. Takes a bit of pressure off the rest."

Sima took out her phone and Googled Margaret Atwood. "You don't exactly look alike…" she said.

"Come Thursday I will; I promise you. I guarantee that once the evening is over, even you'll believe you heard her speak."

"The authors themselves don't even look like their headshots," Berit conceded. "Once every other year or so, the publisher will dust us down, slap some makeup onto us, smarten us up, and sit us down in a flattering light in front of a photographer. The pictures are never very representative. But what about eye color? Hair? Facial features in general? Surely they have to be similar at the very least?"

"Eye color doesn't matter," said Eleanor. "People almost never look anyone else in the eye, far less often than you might think. For example, Harry, what color eyes does Sima have?"

"Mahogany, though they look almost golden in certain lights, like amber."

"OK, bad example," Eleanor muttered. "What color are mine?"

"Uhh…blue? Brown? Green?"

"You see? Besides, we can take our own photos for the program we send out to the ticketholders. That way they'll recognize the fake authors when they arrive. It'll be as though they've always known that Ian Rankin looks like so-and-so."

"And what happens when they open their mouths?" asked Berit.

Eleanor shrugged. "Like I said, I'll coach them."

She seemed excited to play Margaret Atwood, her body brimming with a new energy, glowing with a sudden, intense sense of purpose. It was so powerful that even Berit found herself thinking that their crazy plan might work, though she still couldn't understand what they hoped to get out of it.

"It won't solve anything," she said. "Even if you manage to get through Thursday evening, what are you going to do on the rest of the days? These people will be here until the Sunday. You'll never be able to coach the volunteers well enough to keep up the act all weekend."

"One day at a time," said Sima. "We'll just have to come up with something else for Friday and Saturday."

"I just mean that you have other things to offer than a bunch of fake authors," Berit insisted.

"Like what?" asked Sima.

Berit couldn't come up with a single idea, not off the top of her head, but she knew there had to be a better solution. She had been to enough book festivals in her time, and she knew the type of people who went to them—kind, friendly people, the same ones who went to the theater, to art galleries and concerts. These women—for they were almost exclusively women—carried a large chunk of the cultural sector on their unpretentious shoulders, and they deserved more than a handful of hastily cobbled-together frauds.

"Something else," she said. "Something *real.*"

"Nothing we can pull off in four days," said Sima. She had already made up her mind. "OK, let's do it."

22

SIMA SPENT THE WHOLE OF Monday and half of Tuesday trying to find her prospective authors. By lunchtime on Tuesday, she had managed to convince several reluctant villagers to step up.

Those volunteers were now looking around the pub as though they couldn't quite work out what they were doing there, but Harry had promised beer and lunch to everyone who helped out with the festival, and in the face of a pint and Sima's determination, no one put up much of a fight.

"So," Sima said proudly, "what do you think? I figured we might need a few reserves, just in case anyone can't cope with the idea of getting up onstage."

"Onstage?" a man asked. He polished off his pint in three deep gulps, then made a dash for the exit. Harry glanced at Sima, but when she shrugged, he let the man go.

"There are plenty of others," she said. "Technically you won't even have to stand on a stage. You can sit down the whole time. It's just a little panel discussion."

"A panel discussion!" someone else blurted out. He too would have bolted if it wasn't for Harry grabbing his collar.

"For God's sake, Sima. You're scaring them," said Eleanor. "Who the hell wants to take part in a panel discussion?"

Several people nodded nervously.

"All we're really going to do is sit here in the pub and play a prank on a few Londoners," Eleanor assured them. "That's not so bad, is it?"

Several people began to look interested, albeit reluctantly, and Harry quickly poured more pints.

Mr. Carew, from the antiques shop, and Mrs. Pearce, from the village's only remaining clothes shop, came into the pub together, though it was hard to see them under their enormous heaps of clothing.

"I ransacked my private collection," Mr. Carew explained. His offering consisted of tweed and black turtlenecks, and Mrs. Pearce seemed to have brought all the black clothes she could find: jeans, T-shirts, and blazers.

"Try to look sort of…deep and complex," Sima directed them. She'd printed out photographs of their authors and was now walking in front on the volunteers comparing them to the photos. "Stroke your chin and make it seem like you're thinking something smart. Maybe gaze off into the distance? Look intellectual. *Intellectual*, not constipated."

"Same thing," said Eleanor.

"Thank you, that's enough for now," said Sima, and the lucky ones who hadn't been selected hurried away.

Sima gave the printouts to the local hairdresser, who got to work cutting and dyeing the fake authors' hair in the pub toilets. Eleanor grinned from ear to ear as her hair was being done.

Once they were all ready, Harry set up a camera to take some new photos for the website. Sima then left the two volunteers in Eleanor's hands for their first coaching session.

"I've done a lot of—amateur theater, shall we say?—in the past," she said. "We'll give you a few lines to use if you get stuck, but otherwise you should feel free to improvise. Don't worry. I'll teach you what to do. First things first: relax. Shake your shoulders a little. Have a sip of beer." She gave them both an encouraging smile. "We're here to have fun."

Over by the bar, Berit was watching them work. She was still convinced the plan was a terrible idea, but she couldn't quite bring herself to leave. Something, possibly her innate fondness for watching and observing—or maybe it was her writer's enthusiasm for absurd situations—meant she couldn't tear her eyes away.

Sima came over. "Is what we're doing really so bad?" she asked.

"You're deceiving people."

"They're coming here to have a good time, and we'll show them a good time. Everyone will be happy; I promise you."

Just because people don't know they're being duped doesn't make it right, Berit thought.

"No one is getting hurt, not really," Sima continued. "The people coming here can afford it, and I'll make sure they all enjoy themselves. I mean, just look at how much effort we're putting into this. Everyone is working so hard to make sure the festivalgoers will have the best possible experience."

That was true, but it really only made things worse. Imagine what they could have achieved if they channeled all this enthusiasm and creative energy into something genuine instead, thought Berit.

"You make up things yourself, in your books," Sima pointed out.

"That's different. The reader knows it's fiction. This is like making things up and telling everyone it's a true story."

"People do that all the time. You know, like the movies. *Based on a true story*, it says, but everyone knows they've made a lot of it up. Just think of this as…as a bit of dramatic license, if you will."

Eleanor's coaching session was still underway at a table nearby. "No con artist has ever had their cover blown by saying too little," she said. "If at any point you're not sure what to say, just lean back and look brooding. And if all else fails, just take a sip of beer to win some time, and I'll rescue you."

"I'll be drinking beer nonstop then," said their would-be Ian Rankin. His hair had been dyed dark brown and combed forward into a fringe.

"It's not right," Berit said firmly. "The truth still matters."

She studied Sima. There was no sign of the nervousness or anxiety she had glimpsed earlier. The younger woman's eyes were shining, her posture upright and confident.

She's happy, thought Berit. Maybe a big challenge was what she had been looking for all along.

"Why did you come to Great Diddling?" she asked.

"Have you ever lost yourself?" Sima asked in response.

"Yes," said Berit. "It's easily done if you're not careful."

"I guess it happens to everyone at some stage. You know, you get a new job, start hanging out with new people, and that means you have to buy new clothes, get a new haircut—a new style to match your new dreams, you know? But then you wake up six months later and realize you no longer know who you are."

"You got lucky," said Berit. "Some people lose their entire lives that way and only realize it when it's much too late."

"Well, I didn't feel lucky. But I picked myself up, and I regrouped. It's what you have to do, right? Start over someplace else. Try again."

But picked yourself up from what? Berit thought.

"What's your opinion about Reginald Trent?" she asked.

"I didn't know him," Sima answered quickly.

Too quickly.

"You met the man. He interrupted your tourist board meeting, and you saw him again at the tea party. The entire village was in an uproar about him. You must have formed an opinion."

"He was someone who thought his privilege made him untouchable." Sima seemed surprised by her answer, though she made no attempt to take it back.

"He always got away with things," she continued. She sounded disapproving yet fascinated, as though it was a phenomenon she had spent a good deal of time trying to understand without ever quite managing. "Not just because he was rich or had the right contacts, education, and background, but because of the person he was. He thought he was untouchable, which meant he was. I don't know if it's down to pride or shamelessness, but the rest of us can't do that. We get sent down for the most minor of crimes, while people like him always come through completely unscathed."

"Until he didn't," Berit pointed out.

"Maybe justice caught up with him in the end," said Sima, looking away. It didn't sound like she had the highest opinion of the justice system.

Berit found herself thinking about the way people generalized based on their own experience, and she took out her notepad and wrote, Has Sima committed a crime? Then she took out her phone and texted DCI Ahmed the same question.

Sima was right about one thing, though, Berit thought as she headed home. *The festival was good for the village. There was a palpable sense of anticipation hanging over the entire High Street.*

All over Great Diddling, people were talking excitedly about the festivalgoers who would soon arrive en masse, and in several buildings she passed, the washing machines whirred nonstop as their owners laundered sheets and towels for use in their new guest rooms. Floors were being vacuumed and washed, and guest bedrooms were inspected with pride, nerves, or nonchalance, depending on the host's personality.

The air was warm and heavy with the scent of all the flowers that had been planted outside every shop, the streets were swept, and the windows were sparkling.

At the hotel, several windows were open, and she could hear Penny's voice barking out orders over the roar of the vacuum cleaner inside, swearing as the through breeze made doors slam. The front door to the hotel was wide open to let in light and fresh air.

Berit almost walked straight into a man in a white linen suit. He was standing right in front of the hotel, gazing intently at the open doors ahead of him. For some reason, he reminded her of an actor as he was preparing to play a part. Even when he was at rest, his body seemed primed to react to the next cue.

A vain man, thought Berit. Tall, well dressed, and with a hint of foundation visible on top of his perma-tan.

Without warning, his face broke into a charming smile, his eyes glittering. His teeth were white without being too white, his body confident and lithe.

He walked in through the open doors, straight over to the reception desk. The room was deserted.

Berit heard a series of soft thuds and expletives from the floor above and saw the man's smile falter as he peered around the empty room. She craned her neck to see better.

"They're vacuuming," she called out from the doorway.

"Aha." He gave her a quick glance over his shoulder, dismissed her as unimportant, and relaxed his face again. Berit liked it better without the excessive charm.

After a few minutes, a young girl came through to reception. She was flushed and sweaty, her expression disapproving and her eyes slightly jittery.

"Yeah?" she said in greeting.

The man's smile burst to life again, and he regained the glimmer in his eye. He gave her an old-fashioned bow, which brought a tired smile to the receptionist's face.

"Sorry," she mumbled. "We're busy cleaning. How can I help you?"

"My name," said the man, "is Gerald Corduroy-Smith. I'd like a room." Berit froze.

"Uh, we're fully booked. Haven't you heard? There's a book festival in the village."

He held out his business card. "Please tell the owners that I'd like to talk to them. About a mutual acquaintance who recently passed away."

23

DCI AHMED PUT THE PHONE down.

He had just spoken to the acting agency Gerald Corduroy-Smith had used to hire Alec Rushford. They confirmed that Corduroy-Smith had filled in their web form, claiming to represent a small, independent theater group that was looking for someone to help with a short-term production. Mr. Corduroy-Smith had agreed to their minimum fee, and Alec Rushford had been chosen on the basis of the criteria provided by him. The agency did nothing more than put the two in touch (for a small commission, of course). No one at the agency had actually spoken to Mr. Corduroy-Smith, but that wasn't at all unusual. Everything was done via the website nowadays.

DCI Ahmed was still thinking about precisely what criteria Alec Rushford could have fulfilled when DS Stevens opened the door.

"The author just called," he said. "Berit Gardner. She couldn't get through to you, so she tried the general tip line instead. She said we should go to the hotel right now because Gerald Corduroy-Smith is checking in there at this very moment."

The hotel was already fully booked, but Gerald Corduroy-Smith had been given room twenty-three, the girl behind the reception desk explained to the detectives. That was probably because he seemed to know the owner, she added helpfully.

Mr. Corduroy-Smith himself was just as helpful when he opened the door to his room. DCI Ahmed introduced himself and DS Stevens, and both men held up their ID, but he got the sense that Corduroy-Smith had known they were police officers from the moment they knocked on the door.

"This room is much too small for three," Mr. Corduroy-Smith decided, stepping out into the corridor and closing the door behind him. "But I'm sure the dining room is quiet at this time of day."

He led them back down to reception, pausing briefly to chat with the receptionist. Before long, they were sitting at a table in the dining room. Gerald Corduroy-Smith offered the detectives coffee as though he was their host, but they both declined. He shrugged and ordered himself a cappuccino.

Anyone who saw them would assume that he was the one leading the meeting, DCI Ahmed thought. Mr. Corduroy-Smith seemed perfectly at ease. Clearly not the sort of man who lost his composure easily.

He was wearing a sharp linen suit, a pale-blue shirt, and a Panama hat, his deep tan like an added accessory. His eyes were unnaturally blue, and DCI Ahmed wondered whether he gave nature a helping hand with tinted lenses.

Gerald Corduroy-Smith studied them as openly as they studied him. He smiled amusedly at Stevens's clear irritation, looked at DCI Ahmed with something verging on respect, and then seemed to decide that Stevens was probably his best bet for an ally.

With an open, respectful face, he nodded solemnly and said, "So, how can I help you, officers?"

Stevens reacted instinctively to the solicitous tone. The worst of his irritation drained away. His body language relaxed. DCI Ahmed was fairly sure that the man opposite them noticed the change.

"We'd like to talk to you in connection with the murder of Reginald Trent," said DCI Ahmed. "I understand you were in business with him?"

"I hoped to be, but the idiot went and got himself killed before we had time."

Stevens tensed up again.

"How unfortunate," Ahmed said drily.

"Very." Gerald Corduroy-Smith held up his hands. "Forgive me, but I still don't quite understand why you're here. It isn't against the law to express an interest in buying a couple of properties, is it?"

"You hired an actor to pretend to drop his wallet," said DCI Ahmed.

Gerald shrugged. "That's not a crime either. It was my money, my wallet. If I want to pretend to drop it—or get someone else to drop it for me—then surely that's my right?"

He gave Stevens an open, questioning glance, and the sergeant actually nodded before he could stop himself.

"How well did you know Reginald Trent?" asked DCI Ahmed.

"Not especially well."

"How did you meet him?"

Another shrug. "We had mutual friends, I suppose. I don't really recall at the moment. But that's usually the way, isn't it? You know someone who knows someone."

"We've been trying to get hold of you for some time, Mr. Corduroy-Smith," DCI Ahmed said.

"Well, I had no idea. I try not to watch the news. It's all so depressing these days, don't you think?" He turned to Stevens again. "Makes you wonder where this country is going."

Stevens nodded eagerly.

"Well, unless there was anything else, gentlemen?" Gerald got to his feet, and Stevens automatically did the same. He then had to hover uncomfortably as DCI Ahmed remained seated, eventually slumping back down into his chair as Gerald stood in front of them.

"When was the last time you spoke to Mr. Trent?" asked DCI Ahmed.

"God, how am I supposed to know that? The Friday? Or Saturday? I assume you have his call logs."

"We do. In fact, he called you every day while he was here in Great Diddling."

"The man was homesick; he was never happy here. All he wanted was to moan about everything." Gerald smiled. "And to tell me some juicy gossip about the locals. Perhaps you should be focusing on them instead?"

"Care to elaborate?"

"Ah, but that would spoil the fun."

"The last time he called you was at 3:07 p.m. on the Sunday."

"You see? You knew the answer all along. Well done, you!"

"Ten minutes before he died."

Gerald's smile faltered. "That had nothing to do with me," he said. "And let me tell you, whoever killed him did me no favor. All the time and effort I spent positioning myself clo…bringing about certain negotiations with him. Gone up in smoke! At least, I assume there was some smoke? In the explosion, I mean?"

"Whoever killed him didn't exactly do Mr. Trent a favor either," Ahmed pointed out.

"Well, I can tell you one person who was happy about it," Gerald said. "A woman on the council. What's her name…S-something."

"Sima Kumar?"

"That's the one. Reginald had something on her. He was always talking about it, how he had a hold over a local politician. She'd do whatever he wanted; that's what he said. Perhaps you should be talking to her rather than harassing an innocent citizen."

DCI Ahmed picked up his phone and called the helpful Somalian couple from the hotel in London. Their unsettled bill was one thing he could help with, if nothing else.

"Did Mr. Corduroy-Smith ever reappear to pay the bill?" he asked, looking right at Gerald. His face was completely relaxed, smiling serenely in a way that made DCI Ahmed want to slap him.

"It's funny you called today, of all days," the hotel owners said over the phone. "His card was declined, so at first we were obviously worried. We thought…well, we were afraid Mr. Gerald had tricked us."

"You don't say."

"But it was all just a misunderstanding."

"Oh?"

"He came back yesterday and explained everything."

"And paid?"

"That too."

"Do you know where Mr. Corduroy-Smith was on the evening of Thursday, May 9?"

"Yes, he was here. He ate dinner with us at seven o'clock that evening. He often does."

"And what about that weekend? Was he still with you? Even on the Sunday?"

"He was here for breakfast and dinner, though he often goes out during the day."

Gerald held out his hands, the very picture of innocence. "There we are then, gentlemen," he said pleasantly. "Everything cleared up, I hope?"

"Don't leave the village," DCI Ahmed said. "I'm sure we'll have more questions for you in due course."

"Leave the village? I wouldn't dream of it. After all, I'm only just getting started."

That unnerved DCI Ahmed more than he cared to admit.

Liam had been sent to Truro to do a big shop for all the new B&Bs in Great Diddling, and Sally had gone with him. His Vauxhall Cavalier was packed full of bags, boxes, and bales of toilet roll, and in the footwell in front of Sally, there were several four-pint bottles of milk. Her feet were resting on top of them, which meant her knees kept knocking against the glove compartment.

Through the window, she watched as the pretty green fields raced by. The hedgerows and grass verges were studded with wildflowers, and Sally felt happy, elated, and free in a way she had never felt around anyone else before.

She found herself wondering whether some of Liam's irreverence had rubbed off on her.

"What are we going to do with all this stuff?" she asked. "Until Thursday, I mean."

Liam shrugged. "Hand it out to the new landlords. If they don't have space for it, they'll have to put it in a neighbor's fridge or something. The list of the B&Bs is in the glove compartment."

Sally leaned forward and opened it, rummaging through the petrol station receipts, sunglasses, and broken pens, until she eventually found a sheet of paper with a list of names and addresses written on it. As she pulled it out, she realized there were actually two sheets. A second, crumpled piece of paper was clinging to the back of the list, and Sally wouldn't have paid any attention to it if the word *alibi* hadn't leapt right out at her.

Out of sheer reflex, she glanced down at the bottom of the page. The name *Eleanor* had been signed in a dramatic flourish at the end of the message, which was short and concise.

> *You can't say you were at our place on Thursday evening, but if you need help with an alibi I can sort one out for you. Everything will be OK. They can't prove a thing.*
>
> *Eleanor*

"You find it?" Liam asked, his eyes on the road.

Sally quickly crumpled the note from Eleanor and shoved it into her jacket pocket.

"Yeah," she said, waving the list in the air. Her voice sounded strange, but Liam didn't seem to notice.

24

SALLY SPENT THE REST OF the day in her room, staring at the scrap of paper.

Berit popped her head around the door at lunchtime to ask whether she would like any soup, but when Sally shook her head, she left her in peace.

Around five, she heard Berit leaving the cottage. Sally snuck down to the kitchen and threw the scrap of paper into the bin.

Then she dug it back out again.

What if someone, either Berit or the police, went through the rubbish and found it there? They would know that Liam and Eleanor had been up to something, and they would know that she, Sally, had helped them.

Before she knew what she was doing, she had torn the piece of paper into tiny pieces.

Could she burn them? No, the smoke would be as suspicious as the note itself. One of the nosy neighbors on either side could notice.

She shoved the pieces of paper into her pocket and left the cottage.

All over High Street, preparation for the big day tomorrow was in full swing. Sally made sure to look to both sides before dropping some pieces in the first bin she saw. Then she continued down the streets, dropping a couple into every bin she passed. Once she had gotten rid of the last one, she turned around and hurried home.

Right, she thought. She had done it. There was no turning back now.

Berit ordered a beer, choose a place in the back of the pub, and took out her notepad.

Harry was rushing around, lifting all of the empty chairs up onto the tables so that he could clean the floor. He snapped at the regulars to get out of the way, for God's sake, but when he got to Berit, he was much more polite, asking whether she wouldn't mind lifting her feet, just for a second or two, if it wasn't too much trouble.

Berit swung her feet up onto the chair in front of her, and Harry poured an entire bucket of warm soapy water onto the floor.

The festival would begin tomorrow.

Sima appeared in the doorway carrying a number of large, unwieldy rolls, so long that they were dragging on the floor behind her. She deftly dodged the wet sections of floor, talking to someone on a Bluetooth headset.

"Yes, mysterious murder in an idyllic setting; that's right. No, obviously we can't guarantee the killer won't strike again… Yes, the police are doing fantastic work. DCI Barnaby himself couldn't do a better job."

Harry's eyes followed Sima as she crossed the pub. But there was more to it than that, thought Berit. Even when he wasn't looking at her, he always seemed to know exactly where Sima was. And when he spoke to her, his face lit up. Whenever she smiled, it was like someone had flicked the switch and brought him to life.

There was something grotesque about the contrast between infatuation and murder. As though they shouldn't be allowed to exist at the same time—or in the same place. And yet Berit knew that few things were more of an aphrodisiac than danger and being in close proximity to death. Countless people had fallen in love during the Blitz.

Harry climbed up onto a chair to help Sima with the banners, but he was so focused on her that he didn't even bother to make sure they were straight. The first of them was now hanging at a jaunty angle above the bar:

GREAT DIDDLING BOOK AND MURDER FESTIVAL!

Berit fought the urge to get up and straighten it. She was filled with foreboding. Gerald's sudden arrival on the scene had made her even more anxious. Things were brewing, and she couldn't shake the feeling that she saw too little and understood even less about the things that were going on around her. The notepad in front of her was filled with thoughts, associations, ideas, and questions, but she lacked clarity. She lacked overview.

And tomorrow the festival would begin.

Everything is spiraling out of control, she thought, and she suddenly wondered if the murderer felt the same way. They couldn't have predicted how the village would use their handiwork to revive tourism, could they? How would they react to it?

Crazy or smart, she thought. And then: *What if it's* both?

Harry clambered up onto the table beside Berit's to fasten the second banner to the ceiling, and this time, she couldn't help herself. She got up onto another of the tables and grabbed the other end to make sure it hung straight.

Not until she got down was she able to make out the text.

NO ONE IS SAFE!

25

THE FIRST VEHICLES IN THE convoy appeared just after four o'clock on Thursday afternoon. Sima hadn't wasted any money on hiring buses to transport the guests from the train station. Instead, she had roped the locals into helping out. She shepherded the visitors from the train station into the waiting transportation and sent them on their way to Great Diddling, where the villagers were waiting eagerly to get a glimpse of them.

The first person to get back to Great Diddling was a pensioner by the name of Arthur, who had decided to use his motorcycle. So the first visitor to Great Diddling's Book and Murder Festival arrived in a cramped sidecar, wearing a helmet that was too small for him and clutching his suitcase on his lap.

After that, the guests began to arrive thick and fast. Some of them did come by bus: an ancient thing, bought by a local enthusiast from the Truro city council, which carried eighty festivalgoers. The rest rode into Great Diddling in everything from estate cars and Volkswagen camper vans full of fishing tackle to an old American sports car that was otherwise only used for weddings.

Some ended up at the wrong houses, one person who wasn't going to the festival had gotten caught up in the excitement and accidentally gotten off the train early instead of continuing to Penzance, and one visitor was left behind at the station after going off to find the toilet, but that was nothing Sima couldn't solve.

"At least no one got chucked off the train," she said to Harry, though far too many of the visitors had joked that they should have taken the 4:50 from Paddington instead. "I just hope they like their rooms."

"Don't worry," he replied. "You've done a brilliant job. They're going to love everything."

Three streets away, one of the hosts sent a silent prayer to whoever might be listening that the lady standing in front of her would enjoy staying in her home.

The guest—a short, determined woman—was currently casting a critical eye around the room. There were crocheted cloths on every surface—including the top of the TV—and a number of framed embroideries hung on the walls.

"My mother loved crafts," the host apologized.

The house was a typical two-up, two-down with a small kitchen and living room on the ground floor and two small bedrooms on either side of the stairs on the second. The spare room where the guest would be sleeping was simply furnished, with a bookshelf, a small armchair, a bed, and a nightstand. And a crocheted bedspread, of course.

The woman nodded. "This will do just fine."

"Will it? I mean, that's wonderful." The host set the woman's suitcase down on the bed and then tried to reverse out of the room without bumping into either her guest or any of the furniture. "If there's anything else you need... Tea! Would you like tea? We could have a nice cup in the living room, unless you'd rather...I often drink it in the kitchen, you see."

"Please, in a little while. In the kitchen. And then you can tell me all about this horrid murder."

"Yes, of course."

In another of the improvised bed-and-breakfasts, the hostess had opened up her best guest room to an out-of-towner, but not—as she kept insisting—because she needed the money, no. She had done it because she wanted to help show what Great Diddling had to offer. She had been looking forward to lively chats over tea and biscuits in the living room, maybe even a nice walk together, a chance for her guest to stretch her legs after the long journey, while she pointed out all the sights.

But so far, their conversation had gone roughly as follows:

Guest: "What a beautiful room, thank you."

Her: "Please just let me know if there's anything you need."

Guest: "No, thank you. This will do nicely."

Her: "Maybe an extra blanket? It's a little warmer here than in London, but it can get chilly at night."

Guest: "Oh, no, there's no need."

Her: "Are you hungry? Shall I make a pot of tea?"

Guest: "No, thank you. I'm fine."

Her: "Biscuits? A little sherry? A sandwich?"

The guest had then lifted her suitcase onto the bed and patted it with a manicured hand. "I have everything I need right here."

If she hadn't known better, the hostess would have said that her guest had practically ushered her out.

Finally.

The woman closed the door on her chatty hostess and pushed a chair beneath the handle to make sure she wouldn't be disturbed.

She immediately got to work unpacking her bags, spreading everything out on the bed. The entire Bridgerton series, plus several novels by Alisha Rai. A couple of new gems she hadn't read yet, and what she hoped would be a charming story about a first son of the U.S. falling in love with an English prince.

There was a bag of truffle-flavor crisps in there too, plus a box of Swiss pralines, a jar of her favorite marmalade, a pack of crackers, twenty individually wrapped shortbreads, some Hobnobs, chocolate digestives, and two boxes of Cadbury's fingers. In the very bottom of her bag, she also had a kettle and a stash of Earl Grey tea bags.

She had let the battery on her phone run right down and had no intention of charging it again before she went home.

The woman lay down on her back, reaching for a book with one hand and the bag of crisps with the other, using her teeth to tear it open.

"'Chapter 1,'" she read. "'The Bridgertons are by far the most prolific family in the upper echelons of society…'"

The mirror was small, old, and grimy, with a thick gilded frame. It seemed to Margaret that there was more gold leaf and ornamentation than actual mirror. Perhaps that was why Daphne had chosen it, she thought cynically. The older woman wasn't so keen on seeing her own reflection these days.

The glass was so dull with dirt and age that the image in it was blurred and hazy. All Margaret could see was a wavy figure with long, straight, silvery hair framing a fuzzy, pink oval where her face should have been. Daphne's reflection felt timeless and ethereal, delicate and brittle somehow, as though the being in the mirror could fade to nothing at any moment.

In the right light—or possibly the right mirror—and in her own head, Daphne was still a young woman, thought Margaret.

She studied the person in front of the mirror instead. It was the middle of the afternoon, but Daphne was still in her dressing gown. They were in her bedroom, where a heap of rejected clothing had been dumped on the enormous four-poster bed.

"A man by the name of Gerald Corduroy-Smith has called several times," said Margaret.

Daphne waved dismissively. "I don't have time," she replied, holding up a silk dress in a shimmering, dusty-pink color. "This shade is a little drab, don't you think?"

"He said he was a good friend of your nephew's."

"Then I definitely don't have time for him. Can you believe that

Margaret Atwood is coming to Great Diddling! Why didn't anyone tell me? You know, we've actually already met once before. I wonder if she remembers me?"

Margaret flinched. "You know that Margaret Atwood isn't really going to be there tonight, don't you? It's some sort of trick. Or a joke."

"Well, whatever it is, I want to see it. I've heard that hundreds of book-lovers are already here—in my little village! Who would have thought it?"

"I wonder what they're hoping to achieve," said Margaret.

"Dior or Chanel? Nothing feels right... We need something cheery for the occasion. I feel like a bit of color, something lively and dramatic! Christian Lacroix, perhaps?"

"Are you sure you don't just want to have dinner here, like usual? It's Thursday, which means fish. And then a spot of poetry in the library? You'll enjoy that."

"Don't be ridiculous. I've no intention of missing this. Whatever happens this evening, we'll be right there in the front row. Relax, Margaret. Live a little. Maybe even smarten yourself up a bit...?"

DCI Ahmed erased the bullet point asking where Gerald Corduroy-Smith was from the list of things they didn't know and added instead:

What is Gerald Corduroy-Smith after?

Outside of the conference room, evening was falling. There were no windows, but he felt it anyway, in the tiredness of his body and the way the automatic lights in the hallway dimmed until someone walked by. Fewer and fewer walked by. The police station never truly slept, but at night, it... rested, Ahmed thought.

"Money," said Rogers. "It's always money."

"Which begs the question of why he would go to Great Diddling now. He must know that Reginald Trent's money is lost to him. Why risk being dragged into a murder inquiry?"

"Maybe he's planning to pull off the same scam on someone else?" Stevens suggested.

"But who?" asked Rogers. "No one in Great Diddling has any money. Not even Daphne Trent."

"Especially not her," muttered Stevens. "She spends it all on books."

"OK, let's start from the beginning," said DCI Ahmed. "What do we know about him?"

Rogers took his words literally. "He was born as plain old Gerald Smith in Liverpool in 1967. His father was in and out of jail, and his mother was an alcoholic who died young. Gerald was put into care at the age of seven, and he left when he was fourteen."

"Great childhood," Stevens muttered.

"After that, there's a blank until the late eighties, when he was convicted of fraud. A classic romance scam. Charmed a lonely woman, took all her savings. He was later investigated for credit card fraud and, interestingly, several online scams."

"A man who moves with the times," DCI Ahmed said drily.

"He did his last stretch inside in the early 2000s, and since then, his name hasn't cropped up in any more investigations."

"So he's managed to fly under the radar somehow, but I think we can probably assume that whatever he's been up to isn't exactly aboveboard. Fast-forward to the present, when he somehow manages to make contact with Reginald Trent and decides to scam him. We agree that he was his target, don't we?"

The others nodded.

"He practically admitted it," said Stevens.

"As part of his scam, he comes up with a fictional financial genius called Raglan Harris, and he hires an actor to play him."

"What I don't understand is why they bothered going through the whole charade of dropping a wallet and letting Reginald find it," said Stevens. "What did they get out of that?"

"It's an old fraudster's trick," DCI Ahmed explained. His former professor had specialized in the psychology of fraud and why people fall for it. "One of the easiest ways of gaining someone's trust is getting them to do you a favor. We're all much more willing to help someone we've already helped once. It's as though we think that because we've helped them before, they must be worth it."

"I think there was another dimension to it too," Rogers spoke up, a note of cynicism in her voice. "I'd bet you anything that wallet was stuffed full of exclusive bank cards. An Amex Black Card or a JP Morgan Reserve Card, maybe even a Coutts Silk Card. An easy way to let Reginald Trent know that Raglan Harris is the real deal, and all incredibly easy to fake. The cards don't even need to work. They just need to look good."

DCI Ahmed nodded. "OK, so everything goes to plan; he reels Reginald Trent in and sends him to Great Diddling. For some reason the scam seems to have hinged on him going there."

"That makes no sense to me either," said Stevens. "What could Corduroy-Smith possibly want there?"

Neither of the others had a good answer.

"Let's put a pin in that for now," said DCI Ahmed. "OK, scenario one: Reginald cottons onto the scam and threatens to cause a scandal or go to the police."

"Unlikely," said Rogers. "Reginald Trent doesn't sound like someone who would willingly admit he'd been duped. He probably wouldn't even admit it to himself."

"Trent could've turned violent rather than threatening with the police," Stevens suggested. "Maybe he threatened to kill Corduroy-Smith. And so, out of self-defense—"

"Corduroy-Smith breaks into the construction firm's cabin, steals the explosives, waits two days, and then plants a bomb?" Rogers sounded skeptical.

"No, it doesn't add up," DCI Ahmed agreed. "And have you thought about the way he behaved around us? He didn't seem the least bit worried. His instinct is to talk his way out of difficult situations. If he felt trapped, I think he would rely on quick thinking rather than violence. I could maybe imagine him killing in self-defense if he panicked, but even that feels like a bit of a stretch. If Reginald Trent had worked out what he was doing, don't you think Corduroy-Smith would have just laughed it off and acted like it was nothing? He's definitely brazen enough to be able to talk his way out of most things."

Without thinking, DCI Ahmed took a sip of the cold, bitter tea in the old cup. He pulled a face. Stevens cleared away as many of the dirty mugs as he could carry and returned with three fresh cups.

DCI Ahmed took a new sip. "And don't forget that Corduroy-Smith has an alibi for the evening when the explosives were stolen," he continued. "If he ate dinner in London, he could hardly have driven the whole way to Great Diddling in time to break in between nine and eleven." He thought for a moment. "But I still think we should check the CCTV cameras near the hotel in London on Sunday anyway. Try to find out when he left the hotel and when he got back, just in case he had time to attend the tea party."

Stevens jotted everything down.

"That still leaves us with the question of why he's in Great Diddling now," DCI Ahmed went on. "What could he be after there, even though Reginald Trent is dead?"

No one spoke.

"And was Reginald Trent killed because of whatever Gerald is looking for?"

Again, no one replied. Ian Ahmed rubbed his weary eyes. He tried a new line of thought. "Do you think...do you think he could have gone to the village for the book festival? Maybe that's why he's there?"

His words were met with complete silence.

"It's the only thing I could think of that was different," Ahmed said. "Since the murder, I mean. He stayed away, then the book festival got lots of attention, and he turns up there."

"It's not quite the only thing that's happened," said Rogers. "Four people also confessed to the murder."

26

BERIT HEARD THE MURMUR FROM the Queen's Head, Arms, and Legs from the other end of High Street, and as she got closer, she saw clusters of smartly dressed people all heading in the same direction.

It must be a long time since Great Diddling's favorite pub was last so busy, she thought. *And there has probably never been this many women inside.*

Berit noted with amusement that a fair few festivalgoers had arrived at the venue in good time, and the mood was already cheerful and expectant. Behind the bar, the extra staff was struggling to quench the booklovers' thirst.

Everyone looked up when Gerald Corduroy-Smith came in, and not just because he was one of only a handful of men inside. *Here is someone who knows how to make an entrance,* thought Berit. Even Daphne, who was no stranger to a bit of drama herself, turned to watch him.

He was wearing a pale-gray double-breasted suit with wide lapels and had a hat perched jauntily on his head, and yet somehow—even with the cane in his hand—he managed to make the whole outfit look perfectly normal. He paused just inside the door to soak up the attention of everyone in the pub.

And to take everything in, thought Berit, at least judging by the way his eyes quickly swept the room. Not counting herself, she had only seen two

other people scan their surroundings in that way since she arrived in Great
Diddling: DCI Ahmed and Eleanor Hartfield.

The regulars made way for Gerald Corduroy-Smith as he strode over to
the bar. They recognized a spectacle when they saw one.

"Champagne. A bottle of your best champagne, barkeep!" he said loud
enough for half the room to hear. He then studied the teenager behind
the bar and added, "In an ice bucket. Lots of ice. There is nothing more
depressing than lukewarm champagne."

The young bartender muttered something inaudible and looked
all around. The only bucket of any description was red and plastic. He
shrugged, filled it with a few heaped scoops of ice, and drove the bottle
down into it.

"Oh well," said Gerald. "So long as it's cold, dry, and free."

"No chance," said the bartender, setting the bucket down on the counter with one hand and pointing to the price on the till with the other.

Gerald reluctantly held out his card. The transaction seemed to bother
him, but perhaps he just wasn't used to actually having to pay for things,
thought Berit.

He grabbed the plastic bucket in one hand and three champagne flutes
in the other and then marched straight over to Daphne's table as though he
was confident he would be welcome there. He gave her the same strange
bow Berit had seen at the hotel.

"Gerald Corduroy-Smith, at your service, Ms. Trent," he said.
"Champagne?"

Daphne clapped her hands in delight and took the glass he held out
to her. She and Gerald drank with the same relish, Berit noticed, whereas
Margaret sipped her champagne as though it were water—with little enjoy-
ment and no interest.

Berit discreetly moved closer to their table in order to eavesdrop on
their conversation.

"As I told your secretary," Gerald began, flashing Margaret a dark look,
"I knew your nephew, Reginald."

It was plain to anyone with a pair of functioning eyes that Daphne had
no interest in this particular topic of conversation. Her gaze began to drift

around the room, looking in every direction but Gerald's. Still, she was drinking his champagne. It was a remarkably effective anchor, a bottle of champagne.

"Perhaps we could arrange a meeting for another time, somewhere a little less busy?" he asked eagerly. "Tomorrow, for example. Reginald told me about your book collection, and I—"

"I highly doubt that." Daphne was still stubbornly staring at the festivalgoers. "The only books he cared about were his account books."

"Reginald said—"

"My nephew is dead, Mr. Corduroy-Smith. Perhaps we could let him rest in peace, at least for this evening?"

"I could come over tomorrow and—"

"Tomorrow? No, I'm afraid that just isn't possible. The book festival will continue all weekend." She gazed around with a thrilled expression on her face. "Isn't it fantastic? So many booklovers, together in one place."

And it really was an enchanted evening, Berit thought. She had been to several literary festivals but not one quite like this. Everyone looked like they were in the beginning of an adventure. They seemed to feel instinctively that they were amongst friends, surrounded by other booklovers, more than willing to be charmed and entertained.

With one exception, Berit noticed. The faux Ian Rankin was standing in the dark hallway by the kitchen, bracing himself against the wall and looking green around the gills.

"Jesus Christ, no one said there'd be so many people," he mumbled. "I can't do it, I…"

Harry slapped the back of his head. "Pull yourself together, man. Don't make me tell Sima you're refusing to do as you're told."

"I don't know which is worse, all those people or Sima."

"Trust me, it's Sima."

Berit wasn't sure Harry would have been able to convince the reluctant Mr. Rankin if it wasn't for the fact that Sima had just stepped up onto the stage. The spotlight was on her, and everyone fell quiet.

The book festival had begun.

Sima looked stunning in her stiletto heels, jeans, bright-red suede jacket, and matching lipstick. Everyone's eyes were drawn to her on the stage, and the authors who would be taking part in the panel seemed pale and colorless in comparison.

Berit wondered what could be behind the councillor's striking new style, but then she realized that although Sima had gone through her entire welcome speech, she still had no real idea what Ian Rankin or Elly Griffiths looked like. It was as though Sima's lipstick and jacket deliberately stole the focus from the authors. That was probably just as well, because Ian Rankin looked like he was about to pass out with nerves, and Elly Griffiths was waving cheerily to a young woman at the back of the pub.

Only Margaret Atwood seemed relaxed.

Four chairs had been set out in a line, with a small table in front of them. There were three pints of beer on the table, and Ian Rankin had already drunk half of his.

The panel had been painstakingly prepared, each equipped with a printout of real quotes from the authors they were pretending to be, and they had been styled to look as similar to them as possible. Of the three, Eleanor's Margaret Atwood was most impressive. Her gray hair had been thinned and curled, dyed bright white and ruffled and sprayed so as to look like the famous author. She was wearing a black silk blouse, a black blazer, and a blue scarf.

She's even picked up the scarf trick, Berit thought. It had taken her several years to learn it herself.

Sima turned to Eleanor first. "Margaret Atwood, tell us: What are you hoping to achieve through your stories?"

"I'd like to be the air that inhabits you for a brief moment in time," Eleanor replied, perfectly capturing Atwood's drawly, North American voice. She gazed off into the distance and dreamily raised one hand. "That's how invisible I want to be, how vital."

Several heads nodded in the audience.

It wasn't just the scarf, thought Berit. Eleanor's version of Atwood radiated something cultured and hard to grasp. Her gaze was piercing, as though she could see something others couldn't. There was a slight hint of amusement on her lips, the corners of her mouth curling upward a fraction, and a glimmer in her eye that somehow showed she didn't take herself too seriously.

She's better at playing the part of an author than I am, thought Berit.

"What about you, Ian Rankin?" asked Sima. "How do you like being an author?"

The local Ian Rankin blinked repeatedly in panic. His sheet of quotes was lying forgotten on the table in front of him, and he drank two deep gulps of his beer in an attempt to win himself more time.

"I once read that you said you would rather be a rock star than an author. Is that true?" asked Sima.

The absurdity of her question seemed to loosen his tongue.

"Well, yeah. Obviously…" he said, as though he didn't understand. "I mean, doesn't everyone wish they were a rock star? Surely there's no one who would rather be a writer than David Bowie?"

Sima quickly turned away from him. "Elly Griffiths, what do you say?"

The woman pretending to be Elly Griffiths looked down at her sheet of paper, desperately searching for a reply among the selected quotations.

"Your lead character, the forensic archaeologist Ruth Galloway, is beloved by hundreds of thousands of people all over the world," Sima continued hastily. "Tell us about your interest in archaeology."

"Yes, ah, well, I've always been fascinated by it. Mud and old bones and that sort of thing. Like the girl from *Bones*, right?" She turned suddenly toward the audience: "Here's a bit of free advice for you: don't eat your supper while you're watching that show. There's always a disgusting corpse within the first ten minutes, right when you're sitting there with your fish and chips."

Several people nodded emphatically. Sima seemed to decide to focus on her strongest card.

"Margaret, what advice would you give to any would-be authors?"

"People today are so focused on being seen and heard and showing off their lives," Eleanor replied calmly and thoughtfully without even looking at her cheat sheet, "but I think there's a certain freedom in living on the margins, in the invisible gap between stories."

"Any advice on how to handle rejection letters?"

Eleanor's eyes shone. "*Nolite te bastardes carborundorum,*" she said, translating the famous line from *The Handmaid's Tale* for the audience: "Don't let the bastards grind you down."

Everyone laughed.

Berit looked around the room. It really seemed like Sima and Eleanor would pull the whole thing off. Several members of the audience were gazing at Ian Rankin with something verging on motherly fondness, others looking up at Margaret Atwood with admiration. One woman nearby turned to her neighbor and said:

"Elly Griffiths is totally right about *Bones.*"

And in the middle of them all: Gerald, flashing his charming smile at anyone who met his eye. He'd only been there since yesterday, and he was already sitting there with Daphne and Margaret, a fox in the henhouse. He was watching the stage with an amused, smug look on his face.

But a short, stubborn-looking woman in the front row caught Berit's eye. She was frowning as she looked down on her phone, and then up again at the people on stage.

Sima had been smart enough to avoid inviting audience questions, and she rounded off the panel discussion by urging everyone in the pub to stay for a while, mingle, order a drink at the bar, chat books, and get to know one another. The fake authors from Great Diddling breathed a collective sigh of relief at having made it through the panel.

The audience began to break up, with some deciding to call it a night and others making a beeline for the bar. Ian Rankin was at the head of the rush.

"He seems to make friends quickly," the woman from the front row muttered to Berit as three of the regulars surrounded him, thumping him on the shoulder and buying him drinks.

"Well, you know what they say, a true booklover is never alone," Berit replied.

The woman was a head shorter than everyone else in the audience, but she was also standing so straight that Berit got the sense she was determined not to have to look up at anyone. A strong brow, thrust forward, as though she was always ready to march into the next battle.

"You know, I listened to Margaret Atwood once. In London. She seems...different, somehow."

"People change," Berit said.

"Something about her voice..."

"A bit of a cold, perhaps?"

"Perhaps," the woman acknowledged. But she kept glancing over at Margaret Atwood as she sipped her sherry. "So what made you come to the festival?" she asked.

"Ah, I live here." Berit held out a hand. "Berit Gardner."

The woman gave her a skeptical look. "Of course you are. And my name is Knausgård."

27

ELEANOR'S EYES SNAPPED OPEN. EVEN in the middle of the night, fast asleep after an intense evening, her senses were still on high alert.

Something is wrong, she thought.

She sniffed the air. Coffee. And toast.

Beside her, Mary stirred.

"Wait here," Eleanor whispered. She got out of bed without a sound, pulling on her dressing gown and reaching for the antique letter opener that Mary kept on her bedside table. That was one of the best things about antiques—people often forgot that even beautiful, old objects could be lethal.

Eleanor followed the scent of coffee, gripping the handle of the knife tight as she weighed up her options.

The fact that someone had made coffee probably meant she was in no imminent physical danger, so the first thing she did was to try to force herself to relax. Whoever had broken in clearly wanted them to know he or she was there—and wanted their knowing it to unsettle them. Better not to give them that satisfaction, she decided.

Eleanor rolled her shoulders until they were as loose as her aging joints would allow, pulled the dressing gown tighter around her waist, and forced her face into a surprised smile before strolling nonchalantly into the bright kitchen, as though there was nothing out of the ordinary about someone turning up to make themselves breakfast at the crack of dawn.

The stylish man from the pub was sitting at the kitchen table with one of Mary's delicate floral cups and a full pot of coffee in front of him, plus a plate of toast.

Eleanor reached for another cup, sat down opposite him, and poured herself some coffee.

"Always good to meet someone else who prefers coffee in the morning," she said. It was strong, hot, and utterly vital. She could feel the weight of the letter opener ready and waiting in her pocket.

"Nice kitchen you've got," the man replied in such a warm tone that Eleanor automatically understood the implied threat: It'd be a shame if anything was to happen to it.

He laughed. "Relax, I'm just messing with you." He introduced himself with a flourish and a little bow.

Eleanor nodded hesitantly and sipped her coffee. "Have we met?"

"Not quite. I showed up a week after you left. In Malaga. We had mutual friends there. The Hutchleys. They showed me their collection of Spanish impressionists. Very impressive work."

Eleanor tensed and then forced herself to relax. "Thanks," she said. "So to what do I owe the honor?"

"We're practically colleagues, you and I," Gerald explained. "I have to say, it was a bit of a setback to show up in Malaga and find you'd already plucked them. After you were through with them, they weren't about to fall for a second scheme."

"Small world," Eleanor said. "So do you specialize?"

"Oh, a bit of this, a bit of that," Gerald said. "I had a great thing planned with Reginald. Until it all went to shit."

Eleanor shrugged. "Some jobs do." She briefly considered coming straight out and asking him what he was doing in her kitchen, but she restrained herself. The advantage of letting someone else lead the conversation was that you could learn a lot from the things they chose to talk about.

Gerald pulled a face. "Damn idiot, getting himself killed like that."

"Amateurish," Eleanor agreed.

Gerald reached into his inside pocket and pulled out a newspaper cutting. It was from one of the local papers at some point in the nineties, yellowed and fragile with age. "Eclectic book collection in Cornwall" was the headline of the article. The collection boasted a Charles Dickens, a Jane Austen, and a signed Oscar Wilde, the last with a personal greeting from the author himself to the current owner's grandfather, the article said, and included a photo of the young and stylish Wilde.

Eleanor's heart began to race as she read the famous names, and she felt her cheeks flush with excitement.

"Interesting, huh?" Gerald said. "I saw this clipping years ago, and I haven't been able to stop thinking about it since. But until I met Reginald, I didn't have any way in. My target is the Oscar Wilde, by the way. And any other valuable books I'm able to lay my hands on."

Eleanor looked up at him with a furrowed brow. It was never a good sign when someone volunteered information like this.

"Why are you showing me this?" she asked.

"Because you're going to help me. Reginald's death threw a wrench in the works. I had to stay away. There's something extremely frightening about getting caught up in a murder inquiry. The police's net can so easily snare fish they're not trying to catch."

"For all I know, you're the one who killed Reginald."

Gerald looked irritated. "Don't be ridiculous," he said. "I needed him alive. In any case, I'd just made up my mind to forget all about the books—or at least hold off for the time being—when I read the news about the confessions. Nice work, by the way. But risky, of course. I recognized you from Spain. And then there was the book festival. Things are starting to look up. The only thing I need to do now is get Daphne Trent to like me. Shouldn't be so difficult. Reginald said she was practically senile."

"No," said Eleanor. "Afraid not."

He shrugged. "No, that's not the feeling I got either. I need to find a way to ingratiate myself. Any advice?"

"Look, we're retired," Eleanor said. "We don't do this sort of job anymore."

"It's not a job. Think of it as a favor, colleague to colleague. I need information. I've tried to charm my way in with Daphne, but every time I mention her nephew—respectfully, I might add—it's as though she just shuts me out."

Eleanor laughed. "OK, well you can have this for free: she hated the man. You'll have far more success if you insult him."

Gerald studied her with a look of interest on his face. "Is that so?" he said. "That's good to know. You see, I knew it was the right decision to come here."

Eleanor didn't say anything.

"I love the setup you've got here," Gerald continued. "Sisters' Café. It's like a magician's distraction technique. Priceless. You were cousins in Spain, weren't you? Have you really found an outlet for your talents here? I mean, Great Diddling isn't exactly a big place. Or are you just waiting for the right opportunity?"

"Like I said, we are retired."

He looked at her sharply. "And see that you stay that way. Or all your new friends and neighbors might find out that the kindly old ladies who run the sweet little café are a couple of international fraudsters who have been conning people for decades on at least three continents. What do you think they would have to say about that?"

Eleanor forced herself to shrug, feigning nonchalance. "They can say what they like. We're not suspected of anything. A bit of gossip can't hurt us."

"Not if you're prepared to move, that's true. But are you? It seems to me like you've made yourselves quite at home here. And once a person is stationary, gossip very much can hurt them."

Gerald got up. "Well, I'm sure we don't have to continue on the tedious, tedious topic of threats."

"No."

"If you have any idea about stealing the books yourself, I seriously advise you to drop them."

28

THE WOMAN SMOOTHED OUT THE crocheted bedspread and looked down at the cup of tea on the nightstand. Her hostess had brought it up earlier, mumbling something about breakfast being served in the kitchen whenever she wanted it before shuffling off again.

Sweet but scatterbrained, thought the woman.

It had been a good evening yesterday, and everyone had had fun. In fact, it was the liveliest first evening she'd ever had at a literary festival. It hadn't been awkward or uncomfortable, and the fact that everything was gathered in one place meant no one had had to worry about missing anything or waver over which events to attend.

The evening hadn't been without its funny sides either. She thought back to the so-called Margaret Atwood drinking beer and telling tall tales to a group of women from Edinburgh and couldn't help but laugh.

Still, once you started to indulge lies, there was no telling where it might end. And the fact of the matter was that they had taken money for this charade. That made it fraud.

Technically speaking.

The scent of fried bacon and toast drifted up from the kitchen. She would decide what she was going to do after breakfast, she thought.

The woman had a quick shower, got dressed, and headed downstairs.

"Just one slice of toast for me, please," she said, taking a seat at the table. Her hostess set down another mug of tea in front of her.

"This Sima woman," she began, "is she the one in charge around here?"

"Oh, yes, Sima is always in charge of everything."

"What's her actual job? Is she the head of the festival? Some sort of politician?"

"I...don't know exactly. I think she's part of the council. Chair, maybe? Either way, she's really shaken things up 'round here. Are you sure I can't tempt you with a little bacon? It's cooked and ready."

"OK, maybe one rasher," said the woman. "So how is she earning money from this? Does she take a share of the profits or something? Or does she get paid a steady wage?"

"Oh, no, I don't think she's earning anything from the festival. How could she? None of us ever does."

"I thought this was the first one?"

"The first time it's been about books, yes. Last year it was birds. I'm so glad they picked books this year! You booklovers are much more fun than the bird-watchers—and there are so many more of you!"

The woman decided that her hostess was more than a little scatterbrained.

Right then, an unpleasant thought struck her.

"But surely you must be getting some money?"

She had paid the full fee to the festival organizers on the assumption that it would be used to pay the locals who were hosting the visitors and everything else included in the program.

Her hostess glanced around in an almost guilty manner, then leaned in toward her.

"Oh, yes," she whispered, "I'm getting two hundred pounds. Can you imagine! And I don't even have to cover the breakfast costs. They came over yesterday with all the supplies, including these sweet little jars of marmalade." She held one up. "Are you sure you don't want some scrambled eggs? It'll only take me a few minutes."

The woman did some quick calculations and decided that the organizers had been surprisingly generous. The ticket price was low—that was why she had decided to give the festival a chance, despite the short notice—and it seemed like most of the fee had gone toward food and lodging.

She sipped her tea and tried to ignore her hostess's chitchat. Why go to all this effort to lure tourists to the village only to give half of the money to the bed-and-breakfast hosts? What did Sima get out of this?

The woman didn't know, but she planned to find out.

She smiled. There was a delicious irony in playing detective at a festival dedicated to books and murder.

Sima had assumed that anyone who chose to attend a literature festival must like reading, and so she had filled one of the gaps in the program with the suitably vague "free reading time."

The whole morning had been set aside for reading, and the program made several suggestions as to where the festivalgoers could go for lunch. A few hosts had offered to help out with that, both out of a sense of hospitality and in exchange for a small fee. As a result, Sima thought she still had time to try to plan something for that afternoon—the so-called "Book-related activity" promised in the program—and work out what the hell she was going to do for tomorrow's "surprise."

Without warning, however, a short, stern-looking woman appeared in front of her.

"Excuse me," said the woman.

"I beg your pardon?" Sima struggled to maintain her professional smile.

"It's all a bluff." The woman's tone wasn't quite as aggressive as her posture, but it was firm. "All this." She waved her hand.

"High Street?" Sima asked, her eyes widening in surprise. "I assure you, it's very much real."

"The festival. The authors. All of it. I just saw Margaret Atwood drinking beer in the pub, and it's not even one o'clock!"

"Ah, yes, well, you know what they say. It's five o'clock somewhere…"

"And your Ian Rankin is cutting the grass outside one of the houses."

"What can I say? Such a sweet, *helpful* man…"

"The woman who lived there called him lazy and inept and accused him of wanting to sneak off to the pub again."

"Yes, well, can you blame him? Margaret Atwood is there! Naturally he wants to spend time with such a distinguished colleague."

The woman's face had turned an alarming shade of red, but then she laughed suddenly, seemingly against her will.

"You're quick; I'll give you that," she said appreciatively. "But it's still fraud. I could report you to the police. I'm sure they'd be interested."

"No!" Sima blurted out, before quickly composing herself and continuing in a more restrained voice: "We didn't mean any harm. We just had so little time to plan things, and no actual authors were willing to attend. I don't know what they do all day, but they're clearly very busy. So we... well, we improvised. But you're going to love the surprise we have in store for you; I promise. Just give us a chance to put everything right and you'll still get the festival you've been hoping for. What do you have to lose? It's a beautiful day. Why not sit down in the sun and read for a while?"

"Mmm, I suppose I did just get here," the woman conceded. "And it is always a pain to have to pack again so soon." She thought for a moment. "Fine. You can have until tomorrow. But if I'm not happy, I want my money back, and I can guarantee I won't be the only one. You should be grateful I haven't already reported the lot of you."

Sima nodded eagerly. "Tomorrow," she said. "You won't be disappointed."

The minute the woman was out of earshot, Sima dug out her phone.

"Harry?" she said, sounding stressed. "Get everyone together. Our cover's blown. I'll be at the pub in ten."

The lunch rush was still in full swing when Berit got there. Daphne and Margaret were there, without Gerald this time, and Berit couldn't quite explain why that came as such a relief to her.

Eleanor ordered herself another beer, but Berit decided to stick to coffee.

Penny hopped up onto a barstool beside them and said, "I can't stay long, need to help tidy up after lunch. It's been nonstop—not just hotel guests but other festivalgoers too." She glanced up at the clock above the bar. "I can spare half an hour, though. Harry, give me a beer. Quick."

Sima didn't waste any time getting to the point. She recapped everything the brusque woman had said and repeated her ultimatum.

"The woman is giving us a chance at the very least," said Sima. "Though it's definitely a long shot. But she seems like a natural leader, which means people will listen to her. If she's happy, they will be too. But if we're going to impress her, we'll have to make sure the rest of festival is fantastic, and we'll have to do it without any more lies."

Silence settled over the room.

After a moment, Penny said what everyone was thinking: "So we're screwed?"

"We could take the money and run," said Eleanor, though when she saw the others' faces she added, "No, no. Of course we can't. Just kidding."

"We still have the surprise in store," said Harry. "The big surprise tomorrow? If we could just hold them off until then…"

"There's no surprise." Sima lowered her face to her hands. "It was just something I wrote. I thought I would be able to come up with something, but I…I haven't gotten that far yet."

Berit had been sitting quietly so far, but she took a sip of coffee and spoke up.

"You can still do this. You just need to focus on what you actually have rather than lying the whole time."

"But we don't have any authors," said Penny.

"Authors are only one part of a literary festival. Personally, I've always found us to be quite overrated. Why are the guests always forced to sit and listen while we drone on? Anything interesting a writer has to say is already in their books; give other people a chance to talk! Or to read."

"For two whole days?" Sima seemed skeptical.

"I've got a few ideas," said Berit, holding out a list to the council leader. "Can you get me this?"

Sima skimmed through it, and Berit saw her brain making quick calculations about availability, time, and people. "I think so," she said. "Yes, I should be able to manage all of it."

"Would anyone like to tell me what the hell is going on here?" asked Penny.

"I've got an idea about how we can get a few more book-related things to happen around the village," said Berit.

"The signs might be a bit tricky," said Sima, "but I'm sure we can do it. Phil, the carpenter, owes me a favor, and his wife is renting out two rooms to guests. She doesn't want to have to pay that money back any more than we do. Phil can do the woodwork, but we'll need a few volunteers to help paint them. Where are we going to get the books, though?"

The two women's eyes drifted over to Daphne's table.

"She'll never agree to it," said Sima.

"I think she will. I'll talk to her and remind her that books are meant to be read. They want to be loved. God knows she has enough books in that house."

A smile began to spread across Sima's face.

"It'll be tough, but I think it could work. We should print out a program to hand out before breakfast tomorrow."

"It's gonna take a lot of cleaning," Berit warned.

"The cleaning won't be a problem," Sima reassured her.

"The only thing I haven't worked out is what we're going to do with them today. We're going to need time to prepare."

"Easy," said Sima. "We can ship them off to Daphne du Maurier's house after lunch."

Penny looked up from her beer. "Can she really handle so many guests at such short notice?" she asked.

"They'll get to see the real-life Manderley, and then they can walk around Fowey and experience an authentic Cornish coastal village. Considering how many books have been written about places like that, it's practically a book-related activity in and of itself. They can stop off in St. Austell for dinner on the way home. It'll cost a bit to hire the buses, but it'll be worth it if it means they're out of our hair for the rest of the day. I'll call Ravi at the bus company."

She grabbed her phone right away, and a few hours later, the festival-goers were being herded onto three buses.

Each one had two representatives from Great Diddling on board, there to take the guests on a guided tour of Cornwall. No one had prepared any sort of script for them to follow, which meant improvisations all around. One of the volunteers pointed out all the best fishing spots, another where her father had proposed to her mother. On the third bus, the tourists got to hear all about the local flora and fauna.

"Right," Sima said once they had driven away. "Finally, a bit of peace and quiet."

She turned to the villagers who had gathered.

"What are you waiting for?" she demanded. "Get to work!"

One visitor did not board any of the buses.

When everyone else had gathered on the outskirts of the village, she had slipped quietly away, evading all her hostess's attempts to convince her to go. Once the coast was clear, she made her way over to the café and ordered an enormous chocolate muffin and a large cup of tea. She then set down three books on the table in front of her, opened one of them, and started reading.

When her tea grew cold, she ordered more hot water, and once her chocolate muffin was gone, she bought a cream cake. When she reached the end of the first book, she opened the second.

As a result, she paid no attention to the white van driving back and forth between Tawny Hall and the village all afternoon. It parked outside one shop after another, unloading multiple boxes, then headed back out to the grand house to pick up yet another load.

The sudden sound of saws and hammers didn't seem to bother her either, and if anyone had asked her afterward, she probably wouldn't have even noticed that half the village seemed to be taking their books for a walk.

29

PENNY HAD ONLY AGREED TO help clean the library at Tawny Hall because she wanted to get away from the hotel—and from James. Things were so tense and awkward between them that she had been on the verge of smashing a few plates just to let out some steam.

Despite that, she already regretted saying yes.

The library was a large, beautiful room, but it was also full of books. There were several sofas and armchairs, yet ironically there was nowhere to actually sit; the books were piled high on every available surface.

It was also desperately in need of dusting and vacuuming, scrubbing and airing. The black-and-white floor needed to be polished, but again that was tricky because there were yet more stacks of books on the ground.

"Christ, it's like someone has eaten the color," Penny whispered to Eleanor, glumly studying the piles of dark-green, brown, black, and gray spines bound in dusty, faded fabric.

The whole room smelled like old paper too. Like the school library had while it was still existed—but worse. At least some of the books there had been new, and the space behind the shelves in the natural sciences section had been perfect for making out. No one ever disturbed you there.

Penny touched one of the books and immediately wiped her grubby fingertips on her top.

"I didn't realize books could be so dull," she said. "No, I did know, but I guess I'd forgotten. It's been a long time since I last saw so many of them in one place. Honestly, who even has books these days?"

Eleanor didn't reply, and Penny gave her a jab in the ribs.

"Huh?" said Eleanor, looking up from the books in the cabinet in front of her. Something strange seemed to have happened to her eyes. They were all watery and distant. Her voice sounded different too. "Biggles."

"What?"

"I loved these books when I was little. Biggles is the reason I got my pilot's license."

"Eleanor, focus!"

"Yes. Right. Of course."

But she didn't move away from the cabinet, still staring down at the signed title page in *Biggles Flies West*.

Gerald would never manage to find the book without help, Eleanor thought as she looked around the library. That gave her a sense of schadenfreude, but she didn't feel the usual satisfaction; he might not find it, but neither would she.

It was impossible.

Not that she necessarily even wanted to steal the books. She hadn't made up her mind yet. She just liked to keep her options open.

Eleanor took out her phone, double-checked that no one could see what she was doing, and then Googled *Jane Austen + first edition + value*.

She whistled to herself. Who knew there even were book nerds with that much money? It just went to show that what Mary had always said was true: there were rich collectors everywhere. Rich, gullible collectors.

Eleanor felt her heart rate pick up again, the familiar excitement at the prospect of a new adventure. Perhaps this was the job that could change everything?

The next one always was.

Berit sniffed the air. It smelled like dust and paper, like forgotten adventures that had been biding their time until they got the chance to sneak up on new readers.

There were stacks of books everywhere at Tawny Hall, including the four bathrooms. The guest rooms might be riddled with damp, but the books had been stored in boxes and were broadly in good condition. The pages of some were a little crinkled, having been in the basement during a flood, but many of them were still readable, which meant they could be used after all. Nothing was thrown out.

Berit had volunteered to lead the effort to get the books down to the village. Margaret was helping too, albeit extremely reluctantly. Her face wasn't openly disapproving—she had far too much self-control for that—but she did look slightly doubtful about the whole project.

Still, disapproving or not, she directed the others with her usual brusque efficiency. Several other villagers had turned up with mops, buckets, and other cleaning products, and Margaret told them where to get water before helping Daphne decide which books she could consider parting with.

At first, Daphne had insisted on approving every single book herself, but she quickly began waving through entire boxes at a time. Their enthusiasm and eagerness seemed to have rubbed off on her, and she proved unexpectedly generous, even with the signed first editions.

"Oh, I loved this one," she said, stroking the cover of a Neil Gaiman book, "but it's probably time it found a new owner who will love it just as much."

She fondly lowered it into a box containing several signed Danielle Steeles. After staring at the gaudy eighties' covers for a moment, she had to blink several times, as though she had accidentally looked directly at the sun.

A while later, she peered down into the cabinet of Dick Francis books.

"My second husband loved Dick Francis," she said. "He claimed he was the only author who really wrote about physical pain. Bruises and broken bones. If the hero got hurt, he felt it. Francis had such a knack for describing the way a bruise changed color over the course of several days. I suppose his time as a jockey had taught him a thing or two about that."

Daphne transferred several of them to the box Margaret was holding.

"Just imagine the pleasure someone will feel if they discover one of their favorites!" she said. "Who could have guessed it would be so fun to give away books? Books really are the best gift. I can't understand why I've spent so long giving people flowers."

She looked briefly at a signed first edition of Agatha Christie, then that too ended up in the box.

Berit and Margaret began loading the boxes into a white van from town. Both quickly grew hot and sweaty in the warm sunshine.

"I can't believe you actually managed to convince her," said Margaret. "Daphne has only grown more and more protective of her books over the years, and yet she's letting you take all these books from Tawny Hall. Actually letting you take them away."

"She wants them to be appreciated," said Berit.

"Yes, maybe…I just hope she doesn't regret it."

They made their way back into the library, pausing in the doorway to watch the others at work cleaning it.

"They're fooling themselves if they think it's going to last," Margaret said suddenly.

"What is?"

"Everything. This, the festival, everyone being such chums all of a sudden. They might be friends now, but one tiny bump in the road is all it takes to drive them apart again."

Berit watched Penny and Eleanor dusting bookshelves together. Mary was drifting around the room with a smile on her face, polishing things at random.

"Do you think so?" she asked.

"Friendship never lasts," said Margaret. "No one likes to admit it, but the truth is that we're all alone. The best way to protect yourself is to avoid making the mistake of relying on anyone. In the end, we only have ourselves."

"And then we die?"

"That too." Margaret picked up a box. "I know what you're thinking. You think I've got a dark, antisocial outlook on life and other people, but I don't. Not at all. There's real freedom in giving up any expectations of other people. It's like…like a whole new world opens up inside you, and you realize that you're far bigger than you thought. We limit ourselves when we cling to things or people."

"This should liberate Daphne nicely, then," Berit said.

Margaret looked doubtful. "Yes, well, some people aren't ready to be free."

They broke for tea just after six, and everyone gathered in the library. Berit felt pleasantly warm and weary after a few hours of hard, physical labor. The french doors onto the terrace had been flung open, and the air smelled like spring and furniture polish.

She took a cup over to Daphne, who was following the work from her chaise longue. With a book in her lap and beautiful twilight outside, she looked happy, carefree, satisfied. As though she didn't have a worry in the world now that her nephew was dead.

Berit was acutely aware that she didn't want to think about the murder. She liked Daphne. If the older woman had killed her nephew, then she must have been seriously provoked.

But questions had to be asked.

Just look at them, said a stubborn voice in Berit's head. Penny and Eleanor were at the far end of the room, each holding a teacup and a mop. In the corridors behind them, Mary kept darting about in the shadows, searching for beautiful objects to dust. She had a plate of biscuits in one hand and a feather duster in the other.

Aren't they all happier now that Reginald is gone? the voice continued. If a man lives his life in such a way that an entire village rejoices when he dies, can you really blame anyone for being tempted to solve all their problems in one fell swoop?

Berit hesitated. "Daphne, can I ask what you were reading the Thursday before…before the tea party. Do you remember?"

"Of course. Thursday is poetry night. I was reading Linton Kwesi Johnson's *Selected Poems*. The very next day I started with *The Woman in Cabin 10* by Ruth Ware. It's so gripping I can hardly put it down, even though life has been getting in the way of my reading lately." She looked around the upheaval in the library with a certain amusement. "And it seems it will continue to do so!"

This time, Gerald Corduroy-Smith's entrance was so discreet that for a moment or two, Berit was the only person who noticed him. He quietly pushed open one of the double doors and slipped into the room, taking a deep breath as he stopped to look around. Berit got the sense that she was witnessing a private moment. His face looked so open—reverent, almost—as he turned around and took in all the bookshelves.

"Remarkable," he said, causing the others to turn their heads.

Berit thought she caught him glancing over to Eleanor, but she struggled to read the look he gave her. It seemed to be somewhere between a question and a warning.

He then turned to Daphne and said, "Your nephew was a boor and a fool with absolutely no taste or manners, but he did lead me here, and for that I will forever be grateful."

Daphne gazed at him with far more goodwill than she had the evening before.

"How did he do that?" Berit asked.

Gerald stared at her, confused. "Do what?"

"Lead you here. Why *are* you here?"

"He mentioned Ms. Trent's book collection, of course, though it pains me to say that he didn't appreciate it as he ought. He was only ever interested in what they were worth. As if you could put a prize on such a literary treasure!"

Daphne beamed at him, and he hurried over to her side, clasping her hand in his. "He told me that you had a signed first edition of Oscar Wilde's *The Importance of Being Earnest*, and I simply must see it. Please tell me that I may," he implored, fixing his eyes on her with boyish excitement.

Daphne nodded. Strong feelings for books was clearly something she understood.

Margaret left the room and returned a short while later with a box. She handed the contents over to Daphne, who walked slowly toward the middle of the room with a small, ordinary-looking book resting in her palms.

Gerald moved toward Daphne, and Mary popped up behind him as though drawn in. Berit realized that she had started to move closer herself, as had Eleanor, until they all ended up in a semicircle around the little book. Even Penny joined in, completing the circle.

Gerald couldn't tear his eyes away from the book. His pupils widened, and he gasped. If he was a poker player, thought Berit, he would have lost right there and then. He swallowed and reached out, quickly pulling his hand back and looking up at Daphne.

"May I…?"

She nodded, and as she held out the book to him, he pulled a pair of white cotton gloves from his pocket and put them on.

The book was bound in pale purple fabric, with gilded text on the spine and a pretty floral pattern on the front.

"This was his last great play," said Gerald. Berit wasn't sure who he was talking to. Himself, perhaps. "It opened to great fanfare on Valentine's Day 1895 but closed following his failed libel case against the Marquess of Queensbury. Wilde's complete and utter fall from grace—not to mention his prison sentence—meant it wasn't published in book form until 1899, after his release. If I'm not mistaken, this is one of just a hundred copies of the first edition. Smithers and Company's publication earned Wilde a little money, just when he needed it the most. He still had a few friends left—and your grandfather seems to have been one of them," he added with a slight bow to Daphne.

Gerald stroked the book, studying it with a strange mix of desire and criticism. Like a man who was in love yet trying to find fault with his beloved, thought Berit. A collector's trait, no doubt. Everything had to be assessed. Good condition. Very good condition. Like new.

"Exquisite," said Gerald. "Just one small blemish on this corner and certain signs of rough treatment on the spine." It sounded as though he thought it was a shame the book had ever been opened. "But other than that: fantastic."

Ideally, of course, it shouldn't have been read at all. A very strange attitude to take about a book, in Berit's opinion.

Gerald dragged it out for as long as he could, but in the end he had no choice but to give the book back to Daphne.

She passed it on to Berit.

It was an odd feeling, to touch something that Oscar Wilde himself had once held. Berit was no collector, so she didn't share Gerald's fascination with rare limited editions. She didn't even feel the historian's interest in objects that were contemporaneous with the period they studied. It didn't matter to her that the book had existed at the same time as the author. In her eyes, Victorian society had taken a free-thinking genius and sentenced him to hard labor. They didn't deserve him. Why should a popular, new edition be worth any less? In fact, she found it encouraging that people still loved Oscar Wilde's books enough to keep printing them in large numbers over a hundred years later. Viewed from that angle, new editions were actually more inspiring. Hardbacks with dust jackets, case laminates, paperbacks, audiobooks—surely they were just as valuable as this pale little thing?

And yet...when she gently opened the cover and actually saw Oscar Wilde's handwriting inside, she couldn't help but be affected by it. His words, written by his very own hand. His writing almost looked like it had been drawn with a brush. Rounded and soft, airy, with plenty of space between the letters and words.

Thank you for a wonderful night took up almost the entire page, followed by his first name in lowercase letters. It wasn't until he got to his surname that he had really shown any flourishes. The *W* was a little larger and slightly more elaborate, and by the time he got to the *e*, he had given it a surprisingly wild and free final flick.

Berit passed the book on to Mary, who studied it with almost as much enthusiasm as Gerald, though Berit was fairly sure she didn't share his or Daphne's interest in books. Not unless they were old, beautiful, and extremely valuable, of course.

Gerald watched as the book moved around the circle. He looked tense and uncomfortable every time a new person took it, possibly because their less-worthy hands were carrying it farther and farther away from him.

"How much is it worth?" Penny asked once her turn came around.

Gerald looked like he wanted to snatch it from her. "Worth!" he snarled. "It's priceless!"

He watched with obvious reluctance as the book was returned to its box. Daphne handed it to Margaret, who took it away. To Berit, it looked as though his eyes were burning holes in the back of her head.

With that, they got back to cleaning.

Eleanor's eyes darted around the room. She was just about to tuck *Biggles: The Camels Are Coming* inside her jacket when she sensed someone come up behind her. She flinched and put the book back.

"Oh, it's just you," she said when she realized it was Penny. Eleanor looked down at the book again, then decided this wasn't the right moment.

"I hate dust," Penny muttered.

"Hmm. What?"

"Dust. All this. I hate it. God knows I do enough cleaning at the hotel."

Eleanor peered around to make sure that Gerald hadn't reappeared. He had hung around Daphne, not helping out with the cleaning, of course, but directing all his energies to charming her into inviting him to tomorrow's party. As soon as he succeeded, he excused himself and left, casting a warning glance at Eleanor on his way out.

He's going to try to use the party to steal the book, Eleanor thought.

If she was to get her hands on it, she would have to do it before then.

Eleanor looked around again, to check that Mary was nowhere nearby this time. She wasn't sure how her wife would feel about her plans to steal from someone in Great Diddling. Mary had developed such strange feelings for the village lately.

"Can I ask you something?" Eleanor turned to Penny, keeping her voice low. "The festival, will it be enough to save the hotel?"

"I don't know."

Eleanor grabbed her arm. "We need to think bigger," she said. "We need to dream big. We need to seize the opportunity when we see it. We need to rob the library."

"You're out of your mind."

"Probably, but it would definitely bring in money. We could split it evenly. Fifty-fifty, as they say. I've done a bit of research. These books are worth *a lot*. And it's not just the Oscar Wilde. She's got a couple of Jane Austens and some Charles Dickenses too…"

"How much are we talking?"

"A signed Oscar Wilde? About fifty grand. A Jane Austen? Even more."

Penny's sudden torrent of expletives made Berit, Margaret, and Daphne turn around with confused looks on their faces.

Eleanor elbowed her in the side.

"Bloody hell," Penny mumbled.

"If the Jane Austen is signed, we're looking at even more. Two, maybe three hundred thousand. Not that we'd be able to sell it for its full market value…"

"Why not?"

"We wouldn't exactly be able to go through the official channels, if you catch my drift. But don't worry. I've got contacts. It's been a while, but I still know how to move something. Your share would be a hundred thousand at the very least. That should be enough to save the hotel—assuming that's what you want. Personally, I don't see the point. Take the money and move somewhere hot; that's my advice."

"This is insane. We can't steal from Daphne."

Eleanor shrugged. "I thought you needed the money."

Penny looked around. "Then again, is she even going to notice if a few books go missing?"

Eleanor gripped her arm. "That's the spirit! But we need to do it soon. Tonight. Are you with me?"

"We can't use my car. It'll attract too much attention."

"Don't worry. I'll come up with something."

30

DCI AHMED RUBBED HIS FACE. It felt as though the stuffy air in the meeting room was clinging to his skin like an oily layer. Beside him, Stevens rolled his shoulders in an attempt to loosen them up.

The leftovers of the kebabs they had eaten for lunch were on the table in front of them, along with a greasy paper bag of Danish pastries and several mugs of cold tea and coffee. At this stage in the investigation, everyone was running on junk food, sugar, and caffeine.

Rogers and Stevens exchanged a glance, then sat down and started going through the documents. An hour later, Stevens called his wife to let her know that he wouldn't be home in time for dinner. Rogers called a local takeaway to order pizza.

DCI Ahmed frowned as he read a sheet of paper.

"What's this?" he asked.

Stevens got up and read over his shoulder. "A reported break-in at 17 Church Lane."

Rogers looked it up in the HOLMES database.

"It's been included because of the link to Liam Slater's alibi. That's Mrs. Ainsley's address. The woman he helped with her computer the evening the explosives were stolen."

DCI Ahmed reached for his phone. He double-checked the name of the police officer who had taken the report, looked up his number, and hit dial.

"I hope I'm not bothering you in the middle of dinner," he said when the man picked up. He heard the sound of a TV, of laughing children, followed by a door being closed. The background noise faded.

"Not at all, sir," the police officer assured him, quickly swallowing the mouthful of food he had clearly been eating in front of the TV.

"I understand you dealt with a reported break-in at the home of one Mrs. Ainsley in Great Diddling?"

"Yes, that's right, but it was nothing much. Nothing was stolen, I mean."

A dead end, in other words, Detective Ahmed thought to himself.

"Then why did she report it?" he asked.

The officer hesitated. "It's kind of ridiculous, but she said someone had broken in and used her tea things. I thought maybe it was a homeless person or something like that, but she said that everything had been washed up properly afterward. Doesn't sound like any homeless person I've ever come across, sir."

"And when was this?"

"That's another thing—she didn't know. She'd been staying with her sister for a month and had just gotten home. I hope I didn't do anything wrong, sir."

"No, not at all. This is extremely helpful. I'll let you get back to your dinner. We'll look into this break-in, I promise you. We'll get to the bottom of Mrs. Ainsley's uninvited guests."

"If you say so, sir," the officer replied, hanging up.

DCI Ahmed already had a sneaking suspicion of who they would turn out to be.

The woman who answered the door at 17 Church Lane looked nothing at all like the person they'd interviewed there earlier. She peered suspiciously at Ian Ahmed and said firmly, "If you're selling something, I'm not interested."

He held up his ID. "I'm Detective Chief Inspector Ian Ahmed from the Devon and Cornwall Police. This is Detective Sergeant Stevens. Sorry to bother you this late at night, but we'd like to ask you a few questions in connection with the break-in you reported earlier today."

She looked surprised but pleased as she opened the door wider to let them in.

The protective cover was gone from the armchair, and the top of the chest of drawers was now cluttered with photographs, a crucifix, several pictures of saints, and a trophy from a riding competition.

This new Mrs. Ainsley managed to find the tea things at her first attempt, taking out three mugs and a tea pot from the right cupboard.

"Sorry if I was a bit brusque earlier," she said, setting down the tray. "I thought you might be door-to-door salesmen. Honestly, I didn't expect anything to happen after I reported the break-in. You hear so much about the police these days, cases being dropped from the very get-go and that sort of thing. Plus, they didn't take anything."

"I understand you've been staying with your daughter for quite some time, Mrs. Ainsley?"

"Yes, not that I liked it. It was a trial run, you see. The plan was that I'd sell the house and move down there for good—her husband's brilliant idea. He's only after my money, I could see that right away. The room they wanted me to live in didn't even have a proper window! And I'd be expected to look after the grandkids all the time. Nice to have company 'at my age,' they said. Well, let me tell you what is nice at my age: peace and quiet."

"Quite right," DCI Ahmed agreed. "So you got home...?"

"Yesterday. Thursday evening. And I knew right away that someone had been here. There was grit on the floor in the hall, and I always give the place a good clean before I go away. And then I noticed a broken window at the back."

Stevens got up and inspected the same window he had attempted to fix on their last visit.

"I understand someone also used your tea things?" said DCI Ahmed.

She nodded. "The kettle, tea pot, mugs, and tray. Everything had been washed up, but they'd put it back in the wrong place."

"But nothing was missing?"

"No," she snapped, seemingly taking his words as criticism. "But it's the principle of the thing. Someone has been inside my home. I don't like it."

DCI Ahmed nodded. "You can rest assured that we're taking this very seriously."

She straightened up with a satisfied look on her face.

"Do you know Liam Slater, Mrs. Ainsley?" he asked.

His question took her by surprise. "I know of him, of course. As one does. It's a small village. But I won't have anything to do with anyone from that family. No good, the lot of them."

"So he hasn't helped you with any computer issues?"

She stared at him. "Computer issues? I've never heard anything more ridiculous in my life! I don't even own a computer. And if I did, I wouldn't let him anywhere near it."

"Thank you," DCI Ahmed said. "We'll put every possible resource into finding out who broke in here, Mrs. Ainsley."

"Well, that's me told!" she exclaimed. "Here I was thinking you didn't care about ordinary folk like me."

31

IT WAS CLOSE TO ELEVEN when the three buses parked up on the edge of the village and the tired but satisfied festivalgoers began to file out. The sun had long since set behind the rosebushes, and several of the tourists shivered in evening chill as they walked along the already-familiar streets to their temporary homes.

Those staying at the hotel made their way straight to the lounge space with its deep, comfortable armchairs. A few ordered one last glass of wine. No one seemed to want the evening to end.

By 2:00 a.m., however, everyone was fast asleep in their beds. The hotel was eerily quiet as Penny snuck out through reception, which meant there was no one around to hear her shout "bloody hell!" as Eleanor appeared out of nowhere on her cargo moped. The older woman was dressed entirely in black, much of her face hidden behind a pair of enormous goggles.

"Hop on," she said quietly.

Penny reluctantly climbed onto the seat behind her. She was freezing already in the cool night air. "I'm not dressed for this," she moaned.

Eleanor reached back with a hip flask. "This might help warm you up a bit."

Penny took a couple of deep swigs and then handed it back. She wrapped her arms around Eleanor's slim waist, and with that they were on their way. The streets were empty, the fields on the edge of the village dark and deserted. The cool breeze made her cheeks ache, but it also felt strangely intoxicating. As though she was breathing in freedom. Penny laughed loudly.

When they turned off onto the little gravel track leading to Tawny Hall, it almost came as a disappointment. She could have kept going forever.

They parked a safe distance from the house and walked the rest of the way. Eleanor stuck to the grass by the side of the track to minimize any noise, and Penny followed in her footsteps.

She glanced up at Tawny Hall. The house towered over them, the doors closed and the windows dark, looking suddenly huge and hostile.

Up ahead, Eleanor was moving through the shadows as though she had been born to do this sort of thing. Somehow she always managed to find the darkest spots, which meant she was practically invisible as she walked. When the moon came out from behind a cloud, she was already pressed up against a tree. Penny followed her clumsily, and as she lifted the sheet of dark plastic that had been taped up over a broken window in the old library, it rustled loudly.

She froze.

"Don't worry," Eleanor whispered. "Old houses are always making noises. If it's not the wind, it's mice or the pipes."

"Or a burglar."

"Let's just hope that's not their first thought. They're guaranteed to have at least one shotgun in a place like this."

Penny moved slowly through the junk the police had left in the bomb-damaged room. She couldn't help but shudder as she made her way into the corridor through the hole in the wall.

Eleanor opened the double doors to the library. Only a few hours had passed since they left, yet the room felt completely different. In the darkness, the bookshelves seemed to loom menacingly over them. The only light was coming from the moon outside, casting a cold, ghostly glow onto the shelves around them.

There was something unsettling about the tall shelves in the strange light. For a split second, it felt as though they were moving, imperceptibly creeping closer behind their backs. As though they were slowly surrounding her. Perhaps they were just waiting for her to lower her guard before they launched themselves at her.

"Don't be ridiculous," she told herself, her voice echoing through her head.

"What did you say?" Penny whispered.

Eleanor blushed at her own weakness. "Nothing," she said. "You start here. I'm going to have a look around."

"Wait!" Penny said. "What if I hear something suspicious, or someone is coming, or …?"

"Hide. Then text me. And for God's sake, make sure your phone is on silent."

Eleanor moved slowly into the corridor, pausing to give her eyes a chance to get used to the darkness. She assumed the bedrooms must be on the floor above. It didn't feel like there were any other living beings down here in any case. Without a sound, Eleanor opened every door she passed, double-checking there were no people or windows in the rooms on the other side before turning on the flashlight on her phone. She quickly scanned each room for valuables, but all she found was junk and dust.

The crazy woman loves her books, she thought. If she kept the most valuable titles somewhere safe, it must still be somewhere she could visit them frequently.

Eleanor paused at the bottom of the stairs, then slowly made her way up, making sure to keep her movements soft and fluid. It was sudden, unexpected sounds that people reacted to, not low, ongoing background noise.

She opened a door and immediately knew there was someone else inside. The room had large windows and thin, billowing curtains. The moonlight spilled across a large four-poster bed in the middle of the room, and she could make out a thin figure lying on their back in it.

Daphne Trent.

Eleanor paused and listened. Daphne's breathing was calm and slow, and so she crept inside, unable to stop herself from grinning like a madwoman. Every one of her senses was refreshingly sharp, and her body felt more supple than it had in years. It must be the adrenaline, she thought, giving her muscles and joints renewed energy and strength.

Christ, she had missed the thrill, the danger.

A bedroom was an excellent place to hide books. Suitably close to hand. It wouldn't have surprised her if Daphne slept with the most valuable titles actually in her bed, like Prince John and his sacks of gold in Disney's *Robin Hood*.

She edged closer. There were no books on the bed in any case. Daphne's breathing was still calm and steady. Eleanor kept smiling as she moved through the room, cautiously opening a door and peering into a wardrobe full of old dresses, pushing a couple to one side to make sure there was nothing hidden behind them. The soft rustling of the silk caused Daphne to roll over in bed.

Eleanor froze, standing perfectly still until she was sure the older woman hadn't woken. She then closed the wardrobe doors and crept out of the room.

Back in the hallway outside, she stood with her ear to the other doors before she opened them, which meant she managed to find Margaret's bedroom without even setting foot inside. She was sure the books wouldn't be there, so she skipped that room and moved on to the next.

Several of the upstairs bedrooms seemed to be entirely unused, and a few of the others were so full of clutter that it was impossible to tell whether the books were inside, though Eleanor doubted it. What each of the rooms had in common was that they felt cold and damp. Surely Daphne would take better care of her valuable books?

The only obvious hiding place in the entire house was the library, thought Eleanor. That was where she would have kept the books, anyway. Hidden in plain sight among all the others. After all, the best place to hide a needle wasn't in a haystack but among other needles. Had Margaret really left the library to fetch the Oscar Wilde book, or was that all just a trick? Maybe it had been there all along.

Eleanor made her way back downstairs, practically scaring the life out of Penny when she reached the library.

"Why didn't you check your phone?!" Penny hissed.

Eleanor dug it out of her pocket. Seventeen messages, all along the lines of *I heard something. Just heard it again. Where are you? Come back now. Heard a sound! No, it was just a branch against the window. HEARD SOMETHING AGAIN!*

"Old houses make noises; I told you."

"This library gives me the creeps."

"Keep looking."

Eleanor climbed one of the ladders, working on the assumption that Daphne and Margaret would want to put the books somewhere they weren't at risk of being spotted by any of the guests, but none of the titles she pulled out seemed any more valuable than the next. They were all old and dusty.

This was ridiculous, she thought. Madness. Insane in the clinical definition of the word. No one person should have this many books.

Right then, Eleanor sneezed so loudly she was sure the sound must have carried to every corner of Tawny Hall. She froze at the top of the ladder, but no one came rushing in to stop her from trying to steal any books—not that it would have mattered if they had because she was never going to find them.

No, that wasn't strictly true. She found plenty of books, just not the right ones.

She climbed back down again, her shoulders and back aching. Daphne's books were heavy. And they were also filthy, despite all their efforts earlier. Beside her, Penny was frantically trying to clean her palms on her trousers.

Eleanor lifted an old book down from the shelf and held it lightly between her fingertips. It looked old, and for a brief moment she thought their luck might be about to change. But no. As she shone her phone light on the cover, she saw that it was written by someone she had never even heard of, Currer Bell.

All around them, the messy piles of books grew as they pulled them down from the shelves to check the title and author, flicking through the first few pages for any dedications before dismissing them and moving on.

Eleanor hadn't realized that books could easily double as oversized dominoes, and if you took out one book, several might topple over. She massaged her arm where a particularly hefty volume had hit her.

It was impossible to know whether any of the books were worth anything. Even when they were signed, you couldn't be sure whether it was by the author or just some random nobody. A book by Helene Hanff, for example, was signed: *To Daphne, from the Duchess of Bloomsbury Street.* Utterly worthless. Everyone knew there was no such thing as a Duchy of Bloomsbury Street.

The only book she found that did actually seem to have a personalized dedication by an author she knew was Harold Robbins's *The Carpetbaggers.* It read as follows: *To my dark-haired beauty, as thanks for many an unforgettable night in Rome—and London, and Paris.*

Eleanor decided to stop reading the dedications after that. By this stage, it wouldn't have surprised her if D. H. Lawrence had been Daphne's gardener.

She closed her eyes, never wanting to see another book in her life.

As she was standing with her eyes shut, she heard the sound of a door opening upstairs.

The two women froze.

"What was that?" Penny hissed.

"Let's go."

They quickly threw the books back onto the shelves, hoping that no one would notice they had been there. Both shoved a few into their bags, but in the darkness and their hurry to leave, they had no idea what they had taken. Moving as quickly as they could, they then made their way out into the corridor, through the hole into the old library, and out into freedom.

They had only just made it outside when the lights in the library came on.

Eleanor dragged Penny deeper into the shadows and clamped a hand over her mouth as Margaret appeared in the doorway. She moved through the room and peered out through the windows. With the lights on, Eleanor knew she wouldn't be able to see anything but her own reflection, but she still couldn't help but tense and hold her breath.

Margaret seemed to realize the flaw in her plan because she switched off the lights and then stood in the darkness, allowing her eyes to acclimate. Through the large windows, Eleanor could see her pale outline in the soft moonlight.

They waited. Penny shifted impatiently. Eleanor knew she was keen to get back to the security of the moped, but she forced her to keep still. Margaret probably couldn't see them, but she would definitely be able to hear them if they started moving too soon.

Eventually, after what felt like an eternity, Margaret seemed to decide that it had all been in her mind. She turned back into the corridor and, Eleanor hoped, headed back up to her room. Luckily for them, her bedroom window was on the other side of the house.

They waited another ten full minutes, and then she finally let Penny move—though she did keep hold of her hand as she led her through the shadows.

Once they were back on the moped, Eleanor drove as slowly as she could down the gravel track, but the sound of the tires on the gravel still echoed through the night.

She was so relieved to finally pull out onto the main road that she almost crashed straight into a car. She swerved, and they went careening into a ditch, tumbling onto the cold ground like a couple of books falling from their shelves.

Eleanor passed the hip flask to Penny. Penny took a couple of swigs before giving it back.

They lay flat out in the damp grass, gazing up at the stars.

"What an evening," said Eleanor and suddenly burst out laughing.

"You can say that again." Penny shook her head and then joined in.

"It's liberating, isn't it? Nothing makes a woman feel more alive than breaking the law and getting away with it."

32

THE WHITE ENVELOPE HAD BEEN standing in the middle of the kitchen table when the resolute woman came down to breakfast, and it was still there now. Thick and inviting, it was leaning against a vase of pretty wildflowers on the middle of a crocheted table runner. As her host prattled on about Rebecca and Manderley, the woman's eye was constantly drawn to the beautiful envelope.

"I've always felt sorry for the second Mrs. de Winter," said her hostess. "Imagine arriving somewhere so hostile, never being able to do anything right—and without even knowing what you've done wrong."

Was it for her? But if so, surely her hostess should have said something?

"I'm not so sure," said the woman. "She's incredibly calm when her husband confesses to murder. Don't you think that suggests a pretty flexible moral code?" It took a real show of strength to tear her eyes away from the envelope. "But I'd love to say a thing or two to the housekeeper. It doesn't matter how young and inexperienced the second Mrs. de Winter is: it's not OK for the housekeeper to be obsessed with her former mistress and mess with the new one. Just one slice of toast for me, please. And maybe a little scrambled egg. Oh, go on, add another egg. Slowly, on a low heat— that's the trick. Add more butter. In the housekeeper's defense, I guess I'd say I don't know whether Mrs. de Winter is entirely innocent. There are some people who always manage to find someone who bosses them around. Leave the tea to steep. No one likes weak tea. And maybe a rasher of bacon, just to keep the eggs company."

At long last, her hostess finally pointed to the envelope across the table. "This is for you."

The woman eagerly tore it open and found a folded sheet of paper inside. In large letters, she read:

WELCOME TO YET ANOTHER GLORIOUS DAY
AT GREAT DIDDLING'S
BOOK AND MURDER FESTIVAL!

10:00—THE BIG SURPRISE
          awaits you on High Street
14:00—Book recommendations and reading
groups
18:00—BALL IN THE LIBRARY AT TAWNY HALL

Just before ten, the festivalgoers gathered on High Street. A number of villagers were also present, spread out along the pavement and leaning nonchalantly against the buildings. They were just as intrigued by the transformation of Great Diddling as the visitors, having seen bookshelves and boxes being lugged around town the day before and the signs put up at the crack of dawn.

Those new signs were now hanging outside every shop, but because the sun was in the crowd's eyes, they couldn't read what they said.

Outside the antiques shop, Mr. Carew couldn't contain himself. He kept popping his graying head outside to see whether or not they were on their way.

By the time Berit arrived, the visitors to the village were standing in line just below the crest of the hill on High Street. They looked like an army waiting to storm the village, and Sima was at their head. She was facing the crowd, the empty street behind her.

Sima tapped her microphone several times, and once the murmur had died down, she said, "As you'll soon see, books have completely taken over our little village. In honor of the festival, we've created not one, not two, not even three bookshops. We've created twenty-seven brand-new bookshops."

The booklovers exchanged glances.

"Feel free to browse the shops in search of inspiration. Buy old and new books at unbeatable prices, and we'll come together later this afternoon to talk about all the incredible titles you've found. Split up into groups and meet in the park, at Sisters' Café, or at the pub, depending on whether you feel like a pint, a scone, or a bit of fresh air."

"I'm for the pub then," someone shouted, making Sima smile.

"Well, it is a beautiful day for it," she said. "And this evening, we've all been invited to a ball in the grand library at Tawny Hall. You'll have a chance to experience a magical space and a legendary book collection. The books you'll find dotted around the village today have all come from Tawny Hall's library and our benefactor, Daphne Trent. Who knows what treasures you might find today? Alongside classics and readers' favorites, there might even be a few valuable signed first editions."

She paused for effect.

"So on behalf of myself and everyone else in the village, welcome to the Great Diddling book hunt!"

She gestured dramatically to the high street behind her, stepping to one side with a hopeful look on her face, almost as though she expected the crowd to charge forward like Americans at a Black Friday sale.

The festivalgoers glanced at one another again. A few craned their necks to see what awaited them, and one brave soul eventually took a step forward, then another. Before long, the others followed.

They moved slowly and hesitantly at first, then slowly and with wonder.

Some chose to start on the left-hand side of the street, which meant that Great Diddling Antiques and Souvenirs was their first port of call. *Affordable Prices—Always! and Books!* boasted the new sign. In the window, there was an Edwardian chair, an elegant mahogany sideboard with florid gold detailing, a pretty Chinese vase, and all of the Stephen Fry books Daphne Trent had donated. The turquoise cover of *Mythos* matched the

Chinese vase, and it had been positioned alongside *Heroes*, with its Grecian figures. There was also a copy of *Making History*, with an image of a dead red rat on the front, matching the red damask that had been draped across one of the small tables.

Mr. Carew stood in the doorway, welcoming people in to browse his pots, garden gnomes, tables, and chairs, plus the latest addition to his shop: four old bookshelves packed full of books. The shelves themselves were also for sale.

Others began on the opposite side of the street, meaning they reached Vivian's Blooms—*and Books!* first. There were a number of beautiful bouquets in the window, bursting with the colors of spring. Vivian had picked out some pretty, old, leather-bound books in earthy tones, providing a nice contrast. A fairly early edition of *The Diary of Samuel Pepys* had been positioned alongside several thin volumes of poetry by Shelley and Keats, and a dull-looking edition of Charles Dickens's collected works provided gravitas and support—quite literally, as several vases had been positioned on top.

The festivalgoers spread out along the street.

The hairdresser, Curl Me Crazy—*and Books!*, didn't typically have any sort of display in the window. Instead, you could see straight through to where the two stylists were at work, cutting, dyeing, and perming hair. The decor was sleek and professional, with faux leather chairs, mirrors, and trolleys containing all the necessary tools to take care of Great Diddling's hair-related needs. Despite that, the owner had gone all-in on the book festival, creating an elaborate display on the theme of books and murder. She had smeared mud and red dye onto a wig to make it look like someone had had their head smashed in, and several pairs of bloody scissors hung on string from the ceiling, dipped in red paint as though they had just been driven into someone's heart.

Death by Scissors wouldn't be a bad name for a book about a murderous hairdresser, Berit thought. *Or a seamstress, for that matter.*

The rest of the high street had been transformed in much the same way. The butcher had a display of crime novels by Stephen King and Val McDermid, and the owner of the clothes shop had taken in all of the Dick Francis books Daphne had donated, plus a number of titles by writers like Graham Greene, Marian Keyes, and Zadie Smith.

At the supermarket, Samson had tried his best to resist being dragged into Sima's project, but eventually even he had been forced to give in. Beside the bags of salt and vinegar crisps, a few books had been stacked on the shelf. The checkout girl was busy reading one of them. There was a man's hand gripping a jodhpur-clad buttock on the cover and a scribbled message on the title page: *Dear Daphne, Sorry to hear about Charles. Perhaps you should have read my first book instead? Much love, Jilly.*

People crowded into the hairdresser. One of the locals smiled patiently when his haircut was interrupted by an enthusiastic festivalgoer who had spotted one of Edmund Crispin's books. Another saw a rare Margery Allingham book and immediately snapped it up. The woman who found the signed first edition of *A Murder Is Announced* seemed to freeze for several minutes, staring blankly ahead with a shocked, glazed look in her eye. She paid twenty pounds for the book, and her hand shook as she handed over the money.

In the women's clothing shop, several of the tourists bought dresses, blouses, and accessories ahead of the evening's festivities. And books.

Berit drifted among them. Everywhere she looked, she could see the thrill of discovery on their faces, and she heard their delighted cries and spontaneous recommendations to complete strangers. "Here! You have to read this!" someone told her, holding out a book. Berit was powerless to say no, of course. She spotted Eleanor coming out of the hobby shop with her arms full of Biggles books, a model plane perched on top.

Berit found her own eye being drawn to a first edition of *Frederica* by Georgette Heyer. On the cover, an enormous red-and-white-striped hot-air balloon was just about to lift off. The colors had faded, but it still radiated humor, romance, and vitality. She bought it right away; she just couldn't help herself.

Over in the pub, an informal P. G. Wodehouse society was just formed. Several people had found his books dotted around the village and had been unable to resist the lure of reading about Galahad Threepwood, the Empress of Blandings, Pongo, Jeeves, and Wooster. The collection of books was as varied as the cast of characters: some were glossy recent publications, one a first edition, and others had bought dog-eared, fabric-bound copies of practically every version in between. They dragged a couple of tables together, ordered pints of ale and cider, and enjoyed a good old-fashioned pub lunch in the company of newfound friends. Harry rushed back and forth between the tables with plates of food—burgers, fish and chips, steak and kidney pies, hearty sandwiches, and plates of lamb served with potatoes, peas, and boiled carrots. From time to time, people laughed out loud to themselves as they read.

A man got up and gathered the empty glasses to buy another round.

"Same again?" he asked.

The others nodded without looking up from their books.

The café proved just as popular as the pub. The festivalgoers sat in groups of four or five, with stacks of books on the tables in front of them, in bags by their feet, or lying in their laps as they enjoyed a bookish afternoon tea of scones, homemade jam, and clotted cream.

The groups had largely organized themselves. One woman had spotted another reading *Gentlemen and Players* by Joanne Harris and had hesitantly held out her own copy of *The Strawberry Thief* and asked whether she would like to discuss them over a pot of tea.

Others had simply been drawn to people they thought looked friendly and asked what they had found on their rounds.

It is a truth universally acknowledged among book clubs that at least half the time will be spent talking about something other than books, and that was definitely the case here. One group was chatting about their various purchases, another about their grandchildren. A woman proudly showed off her freshly permed hair, and a third group was trying to work out what they were supposed to wear to a ball in a grand, old library.

Everyone was ready for the party.

Up at Tawny Hall, the preparations continued to the very last. As soon as the lunch rush was over at the pub, Harry drove over there to get the bar ready. Mary and Eleanor had charge of the kitchen, and huge amounts of onions, carrots, potatoes, and flour were unloaded into the pantry. In the fridge, butter, ground beef, and sausages jostled for space alongside the beers and bottles of wine that had been put in to chill. Harry had brought several large bags of ice, and he stashed them in the empty freezer. In one corner of the ballroom, a four-piece band was busy setting up.

Daphne withdrew to her room early to get ready.

"One simply can't rush these things at my age," she said.

Half an hour later, Margaret went up to check how she was getting on and found Daphne's room empty. A dramatic red dress and a snow-white wig had been laid out on the bed. The effect would be striking.

She made her way to one of the bedrooms a few doors down. It was no longer in use, and though it was the middle of the day, the air felt cold, damp, and dark. The grubby old curtains were drawn, and there was junk covering much of the floor, but Margaret deftly picked her way through it, following an invisible path she knew by heart.

At the very back of the bedroom a wallpapered door led into a smaller room. That space, measuring just five by ten meters, was where Daphne kept everything she loved most.

Margaret found her sitting in an armchair inside.

"Whoever broke in didn't find their way in here," said Daphne.

Margaret nodded, though she didn't feel especially reassured. She knew the would-be thieves may well try again.

The little room was climate controlled, specially adapted to avoid any fluctuations in temperature or humidity. There were no windows, which prevented any sunlight from damaging the books, and several of the most fragile volumes were kept in acid-free boxes. Carefully positioned spotlights illuminated the other editions, as though they were the stars in some sort of show. *There really are some fantastic books here*, Margaret thought. All were first editions, the majority also signed by the authors. It was an inspirational, eclectic mix, including titles by Jane Austen, the Brontë sisters, H. G. Wells, and D. H. Lawrence, Mary Shelley, and Jules Verne. The Oscar Wilde, of course, plus Charles Dickens, Robert Graves, and Walter Scott. The only common denominator was that they were all wonderful stories.

Even Margaret found that her heart started beating that little bit faster whenever she laid eyes on them. She had long wished that Daphne would let her hide them somewhere more secure—or at least make sure that the most valuable titles stayed here. The fact of the matter was that she simply couldn't trust her employer. The woman had a terrible habit of picking up a book to read, taking it elsewhere in the house, and then forgetting it there. It was madness, especially considering she could read a cheap paperback version of the same book instead.

"I'll be glad once this party is over and we all can go back to normal," Margaret said.

"Sima said that people have been reading my books all over the village," Daphne said dreamily. "In the café and at the pub and outside, in the park. People are carrying stacks of books all over High Street."

"I still don't like it."

"Well, I do. It's fantastic. Berit was right. Books deserve to be read, to be treasured. And tonight, my library will be full of people, and they're all going to love it. It's going to be the best party I've thrown in decades."

"A library doesn't care whether it's loved or not," said Margaret. "Rooms don't have feelings."

"Oh, you just don't understand," Daphne said impatiently. "I'm very fond of you, Margaret, but you're such a prosaic soul."

Margaret couldn't argue with that. It was true.

"The only thing that worries me is that whoever broke in might try again," said Daphne. "So I've invited DCI Ahmed to the party. He'll notice if anything untoward happens."

"Are you sure that's…wise?"

"I have nothing to hide," Daphne replied, though she avoided meeting

Margaret's eye. "Besides, he'll never unearth any secrets in a ballroom. It simply isn't the right place. And if he tries anything, he'll quickly discover that it's rather difficult to interview suspects with a live band playing."

"I wish you'd at least let me hide some of your books somewhere safer."

"No!" Daphne's raised voice made them both flinch. "I need my books close, where I can touch them. Just keep your eyes and ears open, and talk to Liam. Make sure he stays alert too." She beamed up at Margaret. "It's going to be a wonderful evening. I can just feel it," said Daphne. Her voice was light and bright as she added, "And if anyone tries anything with my books, I'll kill them."

Rogers and Stevens seemed skeptical as they studied DCI Ahmed in his office at the station.

"What?" he asked, throwing his hands out by his sides. "Is there something wrong with my outfit?"

He was unusually smartly dressed in a dark suit and a shirt that looked like he might even have ironed it.

Rogers shook her head and folded her arms. Stevens pursed his lips disapprovingly, then reached out and straightened DCI Ahmed's collar.

"I managed to track down a few old university pals of Reginald Trent's," said Rogers. "A couple of them remembered Sima. They said Reginald dated her for a short while. They remember her because, I quote, 'she wasn't really one of them' and because she was 'a bit intense.' One of them was actually still in touch with a woman he thought was originally Sima's friend. She remembered—and Reginald's old friends confirmed this—that they were inseparable one summer, but then they broke up suddenly. No one ever heard him mention Sima again after that. She left Oxford—and politics—a few weeks later and moved to Great Diddling. There was a bit of gossip about it because she was so clearly a rising star, and then suddenly she was just gone. People wondered what was behind it."

"A fall from grace always gets people talking," DCI Ahmed said cynically. "Keep digging. Find out whether they thought the two were connected or whether they were separate events. Did Sima have to give up her involvement in national politics because of Reginald Trent? And did anyone get even the slightest sense that there was anything criminal about it?"

"On it, sir." Rogers looked like she wanted to say something else.

DCI Ahmed turned to the window. "I want forensics to comb every centimeter of Mrs. Ainsley's house for fingerprints, hair, clothing fibers. I want real, concrete evidence that can connect our suspects to her living room. If nothing else, this was a clear attempt to pervert the course of justice and hamper a police investigation."

Yet again, it looked like Rogers was on the verge of saying something.

DCI Ahmed sighed. "Come on, Rogers. Spit it out."

"I don't think you should go to the party," she said.

Stevens agreed. "It could affect our investigation."

"It's just a party. I've been invited."

"Yeah, a party virtually all our main suspects will be attending," said Rogers. "The boss isn't going to like this."

"He wants results. And right now, they're toying with us. They're too bloody comfortable. My plan is to light a few fires and see who we can smoke out. If we can put them under enough pressure, then they might start making mistakes and give themselves away."

33

THE CRYSTAL CHANDELIER ILLUMINATED THE bookshelves and made the freshly scrubbed floor gleam. A bar had been set up at one end of the room, and Harry waved to Sima from behind it. He looked handsome and reliable in his white shirt and jacket, ready to serve champagne, beer, and G&Ts.

Ready to help with whatever else she needed too, thought Sima.

She had done it. The festival was a success and Reginald Trent was dead. He had taken his secrets to the grave with him, and that meant she could finally breathe easy.

Beside her, Daphne Trent was radiant in her bright-red evening gown. It looked like it was from the eighties, with a dramatic, high collar that offered a striking contrast to her brilliant-white hair. Daphne had livened up her pale face with a matching shade of red lipstick, and her silver charm bracelet clinked softly every time she moved her arm. Sima glanced down and noticed that the charms were all books.

Sima had always been fascinated by people who dressed to be seen, to stand out from the crowd. Personally, she had only ever dressed to blend in. This evening she was smartly, if dully, dressed in a navy A-line dress that hit just below the knee.

Daphne and Sima were by the doors, welcoming the guests as they arrived. Both women enjoyed the effect the ballroom had on the festival-goers. They were spellbound, that much was clear. The party would be the cherry on top of the cake, the perfect ending to a magical day.

No, Sima told herself, it wasn't an ending. This was just the beginning. The minute they got a moment to themselves, she planned to bring up her new idea with Daphne. Together, they would be able to transform the village going forward—for real this time.

Then, she froze. What the hell was he doing here?

"Chief Inspector Ahmed!" Daphne chirped. "Welcome!"

Sima forced a smile onto her face. "DCI Ahmed," she echoed.

Daphne pulled him over to one side for a quick word, but for Sima it was no more than a brief respite. Just a few minutes later, he was back, and this time she was left alone with him. Daphne was busy chatting with Margaret.

She swallowed.

"It's wonderful to see you here," she said. "I didn't think you would... what I mean is...I assumed you wouldn't have time in the middle of an investigation."

"Oh, I wouldn't miss this for the world," he replied, looking around the room. "You must be incredibly proud of everything you've achieved?"

"Yes."

"You really have done a great job."

Sima smiled uncertainly at him.

"Which makes me wonder why you ever left politics. Surely your talents deserve a bigger outlet than this?"

"I got sick of politics."

"What crime did you commit?"

She was sure she hadn't shown any surprise. In fact, the shock of his question had made her freeze, so she didn't think there was any emotion on her face at all.

There's no way he can know, Sima thought. It was a stab in the dark, that's all.

"I've never been suspected, interviewed in connection with, or charged with any crime," she said firmly. "Now if you'll excuse me, I have guests to welcome."

The Elmers arrived together, but they may as well have come alone, Penny thought glumly.

It felt as though they barely spoke anymore. Whenever she tried to ask James about Gerald or the hotel, he got annoyed and stomped away. She had learned it was best to avoid the subject, but that didn't stop her from worrying nonstop about what was going to happen to them and the hotel.

She said hello to Sima and Daphne as her eyes scanned the room for Eleanor. They needed to talk.

In the end, she spotted her out on the terrace.

"If you'll excuse me for a moment," Penny said abruptly, earning herself a confused look from James, Sima, and Daphne. She must have interrupted them midconversation, she realized, but she didn't care.

She made a beeline for the bar before walking over to Eleanor with two glasses of champagne—both for her. Penny knocked back the first and then made a start on the second.

"We've got a problem," she said. "None of the books I grabbed are worth a thing. I Googled them."

"Neither are mine," Eleanor admitted.

Penny double-checked no one else was within earshot. "Do you think we should try again this evening?" she asked quietly.

"They must have stashed the valuable books somewhere before the party," said Eleanor. "And if they noticed we were here last night, then they're going to be even more cautious now. I need to think."

Gerald Corduroy-Smith had just arrived and was busy ingratiating himself with Daphne.

"I wonder whether he thinks he'll be able to get her to trust him like that," said Eleanor. "Or who knows, maybe he's planning to use the romantic angle…"

"What are you talking about?"

"I'm trying to work out how he's going to try to steal the book," said Eleanor. "If we just knew that, we could turn it to our advantage."

"Are you telling me he's also after these books?"

"Certainly." She was watching him intently, and Penny realized that there was a hint of professional interest in the older woman's eyes.

"You seem to know quite a lot about this sort of thing," she said with a note of suspicion.

Eleanor nodded absentmindedly. "Mary and I are a couple of old fraudsters. It's a long story, but we're retired now, sadly. Oh well, I guess it happens to everyone. You can't stay young forever."

Penny choked on her champagne. "Your parents must have been so proud," she croaked, tears in her eyes. "What did they do? Rob banks?"

"Oh, we're not actually sisters."

Penny held up her hands. "I don't even want to know. Christ, look, the policeman's here now! Do you think he knows about the break-in? I can't handle being arrested again. James would never forgive me if he had to confess to a second crime."

"Technically we weren't arrested last time. Besides, if he was here to investigate a break-in, he wouldn't exactly turn up on his own, dressed for a party."

"You seem to know quite a bit about that too," Penny muttered. "All I wanted was to earn enough money to save the hotel and make James love me again."

"Well, that's your first mistake," said Eleanor, still watching Gerald Corduroy-Smith as he moved across the room. "Love isn't about solving someone else's problems; it's about sharing them. Stop trying to save the hotel on your own and talk to him instead. Tell him how you feel."

"Love advice from Eleanor Hartfield. I've heard it all now. So I take it you and Mary are a couple?"

"Yes, but there's no need to shout it from the rooftops," Eleanor muttered.

"And that's how the two of you live, is it? Sharing all your problems?"

Eleanor looked away. "Not exactly. Not right now, anyway. But we'll find our way back to each other; I promise you that."

It sounded like she was trying to convince herself.

"When, exactly?" Penny asked sarcastically.

"As soon as I've solved all her problems."

Sally made her way into the ballroom two steps behind Berit, as ever, but when Berit stopped without warning, she automatically continued until they were standing side by side. She peered around the room in confusion.

It was as though the ballroom had tilted. All the guests were pressed up against one wall, and Sally could see the fascination and wonder on their faces as they gazed up at the tall bookshelves.

The woman who had come into the room after them followed her gaze and stopped dead, mouthing a silent *wow* to herself. Several others nearby craned their necks or slowly turned around to take it all in. One man was so busy looking at the shelves that he actually walked straight into a woman. Fortunately, the woman assured him that she understood. She then accompanied him as he made his way over to inspect the titles.

"There should be a ladder somewhere," she said.

"That's the only thing missing!" he agreed, looking around. "And possibly a bar… Ah, there it is! Can I tempt you with a glass?"

"I'm going to go and say hello to Daphne and Sima," said Berit.

Sally nodded weakly. She had spent her life hovering by the walls at events like this, and for the first time ever, that was where the real party seemed to be. She barely even noticed that she had been left on her own once Berit walked away.

No, not alone. She was surrounded by booklovers.

Sally spotted Liam on the other side of the room, wearing jeans, a white shirt, and a dark-gray suede jacket. She thought he looked incredibly handsome—plus a little mysterious.

She had come close to telling Berit about the note she had found and destroyed several times over the past few days. She was desperate to confide in someone, to be freed from the burden that knowledge of the note had forced onto her shoulders. She was sure Berit would know what needed to be done, that she would know what was right.

Sally appreciated the author's old-fashioned, slightly blunt moral compass. She had only known her a short time, but she had already learned that

Berit never twisted things to her own advantage. The author wasn't afraid of difficult subjects. She saw the truth, and she refused to shy away from it.

If Sally told her about Liam's lack of an alibi, about her suspicion that he and Eleanor might have done something—something stupid that meant they might be in real trouble—then Berit would tell her what she needed to do; she was confident of that.

And yet something made her hold back. Every time she tried to bring it up, she stopped herself at the very last minute. Maybe it was simply because she felt loyal to Liam. He was her friend, after all, which meant she had certain obligations to him.

She was also painfully aware of what Berit would have to say about that. A person couldn't have one rule for friends and another for everyone else. Or as Dumbledore had put it, "It takes a great deal of bravery to stand up to our enemies, but just as much to stand up to our friends."

Right then, Liam grabbed Sally's arm.

"Why didn't you come over when I waved?" he asked. "Come on. I said I would help out in the kitchen, and we could do with another pair of hands."

He led her down one of the old corridors that bisected the house. They turned right then left, left again, eventually coming out into a dark, unused room that smelled like damp wood. Sally hesitated, but Liam just shook his head and dragged her after him.

She bumped into a man who was lurking in the shadows with his arm raised in a threatening manner, making her shriek and jump closer to Liam. The man didn't move, and Liam switched on the flashlight on his phone.

"Relax," he said. "It's just an old doll. Pretty cool, huh?"

Sure enough, it was an old shop mannequin, dressed in baggy clothing. One of its arms had fallen off and been propped up against its leg, and the other was pointing straight up, as though he had his hand raised in class. Sally shuddered, her heart still racing.

"Come on," said Liam, and she hurried after him, shivering in the cool air.

A moment later, they reached the kitchen. The bright light and bustling activity made Sally blink.

There were so many people in the kitchen that it felt almost as lively as the party. Villagers kept arriving with baking trays, bowls, and covered baskets. The plan was to serve a selection of British classics: mini shepherd's pies, bangers and mash, burgers, fish and chips.

"Here, hold this," someone told Sally. "Portion the ground beef into these muffin trays, then add some mash and grated cheese on top. Great. Now shove them in the oven."

Beside her, Liam was frying miniature sausages for the bangers and mash. Close up, he looked just like her friend again. His hair was still the color of flax, as messy as ever, with too much wax in it. His teeth were slightly crooked, his shirt one size too small. He winked at Sally, and she smiled.

Elvis was playing on the old stereo, and Sally started sweating in the heat. She couldn't ask him now, she thought. Later. She would do it later.

First, she wanted to enjoy this evening. For once in her life, she wanted to have fun with a friend at a party.

Was that really so much to ask?

Eleanor made her way over to DCI Ahmed. She was carrying a silver tray in one hand, and she offered him a mini burger.

He took one and, in a conversational tone, said:

"That's an interesting perfume you're wearing. When I interviewed you at the station, I thought I'd smelled it somewhere before, but I couldn't remember where."

Eleanor gave him a guarded look.

"But then it came to me: it was at Mrs. Ainsley's house. Is she a friend of yours?"

He paused, giving her a chance to fill the gap in their conversation, but Eleanor didn't fall for the classic rookie mistake of saying too much. Maybe she knew that silence was always the hardest response for a police officer to deal with.

"Mrs. Ainsley recently had a break-in at her cottage," he continued unperturbed. "It makes you wonder, doesn't it? What sort of world we live in."

"Indeed." Eleanor's voice sounded gravelly, and she cleared her throat.

"Would you like to know the strangest part about the whole thing?" She gave him a hesitant nod.

"Do say if I'm boring you. I suppose if you don't know her, then it can't be all that interesting."

"No, I want to hear it."

"Well, nothing was stolen. Nothing at all. But here's what's really interesting. Get this: whoever broke in used her tea service! They even did the washing up afterward."

Eleanor's face was impassive, and DCI Ahmed polished off his burger in two bites before he went on.

"But that makes things slightly tricky for Liam Slater because he used Mrs. Ainsley as his alibi for the evening the explosives were stolen. You know Liam, don't you?"

Another guarded nod.

"But it seems it wasn't Mrs. Ainsley who gave him an alibi after all. It was the thief! Someone who had the nerve to break into another woman's home and offer up tea and lies to the police."

DCI Ahmed thought he saw Eleanor's right eye twitch briefly, but that was the only thing that gave her away.

"Weird, huh? I suppose whoever it was assumed Mrs. Ainsley would be away for the duration of the investigation and that Liam Slater would be ruled out of our inquiries without either him or the fake Mrs. Ainsley ever having to testify at trial." He shook his head. "It takes a certain sort of person to manage something like that. They must really be able to think well outside the box to come up with the idea. The solution to all their problems. Risky, yes, but certain people have no problem taking risks. They love them. It's as though they need to live dangerously from time to time."

"That sounds stupid," Eleanor said flatly.

"It can backfire, yes. We now know that not only does Liam lack an alibi, but he also went to great lengths to try to give us a false one. That practically proves he was up to something that evening. We'll have to bring him back in for questioning, and this time he won't be able to lie his way out of it."

"Are you sure you should be telling me this?"

DCI Ahmed shrugged. "What harm could it do? Warn him all you like, it makes no difference to us. We're sending a team of forensic technicians to Mrs. Ainsley's house right now, and they're going to comb every last inch of the place. We'll find physical evidence connecting the perpetrator to the cottage, I promise you that."

Liam Slater was Eleanor's polar opposite. Every single thought and feeling was written plainly across his face, and DCI Ahmed was reminded of just how young he was.

The reactions he displayed as the detective cornered him by the bar were, in order: excessive friendliness, which came across as a kind of social foolhardiness or swagger; a sudden onset of anxiety; and last but not least, sulky stubbornness.

A few meters away, Sally was following their conversation, and DCI Ahmed noticed that she looked worried.

"I know you stole the explosives," he lied. He was far from sure how everything fit together, but he wanted to see what impact his words would have. "And I'm going to prove it."

Liam's face was pale and panicked, and he kept fiddling with his clothing as Ahmed talked.

"You've already got a record for theft," said DCI Ahmed. "Oh, I know it wasn't anything major. Nothing at all like this. And I know the judge only came down so hard on you because you wouldn't testify against your friends. But I implore you, don't make the same mistake twice. This isn't a game, Liam. You won't be able to avoid prison this time."

"I'm not a snitch." Liam's face was surly, but his voice wavered slightly, and he looked around as though he was desperately searching for someone to save him.

No one came to his rescue, and DCI Ahmed could have told him that they never would. For the first time, he actually found himself feeling sorry for Liam.

"Come to the station and tell us your side of what happened," he said.

"I give you my word that I'll do all I can to make sure you get a good deal with the prosecution."

James grabbed Penny's arm and dragged her over to the edge of the room. His tie was somehow even more crooked than it had been last time she saw him.

"You need to stop spending time with that woman," he said.

Penny had to put her hands behind her back to stop herself from reaching out to straighten his tie.

"What's it to you?" Penny replied wearily. She didn't have the energy for another argument. It seemed that fighting was all they did these days.

"The two of you are up to something. I saw you sneak out last night, and I saw her too. I know it was her idea for the three of you to confess. There's no way it could have been yours."

"I can do what I like," said Penny. "Keep your nose out of it. You've already done more than enough."

"You don't understand," he said, a pleading note in his voice.

Penny nodded. "You're right about that: I don't understand a thing. I thought we were supposed to be a team, James. I thought we were in this together. I've been with countless men, but not because I can't handle being on my own. I would much rather be alone with myself than alone with someone else."

His face paled.

"You idiot," she said. "Why did you do it? Why the hell did you borrow money from Reginald of all people?"

"I did it for you, obviously." He sounded surprised, as though that should have been obvious to her.

"For me?"

"I had to save the hotel for your sake. And Reginald was the only way I could do that. Everything ended up being so much more expensive than I'd thought, so I took out loans—big loans—and the interest and repayments were about to break me. He offered good terms, long-term stability, everything. He wasn't supposed to ask for it back until we were on our feet; he swore."

"But that's not what it said in the contract, huh?" Penny said cynically.

James looked confused again, as though he still couldn't quite believe that someone would lie to him. "I just wanted you to be proud of me," he mumbled.

"Idiot," she said, though her voice was much softer this time. He may well be an idiot, but he was *her* idiot.

"I didn't want you to know that I'd failed again. I didn't want…I didn't want you to think any less of me. Or to see me as a loser, like my dad always did. Nothing I did was ever good enough for him. I just couldn't bear the thought that you'd look at me with disappointment on your face, the way he used to."

"I've never needed a man to be perfect," Penny protested. "I've known far too many of them to believe that's even possible—the same goes for us women, of course. If someone wants a perfect exterior, they might as well be with a complete stranger. No, what I want is to be able to hit back at the world together, to laugh at the misery and make the best of the situation together. To grow old together."

"I just didn't want you to regret picking me."

"Regret! I don't go around regretting things. How would I ever get anything done? Besides, I picked you. I set my mind on you. And once I've done that, there's nothing I wouldn't do for you. Nothing. That's just how it is."

Penny put her hands on his cheeks and kissed him firmly on the lips.

James was so taken aback that the self-pitying thoughts immediately disappeared. She could practically see it in his eyes, like an engine that had suddenly died. He seemed confused.

"From now on, we're in this together," Penny said.

DCI Ahmed felt no satisfaction following his conversation with Liam. He didn't exactly enjoy scaring young men, but it had to be done. He needed to unsettle the villagers somehow, to make one or more of them start talking so that he could begin to unravel the countless side plots he was grappling with.

He now knew beyond all doubt that Berit had been right about Sima committing a crime of some sort. Sima hadn't reacted when he asked her about it, and that spoke volumes. An innocent person would have been surprised—and shown it.

Even more telling was the fact that she hadn't asked what he was talking about.

He planned to bring her in for questioning the minute he had enough information to crack the carefully maintained, professional façade she was currently hiding behind.

The real problem was that he couldn't find any link between her, Liam, and Eleanor. Had Liam stolen the explosives for Sima, with Eleanor simply providing him an alibi after the fact?

At the far end of the room, Berit was alone by the bookshelves. She was stylishly dressed in a surprisingly modern navy-blue suit, and she looked calm and solemn, standing with her back to the books.

Ian Ahmed often found himself thinking back to their calm, searching conversation at her cottage, and for a brief moment he imagined himself going over to ask her something now—whether she preferred books or people at a party, for example.

He smiled to himself. He suspected he already knew the answer. She was standing alone by the shelves, after all. But she was also watching the ballroom with a sort of hunger in her eyes that unsettled him.

He frowned. He knew he should have put a stop to their odd partnership a long time ago, but he had been so focused on not allowing it to have a negative impact on the investigation that he hadn't paused to consider how it might affect Berit.

Somehow, she had become involved in the crazy village festival. Now sooner or later, she would have to choose between her new friends and the truth.

DCI Ahmed shook his head and decided that he had done more than enough for one evening. He made his way over to the bar and ordered a beer.

As Harry held it out to him, his gold cuff link caught the light.

"Do you have a bottle opener?" asked DCI Ahmed, looking around. Several booklovers were swaying enthusiastically to the music nearby. "Great party, isn't it?"

"Fantastic," Harry said. He pulled a bottle opener from his pocket, popped the lid, and held the bottle out to the detective again.

This time, the cuff link on his other sleeve shimmered in the light. It wasn't gold, DCI Ahmed noticed. It was made of brass, and it was in the shape of a small anchor.

34

DAPHNE'S EYES TWINKLED IN THE glow of the crystal chandelier. She had a glass of crisp, cool champagne in one hand, and she was surrounded by people who were smiling and nodding, appreciating her library. She looked happy, just how Sima wanted her.

"I have a proposal," Sima said eagerly. "With your permission, I'd like to keep the bookshops in town open and turn this festival into an annual event. Just imagine what we could do with more time to prepare! We could actually book some real authors. Your parties would be legendary in book circles; I promise you that. Everyone would want to be here."

Daphne turned to her. She was interested, Sima could see that, though there was also hesitation. The older woman wasn't convinced yet, not by a long stretch, but she was open to hearing more.

"So my books would have to stay down in the village?" she asked.

"Only the ones you can do without. And if you change your mind, you could always bring them back here whenever you wanted. Think of them as being…on loan. Well, other than the ones we've sold, that is. But there are still plenty left. And just think how much more space you'd have up here at Tawny Hall. You could buy even more books!"

She definitely had Daphne's attention now.

Sima impulsively reached out and put a hand on her arm. "Oh,

Daphne," she said. "You have such an incredible collection. More people should get a chance to see it. It deserves to be celebrated and loved—as do you! You would be at the heart of everything, a host for the entire festival. None of it would be possible without you, after all."

"I'll think about it," Daphne promised her.

Sima nodded eagerly. "That's all I'm asking."

"I don't like this one bit," said Margaret.

Daphne continued to gaze out across her library. "Has anyone tried anything yet?" she asked.

"No, but…"

"Well, then." The band started playing, and Daphne tapped her foot in time with the music, noticing to her delight that as many people were reading as dancing. "I told you that DCI Ahmed's presence would be enough of a deterrent. No one will dare try anything while he's here. Relax, Margaret. Here, have a glass of champagne."

Daphne took two glasses and handed one of them to Margaret, but when she noticed that her secretary didn't take a single sip, she took it back and kept both for herself.

Gerald sauntered over to them with a full bottle. "I was planning to bring you a top-up, but I see you're already well stocked." He took a sip of champagne before he went on in the same chatty tone: "I'd like to buy your library."

Margaret only just managed to save the glasses in Daphne's hands from crashing to the floor, then stood quietly as Daphne stared at Gerald.

"Sell my books?! You want to part me from my books? For money?!" Daphne clutched her chest. "This isn't funny, Mr. Corduroy-Smith. It's not funny at all."

"You misunderstand," Gerald replied. "You'll be paid for them now, but I won't take the books until after your death. You could hang on to every one of them for the remainder of your life—and the money, of course. You'll be parted from them when you die anyway; it's not like you can take them with you."

"Many have tried," Daphne muttered. "And who knows? Perhaps I could turn the library into a mausoleum."

"Just think of all the trips you could take," said Gerald. "The clothes you could buy." He looked down at her dress. "New clothes."

His words gave Daphne the same unpleasant sense of being seen that she had often felt while Reginald was alive. Everyone else thought her dress was dramatic and original; she was sure of that. Only Gerald seemed to realize it was old and dated.

"You could organize more of these magnificent parties. And best of all, you'd still have all your books."

"What happens if you die first?" asked Margaret.

"That's a risk I'm willing to take. All I ask is that we have some sort of insurance policy against the most common issues. Damp, fires." He looked around and added, "Theft."

"And who would pay the premiums?" asked Margaret.

"Me, naturally. With Daphne as the beneficiary. I'd just need to get my insurance broker to examine a few of the titles. The Oscar Wilde in particular."

"You aren't the first person to have come to me with proposals for my books, you know," Daphne said drily. "Sima also has plenty of ideas."

For a moment, Gerald seemed surprised, though he quickly flashed her a charming smile. "Don't worry about Sima. I have a feeling she'll change her tune. So, what do you say? I could take the Wilde and a couple of other books back to London with me and have my expert value them and produce certificates of authenticity for the insurance company. You'd have them back in just a few days' time, the money within a week. I have no intention of haggling with you, either. Name your price."

Daphne's head was spinning. She found herself briefly getting caught up in the vision Gerald had painted. Parties, traveling, being rich again— that was the next best thing after being young.

"You don't need to give an answer now," Margaret interjected, turning to Gerald. "A ballroom isn't the right place for a business meeting, Mr. Corduroy-Smith. Daphne needs more time before she makes a decision either way."

Daphne nodded, looking dazed. "Yes," she said, "I need more time."

Her mind was racing. All she could think about was how many more books she would be able to buy with the money.

Sally had been waiting for Liam to come back over to her, but when he failed to do that, she went over to him.

He started laughing and joking the minute he saw her, but Sally wasn't fooled. Liam was worried. Really worried. She wondered just how much DCI Ahmed knew.

They were standing right by the band, which meant she could hardly hear a word Liam said, and after she asked "what?" for the fourth time, he dragged her outside. The evening air felt refreshingly cool on her hot skin.

Liam continued to mess about like he had while they were cooking in the kitchen, but away from the noise of the party, his cheeriness seemed strained. His eyes were jittery, his shoulders tense.

A sudden realization made Sally pause. "You stole the explosives," she said.

It wasn't just that he lied about where he was on the Thursday evening; she knew that now. He had *needed* to lie. Because he was guilty—of the theft, at the very least. But she couldn't quite bring herself to believe that he'd had anything to do with the murder. Liam could never hurt anyone. Could he?

"What are you talking about?" he asked, not meeting her eyes.

"The tea party. You kept laughing and joking there too, just like you are now. I thought it was because we...well, you know, were getting to know each other, but it's because you were nervous."

"Yeah, obviously I was nervous: you're a cool girl from London."

She shook her head. "No," she said. "That's not why." Sally was surprised her voice sounded so calm.

"Don't start, Sally. I've had enough of people having a go at me this evening. I'm not going to take it from you too."

"I'm not. But if you know who the killer is, you need to tell the police."

"That there's exactly what I mean by having a go at me."

"You have to talk to the police," she pressed him. "They can help you."

"Help me?"

"I know you'd never kill someone. Not on purpose, anyway. But someone killed Reginald Trent with the explosives you helped steal."

"You seem pretty sure I'm guilty. I thought you trusted me."

"So am I wrong?"

He didn't speak.

"Liam, you're my friend, and I—"

"Friend?" he repeated, his voice flat. "We haven't even known each other a month."

Had it really been so little time since she arrived in Great Diddling? Sally gave him a confused look. "We are friends, aren't we?" she asked.

"Friends are people who've grown up together, who've covered for each other and gone through shit together. Not people who nag and lecture like a fucking schoolteacher."

Sally blinked and swallowed. "We are friends," she said. "And friendship means speaking up when the other person does something wrong."

He had already turned and walked away, but he paused for long enough to say, "You're wrong. Friendship means being on someone's side, especially when they make a mistake."

And with that, he was gone.

In the end, it was Berit who approached him.

She was holding two bottles of beer, and she offered one of them to DCI Ahmed.

"Assuming you're not on duty, that is?"

He took it. "No, I'm done for the evening," he said. It was a lie, albeit a necessary one. No one liked to be reminded that one part of him would always be on the job.

Berit smiled and shook her head. "You and I, Chief Inspector. We never stop working."

"Call me Ian."

He felt an infuriating urge to confide in her, to share his latest discovery about Harry's cuff link and ask her whether she thought he and Sima were close.

The thought was tempting, but it was also idiotic. He had a job to do, and it was high time she stopped sticking her nose in, simple as that.

The library was still busy, though some of the guests had started to leave. The band took a break. One man had fallen asleep in an armchair, DCI Ahmed noticed, with an open book in his lap and a half-empty bottle of beer on the floor by his feet.

"Yup, we're always working," Berit continued. "That's probably why we're so good at our jobs. It's not something we do; it's who we are. So you can imagine what it would be like to wake up one day and realize that you've lost whatever it is that makes you a good police officer."

"Has something like that happened to you?"

She nodded. "Before I came to Great Diddling. The voices in my head, the special energy that comes from being inspired, my instinct for a good story—from one day to the next, it all just disappeared. It was like losing a part of myself."

"But now it's back?"

"The people here have really helped me. With their madness and their enthusiasm and their…creativity with the truth. They've filled my head with stories, but I can't use any of them—not until I know who killed Reginald Trent."

"Because one of them is going to turn out to be the killer." *At least one of them*, he thought to himself.

"I know," Berit added, a genuine desperation in her voice. "But *who?*"

DCI fixed his eyes on her. "I need you to let me handle the investigative work from now on, Berit. You've been a real help so far, I'm not denying it, but it's time you took a step back."

Berit didn't reply.

"At least promise me you're not planning to help them with something actively criminal?"

She turned to him with a look of surprise on her face. "Of course I'm not."

"You've let yourself get caught up in their madness. Just don't let them pressure you into doing something illegal, OK? Don't lose your objectivity or your clear-sightedness."

"Clear-sightedness," she repeated, a certain melancholy in her voice. "What a sacrifice it is to have to see things exactly as they are."

"The people here are going to discover just how serious it is to be involved in a murder," said DCI Ahmed. "Or to protect anyone who is. Promise me you won't get mixed up in this. I won't be able to protect you if you do."

Berit stood quietly for what felt like a long time. "I'll do my best," she eventually said.

She sounded reluctant, he thought. And sad. It pained him to hear that, but he knew he had no choice.

Justice would prevail. It didn't care about friendship or bonds of gratitude or loyalties. There was a reason it was depicted by a blindfolded figure, he thought. Rich or poor, friend or foe, everyone would be treated impartially and justly.

Because it was right.

35

THE GUESTS WERE DROPPED OFF at the train station after lunch on Sunday, and once the last car had returned to Great Diddling an hour or so later, it was as though the entire village breathed a sigh of relief.

The shops that had extended their opening hours for the festivalgoers closed their shutters. The guests had shopped until the last minute, and the final sale at the souvenir and antiques shop had been an old 1950s suitcase. The woman who bought it had needed it in order to lug all her new books home.

Even the hairdresser had been busy. Several people had taken up their Readers' Cut offer, turning up with a book to be fussed over for an hour or two. The salon had guaranteed they would be able to read nonstop through the hair washing, head massage, cutting, dyeing, and blow drying, and they had also offered manicures with one of the members of staff holding the book for them while their nails were painted.

All anyone could talk about was Sima's triumph. People immediately began reminiscing over their favorite moments, reading Tripadvisor reviews to one another whenever their paths crossed.

"Five stars. Didn't talk to a single person. Best three days of my life," said one of them.

Another stated, "I don't care what anyone says. Margaret Atwood was incredible!"

And yet the festival wasn't the only thing on people's minds. There was plenty of gossip about the mysterious break-in at Mrs. Ainsley's place too. A team of forensic technicians had descended on the little house on Saturday evening, and Mrs. Ainsley announced to anyone who would listen that if she had realized just how much of a mess the police would make in her home, she wouldn't have bothered reporting it.

Paradoxically, it was Sima's success that convinced Mrs. Tinley to call the police. She had seen the head of the council being praised left, right, and center, strutting about the village as though she owned the place.

And so, on the Monday, she called the police.

DCI Ahmed gazed around the shabby flat. The air smelled stale, like old fabric and dead dreams. Mrs. Tinley herself stank of sweat and cigarettes, and he had been looking forward to leaving since the moment he set foot inside.

This was what police work was all about, he told himself. Coming face-to-face with different people and treating them all with respect.

Mrs. Tinley insisted on making tea, and he had politely accepted. When he first joined the force, his boss had explained that the act of serving it had a calming effect on the people they were talking to, and since then, he had rarely turned down a cup.

While he waited, he took in the room around him. It was a sunny day outside, but the tiny windows didn't seem to let any light in. The walls were clad in old-fashioned brown paper, and the furniture was all made from dark wood.

There were framed pictures of the same man everywhere: on the walls and the chest of drawers and the little side table by her armchair. A wedding photograph showed him as a young, serious man standing beside an equally serious younger version of Mrs. Tinley; their solemn faces made them look oddly timeless.

"My husband," she said. "He's dead."

"My condolences."

"Not before he left me for a little slut half his age. He was with me thirty years, but he couldn't manage six months with her. What do you say about that, hmm?"

"I'm sorry."

"Ha!" Her joyless laugh didn't manage to completely mask her grief. "I suppose you're here to look into what I saw the Thursday before the murder? Mr. Trent. That's who I saw." She looked expectantly at DCI Ahmed, then continued unprompted: "He wasn't the sort of man you could miss. But I'm pretty sure he didn't want to be seen. Not at that time of day. Just after ten in the evening, it was. That's why I noticed. Not exactly the normal time to be making a house call, is it? Not unless the person you're visiting is an extremely good friend."

She emphasized the word "friend," leaving DCI Ahmed with no doubt what she was hinting at.

"I saw him go in, and then I saw him come back out again, a full hour later. Eleven o'clock, I checked." Mrs. Tinley looked slightly embarrassed when she realized that what she had just said made it sound like she spied on her neighbors.

Which you clearly do, thought DCI Ahmed.

"We really appreciate your help, Mrs. Tinley," he said reluctantly.

"Yes, well, I know who he was visiting: Sima Kumar."

Ahmed got up and moved over to the window. He pushed back the dirty curtains. From where he was standing, he had a clear line of sight across to Sima's house. It was a drab, surprisingly modern two-story home, separated from the neighboring next house over by a narrow passageway. Sima's was the only driveway on the entire street that wasn't cluttered with children's toys and bicycles.

He wondered whether Mrs. Tinley would be disappointed if she knew that she had just given Sima Kumar an alibi for the night when the explosives were stolen.

And what an alibi, he thought. *Involving the victim himself.*

Mrs. Tinley wasn't done yet. "And he wasn't the only man who paid her a visit that evening!" she said, giving DCI Ahmed a satisfied look. "What do you have to say about that?"

"Who else visited her?"

"Harry Wilson! The bartender. I don't know how long he stayed. I went to bed before he'd left. For all I know, he could have been there until early the next morning."

Her voice was dripping with so much insinuation that DCI Ahmed felt grubby just listening to her.

"Do you remember what time Harry arrived?"

"Half past eleven, practically the middle of the night! That woman struts around the place, acting like she's better than everyone else, but she certainly doesn't have anything against men running in and out of her place. I'm just doing my civic duty mentioning this to you, Chief Inspector."

"As I said, we're very grateful."

"You're not under arrest," DCI Ahmed clarified. "This is entirely voluntary, and you're free to leave whenever you like. But the quicker we can straighten a few things out, the quicker we can rule you out of our inquiries."

Sima nodded and looked around the interview room. Her expression was neutral, as though she was simply taking in everything she could see without judgment.

The glare from the strip light on the ceiling was so unflattering, it managed to make even Sima look tired and weary, giving her skin a grayish-green hue. She had said no to coffee, tea, and a lawyer; yes to a glass of water.

"How long have you been involved in local politics in Great Diddling?" asked DCI Ahmed.

She attempted to straighten her chair, giving him a crooked smile when she realized it was bolted to the floor.

"Practically since I moved there," Sima said.

"What on earth made you choose to move to Reginald Trent's home village?"

"It wasn't his home village. His aunt just lived here, and one day he'd inherit 'the old pile of stones,' as he called it. I went there with him"—she hesitated, then continued—"when we were dating. And I liked what I saw. The village… They needed me. And I guess you could say that I needed them. I ran for council, and that, as they say, was that. I didn't see Reginald Trent again until that ill-fated tourist board meeting."

"You met at Oxford, didn't you?"

Sima nodded. "We had a few mutual friends. I was young and ambitious, he was young and bored, and we…clicked, oddly enough. I think he liked my hunger."

"The two of you began a relationship."

"A brief one, yes."

"And when it ended, you left Oxford. What happened?"

"I was sick of it all."

"What was the crime you committed?"

Sima repeated the same answer she had given him at the party, that she had never been suspected, interviewed in connection with, or charged with any crime. It was like a mantra she was clinging on to, thought DCI Ahmed.

She pulled a face and looked around the room. "Until now, that is," she corrected herself.

"Tell me about the tourist board meeting."

"Why? Surely that's water under the bridge by now?"

"All right. Tell me what happened the next evening."

Her eyes shot up at him, but she didn't say anything.

"He visited you, didn't he?"

She swallowed. "Yes," she said. She improvised quickly. "He was planning to sell his properties in the village, and he wanted to make sure the new owners would have my full support, politically speaking. I suppose he thought they might want to implement various changes, that they might need planning permits or whatever. But he was pretty vague about everything. In all honesty, I don't think he knew what they wanted. He was just looking for a general promise of support."

"Did he get it?"

She shrugged. "If it would be good for the village, then sure. I have nothing against change. It's inevitable. Either you control it, or it controls you."

"Did he threaten you?"

Sima pulled another face. "I guess that could be what he thought he was doing. Reginald was someone who liked to exert power over people. He probably got a kick out of it. But in this case, like I said, it was irrelevant. I was prepared to give the new owners whatever support I could—for the good of the village, not because he was threatening me."

"I think Reginald knew something about you—something less than flattering—and that he was using it to blackmail you."

"I can't help what you think. That's up to you." Sima looked him straight in the eye. "Only one other person was there that night, DCI Ahmed, and he is now dead."

Harry put his hands on the table in the interview room and leaned forward.

"Whatever you've heard about Sima, it's all false," he said.

The pub landlord knew they had brought her in for questioning earlier that day. The whole village probably did by now, thought DCI Ahmed. He had practically felt Mrs. Tinley's eyes on the back of his neck as he picked up Sima from her home, and he didn't doubt that she had spread the gossip far and wide.

"Tell me about your cuff links," he said.

Harry seemed confused. "What do you mean?"

"At the party. They didn't match."

"Yeah, I've lost one of them. I guess I shouldn't use it now I've only got one, but they were my old man's. He loved fishing, not that he ever had time for it. Too busy working 'round the clock. 'I'll go once I retire,' that's what he always used to say. About everything, to be honest—moving back to Cornwall, opening a pub."

"And did he?"

"He retired, but he didn't have time for any of the other stuff. He died a month later."

"I'm sorry to hear that. Was he from Cornwall?"

"His dad was. Worked down the mines, but he left once that dried up. Sorry, but what does this have to do with Sima? I have to get back to the pub."

"Was that why you opened a pub? To fulfill your dad's dream?"

"It was the first thing I did after he died. As soon as the funeral was over, I quit my job and sold my flat in London, bought the pub, and moved to the village. And I've never regretted it, not for a single second."

DCI Ahmed nodded. "You love her, don't you?" A qualified guess.

"Sima? That's not exactly a secret. The whole village knows I'd do anything for her."

"You were out at Tawny Hall, weren't you?"

"At the tea party? Nope, I was probably the only person who wasn't. Someone had to man the pub."

"Before, then. You visited Reginald Trent in his office in the old library. Did you go there to talk about Sima?"

Harry looked away. "So what if I did?" he asked. "It's not illegal to talk to someone, is it?"

"You found out that Reginald had been threatening her." Yet another qualified guess, and like the first, it proved correct.

"The prick was enjoying it," said Harry. "I could see it on his face. He didn't even try to hide it. 'See you soon,' he told her in front of everyone. What a bastard."

"Where were you between the hours of 10:00 and 11:00 p.m. on Thursday, May 9?"

"I was where I always am: at the pub, serving beer. And there must be at least twenty people who can confirm that. The place was packed. We'd had the tourist board meeting the day before, so everyone wanted to talk shit about your charming murder victim."

"Did Sima plant the bomb herself, or did you help her? Given that you'd do anything for her?"

"Sima would never do something like that," Harry protested. A lock of hair fell into his eyes as he leaned forward, and he shook it back. "She's the most honest person I know."

"OK, so you went to talk to Reginald," said DCI Ahmed. "When was this?"

Harry hesitated for a moment, then he nodded. "Saturday," he said. "I just wanted to warn him about…bothering Sima."

"You got dressed up in a suit?"

"I usually just wear jeans and a T-shirt, but I know when to smarten up a bit. I didn't want him to have the upper hand from the get-go, so I put on one of my old suits from London. I used to wear them all the time back there."

"And what happened?"

Harry seemed tired. "Nothing. Nothing happened. I told him to leave Sima alone, he laughed in my face, and then I went home. Like a mug."

DCI Ahmed nodded. At some point in the conversation, Harry had also lost a cuff link. One that had somehow survived the explosion. He thought back to what the bomb expert had said: more comes out unscathed than you might think.

"Sima looks after the village," Harry continued. "She always has. She works hard for us. I just felt like it was time someone did something for her for a change."

"Do you know what hold Reginald had over her?"

"She wouldn't tell me," he said unhappily. "As though anything she'd done could change my feelings for her. She and Reginald were the only ones who knew, she said."

"And now he's dead."

"Yeah," Harry said, looking away.

36

BERIT ROLLED OUT THE PAPER all over the living room floor. It was the kind of paper you could buy in a toy shop, for children to paint on, but she used it to plot her novels.

And now, her murder investigations.

A cup of coffee stood on the desk, and the patio doors were open to the beautiful afternoon outside. The room smelled like coffee and sunshine.

She began by the kitchen door and wrote in big letters:
REGINALD TRENT ARRIVES UNEXPECTEDLY IN GREAT DIDDLING.

That was followed by: DYNAMITE STOLEN BETWEEN 10–11 THURSDAY NIGHT. Here she added: DAPHNE TRENT READ POETRY.

She felt Sally's presence behind her, but neither of them spoke. Sally went into the kitchen and got a cup of tea, then returned to watch Berit's progress.

Berit drew an arrow to a separate box: *At some point after Reginald Trent arrived in the village, someone decided explosives were the most logical solution to their problem.*

"You're trying to figure out who stole the explosives," Sally said. She sounded nervous.

"I want to understand the circumstances that made it feel like a reasonable path to take."

Berit continued down the paper. TEA PARTY, she wrote and almost immediately after that: REGINALD TRENT IS MURDERED.

She took several steps further down: BOOK FESTIVAL IS ORGANIZED. And then: GERALD CORDUROY-SMITH ARRIVES IN VILLAGE.

Here she paused for quite some time. She remembered the bad feeling she had had when he got there. As if everything was spiraling out of control. The book festival had distracted her, but now that it had ended, that same feeling of imminent threat had returned in full force.

SIMA IS QUESTIONED BY THE POLICE, she wrote.

"Is it a timeline?" Sally asked. "Or an overview of the plot, so to speak?"

"These are the things that have happened so far," Berit replied. "But it doesn't become a plot until we can see a clear, obvious link between them. To count as a plot, things have to happen for a reason; one thing has to lead to another. When things just happen here and there, the whole thing is disjointed and episodic. Incomprehensible."

"So what do you need to make it into a plot?"

"Characters doing things. Their motivation and drive is what makes the difference. And I need to know more."

"You've left so much blank space. Does that mean you think things will keep happening?"

"Without a doubt."

Berit gripped the marker and looked down at the paper. In a separate box she wrote: *Competence and madness. Community and betrayal. Honest lies. Books. The lure of Oscar Wilde.*

Behind her, Sally hesitated before saying in a rush, "Liam stole the explosives."

But he hadn't done it alone, Berit thought, suddenly tired.

"Eleanor covered for him."

Berit wondered if that was all she had done. When Sally didn't say anything more, Berit knelt down in front of the paper again. On the right corner, she put down a single word.

Atonement.

That was what worried her, she realized. She wanted this entire crazy, flawed village to have a chance to atone for their sins without wrecking their lives. But one of them had done something unforgivable, and she was afraid that others might be dragged down with them.

She could feel the net tightening around the people she had come to like, and there was a real risk that everyone would end up getting caught.

Unless she helped them.

"Will you talk to him? Liam, I mean. And convince him that he has to talk to the police?"

Berit sighed and slowly got up. "Yes," she said, "I'll talk to him."

But whether or not it would do any good, she couldn't say.

In a field on the outskirts of the village, someone had dumped an old Ford. No one had ever cared enough to take it away, and it had been slowly stripped of parts. The radio was first to disappear, followed by the tires. At some point in time, a bored group of teenagers had smashed the windows, and all that was now left was a rusty shell, propped up on a few cinder blocks.

Liam was sitting on its roof. "How'd you know I was here?" he asked.

"Sally told me that you like to get away here when you need to think." Berit studied the rusty metal and decided against trying to climb up. She leaned back against the hood of the car instead.

"Don't start lecturing me," he said. "I've had enough of that already."

"She doesn't realize you're protecting someone else. Beer?" Berit held up a bottle.

Surprised, Liam hopped down from the roof and stood beside her.

"But she does have a point," Berit went on. "I know you think the murder of Reginald Trent somehow doesn't matter, because the man was an asshole. But we can't go around killing people just because they're idiots—or no one would be safe. I suspect I'd be one of the first to be offed. You might not believe me, but I can be bloody irritating when I want to be."

"I believe you."

"Have you been friends long, you and Eleanor?"

Liam shot her a quick look. He seemed to decide that her question was innocent enough, either that or he just needed to talk, because after a moment he said:

"Since they moved here. I was thirteen. Eleanor saw what things were like for me at home. She let me crash on their sofa whenever I needed it."

"She suggested it as a joke, didn't she? Stealing the explosives. It's OK," Berit added when he tensed. "You don't have to say anything; I'm just thinking aloud. It feels like the sort of thing Eleanor might do. The whole crazy plan of pretending to be Mrs. Ainsley too."

Liam swigged his beer and stared straight ahead.

"I understand," Berit continued. "I really do. I'm rather fond of her myself."

They stood quietly for a moment, looking out across the dark fields. The sun had set, but the evening air was still warm. Someone was having a barbecue in a yard nearby, and the scent of charcoal and sausages drifted over on the breeze.

"It must have come as a real shock when Reginald Trent was suddenly blown to pieces," she said suddenly.

She could no longer see his expression, but they were so close that she felt the reaction in his slim body as he tensed up. Berit was reminded of just how young he was, and she patted him on the shoulder.

"It's all going to be OK," she said. Right there and then, she was determined to make sure it was.

But Liam didn't relax. On the contrary. He seemed to grow even more tense.

Berit nodded to herself. She understood. There was nothing more dangerous than hope.

37

IT WAS AFTER ELEVEN WHEN Berit got to the hotel. Penny was behind the reception desk, painting her nails.

"Would you mind calling up to Gerald's room to see whether he's still awake and willing to spare me a few minutes?"

Penny answered without looking up. "He is. He just ordered a bottle of cognac, so I'm sure he can spare both a few minutes and a glass. Room twenty-three. If you're going to speak to him, make sure you pass on a message from me. Tell him to go to hell."

Gerald was wearing a thick embroidered smoking jacket when he opened his door. He was also completely bald, a fact that didn't seem to bother him in the slightest.

"Ms. Gardner," he said, sounding surprised.

"Call me Berit," she replied, pushing past him into his room.

The bed was still made, which meant she hadn't woken him. There was a bottle of cognac on the small desk, just as Penny had said, a half-full glass beside it. The wardrobe doors were open, and she could see five suits and three wigs hanging neatly inside.

Gerald followed her eye. "Perhaps you prefer blonds?" he said, holding up a shaggy, blond wig. "It's true what they say: blonds do have more fun. Just look at the difference between Boris Johnson and David Cameron. So what can I do for you, Berit?"

"I'd like to talk to you about Eleanor Hartfield."

"Eleanor?"

She really had surprised him now. His mask slipped slightly, telling her he was genuinely interested. Gerald poured Berit a glass of cognac and topped up his own.

"I think you share a certain…background with her," she said. "So I thought you were probably a good person to ask."

"And what background might that be?"

"As a con artist."

Neither his facial expression nor tone of voiced changed in the slightest. "What makes you think we're con artists?" he asked conversationally.

"Just a hunch. Maybe I'm wrong. You're both very theatrical, as though you're constantly playing a part. Out of habit and profession, I think, like you just can't help yourselves. But you aren't actors. Neither of you has ever mentioned the theater, and I've never come across an actor who hasn't told me all about their various parts within five minutes of meeting. You both prefer listening to talking too. I guess that must be vital in your line of work, but the majority of actors seem overly fond of hearing their own voice."

"And they give away more than they ever learn. You're right about that. Listening is key."

"Did you know Eleanor before you came here?" Berit asked.

"Do you think she's the killer?"

Berit sipped her cognac and waited.

Gerald laughed. "No, we'd never met before I came to Great Diddling, but I had heard of her, through a mutual acquaintance. Her and her…sister. Though they were cousins back then, of course." He raised an eyebrow as he gauged her reaction.

"Yes, I understand they've led rather colorful lives," said Berit. "Do you think they came to Great Diddling because of a job?"

He filled his glass again, but Berit shook her head when he offered her a refill.

"I don't know," he said, sounding annoyed.

"They've been here a few years now. If they'd come to Great Diddling on a job, don't you think they would have done whatever it was by now?"

"What's to say they haven't? Maybe it just hasn't been reported to the police."

"Are those the best robberies? The ones that are never reported?"

"Absolutely." He thought for a moment. "No, actually, the best thefts are those that are never even discovered."

Berit crossed her legs. "Hypothetically speaking, what would you say makes a good con artist?"

Gerald smiled. "Hypothetically? Intelligence, a good judge of character, quick reflexes, flexibility, brilliance…and, yes, a certain theatricality also helps. It's all about selling a story. You have to be the script writer and director in one—and at least one of the actors has no idea he or she is even in a play."

Berit nodded. "But you're still writing their lines for them?"

"You have to."

"Sounds harder than being an author."

"Oh, without doubt. You writers have it easy."

"What's the biggest risk in that line of work?"

Gerald replied without missing a beat: "Hubris."

"That's risky for an author too," she said. "Self-doubt keeps a person on their toes. Though on the other hand, hubris is also important, because if you don't have some sense of being invincible, then no one would ever write anything."

Gerald poured himself another glass. This time Berit said yes to a top-up, but when he turned away from her to push the cork back into the bottle, she tipped half of it into a flowerpot. She wet her lips with the remaining liquid.

"Do you know what I've always wondered?" she asked. "Why bother with cons? If a person has all those qualities that you mentioned, why not just get a normal job and really make a go of it? Become successful without risking prison."

Yet again, he answered right away: "For the challenge. The rush of it all. And because of a certain innate restlessness, I guess. Routine is deadly."

She looked around the room in search of a tangent. She wanted to get him talking about the general things before she asked him about anything specific.

"What's the deal with the wigs?" she asked.

He seemed amused. "You women have it so easy. Just imagine, still hypothetically, of course, that you're being followed and you wanted to disappear into a crowd. What would you do?"

"Run?"

He shot her a disapproving look. "Run?! Honestly, Berit, I expected more of you. Much more. Think, woman."

"Move at the same speed as everyone else."

"Exactly. Or more slowly. It's human instinct to speed up if you think someone is following you, so the first thing that person will be looking for are quick, stressed movements. One of the simplest ways to blend in is to steal a map from a tourist and act confused on a street corner."

Berit nodded him on.

"Though there's still a risk that they'll spot you, of course," he went on. "People focus on particular body types and patterns of movement. Both of those are things that can be changed, but not entirely. A tall man can't make himself short, for example, and a fat man can't suddenly look slim."

"And a bald man can't sprout hair."

He laughed. "Bingo!"

"Fascinating."

"An important life lesson more generally too. There isn't a single disadvantage that can't become an advantage if you're creative enough."

"It must have been frustrating. So much hard work, writing the script and directing the play, and then Reginald dies." She was careful to keep her tone breezy.

"That idiot! Getting himself murdered like that." Gerald sounded whiny and irritated, as though Reginald's death was a personal affront.

"It's not about the money for you, is it?" Berit asked suddenly.

"Of course it's about the money. What else would it be about?"

"Books. Or rather, a particular book. And not because it's valuable, but because it's unique."

"Don't tell anyone, will you?" Gerald said with a smile. "Money is a motive that makes sense, but wanting to own a book? Madness. In my line of work, people don't like things they can't understand."

"So you singled out Reginald Trent because you knew about Daphne's book collection?"

He gazed down into his glass. Berit wondered whether he would answer, though she suspected Gerald probably thought they were still talking hypothetically. That, and the ever-present temptation of someone incredibly smart wanting to let everyone know just how smart they were. What's the biggest risk? Hubris.

"Oscar Wilde has always fascinated me," Gerald said. "He was the ultimate con man. Living off his wit, his intelligence...and then there's his illegal sexual orientation." He knocked back his cognac. "Of course, it doesn't hurt that the book is also worth a fortune."

"But then Reginald died."

"And ruined all my plans. Find me a scriptwriter or a director who'd be happy if someone suddenly set off a bomb right in the middle of the second act!" He was trying hard to seem nonchalant. "Anyway," he went on, waving his hand. "What's done is done. Even the most mediocre of men can come up with a plan, but it takes a genius to improvise when things inevitably go wrong. And fortunately for me, I am a genius."

Berit studied him. Genius or not, he definitely seemed to have fooled Reginald. But was he smart enough to kill and get away with it? She wasn't sure. And what did he stand to gain from Reginald's death?

"Daphne told me about the offer you made her," she said. "At the party."

"Like I said, it's all about being flexible."

"She'll never sell her collection to you. Daphne wants to keep supporting the village, and Sima will make sure that's what happens."

Gerald looked down into his cognac and smirked. "We'll see about that."

38

LIKE SO MUCH ELSE IN life, the rumors about Sima started gradually, a slippery slope, where they gained more and more momentum the further they traveled. Like a stone rolling down a hill, Berit thought.

Or a wildfire.

She could see it happening in the café, on High Street, and in the pub. Slowly, hesitantly, people had started muttering that they had always thought there was something off about Sima. Old grudges were dragged back into the light, and as people found encouragement and agreement with others, they felt empowered enough to suggest that someone really should go to the police.

Berit could just imagine a solemn DCI Ahmed reeling them in. He knew how to make people relax and trust him, she thought. For the first time, she actually found herself wishing he was slightly less competent. The villagers would confide in him, cheeks flushing with excited dismay at everything they knew about their fellow citizen.

To think that they had been living next door to a possible murderer all these years, they said. They had served on committees and in working groups with her, and she had been keeping these secrets from them the whole time. But they'd had their suspicions, they claimed. Oh yes, they all had. Something just wasn't right.

Berit paid close attention to everything they said, and her unease only grew stronger. Something felt off about the way people had suddenly started talking about Sima. It was as though someone was controlling the gossip, or at least adding fuel to the flames. The entire village had rallied around Liam when he was taken in for questioning, but when the same thing happened to Sima, they were all acting like she must be guilty.

"And she was arrested in broad daylight!" Mrs. Tinley told a group of locals who had gathered on High Street. "I saw them take her in for questioning."

Berit moved closer to hear what they were saying. Several of the villagers were nodding eagerly. Mr. Carew of the antique shop was the only one who seemed to be trying to defend Sima.

"In broad daylight," he repeated. "Are you trying to say they should have done it at night? Besides, they didn't arrest her. She's just...assisting them in their inquiries."

"Mmm, that's what they always say," said Mrs. Tinley.

"Don't be ridiculous," Mr. Carew told the group. "This is Sima you're talking about. You've known her for years."

His words were met with silence. Troubled at first, then defiant.

"Not that many years," said Mrs. Tinley, earning herself nods from several of the others. "And what did she do before she came here? That's what I'd like to know. Likely as not committing murders someplace else; that's what I think."

James Elmer came marching out of the hotel and glared at Mrs. Tinley. "Take your gossip somewhere else," he said. "And don't forget that the police have been wrong before."

Mr. Carew nodded eagerly, but Mrs. Tinley simply snorted and put her hands on her hips. "You think so, do you? It wouldn't surprise me if it turned out you were guilty after all!"

"Make your mind up. We can't both have done it," said James, rolling his eyes and turning to make his way back inside.

"What I'd like to know is what you're planning to do with all the books," Gerald Corduroy-Smith spoke up. He had sidled up to the group without anyone noticing.

"Books?" asked Mr. Carew.

"Yes. She filled your shops with old, unsellable books. That's all well and good for one weekend, but are you really going to let them take up so much space going forward?"

"The idea is that customers will buy them," Mr. Carew replied.

"What customers?"

Everyone looked around. Sure enough, the street was deserted.

"I heard she's planning to hold another festival next year," said someone.

"The follow-up is never quite as good, in my experience," Gerald declared. "If you want my advice, you should quit while you're ahead. The festival may have been a success this year, but what are the chances you'll be able to repeat that?" He shrugged. "Not that it's any of my business. You've all been paid, I presume?"

"Not yet," one of the bed-and-breakfast hosts conceded.

Mrs. Tinley's eyes darted between them.

"I don't know any of the details, obviously," said Gerald, "but if a person is capable of murder, then I wouldn't be at all surprised if she was also embezzling money. That's all I'll say."

Berit returned immediately to the cottage.

She felt like washing her hands—and her ears. Having to listen to such malicious gossip made her feel grubby. Flock mentality, ill will, mockery, and cynicism. All the worst aspects of humanity coming together in a poisonous mix.

But there was something odd about the rumors against Sima. It felt as if something was spurring them on. Or, more accurately, someone.

Gerald had been hard at work, fanning the flames.

THE CAMPAIGN AGAINST SIMA.

She frowned. Something was nagging at the back of her mind, but *what?* An idea, not yet fully formed… She had caught a glimpse of it before. Something she'd heard…

Something clicked inside her. She knelt down by the paper and added: *the best theft is one that isn't reported or discovered.*

Then she stood back and studied the timeline.

She just couldn't get it to make sense. Something didn't add up. She'd made a mistake somewhere—either that or someone else had—and a piece of the puzzle had been forced into a hole it simply didn't fit in.

It reminded her of the more hopeless moments in her writing process, when so much was already in place that the remaining pieces became even harder to move.

She spent the entire day pacing back and forth in the living room, without any success. By nine o'clock, she gave up for the night. She decided to solve it the same way she did when she was writing, so she forced herself to go home to bed. Sleep sometimes helped her make connections her waking brain just couldn't manage.

But not tonight. She tossed and turned in bed, and when she finally fell asleep, she slept fitfully as she dreamt about books and rolling stones and rogue bookshelves chasing people across High Street.

She was up again before dawn. She felt clumsy and irritable. No revolutionary ideas had come to her during the night, and Berit couldn't escape the feeling that it was all too late. That she was going to fail to help them and that everything—the village, the festival, her book idea, Sally and Liam's friendship—would be lost.

Sally was still asleep when Berit pulled on her khaki jacket and hurried out. The air was cool and damp, dew glittering in the meadow grass beyond the cottages. She could hear a tractor in a field somewhere nearby, but the village itself was quiet as she made her way through it. Berit watched as the sun rose above the buildings on High Street.

In the gaps between the various shops, she caught glimpses of the fields and hills in the distance. It was all so beautiful that it almost felt like an omen that something bad was coming.

She spotted Eleanor as she was approaching the café. The older woman was walking down High Street in the opposite direction.

"We need to talk," Berit said as they met.

"Are you going to ask if I killed Reginald Trent?"

"Would you tell me the truth if I did?"

"No, probably not."

"It was a mistake to get Liam mixed up in this," said Berit. "You might get off scot-free, but people like him were born to get into trouble."

"Liam will be fine," Eleanor replied curtly. She hesitated for a moment, then sighed. "Come on. We can talk over breakfast."

As though by some unspoken agreement, they walked in silence. It wasn't because they were afraid someone might hear them; there was no one else around. No, it was just that the sunrise was so beautiful that it didn't feel right to ruin it with conversation.

The bright sun made them both turn their heads toward one of the alleyways leading off High Street, and it was that same sun that made them pause and stop, unsure of what exactly they were looking at.

The slanting rays of light illuminated a head of flaxen-colored hair.

Somehow they both knew that the person it belonged to wasn't sleeping. Eleanor reeled and had to grip Berit's arm to remain upright. She took two deep breaths, her hand still on Berit's arm, then let go and marched straight into the alleyway.

Perhaps it was an attempt to compensate for her earlier weakness, thought Berit. She stood and watched as Eleanor dropped to her knees and reached out to the victim's—that was how she referred to him in her head—throat.

"He's dead!" Eleanor shouted. "It's Gerald Corduroy-Smith or whatever he called himself. You should probably dial 999. Someone has smashed his head in."

39

MY NAME IS BERIT GARDNER, and I'd like to report another murder.

This woman will drive me crazy one day, DCI Ahmed thought grimly, slamming the car door a little too hard.

In front of him, a cordon had already been set up at the entrance to the alleyway where Berit claimed that Gerald Corduroy-Smith was lying dead. One lane of the street beyond was closed, and an officer was busy directing the handful of cars and pedestrians that passed.

Berit and Eleanor were standing over by the cordon. Maybe it was the way they just stood there together in silence, but DCI Ahmed couldn't shake the feeling that Berit was both literally and metaphorically on Eleanor's side.

He nodded in greeting, then pushed them out of his thoughts, trying to clear his mind before he got his first proper look at the crime scene. First impressions could be crucial going forward, and he knew that he always saw more when he gave both his conscious and subconscious self free rein.

He stood in silence for a moment, faced with a life that had ended too soon and a world that went on like normal. It was going to be a beautiful day. He could feel it. The air smelled like sunshine, which seemed particularly cruel.

The alleyway in front of him was cramped and dirty. A dead space with no back doors leading out onto it. You could always tell when a space wasn't used, thought DCI Ahmed, and unused places often took on other, less-pleasant purposes. He wasn't at all surprised that Gerald Corduroy-Smith had been found dead somewhere like this.

The victim was lying face down on the ground with his feet toward DCI Ahmed and the high street, and Ahmed couldn't help but think that there was something darkly funny about the way his expensive Italian shoes were pointing outward. The crime scene technicians were already busy photographing the body, documenting every aspect of the scene. All that activity felt like an intrusion somehow, but then again death was almost always undignified.

Gerald Corduroy-Smith was wearing dark chinos and a navy sweater, and even from a distance, it was clear that his blond hair was matted with dry blood.

On the ground beside his body, there was a wallet and a small parcel wrapped in fabric. The two objects seemed to contradict each other. The empty, discarded wallet suggested theft, that someone had rifled through it and then tossed it away. But if that was the case, why leave the parcel? Why not take it away and check its contents later?

Unless the killer had known what was inside because he or she was the one who brought it to the scene in the first place. But if so, why leave it and risk having it traced back to them?

"Has the pathologist been yet?" DCI Ahmed asked.

"En route."

He looked around. The high street was, mercifully, still quiet, but he knew it was only a matter of time until a crowd formed. "I'll start with Eleanor," he decided.

DCI Ahmed asked Berit to wait for a few minutes, then led Eleanor over to the other side of the street, where they could talk a little more privately.

"I was out for a walk," said Eleanor.

"At five thirty in the morning?"

"I woke early." She looked up at the detective. "Berit too, clearly."

"And the two of you met by chance?"

"Yes, we didn't exactly arrange to meet at dawn."

"Tell me what happened."

Eleanor shrugged. "Not much to tell. We were walking along the street, we spotted the body, we called the police."

He noticed that she didn't use Gerald Corduroy-Smith's name.

"Did you know who it was right away?"

"No. But I did as soon as I went over to him."

"So you moved closer to identify him?"

"To see whether there was anything we could do to help. But there wasn't."

It must have taken real courage to walk down a dark alleyway where a man was most likely lying dead, thought DCI Ahmed. He studied Eleanor's face, searching for signs of delayed shock. At her age, she deserved extra consideration—though she would never admit that she needed it, of course.

Assuming she hadn't arranged to have the body dumped there, he thought, searching for signs of that too. He found nothing. In fact, he couldn't see any emotion at all in her face. No hint of horror or adrenaline or even curiosity—none of the hundred or so feelings he had seen at crime scenes over the years. The only sign of any sort of reaction was the way she clenched her right fist. He didn't think she even noticed she was doing it.

"Can I go now?" she asked. "I have to get the café ready for opening. And you know where I am, in case you need me."

He nodded, and Eleanor walked away without looking back. DCI Ahmed turned his attention to Berit.

The minute he reached her, she said, "The wig."

He nodded. He had noticed the victim's sudden change in hair color too.

"You knew he wore one?" he asked.

"Yes, I visited him at his hotel the night before last. He showed me his, well, disguises, I guess they were."

He raised an eyebrow. "And do you mind me asking what you were doing visiting his hotel room at night?"

"Talking," she said firmly. "I know what you're thinking, but I wasn't interfering, I promise." She sounded guilty and realized it. "Not much, anyway. I didn't even ask him about the murder."

"So what did you talk about?"

Berit hesitated. "Eleanor Hartfield," she said reluctantly.

"Of course. And here we are."

"We didn't say anything that could have given her a motive to kill him, if that's what you're getting at."

DCI Ahmed chose to ignore her remarks. "Tell me everything that happened this morning," he said.

He got Berit to show him exactly where she and Eleanor had met, and she told him which direction Eleanor had come from, that she had turned around to join Berit rather than continuing wherever she had been going.

Once he was sure he had a clear picture of their exact movements, he asked, "And how did she seem to you when you met?"

"Seem?"

"Yes. Was she calm, short of breath? Did you get the sense that she'd been running or doing anything physically demanding?"

"No, nothing like that. She seemed calm and relaxed. Strolling along the pavement."

He nodded. "And then you spotted Mr. Corduroy-Smith in the alleyway?"

"Yes."

"Did you both notice him at the same time? Or did one of you see him first and shout or say something that made the other look that way?"

"We both looked that way at the same time. It was so very beautiful, you see."

DCI Ahmed looked skeptically at the dark and dirty alleyway in front of them.

"The sunrise," she explained. "It was shining straight down the alleyway, making it look almost idyllic. The sunlight made his hair glow. I don't think we understood what we were looking at initially, not until we saw his feet. That's when we realized something was wrong. I think we were both hoping he was just drunk, but deep down we'd probably already noticed the blood. Then again, it could have just been the sunlight making it look red... You know how you try to trick yourself sometimes..."

DCI Ahmed didn't think Berit seemed like someone who tried to trick herself particularly often, but he resisted the urge to share that thought. "OK, so Eleanor made her way into the alley. Did she touch anything?"

"Only Gerald. She checked for a pulse, on his throat."

"And you didn't follow her?"

"I suppose I thought it was enough for one of us to do it."

"And what happened next?"

"Eleanor said he was dead and that I should call the police."

My name is Berit Gardner, and I'd like to report another murder.

"I wonder how many other people around here knew he wore a wig," DCI Ahmed mumbled to himself.

Berit nodded eagerly. "I've been thinking about that too. His hair was usually dark. He seems to have arranged to meet someone in the middle of the night, so why bother changing that? Whoever he was meeting would have been expecting him to look the same as he always did. Unless he was meeting someone who knew that his hair color…fluctuated. If that was the case, he might have just grabbed a wig at random."

"If it was dark when he met the other person, he might have been banking on them not noticing the color."

Berit waved dismissively. "It would still be noticeable under the streetlamps or if a car drove by. He would never have been that sloppy. Although he might have done it as a joke. If the person knew. Blonds have more fun?"

"I used to think that this whole case started with Gerald," DCI Ahmed said tiredly. "That he set everything in motion when he chose Reginald Trent as his next victim and sent him down to Tawny Hall. And now it seems it will end with him too."

"If there's one thing I've learned from writing, it's that the beginning is never as obvious as you think. A story can begin in several different places. The trick is knowing which one is right."

"Did Gerald pick Reginald with a specific target?" Ahmed mused. "Or did he just 'plant' himself close to the target and wait for the right opportunity?"

The minute he said it, he realized that Berit knew something. He grabbed her arm. "Tell me," he said. "What was Gerald after? You know, don't you?"

But Berit had gotten a faraway look on her face. She frowned distractedly. "*Planted himself…*" she repeated. "There's something about that word…about waiting for an opportunity…"

He studied her closely, but she just shook her head in frustration.

"I can't figure it out," she said. "Something just doesn't add up."

She looked tired, as though she hadn't got much sleep. He suspected the bags beneath her eyes matched his own. Her forehead was still creased in an irritated frown as a result of that thing that she just couldn't see yet.

"Berit," Ahmed said suddenly, "you really need to give this up."

She looked surprised. And unconvinced.

He held up his hands. "This isn't an official warning. It's not some formal order, which I'm sure you'd just ignore."

"I wouldn't," she said. "I do actually respect your authority and the important job you do, but—"

"I'm asking you as…as a friend, OK? This murder isn't the same as the first. It's sloppier. Spontaneous. More physically violent. That means our killer is ramping up. If you hear anything or think of anything—whatever it is—I want you to give me a call right away. Me. Don't go running off to talk to any suspects alone in their room late at night. Let me take the risks now."

"I'm wondering whether it really was spontaneous," she said. "If I'm right, I think you're going to discover that far more planning went into this murder than you think."

"Berit!"

She held up her hands. "I promise not to interfere."

He nodded gratefully.

"Unless it's absolutely necessary," she added.

This woman is going to drive me insane, he thought.

It was still early, but the pathologist had taken the time to apply red lipstick and put on gold earrings. Beneath her white plastic overalls, she was wearing a pair of smart gray trousers and a practical yet well-cut T-shirt. The overall impression was that she was dressed for something other than a meeting with a dead body in an alleyway. DCI Ahmed self-consciously tugged up the zip on his own windbreaker to hide his creased shirt.

She lowered her bag to the ground and got onto her knees by the body. Her blue plastic gloves looked absurdly bright against his pale skin.

"First impressions?" asked DCI Ahmed.

"Same as yours, I assume. Blunt force trauma to the back of the head. I'm pretty sure we'll find traces of dirt when we analyze the wound. You see here? That's not just blood on the wig. It looks like soil of some kind. A rounded object, no sharp edges."

"Time of death?"

"Two hours ago at least. No earlier than midnight, 4:00 a.m. at the latest. That's all I can say right now."

That probably knocked Eleanor from the top of his list of subjects, thought DCI Ahmed. If she had killed Gerald at four in the morning, why would she hang around the crime scene for at least an hour and a half, if not longer?

"Did he live nearby?" asked the pathologist.

"He was staying at the hotel not too far from here."

She nodded. "Explains why he wasn't wearing a jacket. He looks like someone who just nipped out to run an errand, wouldn't you say?"

"If he was just running an errand, why did he take his wallet with him? Nothing would have been open in the middle of the night."

She shrugged as though to say that was his problem, which it was. Then she straightened up, eyes scanning the alleyway. "I'm sure you'll be conducting a thorough search here," she said. "But I can't see anything straightaway here that could have caused the wound."

"The killer took the murder weapon away with them, then?"

"Looks that way."

She squinted down the alleyway again. "Hell of a place to die," she muttered.

DCI Ahmed nodded, though he knew they had both seen worse.

Eleanor made sure to walk back to the café at a leisurely pace, but once she was safely inside, she ran up the stairs. She closed the door behind her, leaned back against it, and closed her eyes for a few seconds before heading through to the bathroom. She closed that door too.

With her clenched fists on the edge of the sink, she pressed her forehead to the bathroom mirror. The glass felt cool against her skin. *Think, Eleanor*, she told herself as she tried to visualize the alleyway. *Sunshine. Dark walls. Wallet. Parcel. Dead body.*

What had she missed?

She hadn't had time to check the parcel. Or the wallet, for that matter. She hoped everything was still inside it.

There was nothing more she could have done, not with Berit there. It had been tempting to swipe the parcel, but she couldn't guarantee that the author hadn't already noticed it. That woman saw far too bloody much.

Eleanor unclenched her hand, revealing a single hairpin in her palm. She had resisted the urge to throw it into one of the bins on the high street. It had been tempting, but the police would be sure to search them. There was every chance they wouldn't notice a solitary hairpin, but Eleanor didn't want to take any risks. *Not with something as important as this*, she thought.

Instead, she carefully rinsed and dried it off, then put it back into the little jar where Mary kept the rest of them.

What had she missed?

40

SISTERS' CAFÉ WAS A HIVE of activity. The whole village seemed to be crowded around the till, and while they waited to order—with Mary and Eleanor struggling to get all the teapots and sandwiches and scones to their guests—they exchanged what little information they had.

"Have you heard…?" one person asked, and another nodded eagerly.

"She found him. Her and that author."

A third person joined in. "I heard the police don't even have any suspects."

"I know who I'd be looking at if I were them. Someone Mr. Corduroy-Smith shared a few home truths about not long before he was killed."

"Next!" Eleanor shouted. In the face of her anger, the visitors obediently shuffled off toward their tables.

The window seats were the most popular, with people crammed together in large groups. They didn't have a view of the alleyway from there, but they could see anyone who walked by outside, and they could also see everyone who came into the café.

As new guests arrived, they found themselves being hounded by those already inside. *Have you heard? Any news? Are the police still working over there?*

At one point, a young constable entered the café to order tea and sandwiches for the other officers. Every conversation fizzled out until he left.

It always felt tragic to search a hotel room looking for clues about a person's life, thought DCI Ahmed. Hotel rooms were, by definition, impersonal. Whenever he traveled, that was precisely what he liked about staying in hotels. They didn't expect anything of him. There were no everyday concerns, no papers from work, no dirty clothes or old coffee cups. Nothing but crisp, white sheets and bland art hanging on the dark walls. He always slept best in anonymous hotel rooms in cities where no one knew him.

Ironically, it was precisely those things that made his work even harder right now. There was practically nothing in the room that could tell him about Gerald Corduroy-Smith.

The bed was neatly made, suggesting he hadn't slept in it since the room was last cleaned. DCI Ahmed made a mental note to check when that was. There weren't enough clothes in the wardrobe to give any real sense of the man who owned them: three suits, of varying degrees of smartness, ranging from dark wool to white linen; two pairs of navy-blue chinos, several white shirts, and a handful of T-shirts. The only thing that stood out—almost like some sort of protest against his otherwise sober and tasteful wardrobe— were his expensive, brightly colored underpants. Stevens held up a pair of rainbow-colored briefs, and DCI Ahmed shrugged.

A half-empty bottle of cognac stood on a little desk against the wall. Or half-full, depending on how you looked at it.

Other than that, there were no papers, no planner, no helpful notes to tell them who he had arranged to meet in the dark alleyway where he died.

Not long later, the detectives took the receptionist through to the dining room so that they could interview her without anyone else overhearing their conversation.

Her name was Alice, and she leaned toward them with her elbows on the table and an excited look on her face.

She seemed like the sort of person who enjoyed scaring herself with ghost stories, thought DCI Ahmed. Someone who always kept one eye open for mysterious white vans up to no good.

"So was it the boss who did it?" she asked.

"James Elmer?" DCI Ahmed was taken aback.

"No, I meant Penny. Did she do it? I mean, she confessed to the first one. It was in the paper and everything. I don't care what my mum says about needing to support myself, I'm not going to keep working in a place where someone got killed."

"The murder didn't technically take place here."

Alice glared at DCI Ahmed. Facts couldn't be allowed to get in the way of a creepy story.

He knew he would have to proceed with caution if he wanted to avoid adding to her excitement. She was the kind of witness who was so keen to help that she could easily be influenced by anything he said. People like that could convince themselves that they had seen and heard practically anything.

"Were you working the night shift in reception yesterday?" he asked calmly.

"Yeah. I mean, to begin with. But the boss...Penny, she took over." With that, it was as though she couldn't hold back any longer. "Have you found the money yet?"

"The money?"

"Mr. Corduroy-Smith came down earlier in the day yesterday and asked about the closest town with a bank. We don't have one here anymore. Anyway, he came back later with a load of cash. Thousands of pounds. I saw it in his wallet when he paid for us to send a bottle of cognac up to his room."

"Do you typically notice how much money your guests have?" asked DCI Ahmed.

"Sure. It's hard to miss a massive wad of cash, you know? People don't usually have that sort of money these days. Most just pay by card or add it to the tab."

When Harry unlocked the door of his pub at eleven, a small but eager group of locals was already waiting outside, and as the day wore on, more and more villagers found an excuse to stop by.

Berit stopped by the pub in the afternoon, and by then, the place was packed. She noticed one group sitting in a corner at the very back of the room and recognized several of them as shopkeepers and B&B hosts during the festival. She grabbed her beer and moved closer, discreetly sitting down within earshot.

"She killed him," said one of them. "He knew something about her, so she murdered him."

The claim went unchallenged and hung in the air between them.

"What happens to our money now? As far as I know, no one's been paid a penny for renting out their rooms," said someone else.

"I'm sure she'll pay up soon," said Mr. Carew.

"Not if the police arrest her first. What if they…what's it called, freeze her assets?" said someone else.

"It's not her money," Mr. Carew continued. "It belongs to the village. No one paid anything to her personally."

"Easy for you to say; you didn't rent out a room. You shopkeepers have already earned your money." Several of the bed-and-breakfast hosts nodded. "We want someone else to take over."

Berit sat quietly, staring down into her pint glass as she listened tensely to everything they said.

"I can talk to her," said Mr. Carew. "I don't suppose you think I killed anyone, do you?"

Berit left her half-empty glass on the table and snuck out.

She knocked on Sima's front door, but there was no answer.

The house was a slender two-up, two-down painted a contemporary shade of dark gray. It was squeezed in between two considerably older houses built on larger plots, which made it seem even more nondescript.

She knocked again, and after what felt like an eternity, the door finally opened. Sima was wearing black sweatpants and a white tank top. It felt odd to see her so casually dressed. Odd and worrying. *She should be dressed for a fight*, Berit thought.

"I suppose you want to come in," Sima said.

She sounded as though she wanted to stop Berit but had already given in. Perhaps the simple act of opening the door had been her capitulation. Sima must have heard her knocking and hesitated before eventually giving in. She stepped aside to let Berit pass.

The house was quiet. There were thick rugs on the floor, all subtle shades of gray, white, and beige, and the huge cushions on the deep sofas and armchairs dampened all sound.

Sima didn't invite her to sit down—and just as well, thought Berit. She wasn't sure she would be able to get back up from the low sofa if she did; the thing looked like it might swallow her whole. It was late May, but there were still several thick blankets draped over it.

The councillor didn't offer her anything to drink, but Berit could understand that—she was hardly a welcome guest.

"You must be wondering why I'm here," said Berit.

"Not especially," Sima said.

"Don't worry, I won't stay long. I just wanted to say this: you can trust DCI Ahmed. He won't judge you before he has all the facts. Sima, you must tell him everything!"

Sima laughed—a strange, warped sound that seemed to take her by surprise. "Everything," she repeated. "That's a lot to ask of someone."

"And one more thing: *keep fighting*. Don't give up. Nothing has ever been achieved by holding back."

"You don't understand," said Sima. "They don't trust me anymore. I can see it in their eyes. And their trust was all I had."

"I think you'll discover that you had something far more valuable than that: their friendship. And friendship only gets stronger when a person needs help and is brave enough to ask for it."

Berit was fairly sure she hadn't managed to get through to Sima, but at least she had tried. She hoped she had planted a seed inside her, ready to sprout and grow once the conditions were right.

Planted. There was that word again.

Eleanor had spent fifty years brushing Mary's hair, one hundred strokes every evening. Mary sat on the edge of the bed in front of her, with her long, thin locks hanging loose down her back.

Seventeen, eighteen, nineteen, Eleanor counted as she brushed.

"I stole the explosives that killed Reginald," she said.

Mary didn't react. She was sitting so close that Eleanor could feel every shift in her body, but she was completely still.

"You already knew, didn't you?"

"I know everything about you, Eleanor Hartfield."

"I found your hairpin. Beside…beside him, in the alleyway."

She wished she could see Mary's face. Her wife's shoulders were still loose and relaxed, but that didn't mean a thing. Mary had never been someone who got worked up over things. She reacted with total calm in almost every situation. Eleanor grew restless and agitated, having to get up and move around to find an outlet for her energy and emotions, but not Mary. She could remain completely motionless in the heat of the moment, utterly cool even in the most stressful situations.

That was why she had always been such a good liar.

"Why were you in that alleyway, Mary?" Eleanor asked softly.

Mary replied without missing a beat, "To sell a book. Or rather, the idea of a book."

Eleanor remembered the parcel she had seen on the ground by the body. "A pig in a poke," she said suddenly.

Mary laughed, a beautiful, bubbling sound that still had the power to make Eleanor smile. "To think I got to try that old trick one last time!" said Mary. "I was convinced he'd go for it, right down to the wire."

"What was in the bag?"

"A book, of course. The same size and weight as the one he was actually looking for. It wasn't exactly hard to find; the village is teeming with them."

"Which book did he think it was?" Eleanor asked, but she was pretty sure she already knew the answer.

"The Oscar Wilde, of course. Worth at least fifty grand, but I was willing to give it to him for twenty."

"He must have been an idiot if he thought you'd actually sell it that cheaply."

"He thought I was an idiot. Very useful, really. And twenty thousand was more than enough for me. I'll get my rose garden in the end; you'll see!"

"But how the hell did you find it? I mean, he must have asked to inspect the book before you did the switch?"

"Of course. I followed Margaret when she put it back that day we all got to see it. I hid behind the stairs as she went up, and then it was easy enough to work out where she went and how many steps she took. Every single floorboard creaks in old houses like that. It took me a while, but I eventually found a small room connected to a bedroom just past Daphne's. I had plenty of time to look for it too. No one pays any attention to an old lady with a feather duster."

Eleanor thought for a moment. It must have been in one of the rooms she hadn't managed to search the night she and Penny broke in. She'd only had time for a quick scan with her flashlight, looking for books or any other valuable items before moving on.

"It must've been hidden?"

"The door was wallpapered. Simple but effective. At first glance, it blended in with the wall."

Eleanor nodded. Especially in the dark.

"Don't worry," Mary chirped. "I didn't take any other books, though I was tempted. And I left the archival box it was in. They don't have any reason to suspect that it's gone."

"But the old pig-in-a-poke trick, Mary? Surely Gerald would never fall for it."

Eleanor was well aware that she sounded jealous. That was the truth; she missed the old cons. And getting away with that one last time! It was the oldest trick in the book: offer something valuable at a bargain price, let the customer inspect it, put the object into a bag, and then swap out the bag when they're not looking. Quick fingers and audacity were all it took, plus a gullible victim.

"It's always easiest to con a con man," Mary said.

She wasn't wrong. They were so convinced of their own superiority that they were never willing to believe that someone else was capable of conning them. That was also why it was easiest to dupe people in areas they felt comfortable. If you wanted to swindle a banker, you needed a financial bluff, whereas an art lover would readily succumb to the lure of a good forgery. And for a booklover…

"But what about the next day?" Eleanor asked. "Once he got home, opened the bag, and realized he'd been had? It'd be one thing if you'd left town the same evening, but we live here. He would have come straight back to you."

Mary shrugged. "It's not like he could go to the police."

"Christ, Mary, there are far worse things he could have done than that."

She shrugged. "I wasn't worried."

Because you knew I'd fix it, thought Eleanor. *Or because you'd already taken care of it yourself?*

There were certain questions you just didn't ask in a marriage. Especially if you were afraid that the other person would tell you the truth.

41

THE PATHOLOGIST PUSHED A MANILA folder across the table.

"The results of the postmortem," she said, though her eyes weren't on the report. She was focused on her plate of scrambled eggs, baked beans, and bacon, and she must have felt his eyes on her because she looked up and, between chews, said, "What? I started early this morning. Besides, postmortems always make me hungry."

The staff canteen at the station was never empty, not even midway between breakfast and lunch. DCI Ahmed got the sense that everyone who passed their table was staring at him. Or making an effort not to stare, which was worse.

Two murders, almost certainly carried out by the same perpetrator. No matter which way you looked at it, it was a failure on his part. It had been his duty to solve the first and prevent the second, but he hadn't.

She continued: "The cause of death was blunt force trauma to the back of the head. Look for a rounded object, around two centimeters in diameter. Probably some sort of gardening tool. I found traces of rust and soil in the wound. I'd be looking for the handle of something metal if I were you."

"So someone whacked him with the wrong end of a spade?"

"Not necessarily a spade, but yes. Something like that."

The pathologist looked up at him. "I've heard you're happy to take reflections and ideas, even if they're just vague hunches?"

Ian Ahmed was surprised. He had no idea she knew anything about his working style or that it was something people talked about.

"I'm friends with Rogers," she explained. "She speaks highly of you."

"I think very highly of her too," he added truthfully. "So do you have any ideas or reflections?" He would never have taken her for the sort of person who had vague hunches about anything.

"Based on the position of the body, I think he was killed by a woman. Someone he knew and underestimated."

She glanced at him to gauge his reaction. Once she realized that there was nothing but interest on his face, she pushed her half-empty plate away and leaned in closer. Something seemed to shift between them in that moment. Perhaps they had just taken their first tentative step toward a professional friendship, Ahmed thought.

"Firstly, there's their height," she said. "I know, I know, that doesn't necessarily mean it was a woman, but the fact of the matter is that he was killed by someone shorter than him. The blow came at an upward angle from behind and to one side. That's what made me think it was probably the shaft of some garden tool, based on the swing radius."

She acted out what she meant, as though she was gripping a baseball bat.

"And whoever it was, they were determined. This was someone who didn't hold back. It takes real strength to be sure you're going to kill someone like that."

"And that's not something everyone can manage, even if they're afraid for their own life," DCI Ahmed agreed. "But doesn't that almost suggest it wasn't a woman?" He held up his hands in anticipation of her protest. "There are plenty of dangerous women out there, clearly, but socially speaking women are conditioned not to resort to violence. They're more likely to hold back, not to lash out."

The pathologist nodded. "I know. I took a self-defense course once, and the first thing they taught us was that if we wanted to be able to protect ourselves, we had to really want to hurt the other person. That the risk would always be greatest if we hesitated, froze, or held back. But in this case, I believe it was someone your victim underestimated."

He noted that she never used Gerald Corduroy-Smith's name. That distance from the victim was a luxury he didn't have.

"Underestimated?" he repeated.

"He turned his back on your killer in a dark alleyway."

That was it, the thing that had been bothering him with the scene.

"His feet were pointing toward the street," he said. "And he was lying on his stomach. He was attacked from behind as he was walking down the alley."

"Exactly. A person would have to be pretty sure of their own superiority and invulnerability to lead someone down a dark alleyway—especially in the middle of the night. Goes against all of our instincts. Could it be an affair gone wrong?"

"If so, that would make it more likely he was killed by a man," said DCI Ahmed. "But no, I think this was something else. Money was missing from his wallet."

"Then I think it almost must have been a woman. Men of his generation feel comfortable with women behind them. It would never occur to them that we might pose a threat."

She spoke with the slightly smug tone of someone who knew that she very much did pose a threat, and DCI Ahmed found himself thinking about her self-defense course.

"Though it could also have been a friend, of course," she continued. "Someone he knew and trusted."

"I don't think there was a single person he trusted in the whole of Great Diddling."

"Well, then. A woman; that's my best guess. Shorter than him and determined."

Mrs. Tinley cast her critical eye around the interview room.

She seemed to have been expecting more, thought DCI Ahmed.

She took a sip of tea from her paper cup before she spoke: "I saw her!

She won't be able to weasel her way out of it this time. I knew all along, didn't I? Haven't I been saying it from the very beginning? Stuck-up Sima Kumar, guilty of murder!"

DCI Ahmed sighed. Witnesses with their own agenda were always the worst. It made them fundamentally unreliable. Even if they didn't lie outright, their testimonies were often full of wishful thinking. People could convince themselves they'd seen almost anything, if they wanted it enough.

And yet, you also couldn't just dismiss them out of hand. Sometimes they were actually right.

"What did you see, Mrs. Tinley?" he asked, a certain tiredness in his voice.

"I saw her walking home after the murder!"

DCI Ahmed felt himself tense. "What time was this?" he asked.

"Just after four. The sun wasn't up yet, but I don't sleep so well these days. I was standing by the window in the living room when I saw her, clear as anything!"

"How was she dressed?"

"Head to toe in black. Suspicious, don't you think? Black trousers, a black jacket, and a black hat, even though it's June! It's not that cold at night."

"How do you know it was after the murder? Couldn't she have...I don't know, been struggling to sleep, just like you, and decided to go for a walk?"

"With a spade?"

"She was carrying a spade?"

Despite his best efforts to keep his voice neutral, Mrs. Tinley seemed to sense his excitement because she puffed up her chest like a proud bird.

"Mmm, I thought that might make you sit up and listen. She must've buried him somewhere, you see. That was my first thought."

"He was found lying in an alleyway."

"Ah, yes, well, she did something else with it, then. Buried some evidence, perhaps? Whatever it was, she'd been up to no good. Whoever goes out walking with a spade in the middle of the night?"

"And you could clearly see that it was a spade, could you?"

"I saw the shaft."

He nodded. "Thank you for your help, Mrs. Tinley."

He had already begun the process of getting a search warrant for Sima Kumar's house when Stevens popped his head around the door.

"We just got a call on the tip line," he said. "Someone who wanted to remain anonymous said he'd seen Sima chatting with Gerald Corduroy-Smith the day he died."

"I'm sure plenty of people talked to him."

"Yeah, but this was different. The caller—"

"The anonymous caller."

"He said it didn't look like a friendly chat. Gerald was smiling, but Sima seemed upset."

"And I don't suppose he heard any of their actual conversation, did he?"

"That's the thing, they hadn't even bothered to lower their voices. The caller heard Gerald say, 'I know everything Reginald Trent knew about you.' As clear as day."

DCI Ahmed sighed. "Blackmail," he said.

"Pretty powerful motive, no?"

Every door in Sima's house was wide open, and it felt as though the entire village had come barging in through the front door. She heard the cars driving by on the street outside, slowing down as the drivers craned their necks to get a better look, the murmur of everyone who simply happened to be passing by and the laughter of the children playing out front because their parents had gathered right on the street outside. From the rear of the house, she could also hear the police officers' boots trudging around on the grass and the gravel, the chitchat of the constables, and the sudden shouts whenever they found something.

The white rug in the living room was filthy from all the shoes that had already trampled it, and the cushions had been pulled from the sofa. The little side table was covered in a fine layer of dust where they had been looking for fingerprints, and some of it had spilled to the rug below. Sima wondered whether she would ever be able to shake off the feeling of all these people invading her life.

She went out front in an attempt to get away from the police but quickly found herself being stared at by her neighbors, colleagues, and former friends. Her life was being torn to shreds, and here they were trying to get a better look at the wreckage. Everyone was looking straight at her, but no one would meet her eye.

"Rubberneckers," DCI Ahmed muttered. "That's what we call them in the police. People can't get enough of this sort of thing. They should mind their own business."

Sima shot him a look of gratitude.

"If you'll excuse me, I need to get back inside."

She nodded. Somehow she managed to keep standing in front of her house with her head held relatively high as everything she had built crumbled around her.

A woman broke away from the safe anonymity of the crowd and made her way over to the neighboring garden. Mrs. Tinley. Sima briefly considered ignoring her, but something—the sheer pigheadedness Berit had mentioned, perhaps—made her march straight toward her instead. This was her home.

"I knew you'd get your comeuppance in the end," Mrs. Tinley hissed. "The others might act like they're surprised, but not me. We all know what your sort are like." She had lowered her voice, suggesting that despite everything, she clearly wasn't prepared to let the neighbors hear her bile.

"I know exactly what you mean, Mrs. Tinley," Sima said calmly. "I've never had any doubt about the sort of person you are, either."

That upset her, of course. Just because she was a racist, didn't mean Sima was allowed to be rude about it. Sima smiled again, fully aware that nothing would irritate her more. She could deal with the racism, she decided once Mrs. Tinley had moved on. It was the gossip she was defenseless against.

From Sima's living room, DCI Ahmed watched as the uniformed officers crowded the garden. He wished he hadn't seen the intricate patterns raked into the gravel before their boots destroyed them. They reminded him of the Buddhist sand patterns he had seen in Tibet, and he found himself thinking about how the transitory nature of everything was an inescapable part of being human. Nothing lasted forever.

A sudden shout dragged him out of the cool living room, into the hot sun. The officers working outside were already sweating, and one of them beckoned him over from the far side of the garden.

There was a gray fence at the edge of the gravel, a jumble of garden tools on the other side. The next garden was only around half a meter away, separated from Sima's by a low wall. In the other direction, there was nothing but a few straggly bushes marking the boundary line. The police officer was holding the shaft of a rake with a removable head. It had been wiped down—sloppily—and there were traces of soil and rust on it, plus something that looked a lot like blood.

DCI Ahmed nodded. "Great work," he said. "Send it off for analysis."

There was little doubt that they had just found the murder weapon, but DCI Ahmed didn't feel any of the usual excitement that came with moving one step closer to solving a case.

Sima tensed.

Mr. Carew had broken away from the crowd and was slowly making his way over to her. *Oh no*, she thought. Friendliness was far harder to handle than open hostility. If he said something kind to her, there was a real chance she would immediately break down in tears.

He mumbled something that might have been "so sorry" followed by "terrible business, this," but because his eyes were fixed on the ground, it was hard to make out exactly what he said. At least she wouldn't have to worry about what he might see on her face, she thought. Sima felt herself relax as she reminded herself that he meant well. Perhaps Berit was right after all, and she really did have friends here.

"It's very nice of you to come over and give your support," said Sima.

"Yes, the thing is, a few of us...we've been talking..."

"There's no need to worry. This is all just a misunderstanding. Once I've straightened things out with the police, we can get back to planning another brilliant festival and exploring all the exciting opportunities for the village."

Mr. Carew gave her a strained smile. Sima knew just how empty and hollow her words sounded.

"Yes, well, we thought it might be best if you took some time to focus on these…misunderstandings. Maybe it would be a good idea for someone else to…help you with your duties."

"Thank you, but there's no need."

"It's just…a few people feel…" He hesitated, as though he was steeling himself, then blurted it all out so that she wouldn't have time to interject: "We think it would be best if you resigned from your post. Only temporarily, of course. The other members of the tourist board have asked me to help with various things. The festival, for example. And the, um, money."

"They asked you?"

"You can still do everything else! It's just that you have so many irons in the fire."

"And you decided all this behind my back, did you?"

"No! No, what I mean is…we met, and a few people felt…" He lost his train of thought. "Yes."

"Don't worry. You can take over all my responsibilities. And you can tell the others that there's no need to ask me to take a step back because I quit."

Sima turned away from him and the other nosy fucking gossipmongers to prevent them from seeing her reaction.

Friends? Ha! I should have known better, she thought.

As she wheeled around, she almost walked straight into DCI Ahmed.

"Ms. Kumar," he said. "I'm afraid I'm going to have to take up a bit more of your time."

She gave him a joyless smile. "Don't worry. I've got all the time in the world."

Sima didn't make the same mistake of trying to straighten her chair in the interview room this time. She simply slumped down into it as though her legs would no longer support her.

And then she started talking.

"When I first became politically active, I was responsible for a small, local fundraising group. It raised money to build orphanages in India, and they thought I'd be the right person for the job because of my 'background.'"

"Which is…?"

"My parents are from Pakistan—not that the people I worked for knew the difference. It was the kind of charity that really only serves to benefit the people who donate to it. We sent them pictures of cute brown children, and they felt good about themselves. Their own kids got to spend a few weeks over there too, building schools and gaining valuable 'life experience' before moving on to Goa or going diving in the Maldives. No one bothered to stop and ask whether they would be willing to send their own kids to schools built by teenagers."

She waved her hand impatiently. "I'm trying to vindicate myself, I know, I know. There's no point trying to sugarcoat it. I stole five hundred pounds. The cost of my first suit. It's small change in the grand scheme of things but enough to ruin my political career for good. I'd stolen from charity, for God's sake, and it didn't matter that the charity in question held gala dinners that cost more than they brought in. Five hundred quid wouldn't even have covered the napkins. So, that's the truth. I was twenty when I ruined the rest of my life."

"Your summer with Reginald."

"Exactly. My summer with Reginald."

Sima got a distant, dreamy look in her eye, and a smile played on her lips. She suddenly seemed far younger.

"Being part of his world was so magical at first. There were so many opportunities. It was intoxicating to feel like I could belong there, but the truth is I never really fit in. The others could make the shift between dinner parties, mingling, and picnics with zero effort; they looked equally well dressed and elegant everywhere they went. But I was constantly struggling and always got it slightly wrong. I had a big meeting coming up, and Reginald said I should buy something new. A really nice suit so that I'd be taken seriously, despite my age and skin color. I told him I didn't have any money, but I did. I was in charge of the finances for a gala dinner. So I faked an invoice from a florist. The plan was always to pay it back."

"But someone else found out?"

"Someone knew the florist, yeah. The whole thing was handled very discreetly; no one wanted a scandal. I was told to step down from my post, and I did. Afterward, I moved to the village, and…well, I did everything I could to help them with anything they needed. I ran for the council. I've done my duty for that village ever since." She grimaced. "I guess I was trying to make amends, if you believe it."

"I believe it."

Sima looked grateful.

"How did Reginald find out?" DCI Ahmed asked.

"He saw one of my printouts, my test invoices, and he saw the jacket. It didn't take much to put two and two together and make it add up to something pretty fucking compromising. Back then he thought the whole thing was hilarious. I don't think he had any intention of actually using what he knew. Not at the time, anyway. We were so alike, he said, but we both knew the difference between us. People like him get away with things. People like me don't."

"But this was all a long time ago, and you were so young. Surely people today will understand? It's like you said, you were never even charged with a crime!"

She looked him straight in the eye. "I'm a second-generation immigrant woman, DCI Ahmed. We might possibly get one chance, but we never ever get a second."

"So what happened? He came back to Great Diddling and found a way to use what he knew?"

"He threatened to blackmail me, yes. But it was never anything concrete. He kept talking about vague future projects, general political support, that sort of thing. I hoped I'd find a solution before it came to anything."

"But then he died."

"Then he died, taking what he knew to the grave. Or so I thought."

"He'd told Gerald about the hold he had over the local councillor," Ahmed said.

"And Gerald was just as prepared to use that information as Reginald had been. He thought it was so funny that I'd only stolen five hundred pounds. He said, and I quote, *ah, the limited ambitions of the young!*"

"What did he want you to do?"

She seemed surprised. "I don't actually know. He was planning to come and talk to me the day after he died."

"Reginald's death meant he lost the ability to do anything with the properties in the village," said DCI Ahmed. "His children inherit them, and they'll be held in trust until they're eighteen. Gerald couldn't get at them, which means he must have been after something else."

"Like I said, he never got around to telling me."

"Because he died before he had a chance."

"Yes. Because he died."

The car park outside the station was deserted, dimly lit by the soft glow of the streetlamps. DCI Ahmed was in his office, looking down at the row of patrol cars outside, when the door opened behind him.

"Why didn't you arrest her?" Stevens asked. "Sir," he added, a little too late.

"We don't have enough evidence. The murder weapon might have been in her back garden, but there are no prints on it. None, not even the ones we'd expect to find—hers or whoever raked the pattern into the gravel. And it wasn't like she kept it locked away in a shed. Anyone could have taken it, killed Corduroy-Smith, and then put it back."

"You arrested James Elmer on far less than that."

"He confessed."

"Mrs. Tinley saw her with the murder weapon right after the time of death."

"Mrs. Tinley saw someone." DCI Ahmed's eye was drawn back to the parking area. "Look," he said, "if you saw someone dressed in black—and wearing a hat—from this distance, would you be able to tell who it was?"

"I'm not sure," Stevens conceded.

"Did you notice anything about the front of Sima's house?"

"What?"

"She doesn't have a porch lamp, which means that the streetlight several meters away was all the light Mrs. Tinley had."

"It might have been enough. We could at least ask Mrs. Tinley if that's how she recognized her."

"She'd only say yes. She wouldn't even need to lie. The woman can't stand Sima, which means she's convinced herself it was her she saw. Her subconscious will just fill in the details."

Stevens hesitated. Then he said in an unusually respectful tone, "Sir, do you think perhaps... Is it possible that your sympathies have gotten the better of you? You like her."

"I respect her."

"Do you think she's a murderer?"

"I think she's a woman who is prepared to do almost anything to survive." Ahmed looked down at the empty car park. *Had he let his sympathies get the better of him?* "I've stationed a uniformed police officer by her house," he said as a sort of defense. "If she leaves home, I'll know."

Stevens still looked worried. "Yes, sir," he said.

He didn't state the obvious: that if Sima Kumar was their murderer and if she somehow managed to slip away and killed a third time, all the blame would fall squarely on his shoulders.

As it should, DCI Ahmed thought.

The crowd was gone, thank God. Harry didn't like the idea of Sima, who had always been so private, being scrutinized and gossiped about.

The police were gone too.

The streetlamps cast an eerie glow onto part of the house, but all the windows were dark.

He wondered how people could have lost their minds so completely. Earlier that afternoon, he'd had no choice but to throw several of them out of the pub for talking so disparagingly about her. He'd even closed up early, driven by some sort of urge to do something for her. To prove that she wasn't alone.

As she opened the door in her dark house, however, he asked himself whether he shouldn't have left her in peace instead. She looked tired, almost see-through, as though she had been stripped bare. It was a warm evening, but she was shivering. Harry took a step toward her, and she instinctively moved back.

"You know I'd do anything for you," he said.

"I don't think there's much anyone can do for me now."

"I love you."

She smiled mirthlessly. "I lowered my guard to someone once, convincing myself that I might not have to muddle my way through life alone after all, and look how that worked out. I'm not going to make that mistake again. Love is a luxury I can't afford right now."

Harry couldn't think of a response to that, but neither could he tear himself away. Not yet.

In the end, he said, "The festival was fantastic." His voice sounded strange and unsteady. "You did such an amazing job."

Sima looked surprised, as though she had already forgotten all about it. "Yeah," she mumbled, "it was."

42

WHEN SALLY CAME DOWN TO make breakfast the next morning, she found Berit lying flat out on the living room floor. Sally stepped over her outstretched arm and made her way through to the kitchen.

From the doorway, she studied the paper on the floor. Three large new words had been added to the timeline: ALIBI THURSDAY EVENING.

Around it, Berit had written: *Linton Kwesi Johnson* and *incontrovertible alibi*.

The latter was circled several times, followed by a couple of exclamation marks.

Beneath *Tea party* Berit had also added: *Why was Liam nervous?*

"I told you," Sally protested. "Because he stole the dynamite!"

Berit replied without opening her eyes. "That shouldn't have made him nervous a couple of days later. It can hardly have come as a surprise to him that he'd done it."

Sally thought hard. "So do you think he's innocent after all? That he didn't do it? No…you should have seen his face when I asked if he had. He looked guilty. And then he said we weren't friends."

"Unequivocal proof."

"You know what I mean. It was like he lashed out because he felt so guilty. Ugh, I'm not explaining this right."

"Not at all, I know exactly what you mean."

In a new square, in huge letters, Berit had written: THE BEST THEFT IS ONE THAT IS NEVER REPORTED OR DISCOVERED.

That sounded like something someone might cross-stitch, thought Sally.

Beside it, Berit had added a question: Or is it one that hasn't even been carried out yet?

"Why would a theft that hasn't happened yet be the best kind?"

"Oh, that was just a stab in the dark. For an author, the next book is always their best." Berit slowly hit her head against the floor. Thud, thud, thud.

"Tea?" asked Sally.

"I can almost see it, but it just doesn't add up. No matter how I twist and turn it. The time for keeping quiet is over, Sally. Gerald's death changes everything. We need to start putting pressure on people. Go and get Liam."

Sally stared down at her. "I don't think he would do anything for me right now. Like he said, we're not friends."

"Try. Tell him I need to talk to him. And remind him of the promise I made."

Sally found Liam on High Street.

"I need you to come with me," she said, quickly adding, "It's Berit, she wants to speak to you. She told me to remind you of the promise she made."

He gave her a weary nod and started moving toward his car.

Sally got into the passenger seat and glanced over to him. Liam looked older than he had when he gave her a lift on her first day in Great Diddling, as though he had been forced to grow up in a short space of time.

He was quiet the whole drive. When they got out of the car, Sally made her way into the cottage ahead of him. She was relieved to see that Berit was now sitting at the kitchen table. That was probably for the best; she wasn't sure how Liam would have reacted to Berit lying flat out on the living room floor.

"Tea?" Sally asked nervously.

Berit's forehead creased in disapproval. "There's no time for that," she said, pointing to the chair opposite her. "Liam, sit."

He did as he was told.

"I need you to listen carefully now," she began. "There are only two ways to do this, and you're going to have to make up your mind. Either you can talk to the police or you can talk to me. I respect your loyalty, I really do, but this has all gone way too far. You can't stay quiet any longer. I give you my word that if you talk to me, nothing bad will happen to Eleanor. Nothing is going to happen to either of you, I promise."

Liam looked at her with desperation in his eyes. "I know I need to talk," he said. "It's just…Eleanor is the only real friend I've ever had, you know?"

Berit nodded. Sally wanted to protest, but one warning glance from the author made her hold her tongue.

"You need to understand what Eleanor is like too," said Liam. "She doesn't mean any harm. It's just that she'd never be able to live a 'normal' life. 'You've got to go a little crazy sometimes, Liam.' That's what she always says. That and 'Life's too short to never break the law.' Or 'A life without adrenaline isn't worth living.' It's not her fault; that's just who she is. She's always saying that too. That society isn't made for people like us. We're just supposed to drift through life like sleepwalkers. Go to work, spend money, watch TV, go to bed. And repeat, until you retire. Then you can start playing bridge instead."

Liam nodded eagerly before continuing. "And she's right! No one wants us to be free, and there are so many people who just don't fit that mold. Some of them drink or take drugs or get into fights, but others just need to be a little crazy from time to time. But she would never kill anyone. She and Mary have done more for me than my mum and all the teachers and social workers ever have. I'd do anything for her. Besides, it was only ever meant as a joke."

Sally got up without a sound, making the tea without Berit noticing.

Liam flashed her a grateful smile and took a sip from his mug. Berit absentmindedly did the same from her own.

"We'd done that sort of thing before. Stolen stuff, I mean." He gave Berit a defiant glance, as though he expected criticism, but she simply nodded and crossed out a question mark scribbled in her notepad.

Liam seemed to lose his trail of thought at the sight of her pen and pad, but Berit circled another word and impatiently told him to go on.

"It was never because of the money. The challenge was to put whatever we stole back before its owner noticed it was missing. A vase from a neighbor, an ugly painting, that sort of thing. The bigger the better."

"And then she suggested something more serious," said Berit.

"We were drunk. It was a joke. I was sure she wasn't serious."

"But she was."

"She swore nothing would happen. We were going to put the stuff back that weekend. I'd seen the blasting schedule. They weren't planning to use any of it before Monday the next week, so we had all weekend to do it. That's what we thought, anyway. We weren't going to use it. Eleanor was never careless like that. Not when it came to me, anyway."

Now that Liam had started talking, it was as though the floodgates had opened. Maybe he had been longing to confide in someone, thought Sally. She wondered what it must have been like to carry a secret like this for so long.

"The challenge was to break in without anyone noticing but also in a way that, if they did notice, wouldn't lead back to us. That meant we couldn't just use the key or take it while I was alone at the site."

"Of course."

"And I did it! Eleanor was so proud of me."

"But then things went wrong."

"Yeah, pretty much straightaway. Someone must've heard us talking about it too. I still can't work out how they could know."

Berit froze. "Someone found out you had the explosives?" she said.

"I had spent the day at Eleanor's. It was late Friday evening, and I was going home to get the explosives. I didn't know the theft had already been discovered. I wanted to return the explosives straightaway. I wasn't comfortable having them just lying there in my room at my mum's place. But when I went to get them, *they were gone*."

The shock was still visible on his face.

"I looked everywhere…" His voice trailed off.

"Who knew that you kept the explosives in your room?"

"Only Eleanor! I thought at first that she had snuck out and gotten them. To put them back, of course. But she said she hadn't come near them. And she wouldn't lie. Not about something like that. Not to me."

But he didn't seem quite as sure as he wanted to be.

"And then someone used them to kill Reginald Trent."

"Yeah, but I had nothing to do with that! Eleanor didn't either, I swear. She'd never hurt a fly."

"When was the last time you know for sure that the explosives were where you hid them?"

"Friday evening, around five."

"And when did you discover that they were gone?"

"Later that night, when I went to get them so I could take them back. Just after eleven."

"And did you and Eleanor talk about the explosives?"

"Sure. That Friday, when they discovered the theft too soon. I went straight over to the café to tell her all about it."

"Could anyone have overheard you?"

"I don't know!" he said, stressed. "I don't think so. We didn't talk about it in the café. We're not stupid. We were up in their private apartment. But someone must have heard us? Right? There's no other explanation."

Now that he had gotten it all off his chest, Liam seemed to deflate. As Berit analyzed his version of events, Sally moved over and patted him on the shoulder.

Friends? she mouthed.

He nodded. "Friends," he said quietly.

For almost half an hour, Berit sat there quietly. Her tea grew cold, but she didn't notice. Sally and Liam looked at each other, but she ignored them both.

Then suddenly she looked up.

"This changes everything," she said with satisfaction. "That's how she did it. Now we just need to come up with a way of proving it. I suppose that'll be DCI Ahmed's job, but we need to work out how to keep you and Eleanor out of this."

Berit reached for her phone and dialed DCI Ahmed's number, only to hang up before he had time to answer. She needed to come up with a diplomatic way of telling him that she might, just maybe, have broken her promise not to get involved. On top of that, she still needed to solve the problem of Liam and Eleanor's involvement before she spoke to him. Berit needed an edited version of events ready before they talked, because she knew he would realize that she was trying to help them. He would do his utmost to uncover every last weak link in her story. Berit wasn't looking forward to having to lie to him. The man was far too observant, and that made her nervous.

Still, these were all minor details. She had her answers at last. She felt almost giddy at the sudden liberation of knowing.

Just to be on the safe side, she ran through everything in her mind one last time. It worked. It was over. She would hand everything over to the police and get back to her writing.

Liam didn't realize it, but he had given her the last piece of the puzzle there too. Berit now knew exactly what kind of book she was going to write.

"I wonder why Sima was going up to Tawny Hall," Liam mused to himself.

Sally had just started getting ready to make lunch in the kitchen when she saw Berit tense.

"What did you just say?" Berit barked.

"I bumped into Sima on High Street. She said she was heading up to Tawny Hall to 'fix everything.' I don't know what she meant, but there was something weird about her. She didn't sound like her usual self."

"When was this?"

"Uhh…about half an hour ago, I guess? Just before Sally found me."

"And you're only just telling us now? For God's sake, Liam. Where's your car? Is it outside? Come on!"

Berit leapt up and rushed out without stopping to check whether Liam and Sally were with her. By the time they made it outside, she was already sitting in the passenger seat with her face pressed up against the side window.

Hurry up! she mouthed.

Sally jumped into the back seat, and Liam fumbled with the key in the ignition.

"Let's go!" Berit snapped, which only made him fumble even more.

A moment later, they were finally on their way. Berit was hunched over in her seat, her chin jutting out as though she could will the car into going faster.

"Speed up, Liam! Watch out for the cyclist! Don't brake now, for God's sake!"

"But you told me to—"

"This is no time to argue with her," Sally said. "Just drive!"

"But—"

"Drive!" the two women shouted in unison.

When they reached the edge of the village, Liam finally sped up, despite the fact that the hedgerows on either side of the road meant he had virtually no visibility up ahead. They met a van driving in the opposite direction and had to swerve sharply to avoid a crash.

"There can't be any danger so long as they're both at Tawny Hall…" Berit mumbled to herself. "But are they? We have no way of knowing."

She took out her phone and called DCI Ahmed. This time, she allowed it to ring, but when he failed to pick up, she left a message: "This is Berit Gardner, and I'd like to report a murder that might be about to happen." She instructed him to meet her at Tawny Hall and then hung up.

"What did you mean when you said that she didn't sound like her usual self?" she asked Liam.

"She seemed kind of…determined somehow, but in a different way than normal. Usually once she's made up her mind about something, I'd be willing to bet almost anything that she'll make a success of it. She said that she was going to fix everything, but I got the weird sense she didn't really believe it. She sounded too desperate. Not something you'd want to put money on, if you get what I mean. Like a footballer playing their first game after a serious injury, claiming they're back at 100 percent when anyone can see they're not."

Then he skidded onto the gravel track leading to Tawny Hall, and as he pulled up outside, Berit flung the door open before they had even come to a halt. She hurled herself toward the house, and Sally hurried after her. Liam brought up the rear.

Berit didn't bother knocking. She simply tore the double doors open and marched into the entrance hall. It was empty, and their footsteps echoed eerily as they ran down the hallway. Berit seemed to know exactly where she needed to be, and Sally suddenly realized where they were heading.

The library.

"This whole mess started with books," Berit said over her shoulder as she rushed ahead, "and it will end with them too, mark my words."

The doors to the library were open, and Sima was standing in the middle of the black-and-white floor. Her eyes were wide, her chest rising and falling rapidly, and there were huge damp patches beneath her arms on her gray T-shirt. Sally had never seen her look so disheveled before.

"Just take it easy," said Berit.

"I am. It's—"

"I wasn't talking to you." Berit moved deeper into the room, continuing in her normal voice. "Margaret, you've always been smart and cautious. Don't do anything stupid now."

Margaret gave a dry laugh. "A bit late for that, don't you think?"

Sally could now see her too. Margaret was standing beyond Sima, probably around two meters away from her, and in contrast to Sima, she looked perfectly composed. She was wearing a pair of corduroy trousers, canvas shoes, and a white T-shirt, and she was gripping a large kitchen knife in one hand. The light spilling in through the window gleamed on the sharp blade.

Sally shuddered.

She kept expecting someone to laugh and tell her this was all just a joke. Don't be silly, Sally, did you really think Margaret would start waving a knife around? It would be worth having everyone laugh at her, she thought, if everything went back to normal afterward.

But no one was laughing.

Berit kept moving until she was almost parallel with Sima, and without thinking, Sally found herself following her. Berit didn't take her eyes off

Margaret, but Sally caught a disapproving frown on her face as she came closer. The author shook her head almost imperceptibly, but Sally ignored it. Huge knife or not, sticking close to Berit felt like the safest option.

Right then, two strong hands gripped her arms and dragged her back toward the doorway.

"You've got no business in there, my friend," Liam whispered in her ear.

The crease on Berit's brow eased, and she leaned nonchalantly against a pile of books nearby. There was a pretty copy of Huw Lewis-Jones's *The Writer's Map* on the top of the stack, an atlas of imaginary worlds with an illustrated sea chart on the cover. She'd always wanted to read it…

Idiot, Sally thought. *This is not the right moment to think about books.*

But she knew why she was doing it. Her brain was simply trying to distract her from the knife in Margaret's hand.

She forced herself to focus on other details instead, like how strong and capable Berit's hand looked on top of the pile of books and how beautifully the sun was slanting in through the windows, hitting the blade—*No! Don't think about the knife!*

Liam tried to pull her back again, but she shook him off, refusing to go any farther than the doorway. From there, she would still have a clear view of everything that happened in the library.

"You don't stand to gain anything by killing Sima now," said Berit.

"Not anymore, no. It was a long shot from the start, but it was my only option. I tried to think of everything, but I've had to improvise so much. There was never any time to plan."

"You know, ever since the murder, I've been thinking about a particular expression; it just keeps bothering me," said Berit. "You planted yourself here, didn't you? Openly biding your time for a chance to steal Daphne's books?"

"It wouldn't have been stealing!" Margaret snapped. "None of Daphne's relatives care about them. They didn't even know they existed, not until Gerald sent Reginald out here. All I would have had to do was clear out Tawny Hall once Daphne died. No one would ever have known."

"The best theft is one that is never discovered," said Berit. Sally recognized it from the drawing paper. "And then you would have been able to buy your cottage at last."

"I deserved it! I've worked hard all my life, but what do I have to show for it? Nothing! All these fat-cat politicians and bosses, their wages just keep going up and up, but what do ordinary people get? Nothing. No, I decided a long time ago that I would never be loyal to anyone but myself. If no one cared about me, then I wouldn't care about them."

Berit nodded. "So you planted yourself here and then settled in to wait."

"Exactly. I could wait. I've always been patient. Besides, I like working for Daphne. The plan was more a kind of…pension scheme."

"So that's why you never got around to cataloging her library. I thought it seemed odd, given how organized you are."

"It was better no one knew. Daphne didn't care, not really. Before I got here and got to grips with her special collection, she barely knew which books she had or where they were."

"So how did you come up with the idea of selling her books once she died?" asked Berit.

"I sold one of them once. The roof needed to be repaired, and we had all these valuable books just gathering dust. One book paid for the whole thing. The only problem was that Daphne discovered it was missing. She started kicking up a real stink before I managed to distract her, and that's when I realized I wouldn't be able to sell them while she was still alive. Plus, I'd made the same old mistake I always do. Why sell the books to pay for *her* roof?" Margaret sounded annoyed with herself. "It's harder than you might think to stop doing things for other people; it's so instinctive. Indoctrination, you might say. Don't move!"

The latter was directed at Sima, who had attempted to creep closer to Sally and Liam in the doorway. Margaret held up the knife in her direction, blade gleaming yet again.

Sally couldn't tear her eyes away.

"You heard Eleanor and Liam talking about the explosives," Berit continued.

"Idiots. I went over there to talk about the catering with Mary, and she asked me to wait up in the apartment, so that's what I did. Eleanor and Liam were talking so loudly as they climbed the stairs that I heard every word. So I hid in the office and eavesdropped on them in the kitchen."

"And then you stole the explosives, on the Friday night?"

"That's right. Liam has been doing odd jobs for us for years, and you learn certain things about a person over time. I knew exactly what his mother would be up to on a Friday evening. She'd already passed out by the time I arrived, and it didn't exactly take a genius to find the stuff in Liam's room. He'd hidden it under his bed."

"And Daphne was so busy reading *The Woman in Cabin 10* that she didn't notice you leave."

"It wasn't an issue. I told her that I was going to make tea, but I was gone over an hour. She hadn't even noticed I was gone."

"It must have taken nerves of steel to kill Reginald Trent while the entire village was watching."

Margaret seemed pleased with the compliment.

"When the police took Liam in for questioning, you needed to find out whether he'd said anything or not, so you came to me and told me you'd killed someone. Very effective. If a person seems to be confessing to a murder, no one will remember what they said beforehand."

Margaret nodded. "I didn't want you to notice that I was interested in Liam, but like you said, I just had to know."

"And everything went to plan. You banked on the fact that neither Liam nor Eleanor were the kind of people who would cooperate with the police, and they didn't. But then you ran into another problem."

"How was I supposed to know that Sima and the rest of the village would turn the murder into a festival? Daphne started talking about giving her books away, for God's sake! And then Gerald showed up, wanting to buy them."

"That must have been stressful for you."

"Even if Daphne didn't give the books away, people would know they were here. And if the festival continued for year after year, the books in her collection would become famous. People around here had already started talking about them, and Gerald was not going to be satisfied just waiting for her to let him buy them. He was up to something. I knew it. I think he was planning to steal them somehow. So you see, I had no choice but to kill him."

Margaret's cool, calm face and the compelling tone of her voice frightened Sally more than the knife.

"It was much easier than I expected," Margaret said, surprised. "I stole a rake from Sima and was planning to wait for the right opportunity, but then I spotted him as I was sneaking home through the village. Gerald, right outside the hotel. At three in the morning! I followed him, of course, and saw him go down the alleyway with Mary. Then I killed him as soon as she'd left. It wasn't hard at all. He was too busy with the parcel to even try to defend himself. I just whacked him on the back of the head."

Her tone of voice was unsettlingly calm and normal.

"What about Sima?" Berit asked. "Why did you want to frame her?"

"I hoped that if Daphne thought Sima was guilty, she'd forget all about selling or giving away her books, and everything would finally go back to normal. But Sima refused to give up. And the police refused to arrest her. Everything would have worked out just fine if they had."

"So what was your plan?"

"I figured that if Sima disappeared, everything would be OK again. Say her car turned up outside the railway station a few days from now, everyone would just assume she was guilty. It would definitely be enough for Daphne, in any case. And everything would go on like before."

"Providing Sima disappeared."

"Exactly."

Sima's face paled.

Some sort of wordless conversation was going on between Margaret and Berit. Even as they talked, it was clear to Sally that they were saying far more than she could actually hear. Margaret's expression had changed, shifting from calm and determined to something verging on sorrowful.

Sally relaxed. Maybe Margaret was starting to change her mind. Surely she would have to give up soon? There was nowhere left for her to run.

But Berit looked tenser than ever.

"I just wanted a cottage of my own," said Margaret. "I wanted my sea and my sky. I wanted to be *free*."

Her voice sounded so distant. Perhaps she was already there, thought

Sally. Perhaps she could see the bare rocks and feel the salty breeze and hear the waves crashing against the shore.

Margaret moved suddenly, but Berit had already gripped the book on the top of the pile beside her, and she threw it as hard as she could. It flew through the air and hit Margaret square in the chest, with enough force to make her stagger backward and send the knife in her hand clattering to the floor. Before she had time to react, Berit was between her and the knife. She gripped Margaret's wrist and held her back. Sima darted past Sally, her footsteps echoing through the sudden silence, only stopping once she was safely out in the corridor. Sally could hear her nervous breathing behind her.

Margaret and Berit were locked in some sort of macabre dance. Neither of them was moving, and Berit's knuckles had turned white around Margaret's wrist.

"Enough," Berit said. "Enough."

She then leaned forward and whispered something in the other woman's ear, her voice low but insistent, a long speech that only Margaret could hear. With that, Margaret's body finally relaxed. She looked defeated, thought Sally.

Daphne's head popped out from behind one of the bookshelves, as though she had finally decided the coast was clear.

Sally couldn't quite bring herself to relax. She hovered in the doorway, unable even to blink, staring at Berit and Margaret and the knife until her eyes began to sting. Before long, she heard sirens in the distance. She saw DCI Ahmed come running, and with that, the whole thing was finally, finally over.

CASE CLOSED

IT WAS A SUNNY SUNDAY in early August, and the Queen's Head, Arms, and Legs was bustling.

Behind the bar, Sima was pouring a beer with her shirtsleeves rolled up.

Harry was on his knees in front of the counter, trying to convince a young puppy to stop chewing on the lace of a tourist's walking boot. The tourist had tried shaking their foot, but that only egged the dog on. It doubled its efforts, pulling on the lace with its teeth.

Mary and Eleanor were waiting for Berit at a table in the corner, but she was in no rush. She wanted to take in everything she could of the village that had both given and cost her so much.

Sima and the villagers had come to a kind of compromise. She had forgotten that they had suspected her of murder, and they had forgotten the youthful mistake she once committed. If either side had been expecting an apology or an admission of guilt, they would have been disappointed, but Berit decided that a short memory probably wasn't the worst quality to have in a small place like this.

Sima had grown up, she thought. She had learned to give Great Diddling a little less of herself. Nowadays, she made sure to take weekends off. That enabled her to work behind the bar at the pub from time to time, but more often than not, she and Harry simply left the other members of staff to hold the fort and went off fishing.

The young dog was Harry's, and Sima had told Berit she had been the one to suggest it. He needed someone other than her to love, she said. She had started planning next year's festival, and a potential investor had been in touch. The woman in question was the CEO of a large company, and her support came with a single condition: that one day of the festival was given over to a reading retreat at which the participants had to hand over their phones, agree not to speak to one another, and read and eat in silence. And no fake authors!

Sima was still the smartest woman in the room, thought Berit, and she still had no interest in hiding it.

There was no sign of DCI Ahmed. Berit didn't think he had been back to Great Diddling since the police wrapped up their investigation at Tawny Hall. She thought back to her last interview with him.

This time, it had taken place at the police station. DCI Ahmed had recorded everything, and DS Stevens had been by his side throughout. That had made the conversation feel oddly formal somehow. The detective chief inspector had been cool and competent during the first few crazy hours following Margaret's arrest, a reassuring figure amid the crisis. Sally had found his presence comforting, Berit knew. Perhaps she had too, once the adrenaline had faded.

Yet during the interview, he had seemed buttoned-up and stiff. He asked the same questions over and over again, rewording them and changing the order, trying to get her to trip up and contradict herself.

"Why were you so interested in what Daphne had been reading?" he asked suddenly.

The question came so suddenly that Berit found herself telling him the truth. "If Daphne had been reading poetry, then there was no way Margaret could have slipped out to steal the explosives. People read poetry in short bursts, then look up to recite it to someone. But if she'd been reading a page-turner, a thriller, then Margaret could probably have been gone for hours without her noticing."

"But Daphne said she was reading poetry on the Thursday in question."

This time Berit was ready for him. "She must have got her days mixed up," she said. "Ask her again. You know how confused she gets."

Ahmed had studied her for a long time, the silence between them heavy with his disappointment.

"Margaret claims she worked alone," he said after a moment. "She takes sole responsibility for the whole thing. What do you say to that?"

"Nothing," Berit replied. "But it's probably true. She seems like a very independent woman. She told me once that we're all alone in this world."

"Sima mentioned that you spoke to Margaret at the end of the stand-off, that you seemed to say something to her. 'As though she was giving her instructions' is how she put it."

"Nonsense. The only instruction I gave her was not to be a bloody idiot, and that's advice I'd give to anyone."

"So she just came up with the idea of stealing the explosives from the construction firm and knew exactly where they were kept and how to break in?"

Berit had chosen to interpret his words as a statement rather than a question, and held her tongue. She had simply sat there quietly until he shook his head and terminated the interview.

Afterward, he had escorted her out through the station. They stood in silence in the car park outside for what felt like a long time, and then he held out his hand.

She shook it. "DCI Ahmed," she said.

He had smiled at last. "Berit," he said. "It's been…an experience."

But he didn't specify if it had been a positive or a negative one.

For a moment, Berit had thought that he wouldn't say anything else, that the special understanding they had shared would end in that odd, distanced way. Then he surprised her by saying, "You know, I've read several of your books."

"What did you make of them?" she asked, though she wasn't sure she wanted to know.

"I should have done it sooner. I would have understood you better if I had."

Berit pulled a face. You couldn't write a book without exposing part of yourself, but it was never pleasant to be reminded about how much you had revealed.

"I was particularly struck by the fact that you see everyone as dysfunctional, lonely, odd, and yet so fundamentally human. Such clear observations, but almost tender in the way you handle them. You feel real sympathy for your characters, don't you?"

"Yes," she had said guardedly.

"For Margaret too?"

"She must have been very lonely."

"Be careful, Berit. In real life, there are far too many people who don't deserve your sympathy. Evil is real. It exists."

"So do unhappy endings, but that doesn't mean we should give in to them."

"I don't know how Margaret came into possession of the explosives," Ahmed said suddenly. He was like a dog with a bone, Berit thought. "But there's one thing I do know: Liam stole them and Eleanor lied to protect him."

Berit didn't say anything.

"There were traces of explosive on his clothing, and he worked for the construction firm. He had no alibi for the evening when they were stolen, and Eleanor's prints were found in Mrs. Ainsley's living room. If I find a way to prove that they stole the explosives, I'll get them for accessory to murder, so help me God."

When Berit still didn't speak, he shook his head sadly. "I guess we found out which side you were on in the end," he said.

Berit sipped her beer.

Standing there in the busy pub, surrounded by the people of Great Diddling, she guessed DCI Ahmed would have gotten even more proof she was on their side. She felt a lingering regret about how their friendship ended. No, not ended, precisely. It was more a case of a friendship that might have been.

She shook her head. What ifs were for writing, not real life. No point in regretting things. She had done what needed to be done, and that was that.

She and Sima had gone over to Mary and Eleanor's place later the same day. They had sat down in the couple's cozy kitchen, surrounded by all the pictures of the garden Mary had never had, and gone through their options.

"What can they really prove?" Sima said. "That Liam handled explosives? He worked for the construction company!"

"Sooner or later, Margaret will tell them where she stole the explosives. It'll be a little hard to explain what they were doing under Liam's bed, don't you think?" Eleanor signed. "I'll have to take the blame myself. After all, it was my fault. I shouldn't have gotten Liam mixed up in this."

"No," Berit agreed.

Mary had looked around the kitchen.

"We could always leave," she said after a moment. "We've always wanted to see Mongolia. Wouldn't that be a last adventure for us? Or we could go back to Egypt. They don't have an extradition treaty, and the coffee is great."

"No one is going anywhere," Berit said firmly.

"Berit's right. We belong here. You've said it all along, and you were right. Oh, well. At least I've already lived an interesting life. I've done a lot of things, but I've never been to prison. Maybe I should think of it as another new experience?"

"And no one is going to prison," Berit said. "Not if I can help it."

The drab, depressing visitor's room at the prison reminded Berit of a school cafeteria. It had the same bland furniture and the same atmosphere of desperation, intrigue, and suffering. All around her, couples and families were trying to act as though everything was OK. There was a small play area in one corner, and the toys there looked as tragic as the toys in a hospital waiting room. The white-painted walls felt like they were steeped in claustrophobia and authority.

Berit had been frisked on her way in, a police dog quietly watching and sniffing as she passed. All of her personal possessions were now stashed away in a locker. Margaret's too, she presumed.

"Bring a pound for the lockers," she had been instructed when she booked her visit. Prison staff were unable to provide change.

Sitting at the table, Margaret looked relaxed. Her trial was yet to begin, which meant she was still allowed to wear her own clothes. She said yes to a cup of tea and a chocolate biscuit, but when Berit set them down in front of her, she left them untouched on the table. Everyday objects in an absurd setting.

"Did she agree?" Margaret asked.

"Yes."

Daphne hadn't taking much convincing. She was surprisingly sentimental when it came to her former secretary's crimes. Daphne was convinced that Reginald and Gerald had been after her books and that Margaret had killed them both to protect her. She seemed to see Margaret's action as an act of loyal bravery, two murders being a perfectly fitting response to a threat against her books.

"I suppose you've heard that I've confessed? I'm 'cooperating' with the police, as they say."

Berit nodded.

At the next table over, a couple were arguing quietly, though their voices kept rising. One of the guards eventually came over and told them to keep it down, and they started whispering their insults instead, with much the same force as when they had been shouting.

"They say I'll get life."

"Not surprising, really. You did kill two men in cold blood."

"I suppose I did."

"Do you have everything you need?"

Margaret had waved her hand, a gesture that could have meant almost anything. In all likelihood it meant look around; what do you think?

"Is there anything I can do?" Berit asked instead.

"Make sure Daphne sticks to her side of the deal."

"Don't worry."

Daphne had already agreed to leave three valuable books to Margaret in her will, for if and when Margaret was released. In exchange, Margaret had promised not to mention Liam or Eleanor in her confession.

Berit had only had time to whisper a few key words to her on that day in the library, little more than *good behavior, conditional release, I'll talk to Daphne, you could still get your cottage, just keep Liam and Eleanor out of it.*

"You can't guarantee that I'll ever be released on parole," said Margaret. "I might die in here."

That was the truth, and Berit didn't bother trying to deny it. No matter what happened, one thing was certain: Margaret was going to spend a long time behind bars.

"But it's a glimmer of hope, if nothing else," said Margaret. "Something to live for. That makes all the difference in a place like this."

Berit nodded. It made all the difference everywhere.

"One day I'll feel the wind on my face as I listen to the waves."

"Of course you will."

DCI Ahmed would have disapproved, and Berit wasn't sure herself that Margaret deserved it, but she wasn't going to deny anyone hope.

When she got back from her visit, she found Sally waiting in the living room with a gin and tonic. They went out into the garden and listened to the sound of the birds and the insects and the neighbors' children, laughing and shrieking in the gardens nearby. All so very pleasant and normal. The claustrophobic walls of the prison, the couple arguing, the everyday tragedy of it all retreated a little in Berit's mind.

After a while, Sally asked what Margaret's defense mechanism was.

"You know, like you said with Liam he tries to laugh everything off, and I try to hide. Does Margaret have anything like that?"

Berit nodded.

"She saw herself as such a logical, professional, clearheaded person that she never realized just how emotional she was. Her denial of all her feelings made her defenseless against them, time and time again. She was convinced she was acting logically, but anyone could see that it would end in disaster, right from the minute she overheard Liam and Eleanor talking about the explosives they'd stolen and she made that deeply emotional decision to steal them. Margaret was so focused on what she deserved—which is such an illogical, emotional concept—that she just couldn't bear the thought of someone like Reginald Trent or Gerald Corduroy-Smith swooping in under her nose and getting their hands on her books. It was feelings, intense feelings, that led to her utterly logical, tragic downfall."

Sally's phone started ringing just as Berit went over to Mary and Eleanor's table. *Perfect*, she thought. She was ready.

She answered the call as she elbowed her way through the throng, heading outside so that they could talk in peace. But then her mother said, "Hold on a minute" as though it was Sally who had called her, and she heard Olivia's half of another phone call, followed by the tapping of keys as her mother typed furiously.

Sally walked over to the window and gazed in at the people inside the pub as she held the phone to her ear. Berit and Eleanor were chatting, Eleanor with a smile on her face.

This past summer had been a mix of hard work and complete freedom, and despite everything that had happened, Sally couldn't remember a better summer. Berit had spent most of it writing in the back garden, at Tawny Hall or the pub, even at Mary and Eleanor's kitchen table.

Berit had also gone up to Tawny Hall quite frequently at first. She claimed it was because Daphne didn't have anything against her going there to write, but Sally suspected it was because she wanted to make sure Daphne wasn't lonely without Margaret. It wasn't right to leave her all alone up there with her books, Berit had told Sally. People need to be around other people.

But Berit had since been replaced. Sima had taken over the role of keeping Daphne company, and they were already deep at work planning next year's festival.

Sally knew that Berit had sent in more than two hundred pages of her latest manuscript to Sally's mother, and since her mother wasn't currently shouting down the line at her, she was confident that Olivia loved it.

Sally had never doubted that she would. She had been the first person to read the text, and though there was still a lot left to be done, she had felt the familiar, expectant tingle she always got when she had a fantastic reading experience to look forward to. Right from the first page, she had known there were brilliant adventures ahead.

"Darling," her mother said now, "it's fantastic, though I'm sure you already know that. You've always had a good nose for stories. When you were younger, I used to try out children's books on you."

Sally remembered that. Usually, she hadn't even gotten to read the ending, because the author hadn't finished writing yet.

"But we need to do something about the title. It's too damn long."

"Berit likes it."

"*The Free and Loose Memoirs of Eleanor Hartfield* is fine, but does she really have to add *In Eleanor's Own Words, Written by Berit Gardner*? It sounds so old-fashioned."

"That's how she wants it. Oh, there was one more thing. I want a promotion. And a pay rise."

"Do you want to be an editorial assistant? A senior assistant?"

"No, I want to be a literary agent."

There was a brief silence on the other end of the line. Sally could hear her mother's breathing. It sounded calm and relaxed, not agitated. Amused, most likely. When she finally replied, Sally could also hear her smile.

"Junior agent," said Olivia. "And we can discuss a pay rise going forward."

"Deal."

Her mother took a deep breath. "What about PR? Is she still refusing to do any promo work? Do you think you can convince her?"

Sally turned to the window again. Eleanor was now grinning. Berit met Sally's eye and gave her a thumbs-up.

"I've got good news and bad news," she said. "I'm afraid Berit won't be available to do any PR, but her main character will be. Eleanor Hartfield will agree to anything you want her to do: radio, TV, the papers. She's going to be the main draw at Great Diddling's Book and Murder Festival next year."

"If she's half as charmingly bizarre as her memoir, then I'm sure she'll be a great success."

"Oh, but I'd avoid taking it to the *Daily Mirror*, if I were you. They have…history."

Her mother was frantically making notes, and Sally listened to the comforting sound of her typing. For a moment, she wondered whether Olivia had forgotten they were still on the line, but then her mother said, still typing furiously, "Sally?"

"Yeah?"

"Make sure she includes a cat in the next one."

READ ON FOR A PEEK AT ANOTHER
KATARINA BIVALD STORY

The Readers of Broken Wheel Recommend

Broken Wheel, Iowa
April 15, 2009

Sara Lindqvist
Kornvägen 7, 1 tr
136 38 Haninge
Sweden

Dear Sara,

I hope you enjoy Louisa May Alcott's *An Old-Fashioned Girl*. It's a charming story, though perhaps a touch more overtly moralizing than *Little Women*.

In terms of payment, please don't worry about it; I've collected several copies over the years. It's just nice that it's found a new home now, and that it'll be going all the way to Europe! I've never been to Sweden myself, but I'm sure it must be a very beautiful country.

Isn't it funny that my books will have traveled farther than I have? I honestly don't know whether that's comforting or worrying.

With kind regards,
Amy Harris

BOOKS 1–LIFE 0

THE STRANGE WOMAN STANDING ON Hope's main street was so ordinary it was almost scandalous. A thin, plain figure dressed in an autumn coat much too gray and warm for the time of year, a backpack lying on the ground by her feet, an enormous suitcase resting against one of her legs. Those who happened to witness her arrival couldn't help feeling it was inconsiderate for someone to care so little about their appearance. It seemed as though this woman was not the slightest bit interested in making a good impression on them.

Her hair was a nondescript shade of brown, held back with a carelessly placed hair clip that didn't stop it from flowing down over her shoulders in a tangle of curls. Where her face should have been, there was a copy of Louisa May Alcott's *An Old-Fashioned Girl*.

She didn't seem to care at all that she was in Hope. It was as if she had just landed there, with book and luggage and uncombed hair, and might just as well have been in any other town in the world. She was standing on one of the most beautiful streets in Cedar County, maybe even the prettiest in east central Iowa, but the only thing she had eyes for was her book.

But then again, she couldn't be entirely uninterested. Every now and again a pair of big gray eyes peeped up over the edge of the book, like a prairie dog sticking its head up to check whether the coast was clear. She would lower the book further and look sharply to the left, then swing her gaze as far to the right as she could without moving her head. Then she would raise the book and sink back into the story again.

In actual fact, Sara had taken in almost every detail of the street. She would have been able to describe how the last of the afternoon sun was gleaming on the polished SUVs, how even the treetops seemed neat and well organized, and how the hair salon 150 feet away had a sign made from laminated plastic in patriotic red, white, and blue stripes. The scent of freshly baked apple pie filled the air. It was coming from the café behind her, where a couple of middle-aged women were sitting outside and watching her with clear distaste. That was how it looked to Sara, at least. Every time she glanced up from her book, they frowned and shook their heads slightly, as though she was breaking some unwritten rule of etiquette by reading on the street.

She took out her phone and redialed. It rang nine times before she hung up.

So Amy Harris was a bit late. Surely there would be a perfectly reasonable explanation. A flat tire maybe. Out of gas. It was easy to be—she checked her phone again—two hours and thirty-seven minutes late.

She wasn't worried, not yet. Amy Harris wrote proper letters, on real, old-fashioned writing paper, thick and creamy. There wasn't a chance in the world that someone who wrote on proper, cream-colored writing paper would abandon a friend in a strange town or turn out to be a psychopathic serial killer with sadomasochistic tendencies, regardless of what Sara's mother said.

"Excuse me, honey."

A woman had stopped beside her. She gave Sara an artificially patient look.

"Can I help you with anything?" the woman asked. A brown paper bag full of food was resting on her hip, a can of Campbell's tomato soup teetering perilously close to the edge.

"No, thank you," said Sara. "I'm waiting for someone."

"Sure." The woman's tone was amused and indulgent. The women sitting outside the café were following the whole conversation with interest. "First time in Hope?"

"I'm on my way to Broken Wheel."

Maybe it was just Sara's imagination, but the woman didn't seem at all satisfied with that answer.

The can of soup wobbled dangerously. After a moment, the woman said, "It's not much of a town, I'm afraid, Broken Wheel. Do you know someone there?"

"I'm going to stay with Amy Harris."

Silence.

"I'm sure she's on her way," said Sara.

"Seems like you've been abandoned here, honey." The woman looked expectantly at Sara. "Go on, call her."

Sara reluctantly pulled her phone out again. When the strange woman pressed up against Sara's ear to listen to the ringing tone, she had to stop herself from shrinking back.

"Doesn't seem to me like she's going to answer."

Sara put the phone back in her pocket, and the woman moved away a little.

"What're you planning on doing there?"

"Have a holiday. I'm going to rent a room."

"And now you've been abandoned here. That's a good start. I hope you didn't pay in advance." The woman shifted the paper bag over to her other arm and snapped her fingers in the direction of the seats outside the café. "Hank," she said loudly to the only man sitting there. "Give this girl here a ride to Broken Wheel, OK?"

"I haven't finished my coffee."

"So take it with you then."

The man grunted but got obediently to his feet and disappeared into the café.

"If I were you," the woman continued, "I wouldn't hand over any money right away. I'd pay just before I went home. And I'd keep it well hidden until then." She nodded so violently that the can of tomato soup teetered worryingly again. "I'm not saying everyone in Broken Wheel is a thief," she added for safety's sake, "but they're *not* like us."

Hank came back with his coffee in a paper cup, and Sara's suitcase and backpack were thrown onto the backseat of his car. Sara was guided carefully but firmly to the front seat.

"Go on, give her a ride over, Hank," said the woman, hitting the roof of the car twice with her free hand. She leaned toward the open window. "You can always come back here if you change your mind."

❦

"So, Broken Wheel," Hank said disinterestedly.

Sara clasped her hands on top of her book and tried to look relaxed. The car smelled of cheap aftershave and coffee.

"What're you going to do there?"

"Read."

He shook his head.

"As a holiday," she explained.

"We'll see, I guess," Hank said ominously.

She watched the scenery outside the car window change. Lawns became fields, the glittering cars disappeared, and the neat little houses were replaced by an enormous wall of corn looming up on either side of the road, which stretched straight out ahead for miles. Every now and then it was intersected by other roads, also perfectly straight, as though someone had, at some point, looked out over the enormous fields and drawn the roads in with a ruler. *As good a method as any*, Sara thought. But as they drove on, the other roads became fewer and fewer until it felt as though the only thing around them was mile after mile of corn.

"Can't be much of a town left," said Hank. "A friend of mine grew up there. Sells insurance in Des Moines now."

She didn't know what she was meant to say to that. "That's nice," she tried.

"He likes it," the man agreed. "Much better than trying to run the family farm in Broken Wheel, that's for sure."

And that was that.

Sara looked out of the car window, searching for the town of Amy's letters. She had heard so much about Broken Wheel that she was almost expecting Miss Annie to come speeding past on her delivery bicycle at any moment or Robert to be standing at the side of the road, waving the latest edition of his magazine in the air. For a moment, she could practically see them before her, but then they grew faint and whirled away into the dust behind the car. Instead, a battered-looking barn appeared, only to be immediately hidden from view once more by the corn, as though it had never been there in the first place. It was the only building she had seen in the last fifteen minutes.

Would the town look the way she had imagined it? Now that she was finally about to see it with her own eyes, Sara had even forgotten her anxiety about Amy not answering the phone.

But when they eventually arrived, she might have missed it entirely if Hank hadn't pulled over. The main street was nothing more than a few buildings on either side of the road. Most of them seemed to be empty, gray, and depressing. A few of the shops had boarded-up windows, but a diner still appeared to be open.

"So what d'you want to do?" Hank asked. "You want a ride back?"

She glanced around. The diner was definitely open. The word *Diner* was glowing faintly in red neon letters, and a lone man was sitting at the table closest to the window. She shook her head.

"Whatever you want," Hank said in a tone that implied "You'll only have yourself to blame."

She climbed out of the car and pulled her luggage out from the back-seat, her paperback shoved under her arm. Hank drove off the moment she closed the door. He made a sharp U-turn at the only traffic light in town.

It was hanging from a cable in the middle of the street, and it was shining red.

e~

Sara stood in front of the diner with the suitcase at her feet, her backpack slung over one shoulder, and one hand firmly clutching her book.

It's all going to be fine, she said to herself. *Everything will work out. This is not a catastrophe...* She backtracked. As long as she had books and money, nothing could be a catastrophe. She had enough money to check in to a hostel if she needed to. Though she was fairly sure there wouldn't be a hostel in Broken Wheel.

She pushed open the doors—only to be confronted by a set of real saloon doors, how ridiculous—and went in. Other than the man by the window and a woman behind the counter, the diner was empty. The man was thin and wiry, his body practically begging forgiveness for his very existence. He didn't even look up when she came in, just continued turning his coffee cup in his hands, slowly around and around.

The woman, on the other hand, immediately directed all her attention toward the door. She weighed at least three hundred pounds and her huge arms were resting on the high counter in front of her. It was made from dark wood and wouldn't have looked out of place in a bar, but instead of beer coasters, there were stainless-steel napkin holders and laminated menus with pictures of the various rubbery-looking types of food the diner served.

The woman lit a cigarette in one fluid movement.

"You must be the tourist," she said. The smoke from her cigarette hit Sara in the face. It had been years since Sara had seen anyone in Sweden smoking in a restaurant. Clearly they did things differently here.

"I'm Sara. Do you know where Amy Harris lives?"

The woman nodded. "One hell of a day." A lump of ash dropped from her cigarette and landed on the counter. "I'm Grace," she said. "Or truth be told, my name's Madeleine. But there's no point calling me that."

Sara hadn't been planning on calling her anything at all.

"And now you're here."

Sara had a definite feeling that Grace-who-wasn't-really-called-Grace was enjoying the moment, drawing it out. Grace nodded three times to herself, took a deep drag of her cigarette, and let the smoke curl slowly upward from one corner of her mouth. She leaned over the counter.

"Amy's dead," she said.

In Sara's mind, Amy's death would forever be associated with the glow of fluorescent strip lighting, cigarette smoke, and the smell of fried food. It was surreal. Here she was, standing in a diner in a small American town, being told that a woman she had never met had died. The whole situation was much too dreamlike to be scary, much too odd to be a nightmare.

"Dead?" Sara repeated. An extraordinarily stupid question, even for her. She slumped onto a bar stool. She had no idea what to do now. Her thoughts drifted back to the woman in Hope, and she wondered whether she should have gone back with Hank after all.

Amy can't be dead, Sara thought. *She was my friend. She liked* books, *for God's sake.*

It wasn't quite grief that Sara was feeling, but she was struck by how fleeting life was, and the odd feeling grew. She had come to Iowa from Sweden to take a break from life—to get away from it, even—but not to meet death.

How had Amy died? One part of her wanted to ask; another didn't want to know.

Grace continued before Sara had time to make up her mind. "The funeral's probably in full swing. Not particularly festive things nowadays, funerals. Too much religious crap if you ask me. It was different when my grandma died." She glanced at the clock. "You should probably head over there now, though. I'm sure someone who knew her better'll know what to do with you. I try to avoid getting drawn into this town's problems, and you're definitely one of them."

She stubbed out her cigarette. "George, will you give Sara here a ride to Amy's house?"

The man by the window looked up. For a moment, he looked as paralyzed as Sara felt. Then he got to his feet and half carried, half dragged her bags to the car.

Grace grabbed Sara's elbow as she started off after him. "That's Poor George," she said, nodding toward his back.

Amy Harris's house was a little way out of town. It was big enough that the kitchen and living room seemed fairly spacious, but small enough that the little group that had congregated there after the funeral made it seem full. The table and kitchen counters were covered with baking dishes full of food, and someone had prepared bowls of salad and bread, laid out cutlery, and arranged napkins in drinking glasses.

Sara was given a paper plate of food and then left more or less to herself. George was still by her side, and she was touched by that unexpected display of loyalty. He didn't seem to be a particularly brave person at all, not even compared to her, but he had followed her in, and now he was walking around just as hesitantly as she was.

In the dim hallway there was a dark chest of drawers on which someone had arranged a framed photograph of a woman she assumed must be Amy and two worn-looking flags, the one of the United States and the other of Iowa. *Our liberties we prize and our rights we will maintain*, the state flag proclaimed in embroidered white letters, but the flag was faded and one of the edges was frayed.

The woman in the photograph was perhaps twenty years old, with her hair pulled into two thin braids and a standard issue, stiff camera smile. She was a complete stranger. There might have been something in her eyes, a glimmer of laughter that showed she knew it was all a joke, that Sara could recognize from her letters. But that was all.

She wanted to reach out and touch the photograph, but doing that felt much too forward. Instead, she stayed where she was in the dark hallway, carefully balancing her paper plate, her book still under her arm. Her bags had disappeared somewhere, but she didn't have the energy to worry about them.

Three weeks earlier, she had felt so close to Amy that she had been prepared to stay with her for two months, but now it was as though every trace of their friendship had died along with her. Sara had never believed that you had to meet someone in person to be friends—many of her most rewarding relationships had been with people who didn't even exist—but suddenly it all felt so false, disrespectful even, to cling to the idea that she and Amy had, in some way, meant something to each other.

All around her, people were moving slowly and cautiously through the rooms, as though they were wondering what on earth they were doing there, which was almost exactly what Sara was thinking too. Still, they didn't seem shocked. They didn't seem surprised. No one was crying.

Most of them were looking at Sara with curiosity, but something, perhaps respect for the significance of the event, was stopping them from approaching her. They circled around her instead, smiling whenever she accidentally caught their eye.

Suddenly, a woman materialized out of the crowd and cornered Sara halfway between the living room and the kitchen.

"Caroline Rohde."

Her posture and handshake were military, but she was much more beautiful than Sara had imagined. She had deep, almond-shaped eyes and features as pronounced as a statue's. In the glow of the ceiling lamp, her skin was an almost shimmering white across her high cheekbones. Her hair was thick and streaked with gray. Around her neck, she wore a black scarf made from thin, cool silk that would have looked out of place on anyone else, even at a funeral, but on her it looked timeless—almost glamorous.

Her age was hard to guess, but she had the air of someone who had never really been young. Sara had a strong sense that Caroline Rohde didn't have much time for youth.

When Caroline started talking, everyone around her fell silent. Her voice matched her presence: determined, resolute, straight to the point. There was, perhaps, a hint of a welcoming smile in her voice, but it never reached as far as her mouth.

"Amy said you'd be coming," she said. "I won't claim I thought it was a good idea, but it wasn't my place to say anything." Then she added, almost as an afterthought, "You've got to agree that this isn't the most...practical situation."

"Practical," Sara echoed. Though how Amy was meant to know she was going to die, she wasn't sure.

Others gathered around Caroline in a loose half circle, facing Sara as if she were a traveling circus making a brief stop in town.

"We didn't know how to contact you when Amy...passed away. And now you're here," Caroline concluded. "Oh well, we'll just have to see what we can do with you."

"I'm going to need somewhere to stay," said Sara. Everyone leaned forward to hear.

"Stay?" asked Caroline. "You'll stay here, of course! I mean, the house is empty, isn't it?"

"But…"

A man in a minister's collar smiled warmly at Sara, adding, "Amy specifically told us to let you know that nothing would change in that regard."

Nothing would change? She didn't know who was madder—the minister or Amy or the whole of Broken Wheel.

"There's a guest room, of course," said Caroline. "Sleep there tonight, and then we'll work out what we're going to do with you."

The minister nodded, and somehow it was decided. She would stay, alone, in dead Amy Harris's empty house.

She was bustled upstairs. Caroline went first, like a commander at war, followed closely by Sara and then George, a supportive, silent shadow. Behind them, most of the other guests followed. Someone was carrying her bags, she didn't know who, but when she reached the little guest room, her backpack and suitcase miraculously appeared.

"We'll make sure you've got everything you need," Caroline said from the doorway, not at all unkindly. Then she shooed the others away, giving Sara a brief wave before pulling the door closed behind her.

Sara sank onto the bed, suddenly alone again, the paper plate still in her hand and a lonely book lying abandoned on the bedspread next to her.

Oh hell, she thought.

Broken Wheel, Iowa
June 3, 2009

Sara Lindqvist
Kornvägen 7, 1 tr
136 38 Haninge
Sweden

Dear Sara,

Thank you so much for your kind gift! It's a book I probably wouldn't have bought myself, so it was all the more welcome. What an awful tale. I had no idea such things took place in Sweden, though I don't know why they shouldn't. If you ask me, there's much more violence, sex, and scandal in small towns than in the big cities, and if that's true of towns, then I suppose it might also be true of small countries? I presume it's because people get closer to one another there. We've certainly had our fair share of scandal here in Broken Wheel.

But a Lisbeth Salander? That we definitely do not have. A remarkable woman. As I understand it, there are two more books in the series. Would you do me the honor of sending the second and third books? I won't be able to sleep before I find out what happens to her. And that overwrought young man Mr. Blomkvist as well, of course.

I'll pay you for them, naturally. Speaking of small towns, murder, and sex, I'm sending you Harper Lee's *To Kill a Mockingbird* as a first installment.

With kind regards,
Amy Harris

READING GROUP GUIDE

1. Sally feels very nervous going into an unknown situation and a very new job. Have you ever been in her position of trying to figure out how to go about your work, please your boss, and figure out a new portion of your life? How did you work through this?

2. Berit claims that "New mistakes are the most fun." What do you think she means by this statement? Do you agree with her?

3. At the beginning of the novel, Berit is experiencing some extreme writer's block. Have you ever experienced writer's block? How did you get through it, if at all?

4. This book takes place in a very small town where everyone knows each other. What are the benefits to small-town life? What are the drawbacks? Which do you prefer: small town or big city?

5. DCI Ahmed claims he often remembers how a person smelled as clearly as he did their face. How good are you at recognizing scents? How much attention do you pay to your own perfume, cologne, or deodorant?

6. Eleanor and Mary chose not to reveal their relationship upon moving to Great Diddling. Eleanor claims that although the times have changed, they were too old. What do you think of this decision and of Eleanor's justification? Do you agree with her?

7. While the police are looking into Mary's and Eleanor's pasts, they discover their history of fraud cases and how they were rarely caught, as no one wants to admit they've been duped. Have you ever been scammed? Would you be too embarrassed to report it, or would you want to go after whomever did it to you?

8. Margaret wants to find some peace and quiet, a calm and relaxing place to just be. Do you have that place for yourself? It could be a physical location, a room in your house, or even a state of mind.

9. Did you figure out who murdered Reginald (and Gerald) before the reveal? Whom did you suspect and when?

10. In the end, Berit is able to write again. What part of her journey throughout the book enabled her to do this? How much did connecting with Sally and the people of Great Diddling help her?

A CONVERSATION
WITH THE AUTHOR

Where did the inspiration for this book come from?

I first got the idea for *The Murders in Great Diddling* while standing on the quaint cobblestone streets of a small village on the border between Wales and England. I looked around in disbelief and asked myself: Maybe it *is* possible? Maybe you actually *can* have too many books? I had never asked that question before and never have since. It was only temporary insanity. I was in Hay-on-Wye, a village that describes itself as the first "book town." Its founder brags about having handled over a million books in his lifetime. When I visited, the village had two thousand citizens and twenty bookshops. The books had taken over everything: the old cinema, the old fire station, even an old castle ruin. It was a disorienting, magical sight, and right there and then, I had the idea of writing a novel about a village that was overrun with books.

But it took an explosive tea party, a murder, and the introduction in my mind of writer-turned-amateur-sleuth Berit Gardner to really get the idea off the ground.

Is Berit based on you and your own thoughts/processes, or is she more of a caricature?

I think Berit is based on the idea of a person I would like to be. She has a brusque, no-nonsense quality about her that I admire but can never quite live up to myself. She believes that there's no need for writers to bother with boring social expectations of normalcy, because everyone knows writers are a bit strange anyway, and there is freedom in not caring what other people think. (I still care too much.) She sees people clearly for what they are but with a compassionate eye. (I am often compassionate but still see people very much as I want them to be.) In one way, we are only too similar: we are both pulled between standing on the sideline, observing at a distance, and we long to be a part of a community. I think it's that longing for community that drives my writing and Berit Gardner's life.

What gets you through writer's block, if you ever have it?

The story or the characters in it. The only time I have really struggled with writer's block was when writing *Welcome to the Pine Away Motel and Cabins.* Since the story meant so much to me, I found myself struggling with how to do it justice. I had to remind myself of the pure joy—a feeling as old as time—of telling a story and just following my characters and seeing where they take me.

What was your writing process for this book like? Did you know who the murderer was from the start?

In a way, I guess you can say that Great Diddling saved me as much as it saved Berit Gardner. I wrote the first draft of the novel during the pandemic, and it reminded me of the glorious escape that can always be found in books. I have known all my life that books allow us to travel in time and space, to be anywhere and anyone, but I think perhaps I still needed to be reminded about it. When it became impossible to travel any other way, I turned to my bookshelves for new experiences and new worlds. And then I turned to my notebook. Anytime I opened it, anytime I picked up a pen, I could instantly transport myself to my charming English village, to a dark English pub, a cozy English café. My body might have been stuck in my apartment on the outskirts of Stockholm, but my mind could still travel as freely as ever. I mingled at the tea party, I had a pint at the pub—and I happily plotted away at my murders.

What do you want readers to take away from this story?

Oh, I hope it carries you away for a little while. Transports you from whatever problems or bothers exist in your life, gives you a break, makes you smile a little as you move amongst the murderous people in Great Diddling. The villagers of Great Diddling believe that there's no better combination than a charming English village, books, and murders, and I hope you agree with them.

What are you reading right now?

I am currently reading about poison through the ages. Crime writers really do have the most fun research. But if the police ever got their hands on my search history, I am done for.

ABOUT THE AUTHOR

© Peter Knutson

Katarina Bivald grew up working part-time in a bookstore, dreaming of becoming an author. In 2013, the dream came true when she published her *New York Times* bestselling debut, *The Readers of Broken Wheel Recommend*. She lives outside of Stockholm with her dog, Sam; still prefers books over people; and has just found out that life is so much more fun when you're plotting to kill someone.